HARRY'S GRAIL

A NOVEL in FIVE PARTS

A. B. PATTERSON

A. B. Patterson

Published by A. B. Patterson 2025
PO Box 1008
Broadway
NSW 2007
Australia

First Printing 2025

Cover design by J.T. Lindroos
www.oivas.com

Front and back cover photographs from iStock

ABP Logo design by Stephen Hill
www.dylunio.com.au

A catalogue record for this book is available from the National Library of Australia

ISBN: 978-0-9923273-6-1

Also available as an ebook:
ISBN: 978-0-9923273-7-8

Published with the assistance of Publicious P/L (Australia)
www.publicious.com.au

To noble causes …

… and defending freedom and the
values of civilized people.

Other works by A. B. Patterson

Novels:

Harry's World
Harry's Quest

Novella:

Jasper: The Gloves Are Off

Short story collection:

Harry Kenmare, PI – At Your Service

Other short stories published:

"Blue Angel"
"Childhood's End"
"Rights and Wrongs"
"Clean, Green, and Obscene"
"Beelzebub's Bird"
"The Train"

www.abpatterson.com.au

Contents

About the Author

A. B. Patterson is an Australian writer who knows first-hand about corruption, power, crime and sex. He was a Detective Sergeant in the WA Police, working in paedophilia and vice, and later a Chief Investigator with the NSW Independent Commission Against Corruption.

His multiple award-winning, debut novel, *Harry's World*, introduced the jaded and flawed PI Harry Kenmare.

Harry's Quest was the sizzling, award-winning sequel in the PI Harry Kenmare series. *Harry's Grail* is the explosive sequel to the first two Harry Kenmare novels.

His Harry Kenmare short stories, some previously published in the USA in *Switchblade* magazine, were gathered together for the first time in *Harry Kenmare, PI – At Your Service.*

He has had short stories, all dark and mostly crime, published in various anthologies and magazines, including *Switchblade, Pulp Modern,* and *Econoclash Review.*

He has also been the contributing editor and co-editor of two anthologies of crime stories, *To Serve, Protect, and Write* and *Romy Lives.*

His hard-boiled, gritty, and noir writing style has been likened to that of Raymond Chandler and Ken Bruen, whilst his eroticism has been compared to Henry Miller.

He is an ardent supporter of the freedom of expression for writers and other artists, and is a proud committee member of the Independent Fiction Alliance.

In libertate veritas est!

www.abpatterson.com.au

Author's Foreword

I owe all the fans of the first two PI Harry Kenmare novels, *Harry's World* and *Harry's Quest*, something of an apology for the delay in getting this third adventure out there for you. Best laid plans and all that!

Finally, my flawed hero PI Harry Kenmare returns, along with his team, to take up where *Harry's Quest* left us. If you're reading this, then it likely means you're a fan of the earlier stories. If so, I sincerely hope you enjoy the next instalment of action and raunch every bit as much.

I've had a huge amount of creative fun and satisfaction in creating the cast in Harry's world. Inventing characters and developing their stories is a uniquely pleasurable activity. So is weaving in aspects of social commentary and injecting some cold, hard realism into the fictional form. I don't shy away from the facts of life in my writing. But above all, the telling of an entertaining yarn is a joy as old as humankind itself.

My sincere hope is that *Harry's Grail* delivers everything you, the reader, is hankering for as you devour the pages.

If you haven't tried them already, the Harry short stories are also out there. Told in the first person, rather than the third person form of the novels, they are juicy snippets of Harry up to all his usual shenanigans.

And rest assured, there will be another Harry novel.

As with my previous novels, and especially with my overseas readers in mind, I have again included a Glossary to assist with the Australian colloquialisms and the ever-pervasive acronyms that modern society seems to thrive on. You'll find it at the back of the book. But I did want to highlight it before you start your reading adventure, in case you want to peruse it first.

Please enjoy!

Cheers,
Andrew

A. B. Patterson
Sydney, August 2025

HARRY'S GRAIL

PART 1

HARRY'S JUNGLE

Beside her body, you could not dream.

- James Crumley

Sex is one of the nine reasons for reincarnation ... the other eight are unimportant.

- Henry Miller

– 1 –

Drip. Drip. Drip.
Red. Viscous. Metallic tang.
Blood.
Orla's blood dripping onto his face.
Her little body. Naked. Violated.
A shovel sticking up, its blade embedded in her throat.
Her head floating off.
'Daddy! Daddy!'
Blood. Endless blood.
Dripping onto his face, running out of her severed neck.
Reggie Wheeler's face. Smirking. Laughing maniacally.
'You fucking pig! Enjoyed your little girl, pig. Bit of baby bacon on my cock. Oink, oink!'
Orla's face fading, floating away.
'Daddy! Help me, please!'

'Aaagh!'
Harry jerked awake and opened his eyes in the camping cot, bathed in sweat.

The trail in the hunt for Reggie Wheeler had led to the steamy, stifling jungles of Laos.

Water was dripping through the rusty tin roof. Any holier, and it would have had its own followers. There was a steady drumbeat of rain on the metal. The rain seemed to never stop. The cabin was on stilts to raise it off the jungle floor, but the smell of the damp earth and rotting vegetation rose up through the gaps between the rough-hewn floorboards. In the small one-room space, the mustiness ran head on into the pungent aroma of tropical-strength insect repellent: the force of nature versus the chemical ingenuity of mankind. The combination was hideous enough on its own, but the added sweat of the three sleuths camping here, in the makeshift observation post for the last two days, made the air retchworthy. Well, if anyone's nasal receptors had still been functioning, that is.

Tanya had commented that if this was Harry's idea of the first overseas holiday for the sexiest lover he'd ever had, then he was never getting laid again. She finished the edict with a singular, 'Eva!' Tanya didn't make a habit of millennial lingo, despite her young age, but she knew it gave Harry the shits no end.

She was now sound asleep in her narrow cot, two of the massive local mosquitoes hovering malignantly above her, desperately wanting to puncture her flesh and suck her blood, but not having the fortitude to breach the chemical fug around her.

Trev, taking his turn on watch, put down his nightscope and touched the prone Harry's shoulder. The interior of the shack was lit only by the subdued glow of a camping light on its lowest setting.

'You awake, Harry?'

'Yeah, mate,' said Harry, sitting up. 'Just dreaming. Badly.'

'Well, all going to plan, Harry, this time next week you'll be able to relax and have dreams filled with the juicy memories of your victory after we've killed Reggie Wheeler.'

'Yep, hanging out for that, plus I'm sick of this fucking putrid jungle already. Any movement?'

'No, the orphanage has been quiet as,' said Trev. 'Only adult movement has been the two nuns we saw during the day.'

'I'm still appalled Wheeler has got himself a position at an orphanage, of all bloody places.'

'Yeah, but there are bugger all background checks over here, and cash always greases the way through, anyway.'

'Yeah, it's a fucked-up world.'

Harry looked at his watch.

'Shit, after six already. Sun'll be up soon. I can take over early if you like, mate. Don't think I'll be getting back to sleep. The rain on the roof is doing my head in.'

'That's all right, brother. But you could fire up the burner and make us a cup of coffee.'

'Excellent idea. I won't wake Sleeping Beauty just yet.' Harry looked over at Tanya. 'And she is beautiful, too.'

'Yep, Harry, you sure as hell punch above your weight.'

Harry chuckled. 'Well, mate, she's only human and I've got hidden talents.'

Trev chortled quietly.

There was a snort of derision from the apparent sleeping lady of the moment.

'Please, spare me, boys,' she moaned sleepily.

'Oh, you got sprung big time, Harry,' said Trev with obvious enjoyment in his voice.

'Yeah, Harry. You're punching so far above your weight you're at risk of propelling yourself into low-earth orbit,' said Tanya.

'Funny ha ha,' replied Harry.

'Seriously, Mister PI, you should buy yourself a lotto ticket every time you look at my naked body.'

Harry chuckled again. 'I'd go broke.'

They all laughed quietly.

'Although you don't want to be getting up close and personal at the moment with all this bloody insect cream. It'd probably kill you, like a dog licking a cane toad.'

'You're way too stunning for a toad, babe. More like one of those sleek tree frogs,' said Harry.

'Given this jungle hell-hole we're stuck in, I'll settle for that as a compliment. But you owe me once we get back to the hotel in Vientiane.'

'I'll repay you on my knees, O Divine One.'

'While you're on your knees, I've got other ideas.'

Trev groaned. 'Oh, cut it out, you two. I feel like the closet gay in the schoolyard watching the football captain making out with the head cheerleader.'

Tanya smirked at them in the dim light. 'No closet for you, Trev. And I'm sure you can get some hot, steamy action back in the city at that bar we stopped at. There was more Asian leather in there than a Bangkok shoe shop.'

'Ooh, yes,' replied Trev. 'Bring on three consecutive hot showers, and then straight down to the Purple Orchid Pleasure Palace.'

Harry stepped over to the table and lit the camping stove. He poured a large bottle of mineral water into a steel pot and sat it on the blue flame. 'Well, guys, as we always say, as long as it's between consenting adults, anything goes.'

Ten minutes later, as they sipped their coffees out of enamel mugs, the first dappled rays of sunlight crept in through the holes in the eastern wall of the shack.

'Rain's slowing up,' said Trev. 'That'll make it easier if we need to get on the road after Wheeler.'

'Yeah, thank goodness we're not here in the rainy season,' said Harry.

'You mean it gets worse than this?' asked Tanya.

'Yep. This is actually the cool, dry season. Next month is officially the start of the hot, dry season.'

'Not too fricking dry if you ask me,' said Tanya.

'Not wrong there,' said Harry. 'I'm sweatier than a Saigon streetwalker's crack.'

'And smelling about the same,' muttered Trev.

'Oh, as if you'd know.'

'Ah, that would be telling. Some of them only look like girls.'

'Spare me,' said Harry.

Tanya giggled. 'Yeah, you wouldn't want to make a mistake there, Harry.'

'Dead right,' added Trev. 'Harry'd be all hot under the collar for some gorgeous Oriental pussy, then suddenly find himself with a handful of nuts.'

Harry shook his head. 'Only thing I've got any urge for at the moment is catching this fucking rock spider, Wheeler. And in second place is a bloody hot shower.'

'Oh, yes,' said Tanya. 'So how long are we going to sit around here?'

'Well, the drum from Major Vang was that Wheeler was working here. Got a room in Luang Prabang, but always coming out here. Seen here several times in the last fortnight,' said Harry.

'You reckon his info is good?' asked Tanya.

'We paid the arsehole enough,' added Trev.

'Yeah, it'd better be good drum,' said Harry.

'Absolutely, the bastard got six million kip.'

'What's that in real money?' asked Tanya.

'About a thousand Australian,' said Trev. 'But he's a greasy, corrupt arsehole, like most of the cops here, so I for one don't trust him.'

'Nor me, brother, but we had to start somewhere,' said Harry. 'In these countries, everything is lubricated with cash.'

'Not much different back home,' added Trev. 'Only it's better dressed up.'

'Exactly,' said Harry. 'But a fat rat in a tuxedo is still a fat rat.'

'There is a degree of droll irony in our partaking in the corruption, given our disdain for it.'

'Yeah, and droll will turn into delicious when we catch Wheeler,' said Harry. 'And I can sleep just fine with that irony.'

Trev picked up a pair of binoculars and peered over the rice paddy at the orphanage, becoming visible through the steamy mist as the sun clocked on for its shift.

'Shit, a moped has shown up out the front of the main building.'

'Didn't hear any motor.'

'No. Must've been parked around the side or the back and just wheeled out ready to go.'

'Any extra movement inside?' asked Harry.

'Top right-hand window, a light's gone on. Can see a shadow moving around.'

Harry grabbed the extra set of field glasses and joined Trev gazing into the humid, hazy distance.

'Is that him?' asked Trev.

Harry's knuckles were white as he gripped his binoculars. 'Yes,' he hissed, 'that's the mongrel dog.'

Harry's mind flashed back to the confessions they'd extracted from Bernhard Schwarz and Herbert Farr. He saw his little Orla, violated, alone and terrified, lying in the shallow grave as Reggie Wheeler drove a shovel into her throat.

'You're mine, Wheeler, you cunt.'

He put his glasses down.

'He looks as if he's packing a bag,' said Trev.

'Okay, team, we need to move,' said Harry through gritted teeth.

'Is it a coincidence he's on the move two days after we've arrived?' asked Tanya.

'Babe, I don't believe in coincidences. Especially not in our game.'

'Reckon he's been tipped off?' asked Trev. 'After what we paid Major Vang?'

'Who bloody knows around here,' said Harry. 'Everybody and everything is for sale it seems.'

'I'll get our wheels started,' said Trev. 'Tan, can you please collect all the gear and stick it in the jeep?'

'Sure thing,' she replied, standing up from her cot.

'I'll keep watching until he gets on his scooter,' said Harry. 'As soon as he moves, we'll head off and grab him as he comes out of the access track onto the main road.'

'Roger that, big boy.' Trev jumped through the doorless frame into the clearing where the hired Suzuki Vitara was parked.

'Finally, some action,' said Tanya. 'Then a hot shower, hell yes. And after that, my Mister PI, if you play your cards right, there could be a whole lot more action. Starting with that monster tongue of yours doing what it does best.'

She blew him a kiss as she picked up her bag.

Harry chuckled without taking his eyes away from the binoculars. 'You're on, babe. After I've killed this paedophile piece of shit, I'll be ready to party hard.'

'You'd better be rock hard.'

Tanya collected their few bits and pieces of equipment quickly and put them in a plastic crate. She took it out to the jeep.

Harry gazed intently through his optics.

'Before this morning is over, Wheeler, I'm going to fucking have you, and it's going to be slow and horrendously painful. It's time for justice for my Orla.'

He couldn't see Wheeler moving around in the upstairs room anymore. He flicked his glasses downwards to bring the recently arrived moped into view. He watched.

Twenty seconds later, Wheeler emerged from the side door of the orphanage building, a large canvas bag in hand, and a backpack on. He strapped the bag to the moped's carrier rack and got on it.

Harry was out the door and into the passenger seat of the jeep before they heard the moped's engine start across the silent rice paddies.

'Let's go! We've got ourselves a ped to capture,' Harry almost yelled.

Trev threw the jeep into gear.

− 2 −

Trev accelerated along the narrow bitumen strip that passed for a main road in this jungle. Harry was gripping a baseball bat, his knuckles shining white. It was an effective and legal implement, an important consideration in this foreign operating environment. They hadn't wanted to take the chance of dabbling in the local black market for guns, their usual weapons of choice. They didn't know the scene here, unlike back home in Sydney, and the local police often posed as illicit vendors to entrap novice players.

Instead, Jimmy Pao's Sports and Camping Emporium had happily taken cash for two baseball bats, as well as three hunting knives and a large machete from the store's outdoor section.

The dirt side road leading to the orphanage was about 400 metres ahead.

'There he is!' yelled Tanya from the backseat.

Sure enough, between the palm trees and jungle shrubs, there were glimpses of a speeding motorbike. It was only about 200 metres from the road and Wheeler wasn't hanging around, despite the bumpy track he was bouncing along on.

'He knows how to handle a bike, that's for sure,' said Trev.

'He'll have to slow to turn onto the road. That'll close the gap for us.'

Wheeler executed a talented slide onto the sealed main road, casting a glance at the jeep bearing down on him. He righted the bike and gunned the engine, speeding away, a little flourish on the back wheel for a couple of seconds.

Trev put his foot down and the little Suzuki engine whined in protest, like a belligerent lawnmower.

'C'mon, mate,' urged Harry.

'Doing my fricking best,' said Trev, dropping the jeep into third gear as they hit a long curve in the road.

Wheeler disappeared around the bend, obscured by the dense, verdant jungle hemming in each side of the road.

Trev had the Suzuki's four cylinders screaming for their lives.

'Fuck!' he yelled, slamming on the brakes.

'What the fuck?!' shouted Harry, as the jeep slid to a stop on the excuse for a road surface, its wheels locked up.

A police cruiser had pulled out of a side track and blocked the main road in front of them.

Wheeler had slowed and then stopped about 300 metres beyond the cop car. He turned to face his pursuers, stuck his middle finger up at them, then gunned the bike and roared off down the road and out of sight.

A young and scruffy Lao policeman was now standing in front of the jeep with an AK-47.

The three sleuths watched in silence as Major Vang got out of the back seat of the cruiser and strutted over to the jeep. He walked to the passenger side where Harry was sitting speechlessly, mouth agape. Harry got out of the jeep, followed by Trev and Tanya.

'Good morning, Mister Kenmare.' The Oriental face smiled at Harry and there were two gleams of gold in the neat dentition.

Harry fought to regain his composure. 'Major Vang, what the hell is going on?'

'Things change, Mister Kenmare.'

'What do you mean "change"? We paid you good money, that hasn't bloody changed.'

'Ah, yes. Yes, you did. But then Mister Wheeler paid even better money. Especially when I told him who was hunting him.' The gold-toothed grin was smugger than a politician telling a lie under parliamentary privilege.

Harry was ready to explode. 'I told you what he did to my daughter! Where's your damned decency?'

'Tsk, tsk. Watch your mouth, Mister Kenmare. You are in my country, and for less than honest reasons. Do not adopt an attitude with me. Do you understand?'

Harry was seething. He wanted to kill this arsehole. 'Yes,' he hissed, instead.

'Good. As for decency, as you put it in your quaint Western way, the only decent thing here is money. And what it can buy, of course. I am truly sorry for what happened to your little girl. But now, here, none of us can change that. So, all that's left is business. Simple.' That golden glint again.

'What about some justice, Major?' said Harry, trying not to spit on him.

'Another whimsical aspect of your Western liberal democracies. And in complete ignorance of the real force of life: power.' He grinned broadly this time. 'But I am sure you will continue your hunt. I wish you well.'

'Bit hard when we've been double-crossed,' said Trev. 'We used to be cops, too. What about a bit of solidarity?'

'As I said, Mister Matson, it is purely business, nothing personal.'

The junior officer had shouldered his rifle and sidled over to Tanya, standing near the back of the jeep. He said something to her.

'I don't speak your lingo, pal, but the answer is "no", whatever the question,' she said.

Vang was smiling again.

'What did he say to her?' asked Harry.

'He likes her, of course. She's very pretty.'

The young cop reached out and pawed one of Tanya's breasts, straining beneath her damp low-cut T-shirt.

Before Harry or Trev could even open their mouths, let alone make a move, Tanya's fist slammed into the cop's nose and he went down backwards.

Vang cackled like a banshee.

The fallen cop scrabbled to right himself and unshoulder his gun at the same time. The effect resembled an epileptic beetle.

Vang barked something at him.

The junior cop had a dark glare in his eyes as he stood up, reshouldering his weapon and walking sullenly over to his boss.

The Major said something further, more quietly but still acid sharp, and the younger officer snapped to attention in front of him, saluting. He went back to the police car.

'He deserved that,' said Vang to the visitors. 'And I always like entertainment. You have a superb punch, Miss Roberts. Far better than most of my men.' He dipped his head in tribute.

The chastised cop sat in the car's driver's seat, glowering at them. You could taste the cloud of humiliation in the air, and Harry knew all too well retribution often followed close on its heels.

He turned to Tanya, but before he could say anything Vang interjected.

'What I will do for you, Mister Kenmare, is to accompany you to the orphanage and instruct the nuns to allow you to go through Mister Wheeler's room. He left in a rush, so you could find something useful left behind. Interested?'

'Yes, of course.'

'Good. Get in your car and follow us.' He turned on his heel and went over to the police car.

The sleuths got back into the jeep.

Harry turned to Tanya. 'Babe …'

'No! Don't lecture me, Harry. I'm fucking sick of men who think they can take what they want.'

'I get that, Divine One, but …'

'So, what then? He's just lucky I didn't have a gun.'

Trev smiled. 'Yeah, because you are pretty handy with a piece. At least three in the morgue who can attest to that.'

'I'm just saying,' continued Harry softly, 'with corrupt cops who do have guns, and all the cards, we need to tread carefully.'

'Yeah, fine, but I'm not here as a sex toy for the pleasure of some small-dicked wanker in a uniform. No matter how big their guns.'

Harry nodded.

'Let it go, Harry,' said Trev. 'I know where you're coming from, but we wouldn't want our Tan any other way.'

Tanya leant forward and kissed Trev on the cheek.

'True,' said Harry. 'Very true. But we'll need to watch our backs. That maggot had vengeance in his eyes. I know that look. Let's stay sharp. And whilst I hate to agree with fucking Major fucking Vang on anything, that was a pearler of a punch, babe.'

'Thank you, Harry. Fewer lectures and more compliments, you might even get laid tonight.' She grinned at Trev in the rear-vision mirror.

He groaned. 'Jesus, I've got to get lucky at the bar tonight. I'm not spending another night listening to you two howling at the moon whilst I'm lying there hugging thin air.'

'Oh, well, Trev,' said Tanya, 'just a pity you don't play both teams occasionally, because I'd certainly be your sex toy for a night.' She blew a kiss at him.

'I'm flattered, Tan, and the pity is all mine, believe me.' He started the engine.

The police car moved off with Vang signalling them to follow. Trev put the jeep into gear and they fell in behind the cruiser.

– 3 –

Major Vang spoke to the head nun at the Our Sister of Lourdes orphanage, and suggested Harry might like to make a donation to a worthy cause.

Harry shook his head as he pulled out his wallet, turning to Trev. 'In this bloody country, mate, my wallet's getting more traffic than a rent-boy's arse.'

'Want to borrow a rubber, brother?'

'Very bloody funny.' Harry peeled out a bundle of the local Monopoly money, about a hundred Aussie dollars' worth, and handed it to the lady.

'Ah, very generous, Mister Kenmare,' said Vang, glinting his golden smile.

'My pleasure,' said Harry with a sarcastic tone he was sure would be lost on the corrupt Major, but at least it made him feel slightly better.

The Major and the nun exchanged words.

'Mister Kenmare, you follow Sister Véronique and she will let you into the room.'

Harry nodded grudgingly. He followed the diminutive nun as she headed for the central staircase that dominated the hallway of the old French colonial building. At the top of the stairs, they turned left. In the other direction Harry could hear the high-pitched voices of children.

He turned to Trev and Tanya behind him. 'At least we might have spared them more of Wheeler.'

'Yeah, until some other ped arsehole buys his way in here. It's a bit of a frequent problem in these countries, especially the poorer areas.'

Harry shook his head.

'I know you guys are against the death penalty,' said Tanya, 'but frankly I'd happily execute all peds.'

'In case you'd forgotten, Divine One, it's only government executions we've got an objection to.'

'Point taken.'

Sister Véronique opened a door and ushered them towards it. She walked away.

Harry stood on the threshold of the ped's bedroom, grimly wondering how many local kids had been defiled in the small room's humid confines. He wrinkled his nose at the imagined stench of sordidness and stepped in.

'Want a hand, Harry?' asked Trev.

'She's right, mate. Won't take long. I want to do this. It needs to be me. I owe it to Orla.'

There was a bookshelf on the left-hand wall, above a small wooden desk with a classroom chair tucked under it.

Harry sneered as he flicked through the small collection of dog-eared paperbacks. Aside from some guides on South-East Asia, it was a molester's wet-dream library: *Lolita*, of course, *The End of Alice*, *Avoidance*, *Touched*, *The 120 Days of Sodom*, and rounded out by *Dream Children*. Harry read out the titles.

Then he flicked through each of the volumes, in case of any hidden photos or papers, but nothing emerged from between the pages.

The desktop was clear. Harry opened the single drawer and pulled out a writing pad. He flicked through the sheets, all blank.

Over to the bed and the small bamboo bedside table with an old banker's lamp on it. He pulled open its single drawer.

'Aaagh!' yelled Harry. He slapped the wall.

Trev and Tanya came running into the room.

'You okay, Harry?' asked Tanya, putting a hand on his shoulder.

Harry reached into the drawer and pulled out a silver shamrock pendant on a chain.

'Orla's,' was all he said, staring at it.

Tanya hugged him.

'Well, Harry, at least now you've got it, and not that pedo piece of shit,' said Trev.

Harry nodded slowly in acknowledgement.

Tanya took the pendant out of Harry's hand, undid the clasp, and fastened it around Harry's neck. It sat higher than intended, given Harry's beefy neck compared to his late young daughter's.

'It belongs there now,' said Tanya, kissing Harry on the cheek.

'Thank you.' Harry turned back the task at hand.

Trev started rifling through the small wardrobe. 'We'll give you a hand now, brother. Only thing in here is a shoebox with some letters and postcards in it.'

'Bit old school,' said Harry.

'Yeah, but maybe some of the peds are trying to stay away from email now, given all the monitoring.'

'True. Grab them all. We'll go through them at our leisure back at the hotel over a drink or sixteen.'

'Best idea so far today,' added Tanya, crouching to look under the metal-framed single bed.

'Is it a wire-spring base?' asked Trev.

'Yep.'

'Tip from an old copper, Tan, go over the mattress surface to look for any cuts or tears, hiding spots.'

Tanya dropped herself right onto the floor. 'Can't see anything like that, but there is something lying against the wall over in the corner. Looks like a notebook or a diary.'

That instantly got the attention of the men.

'Let's pull the bed out a bit,' said Harry. 'Grab the other end, Trev.'

They dragged the bed out from the wall. Tanya climbed over it and leant into the gap, coming back with a turquoise hardbound notebook, the size of a small pocket diary. She handed it to Harry.

He flicked through it, a smile building. 'Reckon we might have hit gold here, at a quick glance.'

Trev's eyes lit up. 'What's in there?'

'Lots of names of guys, addresses, kids' names and ages. Even a few photos taped in. Add it to the box of papers, Trev.' He handed it across.

'Don't think he meant to leave this,' said Trev. 'Like Orla's pendant, reckon it got dropped in a mad panic to get out of here.'

Tanya snorted. 'Yeah, maybe. And maybe he dropped it while wanking off and forgot to look for it when he was in a hurry.'

'Quite possibly,' said Harry. 'Still, our gain. A consolation for having missed out on Wheeler. It may be what we need to resume the hunt somehow.'

Harry cast a final look around the room. 'All covered, team?'

'Roger that, brother.'

'All good, Mister PI.'

'Okay, let's get the hell out of here. That slimy Major arsehole makes me nervous.'

'Not to mention his fucktard sidekick,' said Tanya.

The three sleuths went back downstairs.

The mother superior was in the large front room, its now dilapidated aura a far cry from its former glory as a grand reception room for some French colonial official.

Harry stopped and said, '*Merci beaucoup, Madame.*'

She smiled, put her hands together, and bowed slightly.

The trio did likewise and walked out onto the verandah.

'Bonus,' said Harry, 'the cops have gone.'

'Yeah, no doubt got their cut out of your donation to the good sisters and have headed off to do some more hard work.'

'Corrupt wankers. Okay, team, let's head back to our salubrious shit-hole hotel. Time to drink and review our little haul.'

'Shower first,' said Tanya. 'We all stink.'

Harry sniffed. 'Yeah.'

'Mind you, Harry, I could smell like an open septic tank in the sun and you'd still be begging for me.' She jabbed him in the ribs.

Trev sniggered. 'Not wrong, she's got you there, mate.'

'Whatever. Let's get out of here.'

They got into their jeep and Trev fired up the engine.

Harry turned to Tanya in the back seat. 'You could never smell bad enough to put me off.'

She blew him a kiss. 'And don't you forget it.'

– 4 –

The freshly showered trio were sitting at a corner table in the bar of their hotel, the Mekong Palais, back in Luang Prabang. Harry had quipped as they arrived that whoever had named the joint needed to be beaten savagely with a dictionary opened to the page containing the word 'palace', whereupon Trev had opined that back in the French colonial era, it may well have lived up to its name. But, as for many things of beauty, the years had not been kind, and the low-key, two-star premises, with its attendant casual management regime, had suited their purposes well.

Now they were enjoying a few post-dinner drinks and chilling out. Tanya had suggested getting into Wheeler's notebook and papers, but the men had said that could wait for at least the one evening: they'd be fresher for the task tomorrow. The ceiling fans thrummed and provided a slightly refreshing breeze. It wasn't a patch on air-conditioning, but that was the cost of staying at a low-brow establishment. The bar was similarly post-colonial in a dilapidated way, but the prices were cheap and the service good.

The young Laotian bartender was talking to three middle-aged, male Eurotrash specimens at the bar, loose floral shirts hiding their guts, but their faces failing to hide their holiday motivations as they ogled every young woman who moved within eyeshot. Various arrangements appeared to be made. The local working girls hadn't bothered with Harry and Trev: Tanya's presence acted like a Doberman at a gate. Plus, the locals knew what outclassed looked like when they saw it. The only other patrons were some feral-looking backpackers in the opposite corner, noisy and sounding like a mixture of Canadian, British, Irish, and Swedish.

Harry ran his finger over Orla's pendant that was currently next to his glass on the chipped antique tabletop.

'Can't believe we missed the bastard.'

'I can't believe how corrupt the bloody cops are,' said Tanya. 'I thought some of ours at home were bad enough, but this lot, wow!'

'Some of our lot can be pretty bad, babe. They just tend to be more discreet about it.'

'Yep, and usually a bit more sophisticated,' joined in Trev. 'Over here it's more like a public badge of honour. Same end result, though.'

He touched Harry's hand on the pendant. 'Mate, we will get him. I don't care if we're still hunting him on our Zimmer frames, we will get him.'

'Thanks, Trev, you're a true mate.'

Tanya stood and leaned into Harry, kissing him on the cheek. 'And I'll be there, too. Only when you two are on Zimmers, my sexy arse will still be rocking like heaven on legs.' She grinned at both of them. 'I'm off to grab a round, my turn again already.'

She walked off, swinging her gorgeous buttocks as she went, and looking back over her shoulder at the guys.

A couple of Lao girls loitering near the door, intermittently pouting at the Eurotrash, gave Tanya bitchy looks.

Harry took a slug of his Scotch, Jameson not being available, and slipped Orla's pendant into his shirt pocket.

'I thought you were going to keep wearing it, mate.'

'I wanted to, but then I decided I wanted to look at it regularly, and that didn't work on my neck.'

'We need to get you a longer chain for it.'

'Maybe.' Harry sighed. 'So, Trev, what thoughts on where to from here, given we know how unreliable and fickle the local cops are?'

'Mate, without being able to buy off some official, we're not going to get access to anything useful. If we knew which town Wheeler was headed to, then maybe we could try to grease up a new bunch of cops, but it'd be complete guesswork on where he might go.'

'Yeah. But let's look at the map and see what the options are. We're here now, and I can sniff my final act of vengeance. I'm not going home empty-handed.'

'Fair point.' Trev opened his iPad.

Tanya arrived back, with a bottle of sparkling wine in a bucket and three flutes.

'What the?' said Harry.

Trev frowned.

'February the eighth. A certain Mister PI is a birthday boy! And I did ask for champagne, but we're not in that sort of joint, so New Zealand sparkling white it is.'

Harry looked surprised. 'Bugger me. I'd totally forgotten in all this excitement.'

'Must confess me too,' said Trev. 'Well done, Tan.' He turned to Harry. 'So, mate, how old is it today?'

'Piss off.'

Tanya laughed. 'It's forty-seven today.' She slowly poured three glasses of sparkling wine. They chinked glasses.

'Happy birthday,' said Tanya and Trev in unison.

'Cheers, guys. And babe, you are a beautiful and wonderful woman and friend.'

'Don't forget it, big boy.'

'Oh, please, here we go again,' groaned Trev.

'Or,' smirked Tanya, 'I could let the girls over there know that big Aussie man here is a birthday boy. I'm sure they'd give you a treat or three.'

Harry snorted, almost choking on a mouthful of wine. 'Yeah, and possibly a disease or three. Thank you, babe, but the only birthday present of a carnal variety I want is whatever you might have in mind later.'

'We shall see about that.'

Trev groaned into his drink again.

They all laughed and drank the bubbles.

'And,' continued Tanya, 'I do have something on order for you. Might be a while, though.'

'So, tell me,' said Harry.

'No, it's a surprise.'

'And something else we'd lost track of, guys,' said Trev. 'A toast to our big friend, Zanza. His weeks of speech therapy following his successful surgery are well underway now.'

'Shit, that's right,' said Harry. 'Well, here's to Zanza and a successful tongue reconstruction job.'

'Zanza,' they all intoned, and then drank.

'Was Mama Jocasta going to let you know how it's all going?' asked Tanya.

'I messaged her to say we'd be a bit hard to get hold of for a while, and I'd contact her when we were back in civilization.'

'So, text her now, Harry.'

Harry looked at his watch. 'Just after seven here, so add four for Sydney, makes eleven. Yeah, Mama will still be at the Club: early in the night for the illicit breast-feeders.'

Trev sniggered.

Harry felt in his pocket and frowned.

'No, mate,' said Trev. 'We left all the phones on charge upstairs.'

'Oh, yeah. Forgot that in my hurry to get a drink.'

'No worries,' said Tanya. 'I need to go to the loo anyway, and I sure as hell don't fancy that dodgy bathroom at the back over there. I'll go upstairs to my room and bring your phone back. Give me your key.'

'Cool, thanks.' Harry handed her his room key.

Tanya stood and headed for the stairs.

'Looking forward to finally having a chat with big Zanza when he's finished therapy,' said Harry.

'And what a great way to spend a hundred grand,' said Trev. 'Who said dirty money couldn't do noble deeds?'

'Not me brother, that's for sure.'

'To noble causes, brother.'

They chinked glasses.

Tanya stopped outside her room. Harry had suggested they all have separate rooms to have some space, after the close confines of the jungle stake-out. Tanya had agreed and said if he behaved himself, she might allow him to visit, but only for a quickie.

Now she slipped the key into the door of her room and stepped in quickly. She couldn't remember if the lamp shining on the bedside stand had been on when she left. Her bladder was impressing a sense of urgency. She closed the door behind her and moved towards the en suite before her brain registered a warning bell. There was an intruding aroma in the room: rancid sweat wrestling with garlic and beer.

Tanya's alarm went off in the same instant a force struck her in the back and she was propelled headlong onto the bed. As she turned over and tried to get on her feet, she saw the malevolent face of the cop she'd belted earlier that day. He was out of uniform now, wearing jeans and a black Megadeath concert T-shirt. His dress may have been less authoritative, but the twenty-centimetre stainless-steel blade in his right hand looked every bit as threatening as the AK-47 he'd been gripping that morning.

When the slit beneath his nose opened, it couldn't be called a smile or even a grin: a chasm of evil, maybe.

As the man approached, the chasm hissed at her. 'You must learn respect, girl. Me teach you. Me fuck you. Fuck you hard. You learn respect.'

Tanya's mind was racing. 'Over my dead body, you pencil-dicked cunt.'

She had no illusions that he'd understand the slight on his manhood, but it made her feel better. More importantly, it helped drive up her aggression levels. She'd learnt the hard way that the best method to overcome fear was to replace it with channelled rage and cunning.

Okay, girl, she thought, you took control with those Muslim rapists last year, and there were four of them.

Here she was again, but with one assailant. Still, she'd need to channel it all perfectly right now, or over her dead body it would certainly be.

And she was desperate to avoid that blade. She still had vivid memories of her face being slashed open by that paedophile at the piggery last year. The plastic surgeon had done almost flawless work on her cheek, and she wasn't wanting that undone. She looked at the steel, and then back at the cruel, beady eyes above it.

He was moving forward, with that misogynistic sneer stuck to his face like a smear of dried dog shit on the footpath.

Tanya moved quickly, swinging her legs over the other side of the bed. Anticipating, correctly, that the arsehole would follow by lunging at her with the knife, she grabbed the pillow behind her with one hand.

As the cop closed the distance, she brought the pillow round and lunged in his direction, startling him. She got the pillow in front of the blade as he struck out at her and was able to divert his arm enough that the now smothered blade slid past her. As it did so, she lifted her knee fast and hard, hoping to connect with his crotch, but landing in his lower gut. It distracted him, but didn't put him down as she'd wanted, and needed.

His free hand sailed towards her face, so she grabbed it, directed it to her mouth, and bit down as hard as she could on the fleshy outer edge. She tasted blood.

The cop squealed and decided he needed his other hand disentangled from the bundle of impaled pillow.

Just what I wanted, thought Tanya: knife out of the equation.

She released her teeth and concentrated on driving her straightened fingers into the man's eye. This time he shrieked.

Tanya had just wanted to do enough to escape, and now she turned for the door. Before she could move, however, the wailing assailant transformed into a spitting one, and a bloodied, one-eyed ball of anger rushed her.

She went down, back onto the bed, with the enraged cop on top of her, trying to grab her throat with his uninjured hand.

'I kill you, whore!'

Tanya scrabbled on her back, towards the head of the bed. She was trying to release her feet to kick him, but he kept his body on them, grabbing for her throat and face. She hit the headboard: no more room to escape into.

He made a final surge, like a malignant cockroach, and his fingers closed around her larynx. She went to jab his still open eye, but he was ready for that move and slapped her hand away.

She punched him several times, but he kept his vital facial parts turned away and her fist on his cranium had little effect. She could feel her lungs burning from the lack of air.

Girl, it's so not going to bloody end like this. Not after everything you've survived.

She dug deep into her reserves, fighting down the rising panic. Getting raped now was not the concern, getting killed was. And with this piece of shit, he'd no doubt fuck her warm corpse as well.

The arsehole wasn't looking at her, too busy shielding his good eye from her hands, so he didn't see her look to her side and lunge for the bed lamp.

Tanya grabbed the lamp with its flimsy glass shade.

It shattered immediately on his head, but its light-weight glass wasn't enough to stun him. However, it did make him move suddenly, and his grip slackened at the same time.

Tanya wasn't one to miss opportunities. She drove her free knee into his balls and sprang back off the bed, still holding the lamp base with its bare, glaring bulb.

The cop rolled off the bed, clutching at his gonads.

Tanya thought she could make a dash now, but the cop was determined. Back he came, again clutching the knife. He crawled on the bed with surprising speed.

Tanya looked at his blade, then at her lamp. She had a flash of recollection of some movie she'd watched with Harry where some bad guy had got electrocuted. She always remembered Harry's lame line, 'Well, that was a shocking way to go.' As the evil cop reared up to come off the bed at her, she drove the lamp bulb full force into his open eye.

At the same time as the glass globe broke there was a massive flash and the room went dark. In the faint light seeping in from the street, Tanya saw the cop's body slump onto the bed.

She ran for the door.

– 5 –

'Fucky ducky!' said Harry, stepping back from checking the cop's pulse. There was none. What there was was a tinge of burnt electrical and scorched flesh smell. 'Crispy fried bacon,' said Harry, grinning, 'And as dead as a corrupt cop should be.'

'Guess we're changing some plans now,' said Trev. 'We get caught here with a stiff cop, then we ain't ever going home. And as gay as I am, the sexual options available in the local slammer do not appeal.'

'Even less so for me, mate,' said Harry.

'Guys, I'm really sorry, but he was going to rape me and kill me. And not necessarily in that order. I had no choice.'

'You have absolutely nothing to apologize for, Tan.' Trev put his hand on her shoulder.

'Definitely don't apologize, babe. And even if you had had a choice, I'd still vote for this as the right one.'

'Thanks, Harry. I'm sorry, not for dealing with him, but because I know this will stuff up our plans. We're going to have to get out of here.'

'Still the right choice, Tan.' Trev hugged her.

'Yep, sure as shit. You, Divine One, are always more important. Never forget that.' Harry joined in to make it a group hug.

He stepped back. 'Anyway, we'd lost the trail. But you're right, we will need to leave Laos, and sooner rather than later.'

'And we'll need to get rid of the body,' said Trev. 'Left here, they'll find him when the room is cleaned out, find our names on the hotel register, and they won't need to be rocket scientists from there.'

'We can't just report what he did to me and say I was defending myself?' asked Tanya. 'His boss did see him grab me earlier.'

'Babe, Major fucking Vang might not have approved of him groping you, and was even happy for you to punch him, but take it from me, a live cop will always seek to avenge a dead cop.'

'About the only exception to that rule of police life,' added Trev, 'would be for a dead paedophile cop. But that doesn't help us here. There is absolutely no way out of this by any official or legal means, not in this country.'

Harry nodded. 'And even if we did get our names cleared, it would only be after a few months minimum banged up in Vientiane Prison.'

'So, it has to be unofficial and illegal instead,' said Trev.

'Okay,' sighed Tanya. 'But now we have a body to move. Not exactly a subtle activity.'

Trev chuckled. 'Yeah, pity there's not a piggery next door.'

'Ah, memories,' smiled Harry. 'I still always check my bacon packets to make sure it hasn't come from WA.'

'And talking of piggeries, boys, remember Ms Tanya here does not do dead body duties. Remember?'

'Of course, babe. Consider us your dedicated undertaker service.'

She flipped him the bird.

Trev laughed. 'Mate, there was a housekeeping room along the corridor. I noticed a couple of large laundry trolleys with bags. One of them down the service elevator and out the back to the car park could be the go.'

'Yeah,' said Harry. 'You see any staff?'

'No, but I'll go for a quick recce now.'

'Roger that.'

Trev stepped out of the room, closing the door.

'Harry, I am really sorry to stuff up the hunt for Wheeler. I know just how much it means to you.' She took his hands.

'Babe, I'm just so bloody happy that you're okay. We'll bide our time and other opportunities for Wheeler will come along, or we will make them happen, or a combination of both.'

'But we were so close today.'

'Yeah, and we got shafted by a corrupt cop. Occupational hazard in these countries. But we have no leads as to where Wheeler has gone, so we could trawl around here for weeks and be no further advanced.'

'Yeah, I'm definitely over this place.' She smiled at him. 'And I was going to bang you for your birthday tonight, but guess that'll have to be a raincheck.'

'Damn and double damn,' said Harry. 'Well, we will be back in Vientiane at that good hotel before we fly out, so I'm all up for banging then.'

'Cool.' She kissed him on the lips.

'And can't wait to get back home, I'm hankering for our beloved Emerald Bar.'

'That'd be bloody perfect right now,' said Trev, stepping back into the room.

'How's it look, mate?'

'Good, I reckon. Easy run to the service lift with the body. No staff on this level. Only risk I can see downstairs is that security guy who sits next to the reception desk, with a view into the bar.'

'Can he see down the corridor to the back door?'

'Not without sticking his head around the corner, but if he hears the service elevator fire up, he might think that's unusual at this time in the evening.'

'Yeah,' said Harry, 'all the cleaning has been done and unlikely to be any evening deliveries. Plus, he's probably sitting there bored to tears, so will be eager for something to do.'

'Right. So, we need him busy and we need some noise,' said Trev. 'A fight out the front would do it. Or a traffic accident.'

'Can't see us pulling off either at the same time as moving the stiff, mate. And we can't get Tan to take the jeep for a little prang out the front, 'cos we need it to stick the stiff into.'

'Yep. Any other thoughts?'

'You blokes need to think laterally,' teased Tanya.

'What?' came simultaneously from the men.

'I've got a cunning plan.' Tanya smirked at them, rubbing her breasts.

'We're all ears, babe.'

'Relying on the fact that you blokes are all led by your dicks …' She trailed off to allow the indignant snorts and feigned horror.

'So, I'll reluctantly, because I sure ain't feeling sexy right now, get out of this practical outfit and slip into my denim shorts and a boob-tube.'

'I'm getting some movement,' said Harry.

'Oh, please,' muttered Trev.

'I'll strut past the security dude, giving him plenty of arse wiggle and pout, and go fire up the jukebox with some heavy rock tracks. That's the noise part. Then I'll give the whole bar and the guard the raunchiest set of dance moves this shitty town has ever seen.'

'And, meanwhile, we have an uninterrupted run to the jeep with the body,' said Harry. 'Love it, you never cease to impress.'

Tanya laughed. 'Yeah, righto, you're just picturing my arse in those shorts.'

'Mucho impressive, of course, but I was actually referring to your smartness.'

'When you two have finished your flirtations, I do believe we now have a plan,' said Trev.

Ten minutes later, the debris from the fight had been eliminated, and the dead cop was hidden inside a laundry sack on a trolley. Tanya had moved her stuff into Harry's room, saying there was no way she was going to get to sleep in the bed she'd come close to dying in. She was now getting ready to head to the bar.

'On my way down,' came her voice through the door, as she passed the room of death.

'Cool, let's move it,' said Harry.

Trev peeked out into the corridor. 'All clear.'

They trundled their cadaverous cargo out of the room and along the corridor to the back of the hotel.

Harry looked at the antiquated service elevator. 'Looks as if it's probably the original put in by the French back in the day.'

'Not wrong,' said Trev. 'Hopefully it won't be quite as noisy as a French waiter.'

'Or a French whore,' added Harry, grinning in the subdued lighting emanating from a lonely bulb with insects for company.

'Wouldn't know about that,' grinned Trev. 'Now we just need the bloody music to fire up.'

'Yeah, Tanya's taking a while.'

'Or maybe it just feels that way since we're loitering here like a couple of rent boys with a dead body.'

'Maybe, brother.'

'She's probably getting a drink and coins for the jukebox.'

'True,' said Harry, 'or she's been waylaid by a randy security guard.'

Trev chuckled. 'Hope not, we might get a second stiff to deal with.'

As Harry opened his mouth to reply, the relative quiet of the old joint was blasted out of the ballpark by Bon Jovi's 'Bad Medicine' firing up from the bar below.

'Love it, that is noisy,' said Trev. 'Let's go.'

Harry hit the elevator call button and the carriage rattled up towards them. The clunk as it stopped at their floor was loud enough to make both of them flinch, but Bon Jovi were loud enough to wake the local cemetery.

In the lift car, Trev pressed the button 'RC' and their steel box lurched downwards.

'Mate, where's the "G"?'

'It is indeed the old French machine, Harry. "RC" stands for *rez-de-chaussée*, ground floor in the old *français*.'

Harry shook his head, smirking. 'You never cease to amaze. Obviously, too many of those young French men, mate.'

'You can never have too many of them.'

'So, smart-arse, what does the "SS" button mean then?'

'That, my friend, is the basement, or *sous-sol*.'

'Sorry I asked. One floor and the longest lift ride of my life,' said Harry.

Trev smiled. 'True, but at least it's not your last lift ride, unlike Officer Lucky here.'

Tanya had got herself a beer at the bar, and a heap of coins. She desperately wanted a vodka cocktail, but couldn't keep the guys waiting with their corpse in a bag whilst the bartender mixed a drink for her.

On her way to the bar, she'd made sure she slowed as she passed the security desk and beamed at the guard, who had been bored shitless until that moment. She could feel his eyes on her as she went to the bar, giving her butt cheeks a swagger in their obscenely inadequate covering. Her denim shorts were so brief at least a third of her arse cheeks were on display.

She pushed her butt out as she leant on the jukebox making her selections. She fed the coin slot and loaded up five good, loud rock numbers. She loved Bon Jovi, so it wasn't any effort to move to the beat as the music blared. And "It's My Life" suited her mood perfectly.

Her scarlet boob tube was scarcely up to the task of containing her breasts, and her bosom and butt combined garnered the lascivious gaze of every male in the room, and the envious, snarky snarls of the local girls.

The security guy had wandered through to watch Tanya and had perched himself on a stool. She smiled at him, thinking the job was done perfectly as he couldn't see anything down the corridor now. He smiled back, thinking her look was for him.

She could see a bulge in his tight, military-style pants. So predictable, she thought, and so easy to manipulate. She put extra gusto into her air guitar solo.

The noise of the rock music was even louder as the elevator door opened on the ground level.

Harry stuck his head out, but the corridor was dark. There was a pulsing multi-coloured glow coming from the direction of the bar and foyer.

'Clear, let's move.'

'Roger that,' said Trev.

In under a minute, they were out in the dark car park behind their rented jeep. They loaded their corpse and spread some towels from the laundry trolley over the top of the sack with the dead cop in it.

'Hopefully he won't have started smelling too bad by the time we check out in the morning,' said Trev.

'Yeah, it'll be a windows-down drive into the jungle, me thinks. I bet Suzuki never envisaged this little model doubling as a hearse.'

Trev chuckled. 'Kenmare and Matson, undertakers to the corrupt and deservedly deceased.'

'Got a bloody ring to it, brother. Let's go have a drink and appear normal.'

'Best suggestion yet. And one very good thing about these cheap shit-holes, mate.'

'What's that, apart from the cheap booze?'

'No bloody CCTV systems, Mister Kenmare.'

'Ah yes, an oft-underrated benefit of budget travel and perfect for us, Mister Matson.'

They parked the trolley in the ground floor service area and walked towards the bar. By now Aerosmith's "Walk This Way" was blasting the neighbourhood, with Steven Tyler tunefully celebrating cheerleaders and little skirts.

They paused, both smiling, at the entrance to the bar, looking at the same spectacle everyone else was transfixed by.

'Blonde hair aside, Trev, who does Tanya remind you of right now? Think eighties.'

'Ooh, maybe *Baywatch*?'

'Nah, earlier than that. And think the shortest shorts.'

'Mate, I didn't take a huge amount of notice of the girls.' Trev slapped Harry on the shoulder. 'Mostly never been my thing, the odd experimental tasting aside.'

'Of course. But you must remember this show, even if you were ogling the two guys.'

Trev shook his head blankly.

'Mate, there is our very own Daisy Duke from *The Dukes of Hazzard*.'

Trev roared laughing. 'Fucking oath, she's a dead ringer right now, I see it. But I did prefer the blond brother, Bo.'

Harry sniggered and shook his head. 'Of course you did.'

– 6 –

Three tired-looking sleuths checked out of the Mekong Palais shortly after the front desk opened in the morning. Trev had suggested it would be prudent to stay together overnight, just in case, and take turns to stay alert. So, sleep had not been abundant.

'Yuk, he's smelling already,' said Tanya, opening the passenger door of the jeep.

'A little touch of putrefaction, maybe,' said Harry. 'Windows open and we'll get rid of him in the first decent jungle patch we hit. Few kilometres at most, looking at Google maps.'

Trev grinned. 'Love the smell of rotting corpse in the morning.'

Harry chimed in with his best imitation of an incoming Huey chopper.

Tanya looked at Trev, then Harry. 'Sometimes you guys are fricking strange.'

'Movie reference, babe, Vietnam war.'

'Not my kind of movie. Now, being the lady in this weird outfit, I am not sitting in the back seat.'

'Thought you liked to stretch out,' said Trev.

'Yeah, but I'm ready to puke as it is.'

'Fair enough,' said Harry. 'I'll take the mortuary bench until we get rid of him.'

Trev started the engine and Harry loaded their travel bags on top of their smelly cargo. They headed onto the main street.

'Okay, Harry, navigate me to the road heading for Vientiane.'

'Roger that. Next main road on the left.'

Trev followed Harry's instructions and within a couple of minutes they were on a road leading out of town.

'Be glad to see the back of this joint,' said Trev. 'Can't trust any fucker here.'

'Too right,' said Harry. 'Even the hotel bloke slung in an unmentioned extra charge. Smiled at me like a sly rat and said it was a special local tax.'

'Did you pay it?' asked Tanya.

'Yes, of course. We didn't need to argue about anything this morning.'

'Reckon they must teach con-tricks and corruption at school here. Seems so bloody endemic.'

'Yeah, so natural for them. In fact, we should export a whole bunch of them back home. They'd take over the political system in a flash. Make our bunch of bent wankers look angelic by comparison.'

Trev laughed. 'Oh, yes. Would give our trough-feeding fucking thieves a real run for their money.'

'Actually, other people's money, but we won't split hairs. Now, chariot driver, get us the fuck out of here.'

'Roger.' Trev eased the jeep up to the speed limit.

The buildings thinned out as they traversed a mixture of rice paddies and palm plantations, climbing into the hills.

Tanya, gazing out the window, spotted the police car first. 'Don't go speeding up, Trev. Cop car back down that side road.'

Harry turned around, wincing slightly as his nose got closer to the odorous load.

'Can't see anything through the foliage.'

Trev had eased off on the accelerator a touch, glancing repeatedly in the mirror. 'Shit, looks like they're turning onto the road behind us. Don't look around again, Harry, we don't want to appear shifty.'

'Of course, mate, 'cos there's nothing remotely shifty about having a dead cop in the back.'

Trev looked in the mirror again. 'Bugger, they've turned in our direction.'

The police car closed the distance with the jeep.

'They've just flashed their headlights. Think we'd better pull over.'

'Strange it wasn't with the blue lights and siren,' said Harry.

Trev pulled the car onto the dirt verge. 'Right, we'll hop out to go meet them. Don't need them getting their noses in here.' He opened his door.

'Exactly. I'll have my wallet ready. Seems to fix everything except cancer in this bloody country.' Harry got out of the back door.

The pair of them walked towards the police car, Trev making a friendly waving gesture.

A familiar uniformed figure got out of the back seat of the cruiser. The driver stayed put.

'Major Vang,' said Harry. 'Always a pleasure.' He doubted the cop would get the sarcasm.

'Mister Kenmare and Mister Matson, how are you today?'

'Okay thanks, Major, but I'd be better if we'd found Wheeler again,' replied Harry.

'No more leads from your search of his room?'

'No, Major, that's why we're leaving and heading to Bangkok,' said Trev, glancing at Harry.

'Going to talk to our contacts there in the Australian Federal Police. I know the liaison officer stationed there,' lied Harry.

Trev noticed Vang looking past them at the jeep. 'Tell you what, Major, how would it sound if we paid you some money just in case you come across any information on Wheeler in the future? Call it a deposit on your future invaluable assistance.'

'Yeah, we could check in with you every couple of weeks by email,' added Harry.

Vang nodded slowly, as if considering the deal. 'I think we can do business again. What is your proposition?'

Harry pulled his wallet out. 'Let's say five hundred US dollars now, and more if you find Wheeler for us. And an extra bonus if I get him.'

Vang's mouth formed its rat-like grin. 'Let's say a thousand now. I like big round numbers.'

Harry made a pretence of vacillating, not wanting to appear too eager to hurry the deal. 'I don't think I've got a thousand on me. Maybe six hundred at most.'

'No problems,' smiled Vang.

Harry breathed a sigh of relief. It was short lived.

Vang continued, 'We will follow you back into town and you can go to a bank to get the rest. Problem solved and deal done.'

Harry looked at Trev who put his hand on his shoulder. 'No worries, Harry, you give the Major what you've got and I'll grab my emergency reserve cash from the car.'

Trev looked back at Vang. 'You'll have your thousand in just a minute, Major.'

'Excellent.' The gold tooth glinted.

Trev walked back to their car as Harry counted the greenbacks out of his wallet.

Trev opened the back flap of the jeep, wrinkled his nose at the burgeoning odour, and unzipped his travel bag.

'What's going on?' asked Tanya from the front seat, her hand shading her nose.

'We need more money, Tan, but I think we'll be cool.'

Trev found his washbag, unzipped it and pulled out a plastic envelope stuffed with US dollars. He closed the car flap and strode back to Harry and Vang.

'How much do you need, Harry?'

'Mate, I've given the good Major seven hundred.'

Trev counted out 300 and passed it across to the cop. 'There you go, Major. Will be a good weekend in the Vang household.'

Harry joined in. 'And some nice present for Missus Vang.'

'Excellent, excellent.' Vang caressed the sheaf of banknotes before pocketing it. 'And it would be a gesture of good will to go over and give my driver a hundred dollars.'

It wasn't a suggestion.

Trev took out another 100 and stepped over to the driver's side of the police car. He handed the banknotes to a grinning cop behind the wheel.

'For you,' said Trev.

The cop grabbed the money.

Trev went back to stand next to Harry. Vang was looking as happy as a pig in shit. He shook hands with both the sleuths.

'Safe travels, gentlemen. May our next meeting be equally as lucrative for me and fulfilling for you.'

'Oh, absolutely, Major. We can't wait,' oozed Harry.

Again, despite his flawless English, the Major was oblivious to the sarcasm.

He gave Harry his business card, tipped his peaked cap, and got back into the cop car. The driver did a three-point turn and they headed back in the direction of the town.

'Fuck me,' exhaled Harry.

'Good job the prick doesn't get sarcasm, Harry, you might have really pissed him off.'

'Trev, that was a fraction of what I wanted to say. One day I'd like to take to Major fucking Vang with a baseball bat.'

'He is one slimy, greedy wanker. I'll give him ten out of ten for sheer bloody gall. That's what unchecked corrupt power does.'

'Too right. I think on this trip my wallet has opened its flaps more than the busiest whore in Laos.'

Trev chuckled. 'Well, we got out of that scrape, but I really want to get going and get rid of the stiff.'

'Hell yes. A jungle ravine awaits us, brother.'

The jeep-cum-hearse resumed its journey on Route 13 towards Vientiane, some seven hours away, climbing into the low hills outside Luang Prabang.

'According to Google, mate, there's a lovely, quiet jungle track coming up on your right,' said Harry from the back seat.

Trev slowed the car. 'Ah, yes, I see it. Gotta love Google.'

'Should be quite winding and hilly, and it rejoins the main road in a few klicks.'

'Any houses?'

'None after these first few.'

They rounded a sharp bend heading downhill and then climbing again. Two further hairpin bends and they were invisible to the world despite having travelled only a few hundred metres from the road.

Trev pulled the car to a stop next to a sheer drop into a leafy gully.

'This might do the trick,' he said, getting out of the car.

Harry and Tanya did likewise.

Harry looked over the edge of the track at the dense foliage a few metres below. 'Perfect. He'll go straight through all that greenery and lie beneath it totally out of sight.'

'Yep, and probably forever. Even if someone passing does notice a rotting smell, they'll just think it's an animal.'

'Exactly what he was,' said Tanya. 'But what if he is found? A dead cop after all.'

'More than likely,' said Trev, 'it'll be written off as some corrupt deal gone wrong. The cops here are all into so much criminal shit the only way of telling who's who is the uniform.'

'Totally,' said Harry. 'Corruption deals go sour around here and dead bodies follow. It's not going to raise any unusual red flags.'

'Let's do this, Harry.'

Trev opened the back flap on the jeep and pulled out their travel bags.

'We need to remove any jewelry and his wallet,' said Harry, leaning into the car to grab one end of the dead bundle.

'Better still, we strip him. We can get rid of his clothes down the road, along with the laundry bag.'

'Why?' Tanya had a look of distaste on her face.

'His body will decompose pretty quickly down there, but the clothes will be recognizable for a lot longer,' said Harry.

Trev and Harry stripped the corpse. Then, with Harry holding the ankles and Trev the arms, they swung the body over the edge and watched as it plummeted through the tree canopy. There was a wet slopping sound as it landed beneath.

'Right, let's piss off,' said Harry.

Trev was bundling the cop's clothes into the laundry sack, along with the towels. 'Luckily no hotel name on any of this.'

'Another benefit of low-grade accommodation,' said Harry.

'And we'll chuck his watch and wallet separately.'

'You're driving, so give them here, mate. I'll lob them out as we're moving.'

Tanya took a last look into the verdant ravine and gave the treetops her middle finger. 'Good riddance, cunt.'

Harry touched her face. 'All good?'

'Yep, sure am. I'm so sick of these entitled men who reckon women are just asking for it and reckon they can help themselves.'

'Well, that arsehole got his just desserts thanks to you, Tan,' said Trev.

She grinned. 'And I bet that wasn't anywhere in his entitled songbook.'

Harry chortled. 'Damned right. Let's hit the road, team, it's seven hours to Vientiane. And then we can relax in a much better hotel. Plus, I want to get stuck into Wheeler's stuff over a bucketful of booze.'

'Roger that,' said Trev, starting the car's engine.

– 7 –

The trio made Vientiane shortly before sunset, pulling into their pre-booked Hotel, the Jade Oasis, overlooking the Mekong River.

Harry had showered and was enjoying the first beer, an ice bucket full of bottles having been delivered by room service. They'd had a late lunch on the road, so he wasn't hungry yet. But the cold beer tasted ambrosial. The room's air-conditioning was running hard, and Harry didn't miss the humidity outside as he stared out of the window, watching the orange orb of the setting sun as it descended through the smog towards the horizon. As it sank, the dying rays picked out the various particles polluting the air, creating a radiant pastiche of peach and magenta.

Ironic, thought Harry, that such beauty came about largely from the filth in the atmosphere.

There was a light tap on the door and Harry turned as Tanya walked in. She was back in her Daisy Duke denim shorts and a loose cheesecloth shirt tied in a knot revealing her taut, honed midriff. She'd washed her hair that was now blow-dried and teased out, rather than her practical ponytail out on the job.

Harry beamed at her. 'You look delicious and, frankly, edible.'

'And feeling clean now. But later, Mister PI, I plan on getting totally filthy. It's your belated birthday sex tonight.'

She walked over to him and rubbed her hand down the front of his trousers.

Harry groaned. 'You tease, you. Trev's about to …'

'Exactly,' she grinned. 'And we couldn't have him walking in on us, could we now.'

'Well, I don't think that's the sort of sex Trev would be interested in watching, or joining in.'

'Who knows? Sexual interest isn't black and white for everyone.' She winked at Harry.

'Well, it is for me. Now behave yourself. Wanna a beer, babe?'

'Hell yes.'

Harry opened one and passed it to her.

She looked at all the items spread out on the bed: notebooks, papers, and photos.

'So, anything interesting?'

'Plenty. Now we've had a chance to take a good look.'

There was another tap on the door and Trev walked in, also showered and cleanly shaven.

'Ah, cold beer. You read my mind, Mister Kenmare.'

'Mister Matson, that doesn't exactly make me a genius.' Harry passed him a bottle. 'Here you go, mate.'

He raised his bottle. 'Cheers, team, we certainly earned these.'

The bottles were chinked.

Harry stepped over to the bed. 'I was about to start telling Tanya, this is a bloody treasure trove.'

'Cool, always love those,' said Trev, picking up a bundle of photos and looking through them.

'Fuck me, is that who I think it is?'

'Sure looks like him,' said Harry.

Tanya looked at the photo of a middle-aged, naked, white man with a young, brown-skinned girl, also nude and about eleven or twelve. He was holding her down on a bed. He looked smug. She looked blank. Tanya knew that look, from the inside.

'Give me a gun,' she said. 'I'd shoot the cunt.'

Trev took the photo. 'He's not looking at the camera. You reckon he knew it was being photographed?'

'No,' said Harry. 'I reckon Reggie has discreetly collected himself a whole lot of trophies. A load of wanking material, but also some serious leverage if he needs it, given I recognize more than one Aussie face in the collection.'

'So, is that pedo wanker someone important?' asked Tanya.

'Babe, you've no idea. This is huge. A senior political figure.'

'Shit, yes. Can't wait to get home with this lot,' said Trev. He flicked through a group of photos. 'Ooh, yeah. Know him, and him, and this one looks a dead ringer for that prosecutor Bernhard Schwarz told us about.'

'Simon Abrahams?'

'Yep. I did some research on him before we left and this sure looks like him.'

'Guess he normally wears a bit more for court,' said Harry, pointing at the picture Trev was holding with a naked man and a young girl's head in his crotch. 'And he won't be looking so fricking happy when we're done with him.'

Trev was leafing through a notebook now. 'Lots of contacts and addresses in here, as well as some bank account stuff. This'll keep us busy back at the office in Sydney.'

'No doubt plenty of peds in there for us to "persuade" to assist us in finding Wheeler,' said Harry, doing the air quotes.

'I think I might get some more target practice,' said Tanya. 'Best ped's a dead ped.'

Harry chuckled. 'True. But the priority is to find Wheeler again. And, of course, Trev's Father Barwick.'

Trev had moved over to the window, having grabbed a second beer, and was staring at the twilight over the city.

Tanya walked over, also taking a fresh beer, and chinked bottles with Trev. 'You look a bit distracted, Trev. You dreaming of that gay bar?'

Trev beamed at her. 'No. I was thinking of Jean-Louis. This week's the anniversary of his death.'

'Shit, I'm sorry.' She gave him a hug.

'Yeah, sorry, mate,' said Harry, putting a hand on his shoulder. 'Why don't we get ourselves a feed downstairs and then you can see about that bar.'

'Dinner sounds good,' replied Trev. 'But no bar action for me tonight. Just want to be with friends.'

'Well, that you are.' Tanya kissed him.

– 8 –

The hotel restaurant served a superb feast of the local Lao cuisine, before the three sleuths retired to the hotel bar for a few more drinks and to discuss plans for paedophile hunting back in Australia. They'd secured air tickets for the next afternoon: Harry thought it best to get out of Laos pronto, given Tanya's electrifying experience with the police in Luang Prabang.

A couple of drinks turned into several before Harry, feeling beat after the day's travel, called it a night. 'Okay, team, birthday boy here,' and he winked at Tanya, 'is going to hit the sack.'

Trev was looking into his glass, swirling the ice cubes. 'I'll stay for a couple more. Want to reminisce about Jean-Louis.'

Harry gave him a hug. 'Of course, mate.'

Tanya got up, swallowing her drink, ready to go upstairs with Harry. 'You be okay, Trev?' She put her hand on his.

He leant over and kissed her. 'Thank you, Tan, yes. Just need to mull things over for a while. You go give this rogue his birthday present.'

She poked Harry in the ribs. 'Yeah, I reckon he'll last about fifteen minutes, total, and then be snoring his guts out.'

'Funny!' said Harry. 'But it'll be a wicked fifteen minutes.'

'Bloody hell, fifteen minutes would be a marathon for Harry, wouldn't it?' said Trev.

'And you can piss off, too.' Harry smiled and hugged Trev again.

'And, Tan, if he falls asleep on you, you can always join me back here for another drink or three,' said Trev.

Tanya smiled at him and ran her hand over his thigh as she walked off with Harry.

Trev looked into his glass again. 'Bloody hell, don't know whether it's Arthur or Martha this evening,' he said to the ice cubes. He grinned to himself and took a swig. 'Wouldn't be dead for quids, though.'

Harry lay naked on the bed, having made a world record in undressing. His erection stood like one of Cleopatra's Needles.

Tanya peeled off her G-string and put one knee on the bed. 'Birthday boy want to eat some pussy?'

Before Harry could answer, Tanya planted her crotch on his face.

'It was purely rhetorical. Of course you do!'

She giggled as she ground her pussy on Harry's mouth and groaned as his artistic tongue delved into her vulva and lapped at her clitoris. His tongue really was sheer expert, she considered. Five minutes later she orgasmed on his face, digging her fingers into his scalp and her thighs squeezing his head like a vice.

He was grinning as she slid off his face. 'Utter bliss,' he said.

'For me, too.' Tanya reached behind her and grabbed Harry's rock-hard cock, guiding it into her dripping pussy. She lowered herself down, taking in his cock, and started to ride him.

Harry put his hands on her breasts and gently massaged whilst playing with her nipples that were hard like large pebbles.

'I cannot even conceive a more perfect birthday present.'

'Many happy returns, my wonderful man,' said Tanya, riding him faster now.

'Oh, babe, I'm going to explode!'

'Let me have it, big boy!' Tanya leant back and clutched Harry's scrotum.

That was all he needed. He unloaded inside her, grasping her breasts as he groaned with delight.

Tanya dismounted as Harry's erection waned, and she cuddled next to him.

'Thank you for my birthday pressie, Divine One. Our relationship is far from conventional, but I do love you.'

Tanya tongue kissed him.

'I love you, too. You gave me a life back. And who the hell wants conventional.' She looked at Harry with his drooping eyelids. 'You look beat.'

'I am drained, and you have polished me off beautifully.' He smiled at her. 'Reckon I'll be asleep before I can even get it up again.'

'More's the pity.' She poked him in the ribs.

'Well, young one, you've still got a drinking buddy at the bar if you're wanting to kick on!' He poked her back.

'We'll see.'

Within ten minutes, Harry was out like a light and snoring lightly.

Tanya kissed him on his forehead and slipped off the bed. She went to the bathroom, taking her clothes with her.

A few minutes later, she sauntered back into the bar downstairs.

She sidled up next to Trev who was sitting exactly where they'd left him. Her hand slid onto the inside of his thigh as she kissed his neck.

'Buy a girl a drink?'

Trev turned and grinned. 'For you, Tan, anything.'

'Correct answer, Mister Trev. And I'll hold you to that. Right now, damn it, I'll have a Long Island Iced Tea, please.'

'Ooh, go hard, girlfriend. I might just join you.'

Trev signalled the barman and ordered the drinks.

An hour and three Long Islands later, the pair swayed arm-in-arm to the elevator.

Trev looked wistfully at the mirror in the lift.

Tanya caught the look. 'You thinking of Jean-Louis again?'

Trev nodded. 'Yeah, I still miss the French bugger terribly.'

'Know that feeling with Sash.'

'Shit, sorry, Tan. Didn't mean to make it only about me.'

She leant her head against his shoulder and hugged him. 'Tell me, does the grief get any less?'

'No, Tan, I don't think so. You just learn to cope better, that's all.'

The lift door opened and they stumbled into the corridor.

'I'll always have a spot in my heart for Jean-Louis,' said Trev softly. 'As you will for Sasha. Love does that. Part of it lasts forever. At least that's what I believe.'

'I think I agree.'

They stopped outside Trev's room.

'You want some company, Trev?'

'Shit, not sure I need another drink,' said Trev, opening his door.

Tanya pushed him inside. 'Wasn't thinking of drinking.'

Trev looked quizzically at her as he sat on the bed.

'Meant I might be able to help with you feeling lonely. Bit of loving with a good friend.'

'Not my usual style, Tan, but you know that.'

'I might take offence, Mister Trev. I'm not used to rejection. Am I not sexy enough for you?' She grinned and brushed her bosom across his face, then sat astride his legs.

'Absolutely no offence meant, Tan. Just I'm gay.'

She kissed him on the lips. 'Course I know that, duh! You never slept with a girl?'

'Well, yeah, when I was a teenager and still working things out. And a couple of drunken flings in my twenties.'

'Cool. So, I've got a very, very sweet arse, Trev. You could just pretend I'm whatever you fancy. And we both get some loving feeling. We are two consenting adults, after all.'

Trev opened his mouth, but no words flowed.

'And I go for sex with anyone who makes me feel like it: straight, gay, whatever.'

Trev's voice returned. 'So, a hot pan-sexual lady?'

'Yeah, think that's the word.' Tanya giggled. 'But I'll settle for just hot.'

Her hand went into Trev's crotch.

'Oh, my. By the throbbing feel of that beast, I'd say you have no problem at all with the idea of screwing me.'

'Well …'

Tanya slid off his legs and undid his belt, then lowered his fly.

Trev's erection sprang forth out of the front of his boxer shorts.

Tanya gasped. 'Bloody hell, you are well hung, Mister Trev. You sure were at the front of the queue on the day the schlongs were handed out.' She gripped Trev's huge, hardening cock and stroked it to full erection. 'Or should I say, bugger me, that's huge.' She giggled again.

Trev laughed. 'I've even got supersize rubbers for it.'

'Do you really need one? I know I'm clean.'

'Me, too. Always wear one for the casual encounters, which has been a while, anyway. And I've been tested since.'

'Good, because I much prefer bareback. Love that hot gush inside me. Let's do it, Trev.'

Tanya stood and shed her clothes in an instant. She got on all fours on the bed.

'Get the lube out, lots of it, and enjoy my arse, big boy. Unless you want pussy, but I'm guessing not.'

Trev didn't say a word. He pulled a tube of lube and a small bottle out of the bedside drawer, putting them on the bed, as he caressed Tanya's buttocks. He stood and stripped his clothes off.

Tanya helped herself to lube and started playing with herself.

'Come on, big boy, I want it.'

'Take a sniff, Tan,' he said, passing her the little bottle with the cap off.

Tanya felt a generous dollop of lube get eased into her anus.

She inhaled deeply from the brown bottle, and almost instantly felt her face flush and her sphincter relax as the amyl nitrite took effect.

Trev kissed her butt cheeks. 'And, Tan, tell me if it's too much.'

'Oh, Trev, you have no idea how much I want this. Get on with it.'

'Okay, girlfriend, here it comes.'

Tanya groaned into the pillow as she felt Trev slowly ease his massive member into her rectum.

Her fingers worked faster on her clitoris.

Trev bent over and kissed the back of her neck. 'You good with that, Tan?'

'That is the biggest bloody thing I've ever had up my arse, Trev,' she gasped. 'But all good. Hammer me!'

Trev's thrusting became more rapid and forceful.

'And for the record, Tan, your arse feels utterly superb.'

'I know it is, big boy.'

Tanya screamed into the pillow as she came.

A few seconds later, Trev groaned, fingers digging into Tanya's hips, as he exploded deep inside her.

A minute later they lay next to each other having a cigarette.

'See, Trev, I said you wouldn't have any trouble screwing my gorgeous arse.'

Trev chuckled. 'And what a sweet arse it is, Tan. Still, I don't think that makes me pan-sexual.'

'Who cares about labels? It's so much of the problem with the world now: labels and outrage. All that matters here is that we're great friends and we just had a great fuck. Even if you didn't eat my pussy.' She poked him in the ribs.

'Yeah, I'm not into that.'

'Fair enough, and it's all good. The anal was great, but I'm sure glad you had the rush.'

He laughed. 'Yeah, it goes with the territory, for me anyway. And I loved it, too, Tan. Some intimacy was just what I needed. And not with some stranger picked up at a bar.'

They hugged.

She kissed him on the cheek. 'You're a decent guy, Trev, not to mention good looking and toned. You'll find another lover.'

'Yeah, one day.'

Tanya stubbed out her cigarette, got off the bed, and pulled her clothes on.

Trev looked at her. 'Thanks, Tan.'

'Sleep well, Trev.' She blew him a kiss as she stepped to the door.

* * *

PART 2

HARRY'S POWDER

She threw her arms around my neck and kissed me on the lips. It felt warm, like a belt from a bottle of twelve-year-old Scotch, and tasted just as good.

- Gordon Demarco

'I like a whore best of all because I feel she will never cling to me, never get entangled with me. It makes me feel free.'

- Anaïs Nin

– 1 –

A human scream, even one as prolonged and viscerally penetrating as this one, was not going to raise any eyebrows amongst the distant neighbours. On the off chance they heard something, most of them would be pissed or stoned senseless by this time of night. And all of them were inured to the sounds of shrieking animals departing the planet.

Chow Time Pet Foods pungent processing plant adjoined its equally putrid parent company's premises, Red Meat Abattoirs. Both sat squalidly in the crappiest part of the outskirts of Dubbo, five hours north-west of Sydney. If you got too close, their combined obnoxious odours did to your olfactory glands what a length of barbed wire would do to your anus. For the locals, when Mother Nature was feeling capricious and turned the wind towards town, the reeking cloud was enough to make people dry retch in the streets and was the obvious reminder of the plant. What was not obvious was the proprietorship of the business: the outlaw motorcycle gang, Satan's Hogs.

The screaming tonight emanated from a naked, heavily tattooed man, as his bloodied body was fed feet first into an industrial mincing machine. He'd been injected with a strong stimulant to keep him from passing out during his interrogation. So, he didn't stop screaming until the mincing cogs were up to his waist. Archie

Longman, boss of the Hogs, stood grinning as the gang's chief enforcer The Ratfucker—Rocco Corsi on his birth certificate—used a red-stained and dented baseball bat to push the torso and head into the mix to be canned for canine consumption.

An hour earlier, Longman and Corsi had dragged the trussed and blind-folded man out of a van and into the slaughter room, where he was stripped and tied to a steel chair.

The Ratfucker punched the captive in the face five times. 'That's just a tickle, cunt. You wait to see what we've got in store for you.'

Longman picked up a cattle prod and zapped the guy's genitals. He shrieked.

'So, maggot, we keep an eye on all new members, until they prove themselves. And we caught you out, didn't we?'

'What do you mean?' gasped the man.

'Saw you talking to this dude.' Longman produced a photo from his back jeans pocket. 'So, who is your little bacon-flavoured friend, maggot?'

The man looked at Longman with terror in his eyes.

'Yes, that mate of yours is an undercover pig, isn't he?'

Zap! Another jab with the cattle prod.

The man nodded desperately, when he stopped screaming.

The Ratfucker leant in. 'What did you tell the little piggy?'

'Just what I know about that delivery. He told me we were going down anyway, and if I cooperated, I could stay out of prison.'

Longman almost pissed himself laughing. 'Yeah, fat fucking lot of good that's going to do you, you filthy, double-crossing piece of shit.'

'Well, Arch,' said The Ratfucker, 'guess we know why that import went missing now.'

'Yep. And that's why we've got a gang war on our hands.'

Longman turned back to the captive. 'Zap him again, Rocco.'

The man shrieked as the electrodes hit his genitals.

'So, maggot, what did the piggy say about the gang war? You must have been told stuff: it's front-page news every second day.'

The captive gurgled as he tried not to choke on his own snot and saliva. He spat a yellowish globule on the floor.

'He ... he said it was in everyone's interests for the drugs to be off the streets, and the gang war showed everyone who was responsible for the drug trade.'

'What a pile of shit!' shouted Longman. 'The arsehole pigs want a gang war to distract from them stealing the fucking drugs and selling the gear themselves.'

'Yeah,' said The Ratfucker, 'they're all fucking corrupt.'

'But we need to find that damned shipment. And stop the next one going missing.' Longman turned back to the captive. 'Don't suppose your porky mate said anything about who had taken the shipment?'

'No, honestly, I've no idea,' bleated the man.

'And I think I believe you,' said Longman.

The prisoner looked suddenly relieved, like a child having uttered a gem that pleased the teacher.

Longman tapped the man's face with a dirty and brutal finger. 'And now, maggot, it's goodbye time. You have no further use.'

'No!' wailed the man. 'I've told you everything, just like you wanted.'

'Exactly,' said Corsi, grinning. 'And so, you are now surplus to needs.' He cut the ropes binding the man to the chair.

The man howled continuously as he was carried over to the mincing machine.

'See ya, maggot,' said Longman as he flicked the switch and the metal cogs started their circuitous grinding.

Then the real screaming began.

The Ratfucker grinned all the way through to the head being pushed through the mincer. Rocco Corsi loved his work. The job done, he turned to Longman. 'Okay, Arch, what next?'

'We need to find which pigs are running this scam and then deal with them.'

'Look forward to that, always love handing out some pain.'

'Yeah, but we need to know exactly who's doing what. And that's not our strong set of skills. I reckon we head back to Sydney and get Kenmare to do some work for us.'

'Cool. He sure delivered the goods with those Muslim rapists. I really enjoyed that job.'

'Exactly. The man's a professional, and he likes the cash. Apart from the grog, he's got a very expensive brothel habit.'

'Can't fault a bloke for that, Archie.'

– 2 –

'So let me get this straight, Longman,' said Harry, lighting another cigarette as he sat at his desk looking across at Archie Longman. 'You reckon you've got corrupt cops knocking off your drug shipments and you want us to work out who they are so you can lean on them and get your drugs flowing again. Both activities being highly illegal.'

'About the size of it, Kenmare. The other size being the huge fucking pay packet for you. Hundred large, used notes, of course.'

'Naturally. And that's a big pay cheque, if we're only doing surveillance and target locations.'

'Yeah, because we don't have the skills or the resources to do all the tracking and surveillance you blokes do. So, a hundred large is simply a sound investment in our business.'

'I get that, but there are still some ethical considerations here.' Harry half smiled, looking over at Trev on the couch.

The two bikies guffawed.

'Kenmare,' continued Longman, 'I know you don't give a flying rat's arse about the drug laws, since you reckon it should all be legalized, so you told me once.'

'True.'

'And I know you hate corrupt cops, and the Establishment, who we both know run the top of the drug trade anyway.'

'Again true.'

'And I know your concept of ethics is that arseholes need to get what's coming to them.'

'Yeah, you got me.'

'He sure as hell has, Harry, by the short and curlies,' chipped in Trev.

Longman tapped the desktop. 'Way I see it, helping to take down corrupt senior cops trumps the fucked-up drug laws.'

Harry nodded slowly. 'A fair point, I think.'

'Plus,' said Longman, 'even if you do have qualms about the drugs getting out there, they are out there anyway. If the cops steal our drugs, the only difference on the street is the cops make the money instead of us. Every junkie and every cokehead who wants the gear is still getting it.'

Harry looked him in the eye, staring through a cloud of smoke. Longman held the stare, a smirk on his craggy face.

Harry glanced over at Trev, who gave a slight nod.

'Bugger it,' said Harry. 'Let's have a drink and start planning this shakedown.'

Longman offered his hand over the desk and they shook. 'Good man, Kenmare. Besides, we all work well as a team. We know that from sorting out those Muslim cunts who raped Debbie.'

Trev, now over at the drinks cabinet, filled four glasses with Jameson and passed them around. 'Yeah, we sure did that. Cheers, all.'

They all toasted and moved to sit around the coffee table.

'Okay, so what do we know so far?' asked Harry, opening a notepad.

Longman swallowed a mouthful of whiskey. 'Well, we know some of our recent shipments have been disappearing, along with a load of cash.'

'How much we talking?' asked Trev.

'Three to five mill a pop in gear, both coke and hammer. Times that by four or so. And at least half a mill in cash.'

'Fuck me, the cops must be laughing all the way to the bank,' said Harry.

'Scum,' said Trev. 'For all the decent cops out there working hard, I really hate these corrupt wankstains.'

Longman continued. 'The rest of the info we found out from a rat in the ranks. Our ranks.'

'Dead rat,' smirked The Ratfucker.

'I'm sure,' said Harry. 'And I bet you made him squeal for every last minute of his life.'

Longman grinned and lit another smoke. 'Kenmare, my friend, you've got no idea. Still, we'll skip the details of the interrogation.'

'Yeah, less we know the better.'

'Exactly. So, our snitch was being run by an undercover cop, but apparently the whole thing is managed by someone or ones much higher up.'

'And both the Feds and Customs involved,' added Corsi. 'Or whatever the hell Customs are calling themselves these days.'

'Officially Australian Customs and Border Protection Service,' said Harry, grinning. 'But we'll just stick with Customs.'

'Juicy,' said Trev. 'Liking the taste of this. So, do we have any ideas as to exactly who?'

Longman shook his head. 'No, zilch. Which is where we need you guys. We've got the rat's phone with the contact number for his handler. Need you to arrange a meet and do all your surveillance stuff.'

Corsi chuckled. 'Yeah, 'cos we'd stick out like dog's nuts.'

'Plus, you guys are pros at this shit. We sure as hell aren't,' said Longman.

'Okay,' said Harry. 'But we need to identify the big wigs. The handler alone is bugger-all help. So, that could take a lot of dogging the handler, and even then, he may only talk on the phone.'

Trev leant forward. 'Unless we get real cute. Have the snitch start to get toey and demand to meet the big man before any more deals are done.'

Harry nodded pensively. 'Could work. And in any event, they probably wouldn't discuss anything too complicated or incriminating on the phone.'

'Exactly. So, we make it sound as if it is going to be too detailed for a phone chat and force a meet. Worth a red-hot go anyway,' said Trev.

'Yeah,' said Harry, 'the snitch and the handler might have a bit of detail on the phone, but the top dogs would want it as minimal as a whore's morals.'

Trev cackled. 'More like a politician's morals, Harry. Far more likely to find ethics at the brothel.'

All the men laughed.

Harry looked at the bikie boss. 'Longman, did you get any code names or the like out of the snitch?'

'No, didn't really think of that after he'd told us everything.'

'And after that he wasn't able to talk.' The Ratfucker grinned.

'So, where is the phone?' asked Trev.

Corsi pulled it out of his pocket and passed it over.

'Shit,' said Trev. 'I hope it's been switched off whilst you've been in here. They'll be tracking it.'

'Of course,' said Corsi. 'As soon as we grabbed him, we made him open it and we cancelled the access security to it. It's an older model so just had a four-digit code. Then we switched it off completely. We know all about tracking the bloody things.'

'And we sure didn't want them tracking him to his point of departure,' said Longman.

'Okay,' said Trev. 'We need to move elsewhere before I switch this on, for exactly the same reason.'

Harry drove the VW van with Trev and the two bikies in the back.

'Harry, as soon as we get over the bridge, just keep driving north on the freeway. I'll do what we need as we move.'

'No worries.'

Ten minutes later, Trev turned on the phone.

'Only the one number saved,' said Trev, playing with it. 'So, a dedicated phone for the snitch to contact the cop handler, I would guess, and provided by the cops.'

'That good or bad?' asked Corsi.

Trev smiled. 'Very good indeed, since it means that the handler will be guaranteed to respond.'

He scrolled through the saved messages. 'Okay, nothing specialized, no obvious code words or language.'

Harry sniggered. 'Yeah, the handler probably thought he was too dumb to remember any code lingo.'

'Makes our job all the easier,' said Trev. He tapped an SMS into the snitch's phone.

NEWS! BIG shipment coming. Got sample 4 you.
Need to meet ASAP. Your boss will like this. Need
to meet him and need 50K. 2moro morning.
Can't talk here.

He read it to Harry who nodded. 'Should do the
trick. Let's see what he suggests. You sure about the
money aspect?'

'Two other messages similar in the last six weeks, but
with less cash. Figure the increase might mean the big boys
get involved sooner.'

'Cool, send it, mate.'

– 3 –

The covert handler had taken the bait faster than an alcoholic gulping down the first drink of the day.

Harry and Trev sat in the VW surveillance van in the car park opposite the café the handler had arranged.

'Reckon it'll be inside or out?' said Trev.

'Hard to guess. I'd personally go outside, as harder for eavesdroppers. But the downside is higher visibility.'

Two men in their early fifties sat down at the outermost table along the footpath.

'Not likely handlers at their age,' said Trev. 'Mind you, they don't fit in. No one wears a denim jacket with a short back and sides these days.'

'And the other one's leather jacket is from the bloody eighties. Also with a short back and sides.' Harry looked through his binos. 'Looks as if he's stepped straight off the *Top Gun* set.'

'Not wrong, mate. I reckon we might have two senior cops doing a truly pathetic effort at being incognito.'

'They might as well stick a blue light on the table.'

Trev got on his phone and put it on speaker. 'Tan, see those two older dudes?'

She chuckled. 'Yeah. Someone please call the fashion police and have those wankers arrested. Seriously.'

'Reckon they are the police, babe,' said Harry. 'Although clearly not of the fashion variety.'

'Oh, cool. So glad I got your wardrobe sorted out, Harry. Without my efforts, you'd be looking something like that.'

'Yeah, very funny. So, as soon as you drop that package in the phone booth, cut back and sit yourself at the next table with your phone on transmit with that app.'

'Roger, boys.' She blew them a kiss from the corner next to the phone box and stepped into it.

A minute later she sat at the table next to the retro-dressed men. Both of them noticed her. Even gay guys usually noticed Tanya.

'Pair of pervs,' said Trev.

'Mate, can't blame them. Besides, a bit of distraction might make them sloppy.'

'Oh, here we are. I reckon this new one's a live wire.'

They watched a younger man with a ponytail, a muscle top to show off his tattoos, and Aviator shades, as he sat at the other end of the terrace. He casually scanned the whole café area.

'Looks like a cop,' said Harry.

'Don't we all, brother. Not even the ponytail saves him.'

The younger dude looked at his phone. He looked grim, almost scowling at the waitress as she took his order. He looked at the phone again.

'Time to play, Trev.'

'Roger, Harry.'

Trev pressed 'Send' on a pre-typed text message on the snitch's phone.

> Got a problem. Had to go. Left sample in phone box on corner. Think gang is watching me.

The handler looked at his phone and frowned. He cast a glance at the older guys thirty metres away. One of them raised his eyebrows.

'Sloppy, gents, very sloppy,' said Trev.

'And now he's got to walk past them to the drop.'

With that the handler took a sip of his coffee that had arrived, left his jacket on the back of his chair, and strutted over to the phone box.

'Has he got it?' asked Trev.

Harry was looking through his binos again. 'Can't see, he's in front of the package. Wait, wait, he's turning and, yes, package going into his pocket.'

'Sweet.'

Harry put the field glasses down.

'And the silence from those two is tell-tale,' said Trev, pointing at the receiver recorder propped in front of him. 'I can hear Tanya humming that bloody Taylor Swift tune over and over, but zilch from the two fashion retards.'

'What the fuck?' said Harry, as he looked on the scene of the moment.

Before the handler passed her table, with the two older men looking studiously into space, Tanya slipped open her tied blouse with the appearance of adjusting it. Her more-than-ample breasts greeted the morning sunshine, gloriously, albeit briefly. She was grinning like The Joker.

The handler tripped on the pavement, as deceptively smooth as it was, and the older guys had their mouths hanging open.

Tanya retied her blouse, looked at the nearest older guy who was still transfixed, and turned her face serious. 'You should be ashamed of yourself, mate, you're old enough to be my father.'

'Sorry …' He turned away.

Tanya looked roughly in the direction of the VW van and smirked.

'You naughty girl,' murmured Harry.

'Damn, I love her sense of humour, just wanted to screw with them,' said Trev. 'And her timing is exquisite. She knew damned well none of them could do anything official. Such style.'

'Action!' said Harry.

The handler had picked up his phone. They heard a phone near Tanya ring. The guy in the denim jacket picked up his.

'What's going on?' he said.

Harry was busy snapping away on the Pentax with the big zoom lens. 'He sounds like a Pom.'

The handler obviously said something.

Mr Denim again. 'Okay, leave the sample as you get up. Then you need to get the shipment details from this junkie arsehole.'

'Definitely English,' said Trev.

The handler spoke again.

Mr Denim replied, 'Yeah, I had the money, but he hasn't shown. Set up the meet again for tomorrow.'

The handler put his phone away, got up, and left the small brown parcel on the table.

Mr Top Gun moved quickly, scooping up the parcel, and kept walking away from the café.

'I've got him,' said Trev, jumping out of the van. 'Harry, you take the denim jacket.'

'Roger that.'

Mr Denim had stood up and paid the waitress. He walked away in the opposite direction to Mr Top Gun.

Harry gestured to the watching Tanya, and trotted over the road, slipping Tanya the van keys as he brushed past her. He upped the pace to follow Mr Denim Jacket.

Trev got lucky as his target stopped next to a silver Toyota Camry and appeared to look in at the dashboard, then at his watch.

With a satisfied look on his face, Mr Top Gun walked off and went into a newsagency a few metres away.

Bonus, thought Trev. He took a photo of the rego plate, checked no one else was around, and moved swiftly, stooping slightly as he passed the car. There was a slight clunk as a magnetic lump went up inside the rear wheel arch. Trev kept moving.

Harry's magnetic tracker had to stay in his pocket as his target jumped straight in his car, a white Ford Falcon. He walked past in time to see the 'AFP Police on Duty' sign being slipped off the dashboard as the engine started.

Harry grinned as he kept walking and he called Tanya to come and pick him up.

He hopped in the VW van further along the street as it pulled into the kerb.

'Trev's the other side of the block,' said Tanya, pulling back out into the sparse traffic.

Two turns later and Trev slid open the side door and climbed in.

'Bloody perfect, got the tracker on that bastard.'

'Good work,' said Harry. 'No chance with mine, but the lazy, greedy prick couldn't be bothered feeding the parking meter, so used his "On Duty" sign on the dash.'

Trev howled with laughter. 'Fuck me, you gotta love the arrogance, don't you.'

'Yep. He was from the Feds. So, I'm betting your boy was Customs.'

'Time will tell, but the tracker won't lie.'

'Cool. Babe, let's head for the office.'

Tanya turned and smiled at Harry. 'Roger, boss!' She stuck her tongue out at him.

− 4 −

'Bingo!' said Trev, sitting on the office couch looking at a laptop screen. 'Tracker has got that car pulling into the Australian Customs centre in Mascot.'

'Cool,' said Harry. 'How you going, babe?'

Tanya was sitting at the second desk in front of the iMac, scrolling through image searches online with an iPad next to her with the surveillance photos of the two men from the café.

'Quickly getting sick of looking at arrogant, middle-aged men in uniforms.'

Harry chuckled. 'Hearing you. They're pretty well all arrogant at those senior levels.'

'Yep,' chipped in Trev. 'That's how they get up there. Along with the usual backstabbing and treachery.'

'So glad you two guys got out while you were still decent,' said Tanya.

Harry and Trev burst out laughing.

'Divine One,' said Harry, 'albeit in our differing circumstances, neither of us had a choice.'

'But,' added Trev, 'and the all-important "but", neither of us would have got any higher from where we were as detective sergeants.'

'Too true, brother.' He turned. 'Babe, we were too busy actually being cops, along with all the other decent ones, rather than playing the politics and all the backroom games.'

'Yeah, the backroom heroes I always call them,' said Trev. 'Tan, almost all the ones you see at the really senior levels have never done a decent day's real police work in their lives.'

'Wouldn't know an angry man if one punched them in the mouth,' said Harry.

'Or a crook. The only thing they could catch would be a cold or their next promotion.'

Tanya shook her head. 'I think working with you two makes me the most cynical nineteen-year-old in this city.'

'And therefore, one of the few young people who can recognize all the bullshit they're fed,' said Harry.

'Yep. I definitely belong with you guys. Hang on …'

Tanya scrolled back up the page on her screen.

'Got one, I think. Assistant Commissioner Neil Horley, Feds. Got his mug at a press conference a few months ago.

Harry and Trev both moved to stand behind Tanya.

'Oh, yeah, that's him all right,' said Trev.

Harry squeezed her shoulder. 'Great work, babe, as usual.'

She looked up and smiled. 'Worth a bonus, then, boss? I've got a course I want to do, so the extra cash would be good.'

'For you, anything. And what's the course?'

'Counselling. Something I've been wanting to do since Sash died. Want to learn more about grief and then help others with it.'

'Cool,' said Harry. 'The safe is open for you for anything that worthwhile.'

'Good for you, Tan.' Trev bent down and kissed her on the cheek.

'Thanks, guys, I'll get enrolled then. Now, back to do some research on this douchebag and find the other one.'

'Righto, I'll also see if I can find the Customs bloke's ugly face,' said Trev, returning to the couch and his laptop.

Harry sat back down and lit a smoke. 'No worries, team, you've both got it well in hand. I'll put my feet up and supervise.'

'Get your hand off it, Mister PI.'

Trev sniggered. 'Actually, that bit he could supervise.'

'Well, boss, how about you slide your supervisory backside over to the drinks cabinet and organize some refreshment for us workers. Make yourself useful.'

'Miss Tanya, such employee insolence warrants me bending you over my knee, dropping your jeans, and smacking your arse.'

She chuckled. 'Except I'd enjoy that.'

'True. And our Trev over there probably doesn't want to see your naked butt, as beautiful as it is.'

'I wouldn't be so sure on that,' she said under her breath, as Harry ambled over to the drinks cabinet. His back towards the others meant Harry didn't get to see Trev's beetroot-coloured face.

Tanya winked at Trev and blew him a kiss. He grinned sheepishly and got back to his screen.

Halfway through his second Jameson, Trev broke the silence in the office.

'Got him. Commander Richard Billingham. Only been in Customs a couple of years, transferred over from the Australian Crime Commission. Before that a couple of state agencies in Victoria, and then the London Metropolitan Police. Been in Oz about fifteen years.'

'Looks as if they're both Poms, then,' said Harry, 'since we heard Horley talking over the phone and he sounded like an East End street trader.'

'They're definitely both British,' said Tanya. 'I heard them both talking. Mind you, they didn't sound nearly as poncy as those two clowns from the railway job.'

All of them laughed.

'I have such fond memories of that job,' said Harry.

'Which reminds me, guys, we need to catch up with our friend Zanza.'

Harry scribbled a note on his desk. 'On the list for tomorrow.'

'Here we go,' said Tanya. 'I've found the job history for Mister Horley. He's been in the Feds for the last eight years, New South Wales Crime Commission before that, and a couple of years in the local police. And then guess what?'

'Bloody Met Police is my bet,' said Trev.

'Spot on.'

'So,' said Harry, 'that's how they know each other well enough to be in cahoots on corruption on this scale.'

'A couple of good bent London boys coming out to the colonies for sunshine and graft. The old Mother Country just keeps giving.'

'Yeah, and it's not as if we need to be importing corruption, we do very bloody well on our own.'

'So, what's next?' asked Tanya.

'We get on to Longman and gang and see about setting up a drug drop to tempt our likely lads back out into the open,' said Trev.

Harry pressed a number on his phone, selected loudspeaker, and put it on the desk.

'Kenmare?' Unmistakeably The Ratfucker's gravelly voice.

'Yep, g'day Corsi. Longman there?'

'Yeah, just a sec.'

There was some background noise and Corsi came back on the line. 'Okay, he can hear now as well.'

'Gentlemen, we have results for you. When do you boys want to have a chat?'

'Can't make it this evening, Kenmare, we've got an initiation night for two new members, so the fridges are full of beer and two carloads of sluts have just arrived. How about tomorrow arvo?'

'Yep, works for us.'

'Cool, just for a change of scene, you guys want to come to the clubhouse? That also saves us carrying a large pile of cash to your office.'

'Sure, I know where it is. How about three o'clock?'

'Cool. We'll have whiskey for you blokes, and plenty of vodka if that angel Tanya is coming as well.'

Tanya leant over the phone. 'Oh, Archie honey, I'm *always* coming.'

Through the laughter on the other end, Longman said, 'You got me there, little angel.'

'Not often we see this bloke blush,' said The Ratfucker.

'See you all tomorrow, Kenmare.' They rang off.

'Excellent,' said Harry. 'And even better we've been invited there.'

'Why?' asked Tanya.

'Getting to go into the inner sanctum of the clubhouse means they trust us fully,' said Trev. 'Not that I would have doubted that after the massacre in Punchbowl last year. But great to have this confirmation.'

'Yes, indeed,' said Harry. 'And since our work here is done for the day, I suggest we adjourn to the Emerald Bar for dinner. Let's go.'

– 5 –

The front saloon of the Emerald Bar was quiet when the trio arrived, although it was Monday and not yet six in the evening.

Harry held the door open for Tanya who walked in and then he motioned Trev through. 'After you, mate.'

Trev motioned Harry in. 'No, after you, brother.'

'No, I insist, mate.'

'No, *I* insist, brother.'

Tanya, now a couple of metres inside, turned and shook her head. 'Oh, for fuck's sake, boys. I'll get my own drink, shall I?' With that she strode over to the bar.

At that point both Harry and Trev went to enter and jammed themselves momentarily in the narrow doorway.

'Hi, Shaun.' Tanya greeted the bar manager. 'And I'm not with those two idiots. My usual, please.'

Shaun laughed. 'Coming right up, Tanya.' He picked up a glass and put ice into it as the two guys got to the bar. 'And here's trouble. Even trouble getting in the door, it would seem,' the Irish accent taking the piss out of the sleuths.

'And g'day to you, you Irish bastard,' said Harry.

'Hi, mate,' said Trev.

'Evening, gents. Jameson times two?'

'Please, mate,' said Harry. 'We'll have one here and then head through for a feed.'

'No worries. Kitchen's about to open. And my old compatriot will be here later. He's back from his latest trip.'

'We haven't seen His Eminence since we got back from Laos,' said Trev, suddenly turning his head as a handsome young barman walked in from the back room.

'Ah, Lucien,' said Shaun. 'Let me introduce you to some regulars. You'll be seeing a lot of them.'

The young guy stepped over.

'This is Tanya, the sensible one of the group.'

Lucien dipped his head politely.

'This is Harry, and here's Trev.'

Trev held out his hand, which Lucien shook with a hint of eagerness. They were looking at each other.

The Irish brogue continued, 'Lucien's here for a year, from France.'

'Whereabouts?' asked Trev, still looking at the Frenchman.

Lucien smiled and replied in perfect English awash in his French accent. 'The south-west. A small town between Bordeaux and Toulouse. Not well-known.'

'Which *département*?' Trev got the French pronunciation on the last word.

Lucien's smile broadened. 'The Lot-et-Garonne. The far less famous neighbour of the Dordogne.'

Trev grinned. 'I know it.'

'You are joking?'

'No, I've been through that area and stayed there on holidays. Famous for its prunes amongst other delights. The *pruneaux d'Agen*.'

Lucien beamed his admiration.

At that moment a group arrived at the bar. Before Lucien stepped away to attend to them, Trev slipped a card onto the bar. 'Call me?'

'*Bien sûr.*' His eyes lingered a second and he stepped over to the new arrivals.

Trev was looking smug. He smirked at Tanya and Harry.

'Was that what I thought it was, brother?'

Trev winked at him.

'Mister PI, of course it was. Our Trev here is slicker than satin sheets covered in lube.'

Trev chuckled. 'Can think of some mighty fine uses for both right about now.'

'And I thought I was smooth,' said Harry.

'Look on the bright side, boys, at least you're not competing.'

'True. Let's hit the restaurant. Right now, I could eat the crotch out of a low flying duck.' Harry downed his whiskey and headed off.

As Tanya got off her bar stool, she whispered in Trev's ear. 'Well, maybe just a little bit of competition for my sweet arse. But you're both only human.' She kissed him on the cheek as his face reddened for the second time that day.

Trev followed her to the restaurant.

The three of them shared a large charcuterie platter to open with and the cab sav flowed, as did the banter.

Then the mains arrived. Trev had ordered the eye fillet with *Café de Paris* butter and fries, one of his go-to dishes. 'Love my steak French,' he grinned at them.

'Oh, groan out loud,' said Tanya, tucking into her seafood linguine.

Harry cut into his lamb, done pink as requested. 'Well, I guess that means I like a bit of rump then. Ha ha.'

Tanya shook her head as she swallowed her mouthful. 'Well, Mister PI, that'll have to suit you, because if the chef put pussy on the menu, the animal rights mob would be running a picket line out front.'

They all roared laughing.

After their food, Harry ordered two more bottles of Bordeaux and a cheese platter for them to take out to the beer garden. 'Let's have a smoke to round off the superb meal.'

The waitress came over with the wine. 'Sorry, Harry, but I'll have to get you to collect the cheese platter and take it out there yourself. It's ready over at the servery. New city council rules. I'm not allowed to serve food out there while it's smoking time.'

'The good old nanny state, alive and well. No worries, Carly. You just turn a blind eye whilst I break the rules.'

She grinned. 'No worries, Harry.'

Trev was shaking his head. 'One of the things I always loved about spending time in France. So much less of this nanny state bullshit.'

'And it's only getting worse, brother.'

'Not wrong. Before we know it, we'll be getting arrested for farting in public.'

Ten minutes after they'd settled themselves in the far corner of the deserted beer garden, in walked Liam Doolan, known as His Eminence in this milieu. The Irish accent was as thick as the smile was broad. 'Ah, bloody hell, it's been way too long between drinks, my friends.'

'Liam!' said Harry and Trev in unison.

Tanya beamed at him as he bent down and kissed her on the cheek.

'And a special hello to you, my beautiful angel. You really are the rose stuck between two thorns, aren't you?'

'Fair suck of the sav, Your Eminence,' said Harry.

Trev joined in. 'Yeah, we've got feelings, you know.'

Liam guffawed. 'Piss off. I've met concrete blocks with more sensitivity than you pair of reprobates. Anyway, how are we all? What's happening in the world of sleazy private investigations? I haven't seen you in at least four months.'

'First, let's fill you in on our Laos trip back in February,' said Harry.

'Of course, I was forgetting you've been away, too. Bloody May already, time flies when you're living the drinking life.'

And so, lubricated with red wine, the Laotian escapades were recounted.

When they'd finished, Liam put his hand on Tanya's shoulder. 'So very proud of you, my girl. That cop got exactly what he deserved.'

Harry chuckled. 'Yes, a truly shocking experience.'

'Oh, double groan,' said Tanya. 'Liam, you've no idea how many lame lines I've had to put up with.

'I could hazard a guess.'

'You just have to flow with the current,' said Trev.

'You see what I mean, Liam?'

'Don't give up the day job, lads. You'd fricking starve doing stand-up.'

'Again, feelings.'

'And again, piss off.'

They all laughed.

'I'll go get us another bottle, or are we joining Liam on the heavy stuff?' asked Trev.

Harry emptied his glass. 'Jameson for me, thanks.'

'Vodka lime for me, please,' said Tanya.

When Trev returned with the drinks on a tray, Harry was filling Liam in on the current assignment.

Trev handed around the drinks.

Liam lit a smoke and jumped in before Harry could continue. 'Meant to mention when you were talking about that evil piece of shite Wheeler getting away. I was talking to a cousin of mine who's in the Garda back home.'

Harry frowned. 'Go on.'

'Well, Niall works in the child exploitation area.'

'But in Ireland, so how does that connect?'

'Aha! Yes, and no. He's from the Garda, but not in Ireland now. He's recently started a three-year posting to Interpol in Lyon.'

'And don't tell me,' said Trev, 'he's on the paedophile desk there.'

'Exactly. I was talking to him just last week. He's loving the work.'

Harry took a sip. 'Shit, we desperately need someone with access to intel. Do you think he'd stick his neck out, Liam?'

'As sure as the Irish bathe in Guinness. Our family all believe in blood being thicker, no matter what. If I ask, he'll help. Plus, he's got a personal interest in such matters.'

'How so?' asked Harry.

'Let's just say his early introduction to the good old Catholic Church was as similarly awful as Trev's.'

Trev grinned wryly. 'Liam, I don't suppose your cousin's good looking and gay by any chance?'

Liam roared laughing. 'Hell no. Sorry, Trev. He's a fine-looking lad, all right, but he's bedded more ladies than Casanova on Viagra.'

They laughed.

'And here's something Niall told me that I didn't know before about these fucking child molesters,' continued the big Irishman.

'What's that?' asked Harry.

Liam leant into the group. 'They've even got busy and into bed with the with political correctness hordes and given themselves a fucking new name.'

'Out with it, mate,' said Trev.

'Apparently, they call themselves "minor attracted persons", get that.'

'What the fuck?' gasped Tanya.

The guys were shaking their heads.

'So now the woke brigade wankers are even trying to normalise fucking rock spiders. That label's a new one on me,' said Trev.

Harry nodded. 'Me, too. We've been out of the detective ranks a long while, so not up to speed with the latest lingo.'

'The world's seriously fucked,' said Tanya.

Liam smiled at her. 'It's tragic to hear that coming from someone so young and vibrant, my angel, but alas you are right. We're heading to hell in a hand-basket and the virtue-signalling woke scum have got their feet firmly planted on the accelerator.'

Harry pulled out a notebook, wrote on a page, ripped it out and handed it to Liam. 'All Wheeler's details. Any leads at all would be very appreciated. We've heard nothing more on him since Laos, three months now.'

Liam looked at the paper. 'You reckon this scum would come back to Australia?'

'I doubt it,' said Trev. 'He knows it's Harry after him, we got close enough for him to see us ...'

Tanya interrupted. 'Plus, those bent cops would've told him anyway.'

'For sure,' continued Trev. 'He'd be switched on enough to know that Harry, albeit no longer a cop, would still have enough contacts here, so it'd be way too risky for him.'

'Exactly. My bet is somewhere else in South-East Asia, or maybe Europe with the lack of border controls,' said Harry.

'Leave it with me, lady and gents. Now let's drink.'

– 6 –

The VW van came off the M7 Westlink into the Blacktown industrial area. A couple of streets later, it turned into Alyssa Street and up a driveway lined with closed workshops. Trev drove to the end and halted in front of a rusty roller door with a tatty business sign above it, 'Aardvark Automotive'.

Trev pipped the horn.

Tanya leant forward from the jump seat behind the two guys. 'Is this what a bikies' clubhouse looks like? I was expecting something a bit more wild and outlaw.'

'Don't worry,' said Trev, 'you'll get that shortly. This is where we are swapping vehicles. Longman's boys left a car here for us, so we'll arrive at the clubhouse in a car registered to the Hogs. That way no one who might be watching the clubhouse gets to see our rego details.'

'I see, clever. And who the hell calls a business "aardvark"? Isn't that some African anteater?'

Both the guys cackled.

'Babe, I'm guessing you've never seen a Yellow Pages, have you?'

'No. I know it was a phone book. But, dudes, that's what Google is for.'

'Now, yes. Back in the day, however, the Yellow Pages phone book was the place to find businesses, and it was alphabetical. So, all sorts of places used ways to get at the front of the listings. Some smartarse realized that "aardvark" would do the job nicely.'

'Yep, and so we ended up with all these businesses named after the ant-munching critter from Africa,' added Trev.

'You're shitting me.'

'Honest truth,' said Harry.

The door rose and they drove inside. The nondescript entrance gave way to a massive interior with several car hoists, work areas, and two spray-painting cabins. There were cars everywhere in various states of work and several men in overalls were creating a cacophony of ear-splitting sounds with angle grinders and arc welders. A large, bald Māori guy with a heavily tattooed face leant on the sill as Trev lowered his window.

'Hey, bro, you Kenmare?' came the thick Kiwi accent, floating on a cloud of breath tinged with tobacco and bourbon.

'No, he is.' Trev indicated Harry. 'Archie told us to drop by for some temporary wheels.'

'All sweet, bro. Park over there next to the Mustang. It's your wheels.'

Trev swung the van into a bay beside a shiny, new white Ford Mustang complete with blue GT stripes over its roof and bonnet.

Trev got out of the van and the workshop boss handed him a set of keys.

'We'll be here all evening, bro, so no hurry to get it back. Just don't dent it.' He grinned, showing nicotine-stained teeth.

'Thanks, mate, I'll make sure I don't,' said Trev.

Harry came around from the other side of the van. 'Nice looking machine.'

'Sure is, bro. And it fair fucking moves. Faster than a sheep at a Kiwi stag party. You'll enjoy the drive.'

They laughed.

'I won't be pushing my luck,' said Trev. 'We don't need to get bloody pulled over.'

At that moment Tanya emerged from the far side of the van. A microsecond later, all machinery stopped, to be replaced by a chorus of wolf whistles. Tanya smirked at the audience and did a slow turn for the lads, earning her hoots and applause.

The boss man nodded and grinned. 'Little lady can stay here if she wants.'

'You wish,' said Tanya.

'Sorry, mate,' said Harry. 'She's got work to do with us. She's a hell of a lot more than just bloody gorgeous.'

'Bro, sweet bloody job you blokes have got.'

'It has its upsides.'

Trev lowered his voice. 'But she also kills people, mate, so beware.' He grinned.

The big Māori snorted. 'Yeah, bullshit, bro.'

'I gotta call Longman to let him know we're on our way, so I'll let him tell you,' said Harry, pulling his phone out of his jacket pocket.

'You kidding, bro?'

Harry shook his head and pressed his phone screen, putting it to his ear. 'Longman? We're picking up the car now, so be there in about forty-five.'

There was pause whilst the bikie boss spoke.

'Yeah, all cool. Mate, whilst I've got you, the main man here doesn't believe Tanya is a tough, arse-kicking chick. Care to enlighten him?'

Harry passed the phone to the man.

'Hey, Archie. Rangi here,' he said.

He listened for a few moments. Then his eyes widened until he looked like a giant startled lemur.

'She did fucking what?'

He listened again.

'Fuck me. Thanks, Archie.' He closed off the call and passed the phone back to Harry. He turned to look at Tanya. 'Respect to you, little lady.'

She pouted. 'I have been known to be a bad-arsed bitch.'

Rangi stood there nodding, still looking gobsmacked as the trio of sleuths climbed into the Mustang.

Tanya paused momentarily as she was climbing into the back seat, allowing the still silent workshop to get a fine view of her perfect posterior in the skin-tight denim. She wiggled her butt, which drew another round of hoots and applause.

'See you in a few hours,' said Trev, getting into the driver's seat.

Harry righted the passenger seat now Tanya was in and he got in himself, saying 'thanks for your help, mate,' to the boss man.

'No worries, bro.'

Trev turned the key and the throaty V8 roared into life. He leant across Harry to talk to Rangi. 'And please don't chop up my van by mistake.'

'Yeah, funny, bro.' He smiled and gave Trev the finger.

The Mustang growled its way out of the workshop.

Trev eased the car onto the street.

'Your fan club just got bigger, babe,' said Harry.

'Well, they're only human,' grinned Tanya. 'Hey, Trev, why did you ask him not to chop your van up?'

Trev chuckled. 'That joint, Tan, is what's called a "chop-shop". Stolen cars get chopped into parts or they get rebirthed, given new identifying plates, et cetera.'

'Huge business,' added Harry. 'Must say, there were some damned expensive motors in there. And they'll all be hotter than your sizzling arse, babe.'

Harry texted Longman as they turned into Bailey's Lane in the semi-rural seclusion of Kurrajong Hills. As the Mustang growled into the driveway at the end of the lane, the solid metal gate set into the thick brick wall of the Hogs' compound slid open on its rollers, being pulled by a monster in black leather, the butt of a 9mm automatic openly visible above his belt.

Another almost-as-large bikie in a sleeveless leather vest and black leather peaked cap approached the car.

'Fuck me,' said Trev, 'he looks as if he's straight out of the Blue Oyster Club.'

'Well, mate, I guess you'd know. Not really my scene.' Harry sniggered.

'Piss off.'

'Anyway, I wouldn't say that too loudly around here. A sense of humour might be absent, at least on that issue.'

'Don't worry, I haven't got a death wish. But seriously, look at him.'

The bikie bent down as Trev lowered his window.

'Take it around the back, mate. Park it in the first carport next to the old F-One-Fifty.'

'No worries.' Trev slipped the car back into first gear and slowly cruised around the side of the big double-storey brick house.

The front of the house was innocuous enough, and two old Holden car bodies were rusting on one side of the front yard. A driveway between the house and a massive metal shed was the only way to the back yard, which turned out to be expansive, surrounded on all sides by three-metre-high chain link fences topped with razor wire. There were no neighbours within eyeshot, only bushland on the other side of all three fence lines. Another shed had its roller doors open and two bikies were visible working on Harleys.

Trev swung the Mustang into the two-berth carport attached to the back wall of the house. An old primer-grey Ford F150 sat in the other spot. On the other side of the back door was another larger carport with a brand new gunmetal F250 and two V8 Falcon sedans, one silver and the other dark blue. Another long shed off at right angles housed more vehicles, at least two other dark-coloured F150s with brutal-looking bullbars being visible.

As they got out of the car, The Ratfucker came out of the back door and down the steps.

'G'day guys. How did you enjoy the new Mustang?'

Trev closed the driver's door. 'It's bloody sensational, mate. Would love a look under the bonnet.'

'Can be arranged,' replied the bikie.

'G'day, Corsi,' said Harry. 'I'm hoping I might get to drive it on the way back.'

'Yeah, we'll see,' said Trev. 'I am the better driver, Harry, just as you're the better shot. Gotta play to your strengths.'

Longman appeared as Tanya was climbing out of the back seat.

'Hello, boys. Talking of playing to strengths, at least you brought the attractive one of the team with you.'

Tanya smiled. 'Hello, Archie.'

'Always good to see you, Blondie.'

'Just mentioned to Corsi I'd love a look at the Mustang's motor,' said Trev.

'We'll give you a demo later. But first let's deal with business.'

Longman turned and they all followed him inside.

The air inside the large lounge room of the clubhouse where Longman led them was cloyingly redolent of marijuana, both smoke and fresh leaf.

As they walked in, a woman in her early twenties sauntered in from the adjoining room. She had long curly brown hair and sensational curves, shown off by her scant clothing: a short denim skirt and a translucent chiffon blouse that may as well have been cling wrap. Her large breasts were led by protuberant carmine nipples. Aside from her face, her nipples were the only visible part of her body that wasn't tattooed.

As Harry was thinking to himself she had more ink than the collected works of Shakespeare, and how he'd like to remove what little fabric she was wearing, Tanya seemed to read his mind, whispering beside him.

'I could enjoy that.'

'You and I both,' murmured Harry.

Tanya grinned. 'Ooh, together?'

'Behave, babe, and back to business.'

Longman slapped the girl on her bum as she drew next to him.

'Be a doll, Greta, and fetch us all beers, please.'

'No worries, Arch.' She sauntered off.

Longman caught Harry watching Greta's disappearing derrière. 'Like that, Kenmare?'

'Is the Pope a Catholic?'

The bikie boss laughed. 'We like good sorts around here almost as much as our Harleys.'

'Damned right,' said The Ratfucker.

At that point another girl appeared in the doorway, this one blonde, but also curvy and in shorts with a similarly see-through white cloth top.

'You seen Greta?' she asked Corsi.

'Yeah, she's getting drinks for us, Natty.'

'Cool, I'll go find her.' She walked away.

'Is that transparent top a sort of uniform for the women here, Longman?' asked Harry, grinning.

Longman and Corsi both laughed.

'Could say that, mate,' said Longman. 'Black leather for the blokes and see-through cheesecloth for the girls.'

'Bloody good arrangement,' said Corsi.

'Grab a seat, guys,' said Longman. 'Let's talk a plan.'

As they sat on couches and armchairs, Greta and Natty returned with two ice buckets full of bottled beer.

'Thanks, girls,' said Longman. 'I'll yell if we need anything else.'

The bikie girls left the room.

'Right, what we got so far?' asked Longman. 'Must be some progress for you to ask for a meet, Kenmare?'

'Yep. Obviously didn't want to discuss on the phone, even with a burner. It's not worth the risk on this job.'

'A lot at stake for some very high-level bastards,' said Trev.

'We're all ears, guys.'

Trev spread some photos out on the coffee table and everyone leaned in.

'So, we've got three heads so far,' said Harry, tapping a group photo from their surveillance jaunt. He pointed to the covert handler. 'This one is the contact for the dead snitch. So, he's lower level in the scheme.'

'We'll still deal with him,' said The Ratfucker.

'Sure, but it's these two who, given their high rank, must be running the whole shebang.'

Trev lit a smoke. 'One assistant commissioner from the Feds and one commander from Customs.'

'Whoa, fuck me,' said Longman.

'I'm going to seriously enjoy fucking them up,' growled Corsi.

'This one is Assistant Commissioner Neil Horley with the Feds.' Harry tapped the figure on the left of the café table in the photo. 'And this one's Commander Richard Billingham, Customs.'

'They're both Poms, imports into our law enforcement roles,' said Trev. 'We've found out they used to work together in the Met Police in London.'

'Must be more comfortable being bent in the sun,' said Longman. 'Righto, what we need is to get all the goods on these wankers when they try to knock off the next shipment.'

'When's it due?' asked Trev.

'It's in a container of washing machines from China, still sitting at Botany. It's cleared Customs, so we just need to contact the importer and arrange a meet and exchange.'

Corsi sighed. 'And that seems to be the problem. Doesn't matter where we arrange our meets, the arsehole cops always seem to know.'

'Yeah,' said Harry. 'Reckon they've got the importer's phones off, so you can be as careful as you like with burners, but you're still being listened to.'

'Which this time we'll use to advantage,' said Trev. 'We've got a place in mind that gives us good surveillance spots.'

'Might be a problem,' said Longman. 'Last two times the wankers were waiting for our bloke to take the delivery and then they grabbed him after he'd driven off. Pretended it was a traffic stop.'

'Yeah, swiped the drugs and told our bloke to fuck off and keep his mouth shut,' added Corsi.

'That won't work as a scenario for us,' said Harry. 'We need the shit to go down in a pre-arranged place so we can control the surveillance.'

'Can we assume they only get the intel from the importer's phone being tapped, and not from your pick-up man?' asked Trev.

'No risk there,' said Longman. 'Our bloke, Rory, gets a new phone each time, activated just before he goes to the meet with the drug guy, the Chinaman. So, there's no way in hell they can be listening to our end.'

'Okay,' said Harry. 'That means they find out the meet location from the importer's phone, and then they must have an eyeball on the meet in order to tail your man as he leaves. Would be leaving way too much to chance if they didn't.'

'Makes sense.'

'So, we need some reason to get your bloke to stay in the car park after the importer has gone, instead of leaving straightaway as usual. Then the cops will have to come on in if they want to get the gear.'

'It'll look a bit weird, Kenmare, since Rory has never hung around before.'

'I've got an idea,' said Tanya.

The four men turned to look at her.

'Shoot, Blondie. And I don't mean literally, I've seen your form.'

There was laughter all round.

'Best reason to loiter in a quiet car park is if you're making out.' Tanya pointed in the direction of the door the two bikie girls had disappeared through. 'Get one of your girls to be with the pick-up dude. As soon as the Chinese importer leaves, get her to start making out with Rory. I'm sure they could carry on like that for a while, at least long enough for the cops to get sick of waiting.'

Harry was nodding. 'Stellar, as always, babe.'

'Yeah, I like that one, Blondie.'

'Yep, I reckon that'll do the trick,' said Trev. 'These cops, like all corrupt wankers, will be too eager by half to get their hands on the gear. They won't have any patience at all. Greed will take over, they'll come barrelling in, and we'll get it all on film. And we'll have your bloke's car wired for sound, too, with hidden external mikes, so we'll get anything that's said.'

'What about an LD on Rory?'

'No, Corsi, they could easily search him and then it's blown. So long as he gets them close to his car, it'll be fine. And your two cannot be tooled up either, for the same reason. Under the car seat or in the boot, if you must.'

Longman frowned. 'Yeah, but what if something goes wrong? The other times they've stopped Rory's car on the road, so not too much chance of any real problems: too many witnesses. But in a car park with no one around?'

Corsi opened another beer. 'Yeah. You blokes won't be able to intervene, will you?'

Harry shook his head. 'No, strictly surveillance only. We can't risk a direct open confrontation with the cops, even if they are corrupt.'

'Okay, Kenmare, how's this for size?' said Longman. 'We have two of us in a car a couple of blocks away. If anything is going wrong, you call us and we'll do the rest.'

'Cool, that works fine, but really well out of sight. We don't want any risks to this operation. We'll only ever get this one shot at it.'

'Anyway,' said Trev, 'I think the corrupt wankers will just want to get the drugs and get the hell out of there as fast as they can. I don't think they'd be stupid enough to want any shit going down.'

'I agree, gents. If they wanted to mess with your bloke, they would've done that the first time by arresting him.

They'll want this to be a quick grab of the drugs and no one says anything official. Greed is not only good for these blokes, it is king.'

'Settled then. Rocco, you tee it up with the Chinaman for tomorrow?'

'No worries, Arch. You got the location, Matson?'

'Yes, mate. Here.' Trev passed Corsi a piece of paper. 'But hold off until the last minute before calling the importer with the exact spot. Minimize the time the cops have to get organized.'

'Cool.'

Longman finished his beer in a long swig. 'Excellent, looking forward to bringing these bent pigs unstuck. Now, wanna see under the hood of our Mustang?'

'Shit yes,' said Trev.

They all got up.

Tanya was the last out of the room and she followed the men down the hallway towards the back door.

She stopped as she passed a doorway into the kitchen area. Greta was sitting on the kitchen island, swigging a beer.

Tanya stopped in the opening and smiled at her. 'Greta, isn't it?' She looked down, obviously, at Greta's breasts, and then back into her eyes.

'Yep. And what's your name, baby doll?'

'Tanya.' She stepped into the room.

Greta beckoned her over with her finger. 'Like what you see, do you?'

'As a matter of fact, yes.'

'Really? I thought you might be with one of the guys you came with.'

Tanya giggled. 'Sometimes I am. But I like variety. And you, Greta? What's your story?'

She motioned Tanya closer, until she was standing within reach. She slowly cupped her left hand on Tanya's right breast. 'Is that okay?'

'More than okay.' Tanya took the last step in so she was against the counter edge between Greta's thighs. She caressed Greta's breasts with both her hands. 'So, your story?'

Greta sighed as she locked her legs around Tanya's bum.

Tanya inhaled the beer breath as Greta rested the tip of her nose against Tanya's.

'Well, Archie and Rocco screw me when they want to. And I'm not allowed to fuck anyone else here. Oh, except Natty.' She smirked. 'Outside of here, on the occasions I do go out, I'm allowed to do what I want. Two exceptions: no cops and no other bikies.'

'Cool. I'm neither.' Tanya put her hand behind Greta's head and pulled her lips onto hers. She eased her tongue into Greta's mouth, encountering Greta's tongue coming the other way.

The throaty roaring of a V8 engine came in through the back door, followed by Longman's voice. 'C'mon, Blondie. Come and see the dream machine.'

'Boys and their toys,' Tanya smiled at Greta. She turned to the doorway and yelled, 'Coming, Archie.'

Greta sniggered. 'I wish you were, right on my face.'

Tanya kissed her again. 'Let's make that a date. I've got my own place in Surry Hills. You can come over anytime.'

'Yes, please.' She took out her phone. 'What's your number?'

Tanya told her. A second later her phone buzzed in her back pocket.

'And there's mine.'

'Sweet, let's make it soon, sexy.'

'You bet, baby doll.'

They kissed again and Tanya turned to go outside. Greta smacked her arse as she moved away.

Tanya looked back over her shoulder. 'I'm going to wipe my bedroom with you, Greta.'

'I'll hold you to that.'

Tanya walked off in the direction of the roaring Ford Mustang.

– 7 –

It was Sunday morning, shortly after sunrise. The VW van was parked in Antwerp Street facing south and parallel to the kerb. Trev picked up the binoculars again and leaned in front of Tanya in the passenger seat so he could look out the side window. He scanned the car park on the opposite side of the grassed sports reserve in Bankstown. He continued to pan around the entire field of vision.

'Nothing so far. A couple of dogs being walked, that's all.'

'Still a few minutes before the agreed time,' said Harry from the jump seat. 'I just want to know where the cops will be watching from. They'll absolutely want to have eyes on the drop to call it in when the deal is done.'

Tanya had a video camera ready, aimed out the side window. Its zoom lens was impressive, about the length and girth of a pachyderm's penis. It was secured to a dash-mounted bracket and tripod head. 'Ready to go when the action starts, boys. Any chance of another coffee please, Harry?'

'Me, too,' said Trev, still scanning the distance.

Harry lifted a large Thermos flask and poured coffee into three plastic mugs.

'Not quite our favourite café, but it'll have to do.' He passed two mugs to the front.

Trev put his binos down and took a mouthful of coffee.

'I've had a close scan and can't see any static cameras or anything that looks as if it could house one. So, they'll have to have a bod somewhere close to call it in when the bikie has got the gear and is on the move.'

'Except our bikie won't be on the move.'

'Do you think there'll be any trouble once the bent cops arrive?' said Tanya.

'I doubt it. Most likely they'll just grab the gear they came for and get out of here. Harry?'

'Yeah, I agree. It's hardly an official police operation, so they'll want to get it over and done with and away with their corrupt prize pronto.'

'Ah, we have some movement,' said Trev. 'That's the bikie bloke, Rory, in the blue Falcon sedan. And he's got one of the bikie molls with him.'

'Good, just as planned. Can you see Longman or anyone else from the Hogs?'

Trev scanned around again. 'Nothing else, yet. Rory has parked exactly where we told him to.'

'Something's moving over there to the left,' said Tanya.

Trev focused in on the street beyond the car park. 'Got it. A DHL courier van.' He snorted. 'And a fake one.'

'How can you tell, Trev?'

'Tan, the DHL sign is crooked, so it's a magnetic one. Like the ones I have back there on the rack. Plus, the van's white. DHL are always yellow.'

Harry leant forward between the seats, looking towards the white DHL van in the distance. 'You see, they're so fricking greedy, they got sloppy.'

'Yep, that's arrogance, too. So far up their own arses they're convinced they're untouchable.'

'Yeah, I reckon Longman's going to turn that on its head.'

Trev chuckled. 'You bet. I've got no sympathy for those corrupt wankers, but by the same token I would not want to be in their shoes when the music stops. It'll be A-grade nasty, I reckon.'

Tanya looked over at him. 'You think he'll kill them, those two senior ones?'

'Maybe, and it'd be slow and painful.'

'Or, he'll make horrendous examples of them,' said Harry. At least we only have to work on this surveillance part.'

Trev looked back at the Hogs' pair, Rory and the girl, waiting in the Falcon. 'Hey, Tan, is that bikie moll the same one you were hitting on at the clubhouse?'

Tanya's head snapped around to look at him. 'No, that one over there is Natty, the other girl. My new friend is Greta. Why? What did you see?' She had a slight smirk.

'Before we left, I saw your hand on her arse, and she was looking pretty damned happy about it.'

Tanya opened her mouth, but before she could say anything else, Harry leant forward and kissed her cheek.

'You are unstoppable, aren't you?' He was grinning even more than Trev.

'Shit, looks as if I've been sprung. You don't mind, do you, Mister PI? We've always had an open relationship.' She smirked cheekily at him.

Harry kissed her again. 'Divine one, of course I'm cool with it. What I want most is for you to be the happiest version of you that you can be. You enjoy. I reckon she'll be a dirty one.' He put his hand on her shoulder. 'You lucky thing, you!'

'Oh, yeah, skank with a capital S,' said Trev. 'If I was that way inclined ...' He didn't finish due to Tanya poking his leg.

'Have fun, babe, but stay careful about what you say to her. Her loyalty will be to the Hogs, and we need to keep some barriers up.'

'No worries. Do you want me to film it for you?'

'Yes, please!' came in unison from both the men.

Harry and Tanya looked at Trev.

'Guys, come on. Broad mind and all that.' He grinned.

Harry glanced back through the tinted side window. 'Fuck! We've got action. Camera, please!'

Tanya hit 'Record' on the already positioned video camera.

Trev held the binos back up. 'Okay, a Chinese dude is getting out of that green Honda hatchback and walking over to the Hogs' car.'

Harry was now watching with his own binos.

The Chinese courier walked over to the Falcon as the bikie, Rory, got out. They shook hands. They walked together back to the Honda and the courier opened the hatch.

Harry had swung his glasses over to the DHL van. He cackled. 'Bingo. First DHL driver I've seen using binoculars.'

Trev chuckled, too. 'Yep, definitely the eyes for the cops. Fucking amateurs.'

He sat forward. 'Okay, deal's on.'

They watched as the courier and Rory carried four sports bags from the Honda to the Falcon. Then Rory pulled out a backpack and opened it for the courier who peered inside and rummaged around.

Seemingly satisfied, the Chinese guy took the pack, shook Rory's hand again, and walked back to the Honda.

He left the car park at speed.

Meanwhile, Natty had got out of the car and was all over Rory, as planned.

Trev swung his field glasses over to the DHL van. A couple of minutes passed.

'Ooh, our eyes man is on the phone. Obviously calling in that the gear hasn't left yet.'

The canoodling in the car park continued.

'I'll give them ten out of ten for enthusiasm,' said Harry.

'Not wrong, brother. Anymore gusto and they'll be rooting on the bonnet.'

Tanya giggled. 'And all on camera. Love my job.'

'Okay, DHL man is back on the phone.'

The plan worked. Less than five minutes elapsed and a black king-cab ute roared into the car park.

It screeched to a halt, partly blocking the front of the bikies' car at a diagonal angle.

'That's the UC from the coffee meeting,' said Trev, as a guy got out of the ute. His mate was on the phone still in the driver's seat in the cab.

Another vehicle, a brown Toyota SUV, swung into the car park and stopped next to the ute.

Rory and Natty disengaged from their carnal cavorting.

The lead UC walked over to Rory. The driver of the ute had got out and was standing behind his door, a Glock visible in his hand.

Trev pressed a switch on a transceiver beneath the dash and a recorder started next to it. The voices from the distant car park were crystal clear.

'Rory, isn't it?' said the UC to the bikie guy.

'Who the fuck are you? Your leather outfit attempt as a bikie doesn't cut it, mate. More like something out of the fucking Village People.'

Natty giggled.

There was some sniggering in the surveillance van as well.

The UC shoved Rory in the chest. 'Want to be a smartarse? You'll get a smack in the mouth shortly. Give us the gear.'

'Whatever you say, piggy!'

'Officer to you, arsehole.'

Two more guys in black leather jackets, looking brand new, got out of the SUV, and too clean cut for bikies. They both held Glocks. They surrounded Rory and Natty.

'The gear, Rory,' said the lead UC.

Rory sauntered to the back of his car and opened the boot.

The lead UC, having followed him closely, leant into the boot and whistled. 'Nice haul. Come and grab the bags, Wayne.'

The second UC, the driver from the ute, strutted over and hoisted the sports bags out of the Falcon's boot. He walked back towards the ute.

'Pleasure doing business with you, Rory,' said the UC, giving him a smug sneer.

Wayne threw the bags in the ute and pulled the tonneau back to close it.

The lead UC stepped over to Natty. 'What's your name, bitch?'

'Fuck you.'

The UC nodded. 'Yeah, I think you're going to. You can come with us.'

'Fuck off.'

The lead UC pointed at one of the other dudes. 'Con, you hop in the ute with Wayne and head back to base. I'm going to take this slag for a ride in the SUV with Feng.'

'No worries, Mick,' replied Con.

Mick, the lead UC, grabbed Natty by the arm, but she broke free.

Rory moved in, but Mick levelled his Glock at Rory's face. 'Wanna die, arsehole?'

Rory stopped, holding up his hands.

Mick seized a hold of Natty's hair and propelled her towards the SUV.

His voice was fainter to the listening sleuths as he got further away from Rory and the microphones, but it was audible still.

'Gonna have myself a piece of your skanky tail, slutty girl. And I bet you love it up the arse.'

The SUV's engine started. The black ute took off with the drugs on board.

Mick bundled Natty into the SUV's back seat and got in the vehicle behind her.

Rory ducked into his car and pulled out a sawn-off shotty, pointing it at the bent cops.

'Fucky ducky, here we go,' said Trev.

Mick let two rounds go from his Glock, firing out of the back passenger window of the SUV as it moved off.

Rory fired one blast at the SUV, shattering the front passenger's window, but the vehicle kept moving.

Natty, obviously taking advantage of Mick being occupied with the firefight, threw herself out of the other rear door, landing on the bitumen. She got to her feet and limped away towards Rory.

Rory let the second barrel go, taking out more glass on the SUV, which came to an abrupt halt.

Mick leant out of the door Natty had used, steadied himself with his Glock, and fired two rounds at her, hitting her in the back.

She went down, face first, screaming.

Mick withdrew back into the car, the engine roared, and it burnt rubber leaving the car park.

'Fuck, fuck, fuck!' yelled Harry. 'Let's get in there now! Tan, on the phone for an ambulance! Trev, hit the gas!'

Trev yelled, 'Unfuckingbelievable!' He gunned the VW van's engine and they raced around the park to the opposite side.

Harry jumped out of the van and ran over to Rory, on his knees next to Natty on the ground.

'Look at what those cunts have done!' wailed the big bikie.

'Mate, we've got the ambos on the way. You best get the hell out of here before the circus starts. We'll go with her and let you guys know which hospital.'

Harry put his finger on the side of Natty's neck. 'Still alive, but it's bad.'

Rory still had a hand on the downed girl's face.

'Rory!' yelled Harry. 'Get going, mate, fucking right now! And call Longman and tell him and the crew to disappear fast before this place is swarming with cops.'

A siren sounded in the distance.

'Okay, call me.' He ran for his Falcon and drove off.

'Tan, stay with her. Trev?'

Trev was busying himself in the van, putting away cameras and recorders. 'We need to get out of here, too, Harry.' He threw an evidence bag at Harry. 'Grab those shell cases over there. They're from arsehole's Glock.'

'Yep, okay. Tan, you called in the triple O, so you'll be on tape. You stay with her. When the ambos arrive, your story is that you were out for a walk, heard gunshots, and came over to find this girl on the ground. You saw a couple of vehicles leaving, but didn't get a proper look.'

Harry scooped up the Glock shell cases and bagged them, putting them in his pocket.

'Then, babe, you go with her in the ambulance and keep us posted. All cool?'

'Yep, cool as can be in the circumstances, Harry.' She took hold of Natty's hand.

'We'll see you at the hospital, and we'll let Longman know.'

'Shit, he's going to go ballistic,' she said.

'Not wrong,' said Trev. 'This just went to a whole new level.'

'Yes,' said Harry. 'It's going to get hideous.'

– 8 –

A surgeon with blood smears on her blue smock stepped quietly into the waiting room.

'Who's the next of kin?' she asked.

Archie Longman, in full bikie colours, stood and stepped forward.

'I am, at least the next best thing. Natty's an orphan. She lives with my family.'

The surgeon's placid, slightly grim face—like that of police officers on those notification jobs—looked up at Longman, a clear thirty centimetres taller than her.

'I'm sorry,' she said. 'Natalie didn't make it. One of the bullets hit her pulmonary artery and there was too much blood loss and internal bleeding. She had cardiac arrest as we operated. We really did everything we could. I'm so sorry.'

'I'm sure you did. Thank you for your efforts, doc,' said Longman, a murderous pallor sliding over his face.

'Would you like to see her?'

'Yes, please.'

'She looks quite messed up, so please be prepared for that.'

'Doc, all due respect, but you've no idea what I've seen. I can handle this, believe me.'

Tanya stood up. 'Want me to come with you, Archie?'

'Blondie, that would be grand.' He turned to Harry and Trev. 'And then it's back to your office, 'cos we need to talk.'

He turned and followed the surgeon with Tanya beside him.

Trev sighed. 'I think your word "hideous", Harry, is going to be the understatement of the year.'

'Yep. He might be able to handle seeing Natty dead in there, but I don't think anyone's going to be able to handle him and his rage now.'

'It was already going to be bloody with the stolen drugs and money. Now it's going to go nuclear.'

'And we need to make sure we don't get sucked into a vortex of mutually assured destruction.'

They both sat in silence, pondering the fallout to come.

Longman and Tanya reappeared. She'd been crying. He looked like Satan trying to pass a kidney stone.

'Let's go,' he growled.

Trev pointed at the flat screen on the wall, with some soap opera on low volume doing its best to distract the room.

'The two o'clock news is about to come on. Let's see if there's anything.'

Longman nodded grudgingly.

It was the lead story. There was footage of the car park followed by a cross to the Police Commissioner addressing a media conference. He prattled on about the war on drugs and that this afternoon's shootout was another sordid episode of outlaw bikie gangs fighting over drugs and turf. It wasn't until the bulletin crossed back to the TV reporter that there was mention of a bikie woman being shot.

'And none of the cunts could even manage her name,' hissed Longman.

An hour later, they were all sitting in Harry's office. The Ratfucker had joined them. Harry had briefed the bikies on exactly what went down.

'So, let's have a look at the video, Kenmare.'

Trev played the footage from the part shortly before the arrival of the UC cops in the ute. Trev pointed at the SUV on the screen. 'That's the other one. It moves in a moment.'

They watched in silence. The screen went blank when the footage stopped at the moment Trev fired up the surveillance van to rush in to help Natty.

'Roll it back to when everyone's visible,' said Longman.

He pointed at the lead UC. 'Who is this shithead?'

'Yeah, I'm going to do him myself,' said The Ratfucker.

'That,' said Harry, 'is the main UC. Team leader. Mick, we now know. Don't know his surname yet.'

'But working on it,' added Trev. 'He's the same bloke who was the key go-between for the two head honchos running this gig. The one at the café. Your snitch's handler.'

'So,' said Longman, 'we know who and where they're from. And we've got plans for them. But this boy has a special fucking date with destiny.'

'He might be lured out by another message from the dead snitch's phone,' said Harry.

'If that works, that'll do me,' said Longman. 'We're not going to involve you blokes, and lady,' he grinned at Tanya, 'in anything hands-on, that's our battle.'

'Well, there won't be any other version of justice for Natty,' said Trev. 'They're already publicly attaching her death to another bikie gang, a turf war. And I think that UC will keep a low profile for a while.'

'Maybe,' said The Ratfucker, 'but he's a right greedy prick, so enough of an enticement could still work.'

'Yeah, I'd bet on it,' said Harry. 'Okay, let's work with that idea.'

'Can I contribute a cunning plan?' asked Tanya.

'Of course,' said Harry.

Longman chortled. 'Much rather listen to your voice, Blondie, than these two bastards.'

Everyone laughed.

'Okay,' she said. 'We're not giving this footage to the cops, obviously. But if we leak it to the media, or online, then the UC's face will become that of a bikie, because the wanker Commissioner has already gone public with that: it's all supposedly a bikie gang war. And then when you take out the UC, they can't very well go public about a murdered cop, can they?'

She swallowed her vodka and smiled.

All the men looked at her in admiration, some laced with lust.

'See, Kenmare,' said Longman. 'She's every bit as smart as you and Matson, and she's a shitload better looking.'

Harry grinned. 'Can't argue there, Longman. And babe, that is worth a bonus.'

She blew him a kiss. 'Of course it is. Boss.'

There was laughter all round again.

Longman pointed at a vase of magenta gerberas on the filing cabinet. 'Meant to ask you, Kenmare, you know all about flowers and their meanings and all that shit, don't you? I seem to remember hearing something.'

'Yes, Longman, a hobby of mine. My sensitive side. What's your point?'

'Future planning.' He turned and looked at Corsi.

'Is there a flower that means contempt?'

'Serious piss-on-your-corpse type contempt,' added Corsi.

Harry looked pensive. 'Actually, yes. Yellow carnations.'

'They easy to get?'

'No worries there, Longman, they're available year-round.'

'Thanks, mate. Now let's drink some more.'

– 9 –

Trev's text message to the snitch's phone was a statement of the obvious, but guaranteed to get the UC's interest after the shooting yesterday.

> Whole lotta shit coming down after shooting. Real
> bad shit. Need 2 talk URGENT!

The reply message had mentioned the same café as the previous false start.

Harry and Trev were in the VW van watching. But no camera today.

Tanya had opted to stay at her place to console Greta after Natty's death.

'Consolation of an entirely carnal variety,' had been Trev's comment with a huge smile after Harry repeated Tanya's message.

Harry had laughed. 'Yeah, well at least one of the team can enjoy the memory.'

Now they waited, again.

'And here he is,' said Trev, as the UC walked along the footpath and sat at a table outside the café.

Harry picked up his phone. 'You're on, Longman. He's the only customer outside, so no collateral problems. Same leather as yesterday, the idiot.'

'Thanks, Kenmare. You blokes can go if you like. Chat later,' came over the phone speaker.

Harry rang off.

'And we're not leaving, are we?' said Trev.

'No way. That corrupt cunt of a cop, who's also a murderer, needs his comeuppance. Not often you get a front-row seat at Karma Central, Trev.'

'Lift him or just cap him, you reckon?'

'Ooh, good question. I reckon a straight whack. They'll want to get stuck into the two big prizes.'

As Trev nodded, a throaty engine roar approached.

A black Ford F150 with an uncovered tray screeched to a halt. A masked bikie arose from the bed of the tray to a crouch with an M16.

The UC, who had stood reflexively as the vehicle had stopped, had nowhere to go.

A burst of gunfire blasted into his chest and he went down.

As the F150 accelerated away, a second F150 slammed to a halt. Another masked guy jumped out, ran over to the prone UC, and popped two rounds from a .357 revolver into his head at point blank range.

Then the shooter was back in the truck and it was gone.

Timid faces appeared behind windows. Most had phones to their ears.

'That second shooter was Longman,' said Harry. 'Saw his belt buckle.'

'Just making totally sure he was dead. It was personal. Time for us to disappear,' said Trev, starting the engine.

'Yep, make haste, chariot driver. We've seen enough action for one day.'

***

Tanya, meanwhile, was enjoying action of a wholly different kind, but her neighbours would no doubt have thought murder was afoot, too, given the screams of ecstasy from her and Greta.

The bikies had dropped Greta off in Surry Hills before heading for the UC meeting.

The two girls had multiple shots of vodka in between peeling each other's clothes off, although Tanya had been close to naked to start with. She did most of the undressing of Greta as Greta pashed and fingered her. Then it was frenzied sixty-niner until both girls came, screaming in unison. More orgasms with the double-ender followed.

Now, with half a bottle of vodka gone, and it wasn't even lunchtime, Tanya lay back with Greta's face in her crotch sucking and licking her clitoris, whilst slowly plucking anal beads from her rectum. Tanya was almost delirious with ecstasy.

Greta paused. 'What's that?' Her head lifted from Tanya's pussy.

'What?' said Tanya, coming out of her vaginal reverie.

'Sounded like someone trying the door handle,' whispered Greta.

'Probably just the neighbour sick of our noise. Finish me, please!'

Greta resumed eating Tanya's pussy. As the last anal bead squeezed out of Tanya's arse, she came loudly.

When Tanya let go of her head, Greta slid up her stomach, holding her breasts, and kissed her.

'That, girlfriend, was awesome,' said Tanya.

Greta grinned and licked Tanya's lips. 'Happy to visit again sometime.'

'You're on.'

They were lying in each other's arms when the apartment's front door came crashing inwards.

Tanya instinctively dived for the phone on the bedside table.

***

Harry and Trev walked into the Emerald Bar with the intention of a hearty lunch.

'Cheers,' said Harry, clinking his beer glass with Trev's.

'Cheers, Harry. Here's to the escalating bikie war.'

'Well, I am looking forward to those two corrupt senior bastards getting their just desserts.'

They were speculating a few minutes later on possible means of torture for the corrupt cops when Harry's and Trev's phones simultaneously gave out a sharp siren noise.

'Shit, Harry, it's Tanya's alarm. My tracker says her place.'

Harry was already on his phone.

'No answer.'

'Let's go, Harry. There'll be a cab up at the shopping centre.'

They ran out of the pub with Harry lamenting their lack of weaponry.

'Old school, then,' said Trev to Harry's back.

***

Tanya and Greta clutched the top sheet around their naked bodies, looking at the two men standing inside the doorway of the studio apartment.

A voice yelled along the corridor of the apartment block floor, 'Is everything all right?' At least one neighbour hadn't joined the 'ignore the whores' trope that pervaded level four in the building. That had kicked off when the priggish old spinster, a former convent school principal, who chaired the strata committee had suggested Tanya and Sasha were prostitutes. Well, they had been back then, but not for a long time now. The sanctimonious old bitch hadn't even given her condolences to Tanya when Sasha died. At least most of the neighbours had done that much.

Tanya knew enough of the sleuthing trade now that the fact these men were not wearing masks or balaclavas was not a good sign. Tanya also prided herself on not letting things just happen to her. Fuck being the victim. She'd succeeded in hitting her alarm button on her phone, so hopefully Harry and Trev weren't getting pissed and ignoring their devices.

As Tanya raced to think of a plan for the right here and now, she was stunned when the thinner man stepped back towards the doorway, leant out into the corridor, and said, 'Stay calm. Police business. Remain inside your premises, please.'

'Are they really fricking pigs?' whispered Greta.

'Quite possibly.'

Tanya didn't recognize either of them from the previous day.

The stockier of the two, with a beer gut of a hundred Oktoberfests, pointed at Greta and stepped towards the bed. 'You, bikie slag, on your feet. You're coming with us.'

'What the hell have I done?'

'And where's your warrant, officer?' sneered Tanya.

The two men snorted with derision.

'Ooh, bush lawyer this one, Johnno,' said the beer belly.

'Yeah, but well worth a fuck by the looks of her, Fred. Unlike this filthy bikie skank.'

The fat man, Fred, grabbed Greta's arm and hauled her out of the bed.

'Your scumbag mates shot one of our blokes this morning. So, you are going to be our currency for payback.' He punched Greta in the guts.

She fell on the floor, gasping for air.

'And who are you, bitch?' said the fat man looking at Tanya.

Tanya's phone rang. It was Harry or Trev, no doubt, responding to her alarm.

She didn't move. 'Fuck you!'

As the fat one was laughing at her, a third man, Asian this time, appeared through the door.

Tanya recognized him. He was one of the undercover cops at the drug drop yesterday.

The Asian dude spoke. 'Johnno, the car's ready at the service entrance.'

'Okay, Feng' said fat Fred. 'You two take the bikie slag down. Use the service elevator at this end of the corridor. I need to have a good talk with this other slut.'

Johnno grabbed Greta by her hair. 'Get dressed and make it fast.'

Greta picked up her knickers and jeans and pulled them on.

The fat one was now on his phone. 'Boss, we've got the bikie slag. Bringing her to the safehouse shortly. There's another one here, not one of them.'

'Safe' was definitely not what Greta's destination was going to be, thought Tanya.

'Okay, boss, I'll find out the connections. Then you want a clean slate?'

There was a pause.

'Roger, boss.'

Tanya didn't need to have 'clean slate' explained to her. Shit, she thought, I am so over dealing with corrupt cops who like violence. Plan needed, girl, plan. And like bloody now!

As Greta was hauled away by the other two cops, and the fat one had his back to her watching his mates, Tanya grabbed the string of anal beads.

He turned at that moment. 'Want me to shove them up your arse, darlin'?'

'No. I figure you'd be the anal receiver around here. Bet you like getting your arse punched.'

'Really? Okay you mouthy little tart, what's your connection to the bikie slag?'

Tanya needed to bait him, get him lashing out. He looked hopelessly out of shape, but he sure had a lot of weight if she ended up pinned.

'Fuck you, you fat faggot!' She spat at him and sprang backwards as he lunged wildly.

The edge of the bed took him out at knee level and he went face down on the mattress.

Tanya jumped onto his back and slid the cord of anal beads under his face and pulled it tight around his throat.

Fat Fred was way too slow to get his fingers up before Tanya had a shit-smeared noose around him.

She knew she had to hang on for dear life as he bucked.

She heard her phone ring again.

He tried to roll to get her off him, but she stuck her leg out to rest against the headboard: the advantage of her young, lithe body against his flabby weight. In his growing panic, with his air supply rapidly diminishing, he kept trying to roll the same way, not processing any alternatives. He was trying to get his hand under his chest, but couldn't create a gap.

Tanya leant down behind his head. 'And you know the best bit, fucktard? It's my stinking shit all over these beads. Matches exactly what I think of you.'

Fat Fred couldn't vocalize anything more than a strangled grunt in return. Slowly, his struggling was ebbing.

Tanya was leaving nothing to chance. She kept the beads as tight as a garotte.

When his body went limp, Tanya jumped off the bed and put her underwear on, followed by jeans and a T-shirt.

There was the sound of running feet approaching and she heard Harry call her name before she saw him come bolting through the smashed door, Trev right behind him.

'Glad to see you two.'

Harry pointed at the fat bloke on the bed. 'What the hell? Is he dead?'

'Not sure. And don't care.'

'Given he's fully clothed and definitely not your type, I guess he wasn't here for a social visit?' said Trev, grinning.

'He's another corrupt cop, linked to the crew yesterday. His two mates have taken Greta.'

Harry stepped over to the prone man. He pointed at the anal beads. 'Should I ask?'

'Girl uses whatever is at hand, Mister PI.'

Harry looked at the brown smears around the man's throat and neck. 'Might use his wrist instead.' He checked for a pulse. 'Okay, he's still alive.'

'Thank fuck for that,' said Trev. 'A dead cop in Tanya's room in Laos is one thing. We don't need a repeat here.'

'Damn right,' said Harry. 'But we need to get rid of him.'

Trev bent over and pulled a wallet out of the fat man's trouser pocket. He opened it.

'Badge. Feds.'

Trev rolled him over and opened his jacket. He pulled a Glock out of a shoulder holster.

The man's phone rang in his jacket pocket.

'That'll be his two mates wondering where he is,' said Trev.

'They only left a few minutes ago, using the service elevator,' said Tanya.

'Right,' said Harry. 'Tan, get something to tie this wanker up. We'll strip him and leave him in the dumpster downstairs out back. Trev, now you've got a gat, why don't you go and give the other goons a surprise?'

'Be my pleasure.' He took off.

Five minutes later, Harry dragged the now naked, bound, and gagged Fed to the service elevator. Fortunately, none of the neighbours opened their doors. Trev was waiting at the bottom.

'Mate, as soon as they saw me coming out of the door with a gat, they took off. It was a white Mazda SUV. I couldn't see Greta, but guessing she was laid down in the back.'

'Okay, grab his legs. He's one fat fuck. We'll heave him into the dumpster. Someone'll find him eventually, especially when he comes around and starts making some noise.'

Trev grabbed the Fed's ankles and lifted. 'Geez, way too many half-priced burgers, this bastard.'

After some grunting and swearing, they rolled the unconscious cop over the lip of the dumpster and dropped him into the garbage within.

Trev got on his phone. 'Stefan? Mate, I need an ultra-urgent door repair. Can you?'

Trev rattled off Tanya's address. 'We'll see you shortly.'

The two sleuths went back upstairs to wait.

Harry rang Longman to give him the bad news.

He hung up his phone and turned to the others. 'Longman wants blood.'

'I'll bet,' said Trev. 'Tan, did the other Feds say anything that might give us a clue where they were taking Greta? Did it sound as if they were taking her to their office or the watchhouse to charge her?'

'No. They said the word "safehouse", but that was it. Didn't figure it was an official arrest.'

'Fuck,' said Harry. 'No, they're not arresting her, they're abducting her. We're going to have to go active on this.'

'Yep, brother, otherwise Greta will end up next to Natty in the morgue.'

'So, what exactly is a police safehouse?'

'Tan, it's a secret hidey hole undercover or surveillance cops can use. Even other cops don't know where it is.'

'So how …'

Harry stood up. 'As soon as the repair man is here, looks as if we're going to have to retrieve our naked, fat friend from his bed of trash and make the bastard talk, give up the location. Only chance we've got to help Greta.'

'Longman could do that a treat,' said Trev.

'Yeah, but he'll take a while to get here, and we can't lose any time. How about you grab a cab to the office and get the van. You can be back in ten minutes. We'll do the deed ourselves.'

'Roger, sounds like a plan.'

'And bring the armoury. I sniff the smell of cordite on the horizon.'

'You bet.' Trev ran from the apartment.

***

Forty minutes later, the naked, fat cop, still gagged, was lying on a plastic sheet on the floor of Trev's VW surveillance van. They were parked in an alley next to Tanya's apartment building.

Harry lent over the captive cop. 'Now, you corrupt cunt, you're going to tell us where the bikie girl has been taken. One chance to talk before the serious pain starts. Understand?'

The fat man nodded.

Trev ripped off the tape gagging his mouth. 'Speak, if you know what's good for you.'

'Fuck you,' he wheezed.

Tanya, who was in the jump seat, swivelled around to face the rear of the van. She lifted herself and stomped her heel into the fat man's nose. The scrunching sound of cartilage smashing reverberated in the closed confines of the van, followed by a hissing groan from the cop. Blood ran down his cheeks from his smashed nose.

Harry looked at Tanya. 'I didn't see that one coming.'

Trev laughed. 'Yeah, nor did the retard here.' He picked up a ball hammer from the workbench next to him. 'So, idiot, you were told one chance and you blew it. Where's the girl been taken?'

The cops beady eyes tried to focus on Trev through their watering. Not for long though.

Trev looked at Harry who grabbed a towel. As Harry clamped the cloth over the cop's mouth, Trev swung the hammer into his kneecap.

The fat man, still tied up, shook with pain, his not inconsiderable gut wobbling like a large jelly in an earthquake.

'Plenty more available, mate. Talk!' said Harry, removing the towel.

The cop stared at Harry, tears joining the rivulets of blood on his cheeks.

'No? Nothing?' said Harry. 'All right, more, Trev.'

Trev raised the hammer.

'Okay, okay,' pleaded the cop. 'I'll tell you.'

He stammered out an address.

'Righto, mate,' said Trev. 'Better be true, and we might let you live. But if you're bullshitting us, then more pain.' He raised the hammer again.

'That's the truth, I swear. Please, no more.'

There was a throaty engine noise behind them. Trev flicked open the peep hole in the back window.

'It's the gang.' He opened the door.

Longman and The Ratfucker got out of the black F150.

'Gents,' said Trev. 'We have an address courtesy of the fat man here.'

'He is one ugly fucking pig, isn't he,' said Longman peering in the back of the van.

'Want me to cap him?' asked Corsi.

'Let's make sure he's telling the truth first,' said Harry under his breath. 'Then he'll need to go as he's seen us all and they know Tanya's address.'

'What's the next move, Kenmare?' asked Longman.

Tanya came out of the van with an iPad in her hand. 'Here's the street view, and the satellite view.' She showed Harry the screen.

It was an old terrace house on Derwent Street in Glebe. It had a car area in place of its back yard, running off Derwent Lane behind it.

Trev looked at it. 'I reckon a distraction in the back yard, car fire maybe, or a flashbang, then hit them when they emerge to check it out.'

'Like it,' said Harry.

'We can't just take the bastard door down?' asked Longman.

'Mate, it's an undercover safehouse. The doors are likely to be reinforced. We can see all the bars on the windows. So, unless you've got a bazooka.'

'Well …'

'Yeah, let's cool it,' said Trev. 'We don't want to turn it into downtown Baghdad.'

'So, once we've confirmed the car they took Greta in is there, Trev'll set the trap. We'll be outside the back door ready for them. Take them out and storm on in,' said Harry. 'And no bloody bazookas!'

The bikies laughed.

'Need silencers?' asked Corsi.

'Don't bother,' said Trev. 'By the time I've done my distraction, a bit of gunfire will be nothing.'

Longman chuckled. 'Love working with you blokes. Let's go. But you sure I can't use the bazooka?'

'No!' said Harry and Trev in unison.

– 10 –

The VW van came back along Derwent Lane and stopped next to the F150.

Trev spoke out of his open window next to Longman in the Ford. 'Yep, same car, so we're good. The back gate is open.'

'So, you saw two others, but anymore you reckon?'

'Hard to say,' said Harry, leaning over. 'Given they're all in on this crooked scheme, the numbers are more than likely strictly limited. I reckon it'll only be the two others who took Greta, plus fat boy here. But you never know.'

'What we can be sure of,' said Trev, 'is that anyone in the safehouse is in on the scam, too. They wouldn't take a kidnapped girl there if there were any honest cops inside.'

Harry spoke. 'I agree. Anyone we find is fair game. Any cameras on the back, Trev?'

'Yes, as we'd expect for a safehouse. So, there's no hiding next to the door option. We'll have to run into the yard after they come out.'

Harry leaned over again. 'Longman, pull up just short of the back gate on the opposite side. We'll prop on this side. You guys and me will wait behind the back fence line for them to come out.'

'Let's hope they both do,' said Trev. 'Otherwise, we're storming in for a gunfight.'

The Ratfucker hefted his M16. 'Always up for that, mate.'

The F150 moved off to its position.

Trev turned the van around and followed. 'What was that about another Baghdad?' he said.

Tanya craned forward from the jump-seat. 'Since I'm assuming one of us needs to stay and guard this piece of shit, and I'm the least useful in a gunfight, am I allowed to hurt him while I wait?'

Harry turned to look at her. 'Well …'

She cut him off, smiling. 'That was rhetorical.'

Trev sniggered. 'Damn, wish I could stay and watch.'

There was a muffled noise from the fat captive, now gagged again.

Tanya sneered. 'Another arsehole of a man who thought he could do what he wanted to me. He needs to suffer.'

'No argument here,' said Harry. 'But make it a snappy torture session, 'cos we'll be out in a couple of minutes, tops.'

Trev laughed. 'Yeah, so you don't have time to heat up the soldering iron, Tan.'

Tanya picked up a switchblade from a box and flicked it open. 'Oh, well, cold steel it is, then.'

A more vigorous muffled protest came from the fat cop.

Harry opened the door to climb out. 'At least the plastic sheet's already down.'

'Yep,' said Trev. 'I'm a bit particular about bodily fluids in my van.'

Tanya giggled this time. 'Not what I heard, Trev, you stud.'

Harry sniggered. 'She got you there, mate.' He got out of the van.

As Trev closed his door behind him, Tanya slowly drove the knife blade into the fat man's penis. The van shook as he writhed on the floor.

Longman with a 9mm pistol and The Ratfucker with his trademark M16 were ready to the right of the back gate opening onto Derwent Lane.

Harry hid to the left of the gate with his .38 out.

Trev stepped out from cover. With a low underarm throw, he landed a flashbang under the nearest car in the small yard. He quickly lobbed a smoke grenade over both vehicles towards the back wall of the safehouse.

As the opaque cloud billowed, the flashbang exploded.

'That'll get them out,' said Trev, pulling out his .357 Ruger.

Sure enough, the back door flew open and a guy emerged with a Glock in his hand. He spotted Trev, who was advertising himself, and raised the Glock.

There was a loud crack of a rifle retort as Corsi dropped the guy with one round from the M16.

'No one else coming out?' yelled Longman.

'Think we're going in,' said Harry, taking off for the open back door, .38 at the ready.

The other three followed him, with Longman collecting the fallen cop's Glock.

Harry's shout of 'Gun!' was almost drowned out by the roar of a second guy's Glock at the same time as Harry dived for the floor inside the back door.

Longman, two metres behind Harry, fired off three rounds as he dropped to the ground. Two of the bullets found their mark and the second cop staggered backwards, falling over.

He was trying to regain his stance when he was simultaneously hit by bullets from Trev and Harry.

Trev kicked the Glock away across the floor and checked for a pulse.

'Dead.'

'Okay. Trev, you and Corsi take this level. Longman, you and me upstairs.'

Harry and Longman ran for the staircase. As they got to the top, Trev's voice carried up the stairwell, 'Clear!'

There were three doors, two closed, off the top landing, obviously the two original bedrooms in this colonial-era terrace house. An open door to a bathroom was in front of them.

Longman went low and dived in. 'Clear, mate,' came back.

'Greta?' called Harry.

Silence.

'Greta, baby, it's Arch!'

Silence.

Harry put his finger to his lips and moved to the nearest closed door, putting his ear to it.

He heard a whimper.

He pointed at the door and looked at Longman, gesturing him downwards.

Harry flattened himself against the wall and reached down, hankie over his left hand, trying the door handle a fraction, then snatching his hand back.

Nothing. Silence.

He turned the handle fully and pushed the door open.

Longman, almost prone on the floor, was looking down the sights of his 9mm.

'She's in there,' he whispered. 'Gagged and tied against the far wall.'

Harry looked around the door frame and met eyes with Greta sitting on the floor.

He raised his eyebrows at her and waved his finger from left to right.

Greta looked at Harry, flicked her eyes to her left, and then back at Harry.

Good girl, thought Harry. You are way more switched on than most people double your age: the bikie lifestyle and its lessons.

Harry looked at the chief bikie and pointed to the other side of the door. He lightly tapped the wall next to his head and nodded at Longman. It was plasterboard.

He motioned holding a rifle to Longman who acknowledged his understanding and silently descended the staircase.

He was back within seconds clutching Corsi's M16.

Longman stepped in close to the wall on the opposite side of the door from Harry. He levelled the rifle into his shoulder.

He put four rounds through the wall in quick succession and slightly spread.

Harry swung into the doorway, his .38 ready, as a body crashed to the floor. A Glock was attached to a now lifeless arm.

Harry stepped in, kicking the pistol out of the man's hand. He looked at the cop's back, two bloodied bullet holes visible. One was in the area of the heart.

Longman strode into the room. 'Greta, luv, you okay?'

She bobbed her head as he stepped over to her and slipped off the gag.

'Yes, Arch,' she gasped. 'So good to see you.'

'Nice shooting, Longman.'

'Teamwork, Kenmare.' He grinned as he untied Greta's wrists.

She undid her ankles and stood slowly, shaking her limbs to get the blood flowing again.

'Let's move it,' said Harry, as a faint noise of a siren could be heard in the distance.

They ran out of the house, Longman holding Greta's hand.

Trev and Corsi had opened the car nearest the back door and the reek of petrol hung in the air.

'What's the plan?' said Harry, as Trev went to go back into the house.

'I'm going to get the recorder for that camera, don't need any film of our visit lying around. And when Longman's finished with the fat cop in the van, that plastic sheet he's on needs to be burnt as well.'

'Good thinking,' said Harry. 'I didn't touch anything inside with my fingers. You, Longman?'

'No, all good, mate.'

'Corsi?'

'Nope.'

Longman ran to the VW van where Tanya held the side door open.

Longman looked in at the naked fat cop on the plastic sheet, his genitals now a bloodied mess.

'Blondie, what the fuck?'

'Arch, he was going to rape me.'

'Say no more.' He turned to the cop who was barely conscious. 'And you sure won't be saying anything more, ever.' He put his 9mm to the cop's head and fired one round, putting the man out of the excruciating genital pain he was in.

The Ratfucker arrived.

They wrapped the plastic sheet around the body and hurriedly carried it to the open car, shoving it on the back seat.

As Trev came running out of the back door holding a black box, Corsi lit the car up.

Tanya, having assumed the driver's seat, started the VW van, as Longman, Corsi, and Greta were running for the F150.

The sirens were getting louder.

'Our office this evening,' yelled Harry at the running bikies.

Longman gave a thumbs up as he climbed into the cab of the pick-up, having pushed Greta inside.

Both vehicles sped away in opposite directions.

– 11 –

The news anchor looked gravely at the camera.

> The Federal Police Commissioner has announced that the shootings in inner Sydney this afternoon resulted in three AFP officers dying.

The television image switched to the AFP news conference with the Commissioner looking lethal.

> The police family lost three fine and brave officers today. Our necessary war on drugs and their evils comes at a terrible cost at times, but we will hunt down the outlaw bikie criminals who committed this atrocity. We will win the war on drugs, mark my words. We will prevail.

'Enough,' said Longman, banging his hand on the edge of Harry's desk.

Harry flicked the remote and the wall-mounted screen went dark.

'Fucking lying bastard,' said Longman.

'Yeah, "fine and brave" my hairy arse,' said Corsi. 'Just more corrupt pigs.'

'On the bright side,' said Harry, 'when we're ready, we've got all three of those fine officers on film, all at

Tanya's place and one in the car park deal for Natty's murder. Also starring the UC you knocked. We'll put the record straight whenever you've finished your work.'

'Longman lit a smoke. 'You bet. We're ready to move tomorrow, it's all lined up to grab these two senior wankers.'

He blew smoke across Harry's desk. 'Nice work filming it, Blondie.'

Tanya giggled. 'Yeah, Archie, that was so not the reason.'

The big bikie smiled. 'I bet. That'd be worth a watch.'

'And then it's game on, Hogs' style,' smirked The Ratfucker. 'We'll get our gear back and all the stolen cash. Those two shit stains will sing like birds before I'm done.'

Trev chuckled. 'I'm sure, mate. In your understandable enthusiasm, don't forget to film it carefully, avoiding any backdrops that can be recognized. Then I'll mix it in with the rest of the footage for this year's leading contender for the gold Logie Award.'

'We'll film it all right,' growled Longman. 'Hardest bit'll be not laughing in the background.'

'So, how much gear and dosh are you out?' asked Harry.

Longman looked pensive, his fingers doing the human abacus. 'In total since this started, they've taken about forty kilos of our gear, and over eight hundred in cash.'

'And they've probably got more cash now. No doubt some of our gear's been sold,' added Corsi.

'Big bloody pay day, if you can get it,' said Trev.

'We'll get it, no worries,' said Longman. 'And then back to serious business. Got some heavy profits to make up.'

'You do know that they'll come after you bad?' said Harry. 'Even the ones at the top who are not corrupt will still stick by the ones who are. It's the police brotherhood.'

'It's called the Establishment for a reason,' said Trev.

'Yep, and it's that same Establishment that makes the most profit out of the drug trade by keeping it illegal,' said Longman. 'Dealers like us, we're not at the top of the ladder, you know.'

'Yeah,' said Harry. 'The sooner we stop this stupid bloody war on drugs and legalize it all the better.'

'More like a war on common sense,' said Tanya.

'And that won't change,' replied Longman. 'Precisely because the big end of town are in on the game, controlling it all.'

'It worked in Portugal,' said Trev. 'All legalized and treated as a health issue, not a crime. Been fewer deaths, less crime, and less corruption.'

The Ratfucker guffawed loudly. 'Yeah, one small insignificant country. So what?'

'That's right,' said Longman. 'They did that all those years ago and just how many countries have followed suit?'

'Absolutely zero is the answer,' added Corsi. 'So, no one's interested in the evidence of Portugal. There's simply too much bloody money to be made.'

'Depressing, seriously,' said Harry, 'but I can't agree with the way it is. Prohibition helps no one.'

'It sure helps those in the Establishment, Kenmare. Helps them get very, very fucking rich. Sorry, mate, but that's the game. I get your sentiments and see your point, but none of us are going to change a damned thing here. So, we're going to keep making a business out of it,' said Longman. 'And we'll sling you a half share of any cash we recover. Want to pay our bill for your troubles on this.'

'You already paid us for the surveillance op.'

'Yeah, but that didn't include the undercover piggy roast today.'

'Fair enough, can't have enough cash.'

Longman stood and Corsi followed suit.

'We'll bid you wonderful crew a good night. We've got two abductions to work on.' He grinned broadly.

– 12 –

The stench of the cooking vats stewing the meat invaded every nook and cranny of the Dubbo pet food factory, even overpowering the appalling reek of Commander Billingham's evacuated bowels. The senior Customs officer was naked, aside from a black cloth bag over his head, and spreadeagled against a concrete wall, shackled at the wrists and ankles.

The Ratfucker was laughing as he launched in again with the bull-whip, adding a twelfth livid red welt across the officer's back.

Billingham shrieked as the leather cord bit into his flesh again.

Archie Longman looked on with a smile. The lift of the two corrupt cops had been unexpectedly easy. Perhaps it was down to the extreme arrogance of them, as Kenmare had told him more than once. And it was Kenmare's information that had got them to this point. The PI had told Longman the bent pair of senior coppers usually played golf together on a Friday afternoon. The gang had blocked their car in at a quiet intersection and jacked it with both cops inside. Arrogant wankers hadn't taken their guns with them. Amateur hour, thought Longman as he smiled again.

After they'd bagged the cops' heads, they tranquilized them for the long drive. Then the ski masks came off the bikies. And Longman had instructed all the bikies to use only nicknames when talking in front of the captive cops.

They were now an hour into the torture of Billingham. The AFP guy, Horley, was tied to a chair, also naked and head bagged.

Longman beckoned Corsi over. 'Mate, aside from us only using nicknames, I've also got plans so they'll never be able to visually identify us, and that's if we don't kill them. So, reckon it's time to up the drama and let them watch what's happening to each other.'

'Like your style, boss.' Corsi stepped over to Billingham and ripped the bag off his head. He then walked over to Horley and did the same.

Both cops, squinting in the new light, looked desperately around the room and at each other, Billingham twisting his neck to look behind him from the wall he was facing.

Corsi took hold of the bull-whip again and swung at Billingham's back. The Customs officer screamed.

Longman prodded the AFP cop and told him he was next. Horley had already pissed himself, and The Ratfucker hadn't even started. What a weak prick, thought Longman.

He walked over to the chained Customs Commander, taking care to avoid the puddle of liquid shit around Billingham's feet. 'Now you bent pig, where are our fucking drugs?'

The bloodied Customs officer spat on the ground, a reddish globule merging into the pale brown pool. His London accent croaked, 'Fuck you.'

'Really?' said The Ratfucker, always a man to relish his work. 'Time for your mate to feel some pain, then. Maybe he'll spill the beans.'

'Tell them nothing, Neil,' called the shackled Customs Commander to the Fed.

'I won't, Dick. Old Bill forever!' yelled Horley from his chair.

Longman turned to Corsi. 'You've given them plenty of stimulant?'

'Yep, enough adrenalin to just about give them a heart attack. But not quite.'

'Good work. Righto, fucking hurt him.'

'My pleasure,' said The Ratfucker, igniting an oxyacetylene blowtorch.

The seated Horley looked at it in horror. 'You fucking animals.'

Corsi roared laughing. 'Yep, and I'm really good at it.' He promptly burned the cop's ear off with the roaring torch. Horley's screams were deafening.

Longman picked up a baseball bat. 'Yeah, "Old Bill forever" my hairy arse.' He swung the bat, smashing the cop's right kneecap.

The shrieking climbed to a whole new level.

Longman looked at Corsi. 'Go burn that other wanker, mate.'

The Ratfucker, grinning like a man with genuine job satisfaction, pulled the oxy trolley over to the chained Billingham.

'Any preference for which bit I barbecue first, piggy?'

'Fuck off, scum.'

'Reckon you've got balls, do you? Well, not for much longer. Oink, oink!'

Corsi increased the flame and cooked the cop's scrotum. Billingham's screaming rivalled that of Horley.

'We can keep this up all day, piggies,' said Longman. 'One of you wankers will speak sooner or later.'

'Reckon it's time for some anal treatment, boss,' said Corsi, picking up a piece of slim PVC conduit with barbed wire wrapped around half of it.

He looked at the two cops. 'Eeny meeny miny moe.' He waved his finger between the pair.

'Go for the AFP wanker,' said Longman. He turned to Horley. 'Bet you like getting it up the arse, all that English public-school stuff, but this'll be a whole new experience for you.'

He turned towards the door. 'Boys?!'

Two other bikies came in.

Longman pointed at the AFP cop. 'Untie him and hold him face down on that bench. And remember, nicknames only in front of these two.'

'No, no, no!' screamed Horley as he was dragged to the bench.

The Ratfucker stepped over to him, smacking his butt cheeks with the barbed wire stick. He leant down to the cop. 'Still time to talk, fucker. Or, I can ream your arse out with Mister Barbed Wire here. Last chance.'

'Okay, please, please, I'll tell you.'

Assistant Commissioner Horley spewed out an address and details of a storage unit. He said the address was his home where the cash was kept, and the drugs were at the storage facility.

'This had better check out, wanker, or you've still got an arse-fucking coming your way.' Corsi smacked Horley's buttocks again with the barbed wire.

Longman spoke to the other two bikies. 'Get these wankers secured and silent. But make sure they bloody stay alive. There are syringes of stimulants in that little red case there, if you need them. We'll be back tomorrow.'

'Yes, boss.'

***

Trev put down his burner phone as Harry looked expectantly at him.

'Longman and Corsi are on their way back to Sydney. Got a home address and a storage unit. Longman wants us to sit off the home address and tell them when Horley's wife and kid have gone out. And he wants them filmed.'

Harry frowned. 'I can see why he wants them gone from the house. He's an old-school crook, so he doesn't want to touch the wife or kid.'

'Yeah, not like the newer criminal scum.'

'But I don't know what he wants film for. Still, no problem for us. When does he want us on it?'

'Dawn. He said as soon as she leaves to take junior to school, they'll hit the house. The money's all in there apparently. The drugs are at a Storage King unit. Longman's got another crew hitting that.'

Harry lit a smoke and put his feet up on his desk. 'You know what I'd really like?'

'A wet pussy?' said Tanya.

They all laughed.

'Always want that,' said Harry. 'Later, babe, since you're staying at mine tonight.'

She blew him a kiss.

'Bloody hell, Tan,' said Trev. 'Lusty bikie chick one night, horny debauched PI the next. You are living the life.'

She giggled. 'Just need some thoroughly gay cock now for the trifecta.'

Trev went a radiant shade of scarlet.

'Gay cock?' asked Harry, looking curious.

'Harry, my gorgeous detective, the variety of cock doesn't matter. It's the worth and passion of the man attached to it that counts.'

She smirked at Trev. His fading blush refreshed.

Harry smiled and shook his head. 'Never thought Kenmare and Associates could be such crazy fun.'

'Cheers to that,' said Tanya, raising her glass and drinking.

Harry toasted with his glass. 'Anyway, before the depraved descent into wet pussies and throbbing gay cocks, I was thinking what would be really great would be to sit that bastard Assistant Commissioner Horley in front of a police computer and access all the intel they have on Wheeler.'

Trev whistled. 'That would be gold, mate.'

'But we'd need to get him in front of a computer and hold a bloody gun to his head.'

Trev held up a finger. 'An idea.'

'You usually have good ones, brother.'

'They were playing golf when they were grabbed, right?'

'Yes.'

'So, they wouldn't have left their laptops in the car. They'd be at home.'

'If they took them home.'

'Come on, Harry. Ambitious, career-climbing wankers like these two? Of course they'd take them home. Those types never want to be out of the loop.'

'Conceded, mate. Forgetting how sad these arseholes are.'

'So, Longman and crew are going to hit the house of the AFP arsewipe. They can grab any laptops whilst they're in there.'

Harry nodded pensively. 'And then torture the passwords out of our bent copper friend. I like it, really like it.'

Trev got on the phone to Longman.

***

Hilda Horley shut the back door of her Honda SUV with young Toby inside. Her bloody husband, she cursed inwardly. She didn't want to reveal her disdain to Toby and disturb his idyllic, privileged childhood. Bloody Neil had been out all night and not even a single phone call. Still, it all added to the list of notes for the potential divorce lawyer. No doubt he'd roll in half drunk this evening with some bullshit about being on an all-night, super-secret operation. More like on top of some all-night two-bit syphilitic slag. She was sure the wanker was screwing around. Well, she'd treat herself to an expensive massage after she'd dropped Toby at school.

She was too distracted by her marital-problem thoughts to notice the grey VW van parked further along the street with two men sitting in it, as she pulled out of the driveway and cruised away.

'Longman? She's out. We'll tail and let you know when she's coming back. And don't forget the laptops.' Harry ended the call.

As Trev swung the van around to follow the school mum, a builder's van complete with ladders atop went past them, The Ratfucker grinning at the wheel with Longman next to him.

Trev and Harry hung back as little Toby was dropped at school.

'Ah, looks as if she's not heading straight home,' said Harry, as the Honda took off onto the main road.

'Shops, maybe,' said Trev. 'There's a shopping centre a couple of blocks away.'

'No, she's pulling over there.'

The Honda parked against the kerb outside a small row of suburban shops, the old high-street style.

Trev pulled in fifty metres further on.

Tanya moved to the back of the van and slid open the observation shutter. 'She's out of her car. Walking into that beauty parlour.'

'Okay, Tan, go for a walk past and see what's happening.'

'No worries.' She opened the side door of the van and hopped out, closing the door behind her.

She walked quickly along the street, stopping outside the beautician's shop, pretending to look at the price-list. She got on her phone. 'Okay, she's at the counter. Wait, wait, she's being taken to a booth at the back. Okay, it's a massage table in there. Curtain's now closed with her in there.' Tanya put her phone back in her pocket and walked back to the van.

'Excellent,' said Harry. 'The bikies will have all the time they need.'

Trev nodded. 'Nice to have luck swing it our way once in a while.'

Harry called Longman. 'She's gone for a massage, mate, you've got plenty of time.'

'Beauty,' replied Longman. 'We're bagging the cash now. There's shitloads of it. And Rocco's found two laptops, both with police logos on them.'

'Good stuff. We'll sit on missus until you're done, just in case. Buzz when you're out.'

'No worries.'

Harry's phone rang again fifteen minutes later.

'We're done, Kenmare. Off back to talk to our bent piggy friends. Call you from a fresh burner once we're there. About five hours.'

'Thanks, Longman. Look forward to your call. I really want the info on this pedo fucker.'

'Understand, Kenmare, and we'll do everything we can to help you.'

The call ended.

Harry turned to Trev and Tanya, who was back in the van in the jump-seat. 'Well, team, nothing else to do now. So, I reckon an early lunch at the Emerald Bar.'

'You're the boss,' grinned Trev.

Tanya chuckled. 'Yeah, he wasn't last night, let me tell you. He was one obedient slave.'

'Your wish is always my command, Princess Tanya,' said Harry.

'Oh, spare me,' groaned Trev. 'Let's get to the pub, please.'

– 13 –

The two naked law enforcement captives were huddled together asleep on the concrete floor of a meat room. They didn't stir as the temperature-proof door was yanked open. But they did stir when the bucket of icy water was thrown on them.

A bikie grabbed Commander Billingham by the hair and hauled him upright. 'Boss is back. Time to party again, piggy.' He shoved the Customs officer towards the door where he was grabbed by two more bikies.

He walked back and kicked AC Horley in the guts. 'Get up, arsehole.'

Horley whimpered and struggled to his feet, only to promptly collapse as his shattered knee failed to support him.

The bikie shrugged. 'Have it your way, arsehole.' He grabbed the cop by the ankle and dragged him across the concrete floor as Horley screamed. 'Save the girly shrieking, piggy, you'll be needing it for real shortly.'

Longman and The Ratfucker were standing in the ice-cold torture room, two metal chairs ready for the captives.

'Made the call?' asked Longman.

'Yep. Kenmare and Matson are heading back to their office now,' replied Corsi.

'Bet they were at the bloody pub.'

Corsi chuckled. 'Yep.'

'At least those old-style Ds are human.'

The door opened and the two captives were dragged in.

The Ratfucker picked up a meat cleaver from a large butcher's block on wheels.

'Fuck, boss, I am looking forward to this.'

'You and me, both. But we need to get that sorted first.' He pointed to the police laptops on a camping table near the butcher's block.

'I'll make 'em sing, rest assured. Never failed yet.'

Longman smiled and slapped Corsi's shoulder. 'Oh, I fucking know you will, mate.'

The two cops, amidst whining protests through their gags, were strapped to the chairs by the other bikies.

Longman stepped forward. 'Hello, piggy wankers, how are we today? Have a good sleep, did we?' He punched Billingham in the guts, and then did the same to Horley. 'Hope you're in a talkative mood, my federal piggy.' He gripped Horley's jaw and squeezed until the cop wheezed in pain. Longman removed the cop's gag.

Horley looked at him with the desperate look of a virginal altar boy staring at Father Michael's erection whilst trying to work out how to escape the vestry.

'But we told you where the gear was,' whined Horley.

'Yes, yes you did. And we got the lot. Thank you very much, Assistant Commissioner Fucktard. But see those?'

Corsi picked up one of the computers, tilting it so the police logo was in plain view.

'Your laptops. You're going to tell us how to access your police systems.'

'No! No, I won't!' yelled Horley.

'Ratman, your cue, I believe. And, boys, let's give them another hefty shot of stimulant. They're going to need it.'

One of the bikies grabbed two syringes and injected both of the cops.

The Ratfucker pulled his phone out of his back pocket and tapped the screen. A photo of Hilda Horley and young Toby came up, them getting into the SUV in their Sydney driveway. He put it in front of Horley's face.

'So, fucktard, unless you do exactly what we want, we'll go back to visit your family and little Johnny English there can watch on while we gang-bang your darling wife. Actually, she's quite a good sort, wouldn't mind slipping her a length. And once you've done as you're told, we're going to do a little film of the pair of you confessing to your corrupt deeds. Then you might, and I emphasize "might", get out of here.'

'No ...' wailed Horley.

'Yes, my bacon friend. "Yes" is the answer. Or we're going to find out how much your missus likes it up her arse.' Corsi chuckled. 'And one of our blokes here has no joke got a ten-inch schlong. On the soft, too. On the hard, it looks like a fat fucking salami. That'll make her eyes fucking water, won't it?'

Longman walked over to Billingham, slid the gag off, and held his phone up. 'And here's your missus, Customs piggy, courtesy of Facebook. And what do we have here?' He tapped on an image of a buxom teenage girl in a netball uniform. 'Your daughter would be very sweet meat, Customs piggy. What is she, sixteen, seventeen? You reckon she's still a virgin?'

The Ratfucker cackled again. 'Hell, I love breaking in the virgins.'

Billingham sniffled miserably. 'You must really hate law enforcement. You're barbarians.'

'Maybe, arsehole, maybe. But I don't *hate* you because you're a pig. Dislike, sure, but not *hate* for that reason. To us, you pigs are just an occupational hazard. And I've even met a few along the way who I respect, in a way. No, I bloody *hate* you two because you're bent pigs. It's the fucking hypocrisy I can't stand.'

Corsi had fired up both the laptops on the table. He walked back to Horley.

'Now, as I call out for usernames and passwords, you better play along, otherwise it's party time for your wife.' He slapped Horley across the face. 'Got it?'

Horley nodded, his eyes watering.

Corsi went back to the table, Longman joining him.

Horley spewed out his details and Corsi accessed both machines. One screen showed the AFP logo. The other opened to a screensaver of Ms Horley and young Toby with a backdrop of Tower Bridge in London.

Longman got out his phone and pressed the screen.

A moment later he spoke into the phone, 'You blokes ready? We're into the computer with the police access. Talk us through what you need. The arseholes can hear, we're on speaker, so no names for any of us.'

Back in Sydney, Harry put the phone on the desk in front of him and Trev, on loudspeaker.

'Mate,' said Trev, 'look for an icon for "intelligence" or "crime commission" or something like that.'

Corsi, listening to Longman's phone, played on the screen and clicked on the mousepad. 'Found one. Called "ACC". That's the national crime mob, isn't it?'

'Spot on,' said Trev. 'Now open it.'

'Shit, now it's asking for finger ID.' He looked at Horley.

The cop sniffed. 'My fingerprint is needed. Bring it over.'

Corsi picked it up. 'Which finger?'

'Right index.'

'No! Don't do that, mate!' Trev's voice blasted over the speaker. 'He might have a one-touch disable function. Will wipe the machine in a second.'

'So, what should I do?' asked Corsi.

'You'll need to hold his finger really firmly and make sure it can't touch anything other than the fingerprint ID button.'

The Ratfucker put the computer back down. 'I've got a better bloody idea.'

He picked up a large pair of pliers and walked over to Horley, who was bouncing in his chair trying to break free. He knew what was coming.

'No!' he shrieked, as Corsi bent down behind the chair where Horley's bound wrists were.

'Right index, you said? I'd hate to get it wrong and have to start again.'

'Actually, mate, you'd love to start again, and again, and again,' said Longman.

The Ratfucker grinned. 'Got me there, boss.' He opened the steel jaws and tried to place the wire cutting blades around Horley's finger, but the cop was struggling like an unwilling gimp.

'Hold him,' Longman directed the onlooking bikies.

With Horley pinned and nearly suffocating from a muscly, tattooed arm holding him in a headlock, Corsi slid the pliers around the required digit and jammed the jaws together.

Despite the headlock, Horley screamed like a banshee.

Corsi, with a broad grin of satisfaction, walked back to the computer holding Horley's index finger. Taking care not to get blood drops on the keyboard, he applied the fingertip to the touch key. The screen changed.

'Bingo,' said Longman. 'What next, boys?' he said into the phone.

Trev spent the next little while talking the bikies through the national police intel system, regularly telling them to photograph the screen.

Twenty minutes later, with Longman having sent all the photos to Trev's phone, they were done. The sleuths now had copies of all the intel available to Australian law enforcement on Reggie Wheeler.

Longman picked up his phone and turned off the speaker. He put it back to his ear. 'Okay, mate, you're off speaker at this end. That all for now?'

Harry came back on the line. 'Thanks, Longman, really appreciate this.'

'No worries, buddy, anything to help you find that rock spider. And I mean anything, anytime.'

'Thanks, mate. See you when you get back. When's Natty's funeral?'

'Thursday next week.'

'No worries, we'll be there.'

Longman rang off.

– 14 –

'Okay, piggies, time for confessing on film. They say confession's good for the soul.' Longman paused for effect. 'Never agreed myself, but I'm not the one in the hot seat today. Who's up first?'

Neither of the cops said anything.

Longman turned to The Ratfucker. 'Mate, we're not seeing much enthusiasm here. Might need some of your special TLC.'

Corsi grinned. 'My pleasure.'

He ignited a blowtorch and waved it at the two captives in turn. 'Okay, wankers. Who wants to be barbecued?'

'That's right, piggies,' said Longman. 'Either we get filming, or we're going to smell a lot of fried bacon in here.'

Corsi stepped towards Horley.

'No, no, I'll talk.'

'Good decision.' Corsi turned off the burner and picked up a camcorder mounted on a tripod. He set it down and focused it on Horley's face.

'Ah, shit!' said Longman.

'What?'

'Know what I forgot? Make-up and hair stylist.'

All the bikies roared laughing.

Longman motioned to the others as Corsi returned to the camera controls. 'Grab that one, boys, and stick him next to this one. Side by side.'

A minute later, the two cops faced the video camera, tied to chairs next to each other.

Longman looked at them and shook his head. 'Okay you pair of bent pigs, time to tell the camera here all the corrupt stuff you've done. And take it in turns, I want to hear both of you singing.'

Corsi picked up the dormant blowtorch. 'And remember, bacon boys, any hesitation or any omissions and I'll be providing some flaming encouragement. Understand?' He waved the blowtorch at them.

Both cops nodded sullenly.

Longman pointed at Horley. 'You start, federal piggy.'

Corsi pressed 'Record' and the camera's red light went on.

For the next twenty minutes, Horley and Billingham grudgingly spilled the beans on their corrupt enterprise. It got off to a slow start, but Corsi lighting the blowtorch again injected all the motivation that was required.

When the pair petered out, Corsi looked at Longman who signalled the cut sign with his hand.

Corsi stopped the camera.

'That's plenty, mate.'

Corsi smirked. 'Now for the real fun part, yes?'

'Yes, my bloodthirsty friend.'

Corsi turned to the other bikies slouched against a wall. 'Everything ready next door, boys?'

'Yes, boss.'

'Okay, let's get these two into the branding room.'

The other four bikies moved faster than a politician claiming a pay rise.

'No!' wailed the cops in unison.

'We've done everything you asked,' pleaded Billingham.

'We've got families,' sniffed Horley.

Longman snorted. 'Do I look like the fucking compassionate type?'

'And that was rhetorical,' added The Ratfucker. 'Genghis Khan had more compassion than him.'

'Thanks, mate, I'll take that as a compliment.'

The two blubbing cops were bundled into the adjoining room and held by the bikies.

The room smelled of wood smoke and an extractor fan was humming. There was a raised, half forty-four-gallon drum on its side full of glowing embers with two long metal rods hanging over the end.

Longman picked a rod out of the brazier that was heating the whole concrete room to a comfortably warm level, in contrast to the frigid chamber they had come from.

The glowing head of a branding iron was now visible as Longman swung it out of the brazier. Its head was in the shape of a word.

'Hold his head,' he commanded, pointing at Horley.

One of the bikies, a 190cm man mountain from Tonga, put Horley in an upright headlock, gripping his hair from behind.

'This is so everyone will always know exactly what you are,' said Longman, plunging the red-hot iron onto Horley's forehead.

The sound of the sizzling flesh was almost as loud as Horley's scream.

Longman stood back to admire his handiwork. He frowned. 'CORUPT' now appeared on the cop's head, arising from the steaming flesh.

Longman looked around his assembled troops. 'All right, boys, who made the bastard branding iron?'

A tall, fat bikie with an eye-patch and a scar on his head that made him look lobotomized lifted his chubby hand, albeit half-heartedly.

'Come here, Lurch,' said Longman.

Lurch ambled over to his boss.

Longman pointed at Horley. 'Lurch, how do you spell corrupt?'

'Ah, C O R U P T, I think.'

'It's got two bloody Rs in it, mate! For fuck's sake! Now these wankers will be wearing a spelling mistake forever.'

'Sorry, boss. I left school when I was thirteen. Never much good at spelling. And they didn't teach it in juvie.'

The Ratfucker was cackling. 'Could be worse. Could have started with a K.'

Longman split his sides with laughter. 'I'll pay that.'

'Sorry again, boss,' said Lurch.

'No worries, Lurch. Still a damned good job on the metalwork, though. You can do the other pig, if you'd like?'

Lurch grinned, not expecting a reward. 'Gee, thanks, boss.'

He took the branding iron and stuck it back in the brazier for a couple of minutes, whilst Billingham pleaded for mercy. At least until the Tongan bikie punched him.

Longman looked at the Tongan. 'Okay, Krakatoa, hold that one firm.'

The huge Islander gripped Billingham in a neck-lock, holding his head steady.

Lurch pulled the iron out of the brazier.

Billingham's attempt at a scream was stifled into a wheezing whimper by the muscle-heavy brown forearm across his throat.

Krakatoa looked at Lurch moving in. 'Hey, Lurch?'

'Yeah?'

'Don't you fucking miss, bro, 'cos if that thing gets me, I'll rip your fucking head off, bro, and then shit down your throat.'

'No worries, Krakka, it's only me spelling that's shit, not me aim.'

Lurch closed the remaining metres and carefully lined up the branding iron in front of the Customs Commander's face.

'Hold tight, Krakka. Now take this, pig.'

The glowing metal hit Billingham's forehead with a sickening sizzle. The cop bucked and tried to scream, but the Tongan's grip stymied any physical action.

Lurch stood back and looked at Longman for approval.

'Good work, Lurch.'

'Thanks, boss.'

Longman looked at the cops. 'Okay, bacon boys, that's the first procedure done and dusted. Let everyone in the world know that you're corrupt wankers. Now, the sun's coming up soon, so time to do two more procedures and then say goodbye and thanks for your company.'

'Which procedure next?' asked Corsi.

'What do those Muslim wankers do to thieves, mate?'

Corsi grinned. 'Off with a hand.' He picked up a machete. 'Krakka, hold him and the hand at the block. Lurch, push it over.'

Lurch wheeled over a butcher's block to Horley, who tried desperately to struggle against the Tongan, but it was like watching a marmoset resist a gorilla.

Lurch pulled another shaft from the brazier, this one with a red-hot, small round plate on its end.

Corsi swung the machete down, taking Horley's right hand clean off at the wrist.

Lurch lunged in with his glowing rod, the hot metal plate searing the exposed wrist sealed, the sizzling again competing with the screaming.

Billingham struggled even harder as his arm was put onto the block.

Corsi sneered at him and there was a thwomp as another right hand was cleaved from its owner. Then more sizzling flesh.

'Right,' announced Longman, 'good work, men. Now for the third and final procedure. Let's make sure they can never, ever identify any of us in a line-up.'

Corsi grinned. 'Sweet, I've been waiting for this bit. What do the French say? The *pièce de résistance?*'

'A man of many talents, Ratman.'

Corsi produced a small satchel from a sports bag on the ground next to the table. He opened the satchel on the butcher's block, avoiding the blood. It held four large glass syringes with needles attached. They were full of a clear liquid.

'Yep,' said Longman, 'you two piggies won't ever see another face, let alone identify ours. Sulphuric acid straight into your eyeballs. And then darkness, irreversible and forever.'

'Perfect match for your souls of darkness, fuckers,' added Corsi. 'Krakka? Him again, please.' He pointed at Horley.

'No! Please! For the love of god, no!' cried the cop.

The Ratfucker snorted. 'There ain't no god in here, arsehole. Plus, you should really have thought about consequences before all your greed and corruption.'

'And,' said Longman, 'to reinforce our point, gentlemen, while you won't ever be able to pick us out of a line-up, if there is ever any sniff of us getting caught, your lovely wives will be getting gang-banged by the whole clubhouse.'

The Ratfucker plunged one needle into Horley's left eye and slowly depressed the plunger. He did the same for the right eye.

Horley was dragged away by Lurch and another bikie.

Krakka grabbed Billingham, cutting off his screaming.

Corsi emptied the remaining two syringes.

Longman nodded approvingly. 'Good work, everyone. Now let's go. Get them in the van.'

***

Senior Constable Tommy Motu and Constable Joe DiLallo of the Dubbo Highway Patrol were in the last hour of their night shift, closing in on their seven-a.m. finish. It'd been a quiet night, no accidents, only two DUIs, and a handful of speeding tickets. The pair of traffic cops were cruising back towards town on the Mitchell Highway from Wellington, the sun breaking over the horizon, and contemplating a large breakfast at McDonald's before heading back to the station to complete paperwork and knock off.

Joe had flicked on the indicator to turn off the highway into the Macca's car park when Tommy said, 'Hang on, Joey. Keep going straight. There's something up at the roundabout.'

'Roger that.'

Joe cancelled the turn and eased the V8 Commodore onwards to the roundabout.

'What the fuck?' said Tommy.

Joe stopped the cop car against the kerb and put the red and blue lights on.

The two patrolmen sat in stunned silence looking at the spectacle before them: two naked and visibly injured men chained to a direction sign a metre in from the edge of the roundabout.

Without saying a word, Tommy got out of the car. He took out his phone and took a photograph.

He leant back into the car. 'Want you to video this as I move in.'

'Roger.' Joe hit the switch for the dashcam. He opened his door and stood outside the car as Tommy walked over to the bizarre scene.

'Jesus fucking Christ,' was all Tommy could utter as he stepped towards the two men, both mewling like beaten kittens.

Apart from the chains, the only thing they were wearing were garlands of yellow carnations around their necks.

Joe walked over. 'Fuck me. What the hell is this?'

Tommy, wide-eyed, shook his head. 'Beats me.' He took the radio from his belt, pressed transmit, and called for two ambulances and back up.

'Well, Tommy,' said Joe, 'I sure don't feel like Macca's anymore.'

'You and me both, bro.'

– 15 –

The service chapel of the crematorium looked like an AGM of the Satan's Hogs gang.

Archie Longman and Rocco Corsi stood in front of eight of their most senior men. All ten were in full leather and gang colours. A large cloth with the colours was draped over the coffin on its bier. Greta was sitting next to Corsi, dressed in a black blouse and short black skirt, with black stockings. As skimpy as her outfit was, it was the most respectable she had ever looked. Two other bikie molls were with the gang, also in black, and also skimpy.

As Longman looked at his watch, the main entrance door opened. Longman turned to watch Tanya step in, dressed in black although less provocatively than Greta. She was followed by Harry and Trev, and an enormous black man.

The Ratfucker had turned as well. 'Who the fuck?'

The sleuths walked to the front and all shook hands. Greta and Tanya hugged.

Zanza, in a magnificent charcoal Hugo Boss suit, stood next to Harry.

Corsi, not accustomed to having to look upwards to any man, held out his hand. 'I'm guessing you're with these blokes, who are our friends. So, pleased to meet you, mate.'

They shook hands.

Longman, not as tall as The Ratfucker, had to crane his neck even more. 'Bugger me, you're huge, mate.' He held out his hand.

Zanza grinned. 'I'm working with Harry now.' His voice was African-accented and slightly laboured as he formed his words.

'Meet Zanza, gentlemen. Our new team member. Adds a new dimension to our professional capabilities, don't you think?' Harry grinned.

Before Longman or Corsi could reply, the funeral celebrant came in from the door behind the bier.

'Good afternoon, everyone,' she said.

The motley crew fell silent.

An hour later, the same crowd gathered in a private function room upstairs at the Cambridge Tavern in Stanmore. Two topless barmaids were serving drinks.

Harry and his crew arrived and walked over to the bar.

Glasses in hand, they chinked.

'Zanza, mate, it's fantastic to hear your voice. You used to it yet?' asked Harry.

'Getting there, Harry. And thank you with all my heart to you guys for arranging it all with the surgery in America.' His enunciation was clearly a work in progress.

Longman and The Ratfucker arrived next to them.

'So, Longman,' said Trev, 'our new bloke, Zanza, couldn't speak before. He had his tongue cut out in the Congo.'

'Fuck me,' said Longman. 'But now?'

'Yes,' said Harry. 'Remember that hundred K we got from those jihadist mongrel bastards?'

'Oh, yeah. Bet that paid for a lot of booze and women.' Corsi and Longman laughed.

'No, actually, although ordinarily it would.'

'Kenmare, please do not tell us you're reformed.' Longman winked at Tanya.

It was Harry's and Trev's turn to laugh.

'No way, Longman.' Harry raised his glass to Zanza. 'No, that cash paid for an operation in America and many weeks of intensive speech therapy.' He put his hand onto Zanza's shoulder. 'Best hundred grand we ever spent.'

Zanza smiled. 'Thank you.' He turned to the two bikies. 'And please excuse my way of talking. The operation was a complete success and the speech therapy has been great, but I still need more practice.'

'No excusing needed, mate. You sound all right to me, and good on you,' said Longman.

Harry looked at Longman. 'Mate, so sorry about Natty. And sorry it was our plan that ended up like this. We never saw anything like this happening.'

'Kenmare, the plan was damned fine. It's the bent pigs that are the problem.'

'Yeah, in so many ways.'

'In this case, *were* the problem,' added Corsi, grinning.

'Drink to that, guys,' said Longman raising his beer.

Everyone chinked.

Longman looked at Harry. 'I didn't used to like you, Kenmare. You banged me up. But, mate, I always bloody respected you.'

'How so?'

'You were a hard cunt in that interview room, but that was what we expected from the demons in those days. Biggest thing, you were honest. All that cash you recovered from our last robbery, it all turned up at the trial. Every single damned dollar of close to six hundred grand.'

'Yeah, old school detective ethics in my book, Longman. Okay to give a bloke a tickle, especially when he deserves it. And you fucking did, by the way. But not okay to steal.'

'A distinction that doesn't exist in this vomit-inducing woke age,' said Trev.

Tanya spoke. 'One thing I've learned working with these guys is that not all cops stick together as the same group.'

'No, that façade is used, especially in the media, but it's not solid, that's for sure,' said Harry.

'And so, is that how you two are okay with shooting corrupt cops?' asked Tanya.

'Exactly,' said Trev.

'At least when put in a situation,' added Harry. 'Now, enough philosophy. Let's drink to celebrate Natty's all-too-short life.'

'More beers!' shouted The Ratfucker.

Breasts bounced behind the bar as the two girls filled beer glasses and jugs.

Three hours later, and half an hour after the arrival of four hookers, Harry swallowed the whiskey in his hand. He looked at one hooker who was eating the pussy of a bikie moll laid back on a pool table, whilst a male bikie was hammering her from behind, two more bikies cheering as they waited their turn. Another hooker was being spit-roasted on a leatherette couch. The other two were both on their knees giving head.

Harry grinned at Trev. 'Gotta love debauchery, fuck the woke brigade. But time for us to go, brother.'

'Roger that.'

Harry waved at Longman and Corsi.

'You guys off?' called Longman across the depraved room.

'Yeah, we'll let you party. Talk soon.'

'Okay, but more girls are on the way.'

'All good. Enjoy.'

'And I'll release the video tomorrow,' yelled Trev.

The sleuths left the debauchery, passing another quartet of hookers coming up the stairs.

Outside the pub, the four sleuths stood on Parramatta Road waiting for taxis.

Trev had announced he needed to head for his sort of bar as the upstairs action, whilst not of his exact variety, had nonetheless got him horny.

Zanza was heading for Club Mammary to help Mama Jocasta with a couple of last-minute bookings.

Tanya said she was coming with Harry. 'I've got a very belated birthday present for you, Mister PI.'

Trev sniggered. 'I bet you bloody have.'

Tanya poked him in the ribs. 'This present is actually wrapped.'

'Yeah, you in your underwear.'

'Ha ha, funny man. There will, however, be a side serve of pussy.'

The first cab arrived.

'You go first, Zanza,' said Harry, 'since you've got work to do. Say "hi" to Mama for us.'

'Will do. At your office tomorrow?'

'Yep. Let's make it midday. Sleep in. Then we start a new chapter entirely.'

Trev smiled. 'The hunt is back on for Wheeler. Can't wait.'

Harry let Tanya step into his apartment in front of him, as usual.

'Now, Harry, your present.' She picked up a large, rectangular wrapped item sitting next to the hall stand.

'How did that get here?'

'I dropped it in when you were in the office this morning.' She handed it to him. 'Happy birthday, my gorgeous Harry.' She kissed him with plenty of tongue, leaning over the top of the package.

Harry ripped the paper off his gift and held a framed sepia-toned photographic print.

He whistled. 'Far out, where did you get this? *Centurion and Slave* by Bob Carlos Clarke. One of my all-time favourites.'

'Sorry it took so long, I had to order it from Europe and have it printed specially. But I figured it would be worth the wait for you.'

Harry gazed at the image of the two girls, one partially clad in Roman armour, breasts exposed, the other on her knees, clutching the centurion's naked thigh.

'Thank you, so much, Divine One. Best pressie I've ever had. Apart from you, of course.'

'My pleasure. Now, Harry, see the centurion? That is me.' She put her fingertip on the standing girl in armour. Her finger moved to the girl on her knees. 'And you, Harry, are going to be my slave. Get in there, now!'

She pointed dramatically at the bedroom doorway.

'Yes, ma'am,' said Harry, mock running for his room.

Tanya ran after him.

A minute later, no more, Tanya held the back of Harry's head as she forced his face into her pussy.

'Now eat me, slave. And pretend I said that in Latin.'

Harry's muffled voice said something that could well have been Swahili for all Tanya knew.

Then his tongue massaged her clitoris. And she closed her eyes and rode his face.

* * *

PART 3

HARRY'S STING

This was really a dish. Seen close up she was almost paralyzing.

- Raymond Chandler

She was a dull person, but a sensational invitation to make babies. Men looked at her and wanted to fill her up with babies right away.

- Kurt Vonnegut

– 1 –

Harry could still smell Tanya on his face as he walked from his apartment to his office. He inhaled deeply through his nose and smirked. Life is great, he thought. Wouldn't be dead for quids. And now he could sniff the hunt for Wheeler getting back on track.

As he walked through the Jones Street Park and past the TAFE college, he admired the hibiscus flowers providing a colourful splash in the urban landscape. He walked onto the downward slope of Mary Ann Street. Winter was kicking off and it was a crisp, cool morning.

Coming up the hill on the pavement was a young woman, whose pace was almost as brisk as the morning air. She was petite with a huge bust, covered in a thin beige jumper. She was closing the gap rapidly, as Harry slowed his pace to admire her.

There was no mistaking her lack of bra under the jumper and the high beam was resplendent. In fact, high beam was an inadequate description, thought Harry, there had to be fog lamps attached.

Harry smiled as his eyes flicked back up to a height of propriety. She still caught him. He said, 'Morning.'

She smirked in return and met his gaze for a second. Then she was past him on her journey, leaving him to smell her floral perfume on top of Tanya's sex.

Definitely would not be dead for quids, he thought.

He stopped at the French café on the corner of the block where his office was and ordered coffees and croissants for him and Trev.

He smiled at a tall blonde in her twenties standing waiting for her order.

She returned the look.

Nothing ventured, thought Harry. 'Great coffee here,' he said.

'My first time.'

'Ooh, a Scandinavian accent, I think.'

She grinned broadly. 'I'm from Finland.'

'Holiday?'

'No, study.'

'I've been to Helsinki once, on a tour. When I was much younger.'

'That's where I'm from. Did you like it?'

'Loved it, at least what I can remember. Met some locals on my first evening and ended up drunk for the rest of the three days.'

She laughed. One of those easy, genuine ones. 'Finnish people are very friendly.'

Damn, I hope you are, thought Harry. 'So are some Australians. I'm Harry.'

He held out his hand and she shook it.

'Anna.'

'Lovely to meet you, Anna from Helsinki. I've read that eighty-five percent of Finns are blonde, the blondest race on Earth.'

She looked at him, pouted noticeably and winked. 'Harry, I'm one hundred percent blonde.'

Harry felt movement in his loins.

'So, what are you studying?'

'My Masters at Sydney Uni. In Gender Studies.'

'I see.' Harry definitely did not see. This was confusing. Female Gender Studies students did not look like Anna, and they sure as hell didn't get flirty with men like Harry: too busy keeping their crew cuts attractive to the next bit of carpet they could munch on and maintaining their confected outrage at whatever cause held the day.

Anna's smile returned, as if it were her default expression. 'But I'm not one of *those* women, the ones who hate men. And there are a lot of them in the class, believe me.' She rolled her crystalline blue eyes.

Harry recovered his composure instantaneously, the legacy of years of experience in the witness box as a detective. 'Well, Anna, I'm a postmodern metrosexual who believes a woman's pleasure is the paragon of lovemaking.'

Her laugh was louder this time. 'How does that line usually work for you?'

'Mixed results, but my tongue does always make that pleasure the number one priority.'

'Wow, you don't waste time. That added line is far better, by the way.'

'Life's short, play hard. That's what I reckon. Time's too precious to waste.'

Her coffee arrived.

'Well, lovely to meet you, Harry.' She didn't move immediately, taking a sip of coffee.

So, Harry pulled out his wallet and handed her a business card. 'I'm probably a lot older than your usual dates, but just in case.'

She examined the card, before looking back at his face. 'Private investigator? Interesting.'

'It has its moments, detective work.'

'So, you could help me find something?'

'Of course. Are you missing something?'

'Multiple orgasms.' Her face could have been over a poker table.

Harry swallowed. This girl was right up his alley, he thought, and he fancied being up hers.

'Actually, that's a speciality of mine.'

She stepped into his space. 'I'll call you,' she whispered in his ear. 'I've never been out with a detective.'

'I'll be at your service, Anna.'

Harry inhaled her scent deeply. It was an exotic floral fragrance, and it was magnificent.

'God, you smell as wonderful as you look. What is that?'

'Chanel Beige. Frangipani flowers. See you, Mister Detective.'

And she was gone out onto George Street.

Well, bugger me, thought Harry.

***

Harry walked into his office with the two coffees and pastries.

'Oh look, the afternoon shift's arrived!' Trev greeted him.

'Funny man. It's only ten.'

'And he's brought afternoon tea with him. Good man, Harry.'

Harry handed him a coffee and one of the brown bags with a chocolate croissant inside. 'Don't choke on it, my comedian partner!' Harry grinned.

'Tanya not coming in?'

Harry chuckled. 'Too much fun last night.'

'Ooh, you brute. Have you worn her out?'

'This old dog's still got some life in him. No, she's got some stuff she wants to sort out with Tessa. She's keen to keep a finger in the rag trade.'

'Cool. So, we have a morning, or what's left of it, to do planning, Mister Kenmare.'

'That we have, Mister Matson. Let's get into it.' Harry sat at his desk and lit a smoke. 'So, what intel have we got on Wheeler courtesy of the AFP computer hack?'

'Well, his entire crim history, although no surprises there. Several convictions. Only one prison stretch years back. And his family address down in Nowra.'

'Ah, the glorious Penrith-by-the-sea.'

Trev laughed. 'Never been there, yet.'

'Might be about to change. What else?'

'A few associates, but same names we got from his notebook in Laos. Still, we've now got addresses.'

'But Abrahams and Hayes aren't listed as associates, I bet.'

'Nope. We need to change that.'

'Trev, I feel a bloody big sting coming on.'

'Also, from his notebook we know he banks with CommBank.'

'Hell, it'd be great to have an insider to monitor his account. That'd tell us exactly the area he's hiding out in, since he'd be using an ATM at some stage.'

'And thanks to the AFP intel, we know he's now back in the country. He'll be trying to renew his visa for Laos, I reckon. He'll be on a work visa for the orphanage and he'll need to renew it from outside the country.'

'For sure. So, we need to move quickly before he fucks off back there. We're sure as hell not going back anytime soon.'

'Not wrong, mate. Now, how do we get a bank insider? Know anyone?'

'No, mate. I avoid banks and bankers like the plague.'

The lock turned in the door and in walked Tanya, holding a coffee.

'Hi, my PI guys.'

'Hi babe, you're earlier than I expected.'

'Yep. Tessa had to go to an unplanned meeting.'

'And how is the lovely English rose?' Harry grinned.

'Pining for your cock, Mister PI. Like every woman in Sydney.' She rolled her eyes at Trev.

Trev chortled. 'Keep rubbing his ego, Tan, 'cos that's all we need: Harry Kenmare thinking even more of what a ladies' man he is.'

'Bugger off, the pair of you. My return invitations have always outnumbered complaints.'

'He does have a point,' said Tanya. 'Speaking from a randy girl's perspective.'

'Back to work, gang, we've a rock spider to catch,' said Harry.

'What leads have we got?'

'Well, Tan,' said Trev, 'we know his likely haunts given his family connections. I've looked at two or three, but his grandmother's place is the most likely hiding hole, given she probably wouldn't say anything to anyone if Wheeler told her to keep it quiet.'

'No parents or siblings?'

'None relevant, babe. AFP records showed no brothers or sisters, and the mother suicided after the father went inside for, guess what?'

Tanya groaned. 'Molesting.'

'Bang on,' said Trev. 'Ran a school in the Philippines. Got done for rape and child porn. He's halfway through a twenty-five-year stretch in prison in Manila.'

'So, where's granny live?'

'In Nowra.'

'Are we going to do surveillance?'

'Not feasible, babe. We might get lucky, if he is at granny's, but he could be staying with another contact, or some family member we don't know about, so we'd be wasting our time. And that's what we don't have much of.

We're sure he's only back for a couple of weeks to renew his visa for Laos. Then he'll be off again to ruin more young lives in South-East Asia.'

'And we don't want to meet the Laos Police Force again, do we, Tan?'

'Ugh! I can still smell that cunt's breath. Garlic, ginger, and malicious masculinity.'

'All I can smell is electrical burning,' said Harry.

They all laughed.

'So, Tan,' said Trev, 'we're looking for ways to get his bank account info, since he'll have to be using it to survive here. We know which bank from his notebook. Got the account number and the branch. But we really need live-time tracking of his transactions.'

'Don't you guys between you have any police mates who could help?'

'Too risky, even if they would, and that's far from certain,' said Harry. 'Also, it'd establish a link to us when we catch and kill him.'

'And likewise, we don't know which phone company his mobile is with, so we're stuck on that, too.'

'What we really need,' said Harry, 'is an insider in CommBank.'

'And one who can be persuaded to help out.'

'Social media,' said Tanya.

'So, what are you thinking, Tan?' said Harry.

'Well, there are all these groups on Facebook, for instance. Different interests, professional groups, et cetera. We could go trawling for banking people. It's seriously amazing what people put out there.'

'Yeah, true. Like your thinking, Tan,' said Trev.

'Mmm, too techie for me,' said Harry. 'I'll drink and supervise.'

Tanya sat at her desk and signed into the iMac. 'Gather round, boys.' She started surfing Facebook. 'See, here's a group, "Bank Johnnies Social". And another, "Finance Professionals Forum".' She kept trawling. 'Ooh, I like this one, "Banking Bitches Being Bad".'

'Nice alliteration,' said Harry.

'I've always considered bankers as boring,' said Trev. 'Certainly never shagged one.'

'Not all, mate. Years ago, as a young copper, I met one at a party. She was CommBank, actually. Her place was all satin sheets, leather straps, and orgasmic punishment. Then she got her flatmate, also a CommBank girl, to join in. I could hardly bloody walk the next morning. Makes me nostalgic every time I go past a CommBank branch. Damn, she was feral, mate.'

'Okay, you big stud, I accept they are not all boring then. I don't suppose you still know her?'

Harry chortled. 'Get real, Trev. Strictly a one-night shag fest, that one. You'd understand, I'm sure.'

Trev grinned and nodded.

Tanya was still trawling Facebook. 'So, boys, when we've quite finished reminiscing about previous conquests, this group is a private one for female bankers to talk sex and fantasies.'

'Shit, who would've thought,' said Harry. 'The world we live in.'

Trev chuckled. 'Don't worry my Jurassic friend, the next mass extinction event is just around the corner. You'll be out of your pain then.'

'Funny man. My idea of feeling the earth move does not involve a meteor.'

'You still operating those fake profiles, Tan?'

'Of course, Trev. Which one do you reckon I should use for this?' She clicked on the keyboard and up came Karla Sayers from Melbourne, then Léa Frichot from Bondi, and finally Zoe Heath from Brisbane. 'I need to update one of them to be working for a bank and then apply to join the group.'

'Don't pick one of the Aussie girls,' said Harry. 'Too likely one of them could come unstuck with some hard research.'

'Yep, good thinking, mate. Tan, go for BNP Paribas and the French girl's identity. And your cover story is you've been seconded to Sydney on an internal project you can't discuss.'

Tanya opened Léa Frichot's profile and updated it with working at BNP Paribas in Sydney. She even grabbed the company logo and added it. Then she applied to join the Banking Bitches private group.

'And they have a joining question subject to administrator approval: detail an erotic fantasy I have.'

'That might take a while,' said Harry, grinning at her.

She stuck her tongue out at him. 'Okay, here goes.' She was typing and verbalizing it. 'I want a woman going down on me at the same time as a big cock is in my arse.'

Trev nodded approvingly. 'Yep, reckon that'll get you membership. I'll get the drinks whilst we wait.'

– 2 –

Fifteen minutes later, Tanya clicked on her Léa account and smiled. 'Well, that didn't take long. I'm now a member.'

'Good work, Tan. Now let's start looking for members who work for CommBank and are looking for action.'

The three sleuths crowded around Tanya's iMac screen as she clicked on various female profiles in the group.

'Bugger me,' said Harry, 'there is some serious horniness going on in there. I can smell the juices from here. Who knew?'

'Not wrong, brother. Fantasies I'm seeing so far include three gang-bangs, two for fisting, one anal, three for felching, and that one wants to bathe in a bathtub of jism,' said Trev. 'That last one sounds like a hot scene from a John Rechy novel, only she's clearly not gay.'

'But is it all just idle talk, mate?'

'Some will be,' said Tanya. 'But I reckon a lot of these women would go through with it if a discreet, safe chance arose.'

Harry pointed at the latest profile on screen, a thirty-something redhead who desired a threesome and to felch the other girl. 'Babe, we could do that one, you and me, what do you reckon? I'll have anal with you and then we can both watch as she felches you.'

Tanya grinned. 'You know, I'd go for that. She's sexy.'

She kept scrolling and clicking. 'Hey, look at this one with CommBank. Youngish, cute, and says she has a lifelong fantasy to be shafted by an enormous black cock. And while her husband is away on business.'

Harry looked at Trev. 'You thinking what I'm thinking?'

'On it.' Trev picked up his phone.

Tanya raised her head and her eyebrows.

'Zanza, of course,' said Harry. 'And if she's married, it's the ideal scenario because she will want complete discretion.'

Tanya laughed. 'Shit, she'd never in her wildest dreams be able to imagine a cock that big.

'Zanza? Mate, quick question.' Trev explained the scenario in brief terms. 'So, will you take one for the team?'

On the other end of the phone that Trev switched to loudspeaker, Zanza gave one of his mellifluous chuckles. 'Hey, Trev, I get to have sex with a lovely lady, and I'm taking your word for the lovely bit, and you call that work?'

'Big fella, the work part is the persuasion to get her to access the info we need. The rest is a perk of the job.'

'I'm in,' boomed the big African's voice.

'Cool, we'll be back in touch shortly. And mate, she'll probably want to see a dick pic before she agrees, so get that big boy primed and on film in preparation.'

'You can use a wide-angle lens,' Harry called out.

Zanza laughed and rang off.

'Mister PI, more like a fish-eye lens needed there, I've seen that big boy.'

It was Harry's turn to raise his eyebrows.

She smiled with a tinge of sadness tarnishing her beautiful face. 'Sasha. She kept a picture of Zanza on her phone, and one of his beast. And it's huge, seriously.'

'I smell a cunning plan,' said Trev. 'Time to make contact, Tan, or should I say Léa.'

Tanya got busy with a direct message.

> Bonjour, Lorraine. I'm new to the group. Just saw your fantasy on your profile. If you're keen on living it, I have an African friend here in Sydney. He's HUGE, especially where it matters. And he's a lovely, gentle man. Let me know if you want an intro. And you look hot. I swing both ways, so if you ever want some girl action, please think of me.

Harry whistled.

'As you taught me, Mister PI, go hard or go home.'

'If she is serious about the fantasy, I reckon this will get a bite,' said Trev.

'So, now we wait,' said Tanya. 'Although I bet most of these women check their Facebook on their phones while they're at work.'

Harry lit another smoke and sat back at his desk. 'So, once we have confirmed Wheeler is active here with his bank account, we need to lure him somehow. We could hang around his general area, but it'd be too hit and miss, unless we have an exact address.'

'Yep, I agree,' said Trev. 'Perfect option would be to arrange a meet between Wheeler and Abrahams.'

'But how? We can only confront one half of the pair with a bogus message, not both.'

'Indeed.' Trev grinned.

'Uh oh. I smell a nasty plan coming,' said Tanya.

'You bet, Tan. We email Abrahams from a Wheeler lookalike email account and ask to meet urgently. Then we grab Abrahams. After much nastiness, in the true style of

Kenmare and Associates, he contacts Wheeler for us and sets up a meet. Then we grab our target.'

'Sounds good in theory, brother, but emailing Abrahams? Whilst we know his office email at the Commonwealth DPP, Wheeler wouldn't be likely to use that one.'

'Correct. But I already have a personal email address.' Trev's grin was even wider.

'How?' asked Tanya.

'He goes to a gym in Darlinghurst where I sometimes go. Found that when I did a bit of casual surveillance of him and Hayes after we got back from Laos. I know the gym manager, one of my gay casuals. I was able to look at the membership list.'

'Nice work, mate. But we need to know Wheeler's rough whereabouts ASAP, so we can be in a position to use Abrahams in the right area and under our control.'

'Let's hope Zanza can work fast.'

'I'll message him to come in pronto.' Harry picked up his phone.

'And I'll set up a bogus email account for him in case that's how the wanton bank wench wants to be contacted. If not, we'll use one of the burner phones.'

'Hey, guys, luscious Lorraine is keen. She's just messaged. And she wants an introduction.'

'Babe, you go back and ask if she'll give you an email address or mobile number. Or would she prefer to be given your African friend's details? What's his cover name, Trev?'

'Alphonse. Common name for the Congo.'

'That sounds exotic enough,' said Tanya. She started typing.

Ah, Lorraine. Alphonse will make your fantasy come true, believe me. Do you want to give me a contact for you, or would you rather I gave you his email, if you'd prefer to initiate the contact. I can speak to him today.

Hey Léa. I'm free tonight as my husband went away for work yesterday. Great timing, eh? Otherwise it'll be a fortnight before another opportunity. I don't want to wait. 0485 993 919. And thank you for your offer. I've only ever been with men. But if I want to experiment, I'll be sure to drop you a line. You're beautiful. X

Okay, I understand. I'll give your number to big Alphonse. And I mean BIG! Enjoy your fantasy, Lorraine. Give me some juicy details later. And do message me if you want to try it differently. You're so hot, I'd love to pleasure you for hours. Léa X

'You're laying it on thick there, Tan.'

'Trev, I'm making the lady feel great about herself, so she feels wanted, really wanted. Her juices will be flowing already, trust me. Reduces the chance of her getting cold feet.'

'And, mate, ditch the email set up. We'll give the big fella a burner for the job.'

'Roger that.'

***

The door opened and Zanza stepped in. He grinned at the trio sitting there.

'Hey, guys.'

'Mate, welcome to your first field assignment officially as one of our team,' said Harry.

'Harry, I can't believe you're going to pay me to have sex with a hot woman.'

'That's how Harry met me.' Tanya blew Harry a kiss.

Harry laughed. 'Zanza, it's the information bit you're getting paid for. But I wouldn't say no to this mission myself. Except I'm not black.'

'Or huge,' added Tanya.

'Bugger off.'

Everyone cackled.

'Here's your lady, Zanza.' Tanya pointed to her screen.

Zanza leant in and looked at Lorraine's profile. 'Yes, I will enjoy her.'

'Well, she's gagging for it, Alphonse,' said Trev.

'Alphonse?'

'That's your name for this. You never use your real one.' Trev handed him a mobile. 'And this is a burner phone, just for this assignment. I've already put her details into the contacts. So, send your photos to this burner phone and then contact lusty Lorraine. Easy. Here's the burner number.'

'Cool.' Zanza pulled out his own phone and tapped on the screen.

The burner phone buzzed.

Trev gawked at the burner's screen. 'Fucking hell, mate, you are well hung, aren't you. Don't suppose you like guys as well?'

Zanza chuckled. 'Sorry, Trev, only the ladies for me.'

'More's the pity, mate. Still luscious Lorraine is going to be putty in your hands. Mind you, I'm not sure she knew exactly what was coming her way when she put this fantasy out there. Time to message her.'

Zanza took the burner and typed on it.

> Bonjour Lorraine! Alphonse here. Would love to meet you. Want to see my picture first? X

The reply was immediate.

> Hi Alphonse! Thank you so much for contacting me, I'm so excited. Would love to see a photo of you. And I mean ALL of you! LOL XXX

Zanza tapped again, attaching his portrait picture and the dick pic.

> Lorraine my lovely, here you go then.

The other sleuths were watching the exchange on an iPad Trev had linked to the burner phone.

Tanya gasped. 'Wow, Zanza! No wonder Sasha couldn't stop talking about your package.'

> OMFG! Alphonse. OMFFFG! I'm dripping wet already. Can you be free tonight for me? Please, please, please!!! XXXXXXX

> Lovely Lorraine, your desire is my command. Let me know when and where. I'm free all evening. And I am going to make you howl with pleasure. X

> Thank you, Alphonse! XXX I'll book a room and go there after work. I'll be there by six. I'm in the

city so hotel will be around here. Will send details.
Oh god, I can't wait! XXXXXXX

See you soon, my lovely. Stay wet! X

'Superb work, mate, you're a bloody natural.' Harry patted Zanza's shoulder. 'Okay. So, she's a bank manager with CommBank. I'll put money on her being able to access the bank systems from her laptop, which I'm equally sure she'll bring with her since she's coming straight from work.'

'Coming won't begin to describe what she'll be doing, Mister PI.'

There was laughter around the room.

'They all have their work stuff after hours these days,' added Harry.

Trev snorted. 'Yeah, the charade of work-life balance and all that managerial shit-talk.'

Harry resumed. 'All we need from her, Zanza, is the account activity and locations for this paedophile Wheeler. Here's his details and account number.'

'So, what's my reason and backstory?'

'All sorted,' said Trev. 'Here's your business card.'

Trev handed Zanza a small bundle of half a dozen cards, plain white with neat black font.

Zanza studied the top one. 'Alphonse Leclerc – Private Investigator.'

'And the phone number is the burner.'

'Your backstory, then,' said Harry. 'Version one is you're trying to track down Wheeler as he skipped on his wife and kids after beating her senseless and putting her in hospital. Now she's got no way to support the three young kids. You're laying on a big sob story to tug at any decent woman's conscience. Get the idea?'

'Yes. Can I improvise if I need to?'

'Of course, mate. That's why we've kept it quite general. You just need her feeling sorry for another woman who's been a victim of violence from an arsehole man. Your need for his bank details is to see what means he has to pay child support and also where he might be hanging around. That's all we need.'

'And version two?'

'Yep, another good option for working on a woman's conscience. You say Wheeler is a paedophile, which he is, and some victims are wanting to sue for compensation and so, again, you need his financial details and whereabouts.'

'Any preference on which version I use?'

'No, mate. Sound her out a bit first, try to get a feel for her soft spots. Then you decide which one to go with. And in the general chat first, tell her most of your PI work is tracking down cheating or abusive husbands, and paedophiles. See if she has any strong reaction to guide you.'

'And whether you get the info before or after the sex is entirely up to you,' said Trev. 'Play it by ear.'

'Probably before, Zanza,' said Tanya. 'Because after that big beast has done its work, luscious Lorraine probably won't be able to walk or talk!'

They all laughed again.

– 3 –

Zanza smiled at the faces who turned to look at him as he strode into the lobby of the Saturn Hotel in Railway Square. He was used to turning heads: black African men were not that common in Sydney, and his sheer size would even stick out in a Harlem Globetrotters team meeting. He knew some of the people looking were simply stunned by his physique. And he accepted a few had an issue with his race. But he always smiled. The simply stunned ones invariably returned the look. The racist ones were lost for a reaction, as his smiling offended every aspect of their stereotype. And as he smiled, he always had the same thought: fuck you. But he also knew hatred of the 'other' didn't only come from white people. He'd learnt that the brutally hard way as a child soldier in the Congo. There was no shortage of lethal hatred of the 'other' back there in that murderous civil war, and everyone had been black.

As he headed for the lifts, a male concierge slithered over to him.

'Excuse me, sir. Are you a guest at the hotel?'

Zanza stopped and deliberately stepped close to the man in the burgundy uniform. He looked at his name badge.

'No, Hector, I'm not. I'm visiting a friend. Is that quite all right with you?'

Hector took a couple of steps back and was blocked by the reception counter.

'The hotel takes security very seriously, sir. Which room is your friend in?'

Zanza glanced around and made sure plenty of eyes were turned in their direction. Something of a hush had fallen over the lobby.

Zanza raised his deep voice for effect. 'First, my friend's room number and therefore her identity are none of your business. Second, is this a black thing? Would you be confronting a white man with the same questions?'

Now there was complete and utter silence. And all eyes were turned on the pair.

Zanza smiled.

Hector swallowed hard. Before he could muster any reply, a large Chinese man in a slate-grey suit came rushing out of the door behind the counter and stepped over to the stand-off.

'My office, please, Hector. Now.'

'Yes, Mister Zhao.' Hector scuttled away through the door.

'I'm Quang Zhao, sir, the hotel manager.' He held out his hand.

Zanza shook it.

'On behalf of the Saturn Hotel, I apologize unreservedly for the unacceptable behaviour of our staff member. I will deal with him, rest assured.'

'Thank you for the apology, Quang. The irony of it coming from an Asian man is not lost on me. I appreciate it anyway.'

Quang handed him a business card.

'Sir, if you would like to let me know your contact details, I'll be happy to send you a written apology and one from the staff member. Plus, I'll give you a voucher for a weekend here.'

Zanza took the card. 'Thank you, Quang. I'll bear that in mind.'

'Thank you, sir. Please enjoy the rest of your day.'

The background hum of noise resumed as Zanza walked to the lifts.

***

Lorraine Farquharson was shivering with anticipation as she heard the knock on the door of her hotel room. She'd been attending to emails on her laptop and polishing off a bottle of Chardonnay to bolster her courage. Her husband and her had ceased any intimacy a few years ago, only staying together for financial convenience, like so many past-the-due-date couples, and since there would be a substantial inheritance coming from his parents. As the latter were staunch Catholics, a divorce would put paid to the benefits of the will.

Still, she didn't need hubby knowing about her fantasies, let alone her dalliances. This wouldn't be her first tryst, but it sure was the one she was going to brag about loudest to her girlfriends.

She opened the door.

'Bonjour, Lorraine.' The huge African man beamed at her. 'I'm Alphonse.'

She levitated her eyes from his magnificent chest, the bulging contours of muscle accentuated by a tight maroon T-shirt over which he wore a caramel-coloured sports jacket. Her eyes settled on his smiling face.

'Hi, Alphonse,' she almost whispered, her voice catching in her dry throat. 'Come in.'

'Thank you.' He stepped inside. 'And please excuse some of my words sounding a bit strange, I've been doing speech therapy after an operation. Long story.'

She closed the door and put her hand on his face. 'Oh, your accent sounds wonderful to me.'

She walked over to the bed and sat down, lifting her wine glass and taking a sip. 'So, Alphonse, what do you do when you're not fulfilling fantasies of wanton wenches like me?' She gave him a cheeky grin and ran her tongue along her lips. At the same time, she opened her thighs invitingly.

'I'm a private investigator.' He sat next to her. His manly bulk dwarfed her sexy feminine frame.

'Ooh, that sounds exciting. Lots of cheating spouses, I bet.'

Zanza chuckled. 'Occasionally. Most of my work is tracking people down.'

She put her hand on his thigh and slowly slid it along to his bulging crotch.

'You mean for debts, that sort of stuff?'

'Usually deserting fathers who are running away from child support payments. Sometimes abusive men who need court orders served on them. And some other jobs.'

She swivelled off the bed to kneel in front of him. She smirked and undid his belt. 'Anything interesting at the moment?'

'Yes, actually. I'm looking for a paedophile.'

'Ugh, I hate child molesters. I hope you find him. I reckon they should bring back the death penalty for scum like that.'

'Yeah, they are scum. I hate them, too.'

His explanation was interrupted by her undoing his zipper and unleashing his semi-erect cock out of his boxer shorts. In her grip, it immediately swelled to its full potential.

She gasped. 'God, you are huge. I've never seen one this big.'

She stroked his cock and kissed the glans. 'Isn't chasing paedophiles a police job?'

'Usually. But I'm looking for this one so his victims, and there are lots of them, can file a compensation claim.'

'Well, as I said, I hope you find him. I was abused as a little girl.'

'I'm sorry.' He stroked her face.

'Can I ask you a big favour, Alphonse?'

'Of course, my beautiful Lorraine.'

'When we screw, can you please do a video on my phone of me with your cock sliding into me? You don't have to show your face or anything to identify you, unless you want to, but I really want to show my girlfriends this. Please?'

'No problem at all, baby.' He thrust his pelvis forward slightly so his massive member was nearer her face.

She took the hint and lowered her open mouth over the head of his hard rod.

'So, Lorraine, can I ask you for a favour in return?'

She left a saliva trail hanging off her bottom lip as she lifted her face off his cock.

'Anything, Alphonse, seriously anything.'

'Can you check for any bank record for this paedophile I'm tracking?'

'Oh, so easy, no worries. Let's screw and then I'll get any information you want.'

'Thank you, baby. Now, time to get naked and get dirty.'

'Oh, yes!'

Lorraine peeled off her underwear and lay back on the bed, spreading her legs wide. She grabbed a tube of lube and squeezed a large dollop into her left hand. She saturated her pussy with it and rubbed her clitoris as she gazed at the 25cm rigid black rod that was now poised above her pelvis.

'Please be gentle, Alphonse. I've never had anything that huge in me. And don't forget the video.' She pointed to her phone lying on the bed.

'I'll be slow and gentle, baby, at least until you're into the rhythm of it.' He took the phone and got the camera rolling, holding it up to film the whole of Lorraine's body and face and with his cock in the frame.

She groaned as Zanza eased his massive rod into her pussy.

As he gathered speed, Lorraine's groans turned to loud moans, and finally a howling into a pillow she grabbed as she orgasmed. She pulled the pillow off her face. 'Alphonse, pull out and blow all over my face.'

'No problems, baby.' Zanza pulled his member out of her, manoeuvred up to straddle her body, and gave his erection a few finishing strokes. The ensuing torrent of come nearly drowned Lorraine. Zanza was still filming as she giggled and gurgled.

'Like that, baby?'

'Loved it, big boy. I think I'll call you Alphonse the Awesome.'

'Here's the video.' He handed her the phone.

She pressed 'Play'. 'Oh, yes, that will impress the hell out of the girls. Thank you.'

'My pleasure.'

'Mine, too, rest assured. Now, let's have a look at my computer for what you need. Let you recharge your batteries. Then I want you to do me doggy-style. I'm getting a taste for that beautiful beast.' She lifted her head and kissed his cock.

'Your wish is my command, Lorraine.'

Five minutes later, with towels wrapped around them and Lorraine no longer dripping jism from her chin, they sat at the table. Lorraine went through Wheeler's account as Zanza took copious notes for ten minutes.

'That what you need, awesome Alphonse?'

'Perfect, baby, just perfect. Thank you.'

'Cool.' She closed the laptop. 'Now shag me again.'

'Yes, baby.'

– 4 –

Zanza was beaming as he walked into Harry's office.

'Hey, hey, our Congo charmer returns, and he's smiling,' said Harry.

'Is luscious Lorraine still able to walk?' asked Trev.

'Yes, although perhaps not quite as before.'

They all laughed.

'Most importantly, aside from you enjoying your assignment, what do we have on Reggie Wheeler?' asked Harry.

'He's definitely here still. He used his ATM card yesterday at Randwick shopping centre.'

'Excellent. So, now we know he's not at granny's in Nowra. We need to move fast. Trev, time to email Abrahams.'

'Yep. We just need to sort out a meeting place. And one where an abduction will be easy.'

Harry nodded. 'I reckon a car park after dark. We know where Abrahams lives in the eastern suburbs, and we can hire a car. Lure him into it and knock him out before he realises it's not Wheeler in the car.'

'Yes, way to go. Tan, you're the smallest of us, so can you handle being crouched in the back seat with the chloroform?'

She smiled. 'Do bears shit in the woods? That will be fun and satisfying.'

'And Trev,' added Harry, 'you're a similar build to Wheeler, so you're in the driver's seat in a hoodie.'

Trev chuckled. 'Ah, a hoodie, the uniform of scum everywhere.'

'Indeed, although good for our covert work. Anyway, give him the instruction in the email to get into the front passenger seat of the car. Then whammo, he's ours.'

'Where will we take him?' asked Tanya.

'Needs to be somewhere no one will hear him scream, if we need to get down and dirty. Plus, it'll need a good phone signal for when he agrees to email Wheeler for us.'

'I have just the place,' said Zanza.

They all turned towards him.

'Do tell mate,' said Trev.

'Club Mammary, of course. All the rooms are soundproofed and the phone signal and Wi-Fi are perfect.'

Harry nodded. 'And Mama Jocasta will be okay with it?'

Zanza's grin broke out as brightly as a glorious sunrise. 'Harry, man, she loves you. And she hates pedos. I'll call her and ask her to set aside the best room for our job.' And I have a key for the side door, so even more discreet access from the laneway.'

'Bloody outstanding,' said Trev. 'I'll get an email happening.'

***

Crown Prosecutor Simon Abrahams was sitting in the darkened lounge room of his penthouse apartment in Double Bay. His salary as a senior prosecutor for the CDPP paid handsomely, plus he had a bulging pot of family money. On the non-material side, what he possessed was an insatiable predilection for young girls. And always young flesh well below the age of consent.

He was exceedingly comfortable this evening following a win in court today in a drug importation trial that also involved a corrupt cop. He was an ardent and articulate supporter of the war on drugs and its associated police corruption. What better way to distract resources away from crimes in the prepubescent realm. Not that they should be crimes, he thought. So much for progress. Those ancient civilizations were the truly civilized and progressive societies. The deflowering of children was celebrated in Rome and Athens back in the day. That was his take on history, anyway. There was no stigma back in those more civilized times for a man like him: a lover of children, or a 'minor attracted person' in more contemporary and correct language. God, he loved the progressive nature of wokeism.

He leaned back in his expensive Bellini recliner, feeling the Italian leather against his skin. He was naked and had an ice bucket next to the chair with a bottle of rosé in it. The wide armrest of his chair had a full glass of the pink wine resting on it. A tray table over the chair had a laptop on it. He took a long sip of his wine and pressed 'Play'. One of his favourite banned movies, *Old Macdonald had a Chicken Farm*, started. What the old farmer did to the little girls in the hay loft never ceased to raise a raging erection for him. He did the rest himself. But as much as he derived pleasure and satisfaction from his small but high-quality child-porn film collection, it was a poor substitute for live virginal flesh.

Ten minutes later, he wiped up his orgasm and poured himself a second glass of wine. He'd watched the scene with the old farmer and his two farmhands gang-banging the ten-year-old girl. Thank God for digital technologies, he thought. If they still depended on video cassettes, that film would have been worn out years ago, with the number of times he had watched it.

As he sipped his wine in post-ejaculatory peace, his mind drifting through a mixture of lascivious recollections and depraved fantasies, he saw an email notification on his mobile phone screen. He picked it up from the side-table and clicked on the email. It was from an address he wasn't familiar with, some gmail.com address, although it had 'Reg' in the username. He opened it.

> Hi Roy Rooster, Foghorn Leghorn here. Sorry for new email address, think other one is being watched. Need to see you, visa time of year again. Am back in Oz until visa renewed. FL

Abrahams looked at the message as he swallowed his wine and poured himself a refill. Bloody Reggie, he thought. Always needed help with his visas, but he sure seemed to enjoy living in South-East Asia with all the young flesh there. Abrahams felt a twinge of envy. His public position required more care and discretion than rampant Reggie. Anyway, the nickname usage in the email seemed to verify it was indeed Reggie. Best to double-check, though.

> Hey Leghorn! Great to hear from you. To confirm ID, what's the name of the young chicken farm in the jungle? RR

In the Kenmare office, Trev chuckled. 'He's cautious is our pedo prosecutor. He wants the name of the orphanage.'

Harry nodded. 'He can be as cautious as he bloody wants, we're a few steps in front.'

Trev smiled. 'Yep, such a bonus getting the chicken nicknames out of Farr before we snuffed him. And then finding them in Reggie's notebook.'

'And what's with these chicken names?' asked Tanya. 'I didn't get a chance to ask over in Laos.'

'These low-life scum refer to their child victims as chickens,' said Harry, scowling.

'Sick fuckers,' said Tanya.

'One of the reasons it's so pleasurable to eradicate them,' said Trev. He went back to his keyboard and typed.

> No worries Big Roy. Chicken meals at Our Sister of Lourdes. And finger lickin' good! FL

Tanya was looking over Trev's shoulder. 'Trev, you are a sicko.' 'Tan, realism is everything in this game.'

Back in Double Bay, Abrahams looked at his screen and smirked. Very cool, he thought. He could help Reggie with his visa again and Reggie could hopefully line him up with some action. He emptied the rosé bottle into his glass.

> Tell me where and when, Leghorn. And I could do with a fix. Nudge, nudge! RR

In the city, Trev let out a whoop. 'Got him!'

Harry joined Tanya watching Trev's screen. 'Let's try for tonight. I don't want to ever contemplate losing Wheeler again.'

'No worries.' Trev hit the keyboard again.

> How about this evening Rooster? Have some action available at a mate's place. Take you there? FL

In the penthouse, Abrahams swallowed an extra-large mouthful of wine as he barred up at the prospect.

> Excellent, Leghorn! Excellent. Can meet you by 8
> if not too far. RR

Harry leaned into the screen. 'He lives in Double Bay, doesn't he, Trev?'

'Yep. I reckon the car park at Rose Bay will be perfect. Close enough, pretty poorly lit, and very quiet after dark.'

'Do it, brother.'

> Big Roy Rooster, car park at Rose Bay, behind
> tennis courts, Vickery Ave. 8 PM. I'll be in a white
> Corolla with a pride ribbon on radio aerial. FL

Abrahams smirked.

> See you there. RR

He headed for his bedroom to get dressed.

Trev closed the email account, did some more typing and closed his laptop.

'Righto, team, I've got a white Corolla booked from GoGet around the corner. And ta da!' He pulled a rainbow ribbon from his briefcase.

Zanza stood up. 'I'll get going to the Club to get the room organized. I'm guessing one chair with some ropes?'

'Mate, you are truly a fast learner,' said Trev.

Harry laughed. 'Yep, big future with us, mate.'

Zanza headed for the door. 'Text me when you're on the way with the ped.'

'Roger that, big fella,' said Harry.

Simon Abrahams was early to the meet, spurred on by the eagerness oozing from his pores. And it was the sort of depraved zeal that trumped caution. He got the Uber driver to drop him at the entrance to the dark car park and pretended to fiddle with his phone until the driver left. He scanned the parking lot in the darkness, spotting a small white car in the far corner. There were a couple of other cars closer, but he couldn't see any figures in the gloom.

He walked casually into the car park, spotting a shape in the driver's seat of the white car as he was about halfway towards it. He glanced to either side and didn't see any people in the other cars. There was a grey van in the opposite corner, but he couldn't see anyone in the front of it. Probably a couple in the back, he thought.

He slowed his pace as he approached the white Toyota, checking for the rainbow ribbon on the aerial. The colourful pennant fluttered in the breeze.

He stepped quickly to the passenger door, opened it and jumped into the seat.

'Leghorn, so good to see you.'

Reggie didn't reply and didn't turn around. From the side, a hood covered his face.

The next thing Abrahams knew was a cloth reeking of a chemical was over his mouth and nose. He tried to pull his head forward and raise his hands, but darkness descended on him.

Tanya and Trev had planned it so as soon as Abrahams was in and the door was shut, Tanya would strike from the back seat.

So, the moment the door closed and Abrahams greeted Reggie, Tanya launched up and shot both her hands around the headrest of the passenger seat, clasping the chloroform rag she'd pulled from its plastic bag over Abrahams's face and using her other arm to lock around his throat and pull his head back. She clung on like a limpet until he stopped moving and went limp.

As soon as Abrahams slumped in the seat, Trev hit the button to lower all the windows. Both he and Tanya gasped for some fresh air. The lowered windows was also the sign to Harry.

The grey VW van started and slid over to the car, stopping next to the passenger side of the Corolla. Harry angled it in at the rear to obscure any view from the street.

With the van angled as it was, Tanya had to climb out of the opposite side. Both she and Trev walked around the front. Harry slid open the van's side door, and the two guys dragged the unconscious paedophilic prosecutor from the passenger seat of the car and dumped him in the van.

Harry closed the side door. 'Okay, babe, Trev and I'll head for the Club. You know where to drop the car?'

'Yep. See you at the Club after that.'

'And, Tan, keep the windows down all the way to clear out any smell.'

'No worries. And please don't start the really painful part until I'm there.'

'Babe, as if we would.'

– 6 –

The first sensation Simon Abrahams had as he came to was of an overpowering smell of baby powder. His eyes began to focus. He also realized he was sitting and his hands were secured behind him and the chair he was on. He could see a large couch against the wall with a huge teddy bear sitting on it, glass eyes staring inanely at him. The walls were a pastel blue and a large mobile hung from the ceiling, with half a dozen unicorns dangling from it.

'What the fuck?' he said to himself.

He tried to stand, but found his ankles were bound to the chair legs. The chair was a heavy wooden one, so the half stoop he attempted made him look like a shuffling, bent-double hunchback. He gave in to gravity and the chair legs thudded on the carpet. He noticed this was also pastel blue.

'Help!'

He was about to repeat his desperate call when the door opened. Two figures in clown masks walked in. From their physiques, they both appeared to Abrahams to be men. One was stocky with orange-red, frizzy clown hair. The other was slender but muscled. His clown mask had bright blue hair.

Abrahams heard himself say, 'What the fuck?!' again.

As the two clowns did a brief but bizarre synchronized dance routine, in total silence, Abrahams couldn't even utter the question a third time. He stared at the surreal spectacle before him.

It didn't stay surreal for long.

The red clown lunged in and punched him in the guts. The blue clown guffawed, waving his arms around.

Abrahams was in pain from the punch, but he feared it could get much worse. He also suspected some sort of dark nightmare was beginning.

He was right, of course. What Harry and Trev had in mind was a nightmare of Bram Stoker proportions.

Tanya and Zanza were watching and listening on a monitor in Mama's office.

'Well good evening, Mister Simon Abrahams, respectable government lawyer and child-molesting piece of shit,' said Harry. He wanted to look the arsehole in the eyes, face-to-face, but needs dictated the masks. Getting identified for abducting and assaulting a crown prosecutor was not a good move on any planet.

The respectable molester looked at him, his face a conflicted mixture of anxiety and outrage.

The latter won out. It usually did, thought Harry, especially amongst the narcissistic and sociopathic. And those types were seriously over-represented in the higher echelons of society.

Abrahams roared at the clowns, 'Do you arseholes know who I am?!'

Harry and Trev looked at each other and clutched their faces in mock dismay. It resembled a Marcel Marceau sketch but less benign.

Abrahams went silent as the blue clown leant in towards him.

'Yes, cunty. We know exactly who you are: a senior CDPP prosecutor. And we know who your associates are. Lovely crowd, I must say. And we know who you like to fuck, all underage.'

The bravado slinked back. 'You can't prove anything.'

'I wouldn't be so sure,' said Harry. 'Reggie Wheeler ring a bell?'

'Or perhaps Leghorn from a Laos orphanage?' added Trev.

Abrahams not only looked gobsmacked, he was utterly flummoxed.

'Brother,' said Harry, 'no one's looked that stunned since Little Red Riding Hood saw the Big Bad Wolf had a massive erection.'

'Too true, brother, until she gasped, "My oh my, Mister Wolf, what a massive schlong you have".'

'Ah, yes. Which was followed by, "So give it to me now, you lupine scoundrel, you".'

Both clowns laughed.

The moment of banter enabled Abrahams to regain some composure. He was an expert at recovering his position, thanks to years of courtroom work as a prosecutor.

'I don't know what you're talking about.'

The blue clown launched in and the punch to his face nearly broke his jaw. It was a solid antidote to his verbal bravado.

'We had a little encounter with your friend Reggie over in Laos,' said the blue clown.

'And we want another meeting, which you're going to arrange, 'cos we know he's back in Oz at the moment,' said the red one. 'Getting his annual visa sorted out no doubt.'

'So, tell us, Abrahams, why do you help out Reggie? We know you're both peds, but what's in it for you? Especially with the risk for you in your lofty position.'

Abrahams looked at the pair of clowns and considered silence was more prudent than anymore bravado.

The red clown pulled a pair of pliers from his trouser pocket. 'Silence, my prosecutorial paedophile, equals pain. An endless supply of gratuitous, excruciating pain.'

He stepped behind Abrahams and bent down, grabbing the captive's right hand. 'Which fingernail first, arsehole?'

Abrahams simply couldn't abide pain, of any sort. It was an ingrained trait ever since school and the beatings in the toilets. The other boys at his elite private school had been able to smell his difference: animal instinct. And they tortured him for it.

He now rapidly reconsidered silence versus pain. 'Okay, please, don't hurt me. I'll talk.'

'Ah, very wise, Mister Crown Prosecutor,' said the blue clown.

'So, what does Reggie need your help with?' The red clown was back in front of him and, much to Abrahams's relief, the pliers went back into the trouser pocket.

'He's got criminal convictions, so that's a problem with his visa application each year. A letter from me on CDPP letterhead vouches for his reformed behaviour. It seems to work, along with some cash.'

'But why?' said the blue clown. 'Why bother and risk yourself? It's not as if he's here providing you with victims.'

Abrahams paused and swallowed hard. 'He's got an old video tape of us, from years ago.'

'You mean a sex tape with a kid?'

The prosecutor nodded.

The red clown slapped his face. 'Say it, cunty! Say out loud what you are.'

'Okay, okay. Please don't hit me anymore.'

'Well smarten up then.'

'Okay, yes. It's a sex tape of Reggie and I with a girl.'

'You mean a child girl, yes?'

'Yes.'

'That's better, Mister Prosecutor.'

'But how do you know I help him?'

The red clown laughed. 'Ah, Mister Prosecutor, we know a shit load of stuff about you and Reggie. Like we said, we encountered him in Laos.'

'Has he been in touch this visit?' asked the blue clown.

'Well, I thought he had, but that was obviously you. So, no.'

'Okay, here's how this is going to play out,' said the red clown. 'And it's very simple, so listen up. You're going to contact Reggie, however you usually do so, and you're going to arrange to meet him. You can say you know from police intel that he was back in Oz again, and you wanted to get his visa sorted out pronto 'cos you're heading overseas for a long holiday. So, that should cover off why you're being proactive and reaching out to him.'

'Pretty straightforward, yes?' The blue clown poked him in his ribs.

Abrahams nodded.

The red clown continued. 'And once we've got Reggie Wheeler, you'll be in the clear, at least as far as we're concerned. Got it?'

'Yes. I normally use another private email account. It's also on my phone that I assume you have taken.'

'Good, that makes it easy. I'll get your phone and you'll send him a message. I'll be watching over your shoulder, so any funny stuff, we will seriously fuck you up. Like pain so dire you'll wish you'd never been born. Understand?'

'Yes, yes.'

Abrahams sat there glumly as the two clowns left the room. Maybe he could benefit from this, despite how his current predicament looked. He'd always resented Reggie having that damned video tape, secretly recorded as it was. An idea germinated quickly in his head. Yes, that's what he'd do. He'd tell Reggie the letter for his visa this time meant that the video had to be handed over. Sure, Reggie could possibly have had a copy made, but it was unlikely. He'd had to flee Australia almost straight after the depraved filming in question, and Abrahams knew the video tape was in safe storage here in Oz. To get anyone to copy that sort of film was fraught with danger. The avenues were so limited it would take a lot of careful arranging, and Reggie had not had that sort of luxury, or time. And if he'd done anything recently of that ilk, the chances were it would be a digital copy. And that always gave Abrahams an easy out to say it was fabricated. The digital age had brought not only more ready availability, but a whole new world of deniability. An old original video tape was more convincing, as fakes were more easily discernible. And any such tape would be terminal for his career and lifestyle.

– 7 –

Crown Prosecutor Simon Abrahams breathed in the fresh, salty air blowing in off the Pacific Ocean as he sat outside a small café along from the beachfront at Coogee. Seagulls squawked as they cruised the air streams on the lookout for any breakfast scraps.

Abrahams was exhausted and he could smell himself. His overnight captivity had been uncomfortable and his captors had insisted on an immediate meeting. Still, he'd be glad to get his bit done and return home. Reggie had been resistant to start with, wanting to leave it a couple of days as he was 'on a mission' in his words. Abrahams knew that meant he was stalking or grooming some little girl. But Abrahams stuck to the script the men had given him about going overseas imminently, so Reggie would have no other opportunity. Abrahams had also slipped in the demand for the video tape, previously telling the watching captors he was referring to a favourite child porn video they had watched years previously. When one of them quizzed him for more detail, he fed them a line about it being harder to get videos now he was a crown prosecutor, and he loved the old-fashioned tape format. He omitted to mention he was a star performer in the film. They seemed to accept his ruse. And if they did suspect it was really the video that Reggie effectively kept as insurance that he'd mentioned to them, he guessed they were only interested in capturing Reggie.

He glanced at the grey VW van parked in a loading zone a short distance along Havelock Avenue, at right angles to Arden Street where the café was. It was the back of the van facing his direction, but he knew they were watching him. The stocky one had made it abundantly clear if he did not follow his instructions, he would be tortured and mutilated when they caught him. The line about being forced to eat his own testicles particularly stuck in his mind. So, he needed to be clever to get away from this situation and not leave them any chance to grab him again once he had the tape.

His instructions were clear: have his discussion and a coffee with Reggie and give him his letter. He was kicking himself now for having had the letter with him when he went to the car park meeting, but he wasn't to know it was a set up. But he'd unfortunately made it easier for the thugs to carry out this part of their plan. Once the letter was handed over, that was the signal to the watchers in the van and then Abrahams was to bid Reggie farewell and walk to the nearest taxi on the beachfront and go home.

Internally, he was torn between urges. Part of him wanted to be the supposed upstanding prosecutor and call in the cops to arrest his abductors, although he still hadn't seen their faces. And his story of going to a car park meeting after dark from whence he was abducted would have the cops immediately suspecting him of dogging. And that sort of info would leak from the cops to the prosecutor's office at warp speed. Another part of him was obsessed with the threats of violence. The two thugs seemed too keen on their exploits to be amateurs. Plus, there was the overriding fear of being exposed and his dirty secrets hitting the public domain. But the aspect that was most pushing him into doing exactly as demanded was the prospect of getting that damned video cassette off Reggie. Then he'd be able to cut forever the association that was now simply inconvenient in the extreme. It'd been useful back in the day because Reggie had been able to regularly provide kids for him and his police mates, Bevan and Malcolm. But now Reggie was always overseas he served no purpose for Abrahams. He was purely a risk.

His contemplation was terminated by the chair opposite being pulled out and Reggie Wheeler plonking himself down.

Reggie held out his hand. 'Well, hello Big Rooster. Great to see you.'

'Hello, Leghorn.' Abrahams shook Reggie's hand. 'Coffee?'

'Yes, please. Lots to talk about. Laos is *so* much fun.'

Abrahams waved to the young waitress doing nothing inside the deserted café. When she stood and looked over, he pointed at his cup and indicated two more.

He sure as hell needed as much caffeine as he could get after the nocturnal ordeal he'd had, so he didn't want to do anything precipitous yet. He had to take things slowly.

'So, how is Laos, Leghorn?'

'Rooster, it's a kindergarten smorgasbord, seriously. You would love it. Should come and have a holiday *chez moi!*'

'Maybe. I know I'd enjoy it. But a visit is a bit trickier for me, now. Mind you, I wouldn't mind some films from you from over there.'

'That can be arranged.'

Their coffees arrived.

Abrahams took an over-eager gulp and burned his tongue. He took a mouthful of water, refilling his glass and pouring some for Reggie.

He exposed the corner of the envelope in his inside jacket pocket and tapped it.

'I've got your letter for you, as usual.' He put it on the table in front of him. 'Now listen, Reggie, it might be a lot harder in future to do this, if not impossible.'

'Why? What's the problem, Rooster? We're still mates, aren't we?'

'Reggie, don't be such a drama queen.' He patted the back of Reggie's hand resting on the table. 'Of course we are still friends. Chicken buddies always.'

Reggie looked relieved and smiled. 'Chicken buddies, yes.'

'No, the problem is I'm in line for promotion to the Deputy Director of Prosecutions position. There will be a heap more scrutiny on me, so anything like this will become incredibly risky.'

Wheeler frowned. 'No worries, understand that. I can probably get away without the letter from now on if I add a whole lot of cash to the greasy palms in Vientiane. I just don't have a lot of spare cash these days.'

'Relax on that, I can help you out with cash next year and we can do that very discreetly, no risks.'

'Thanks, Rooster, you're a true friend. And here's that video you wanted. Dug it out of my trunk at my cousin's place where I've crashed a few nights.'

He put a plastic shopping bag on the table.

'I enjoyed watching it again, Rooster. We gave that little girl a real going over.' A globule of saliva dribbled from the corner of Reggie's grin.

Abrahams smirked. 'Yes. Fond memories of that one, Leghorn. And she never reported anything.'

'That's because I can pick them well, Rooster. Single mothers, always needy, especially the druggie ones. Gold mine.'

'Not my social circles, unfortunately,' said Abrahams.

'Roy Rooster, you really must come for a trip to South-East Asia.'

'All in good time. Now listen, Leghorn, apart from your letter, I need to help you out here.'

'How so?' Wheeler leaned in.

'Did you have some guys come after you in Laos recently?'

Wheeler stared at him. 'How do you know about that? Are the cops after me?'

'Not that I'm aware of. And, anyway, if they were you probably would've been grabbed at the airport when you came in.'

'True. So why do you ask?'

'Okay. I got lured to a bogus meeting last night. I thought I was meeting you. But I then got abducted. And these guys made me set this up.'

Wheeler's eyes darted to each side.

'Do *not*, I repeat *not*, turn around, Leghorn. Do *not*, okay? *Keep* looking at me, for fuck's sake.'

Wheeler nodded slowly, his eyes still twitching. 'All right. What do these people look like?'

'I don't know. They had masks on. But there are two men, one stocky and one slender, both about one-eighty in height. And there's a younger female with them.'

Wheeler grimaced. 'That's them. They came for me in Luang Prabang at the orphanage. The local cops tipped me off just in time. The benefit of regularly greasing those palms.'

Wheeler moved his eyes from side to side again, straining to look around.

'Reggie, I said do *not* turn around. We can't have these men getting suspicious.'

'So, what are you supposed to do?'

'I'm supposed to signal them with handing you the letter. Then they'll come from behind you. I can see their van from here. I guess they'll tell you to go with them. They are armed, Reggie. I had a bloody gun pointed at me in the back of their van.'

'And what do you do after you've signalled them?'

'I walk off to the cab rank down on the beachfront without turning around. And I disappear. I'm free to go, apparently, after I've given the signal. And I'm to tell you to wait a clear ten minutes after I've gone.'

'Shit, Rooster, they'll fucking kill me. I think one of them could be an ex-cop whose daughter I did years ago.' Wheeler grimaced with desperation.

Abrahams shook his head. 'Okay, not your smartest move, Leghorn. For now, relax. We'll give them a surprise. Plans don't always work out. Just remember, they are behind you up that side street, so do not run in that direction. Got it?'

***

The trio in the VW van parked in Havelock Avenue and facing the opposite direction were watching intently through the heavily tinted rear windows. They'd all taken their masks off as soon as Abrahams was sent to the café so as to minimize any unwanted attention. Even at this time in the morning, anyone who saw two clowns and Marilyn Monroe in the back of a van would likely be on the phone to the cops saying a heist was about to go down or some strange porno film was being made.

When Tanya had come back to the office from the fancy dress shop the previous morning with the masks, both the guys had raised their eyebrows when she pulled Marilyn Monroe out of the bag as they were examining their clown faces.

'And why are we clowns?' asked Harry.

'Because, boss, I wanted a giggle. And seeing you two in those, I think I'll piss my pants with laughter.'

'So why aren't you also a clown?'

'Mister PI, as you well know, and on every carnal level, I am way too sexy for that. Marilyn is so much more my style.'

Harry nodded.

'She's got a point there, Harry,' said Trev.

'Shit, you could have got us JFK or something like that.'

Tanya giggled. 'Try them on, boys.'

Harry and Trev slid their masks over their faces. Tanya burst out laughing. 'Fricking gold!'

Now, they were all glad to be out of the masks and breathing unhindered, without the pervasive rubbery-plastic smell. But it also meant they were confined to the interior of the van. In their careful plan, they didn't want Abrahams to have any chance of seeing their faces. Plus, there was a risk Reggie Wheeler could spot them as he arrived for the meet. So, they sat in the back of the van, watching and waiting for the signal.

Harry turned his head slightly towards Tanya, who was sitting in the swivel jump seat, facing towards the back doors where the two guys were crouching. 'And, for the record, you are way sexier than Miss Monroe, and she was pretty damned hot.'

'Oh, thank you, Harry.' She blew him a kiss.

'Leave it out, you two,' said Trev. He grinned at them. 'I didn't bring the mattress for today's operation.'

Tanya giggled. 'Who needs a mattress when I've got Harry's face.'

Harry beamed with a smug expression whilst Trev groaned.

'Fuck! What's happening?!' yelled Harry, his face crammed against the glass of the back window.

In the distance, Wheeler was running, heading in the opposite direction down Arden Street. Abrahams was on his feet, too, moving away from the café. He went out of sight as well.

'Tan, in the driver's seat now! Let's go!' yelled Trev.

Tanya launched herself into the front seat and fired up the van's engine. She threw it in gear and was about to pull out from the kerb when a bus trundled to a stop in front of them, awkwardly angling itself into the bus stop space leaving its rear end hanging out in the road. A large delivery truck that had been following came to a stop as it couldn't negotiate its way around the protruding bus.

'Fuck, fuck, fuck!' yelled Harry and Trev in almost perfect harmony.

Harry grabbed for the handle of the side door. 'Right, on foot, Trev. A good old-fashioned foot chase.'

'Roger, mate, but hopefully without the back fences. Tan, get this limo on the road ASAP and if you see Abrahams, go after him. We'll call you when we've caught up with Wheeler.'

The two guys jumped out of the van's side door and ran in the direction Wheeler had disappeared.

Tanya was riding the clutch in first gear and screaming abuse at the bus. It signalled and pulled out onto the road, the truck falling in behind it. As luck would have it, there were no other vehicles in the lane, so Tanya was able to accelerate the van into a U-turn to head for Arden Street and all the action.

As the two guys ran onto Arden Street, Wheeler was legging it towards the beachfront. He made the mistake of turning his head to look for his pursuers. As he glimpsed the two running sleuths, he ran headlong into a woman pushing a stroller with an infant in it. Wheeler went arse over onto the pavement, and so did the child in the stroller. The mother shrieked.

'Oh, shit,' said Harry. 'That'll have a call going into the cops.'

'He's crossing over,' yelled Trev.

Wheeler had regained his feet more swiftly than a fallen cat and was running across the road towards the shop side, away from the beach. But it was also the side the two sleuths were on.

Harry was breathing hard and hating the running. The fitter Trev was pulling in front of him.

Wheeler ducked left into Carr Street heading away from the beachfront.

The sleuths were still about fifty metres behind him. Trev turned the corner with Harry a few metres back.

Wheeler ran across the street, heading for the first cross street, Brook Street.

As they entered it, Trev was gaining quickly on Wheeler, whose prolonged and depraved holiday in South-East Asia clearly did not involve any form of gym regime.

Harry was now about thirty metres back.

Wheeler turned his head again, and again it was a mistake, as he careened into a wheelie bin, knocking it and himself over.

Trev could see the look of terror on the ped's face as he closed the gap between them.

Wheeler scrabbled over the bin and was running again, but Trev was now fewer than twenty metres away and closing. He did have a solid gym regime.

The next thing Harry saw, bringing up the rear, was an airborne Trev hurtling off the bonnet of a car that had emerged from a driveway obscured by shrubbery.

***

Tanya, meanwhile, swung the van onto Arden Street and headed north. Scanning ahead she could see the two guys chasing Wheeler. She was in time to see Wheeler sprint into the second side street on the left running away from the beachfront. But there was no sign of Abrahams. She slowed the van as she drew next to the first street on the left, Waltham Street.

'Got you, fucker!' She swung the wheel hard and accelerated into the side street, towards the back of Abrahams's figure now walking briskly along the street.

He turned at the noise of the van's engine.

Tanya smiled as she saw the look of fear wash over his tired face. She was closing the gap rapidly.

Abrahams turned and ran. He ducked left into Asher Street as Tanya was almost on him. She hurled the van around the corner and sped in front of the running man, swinging the van to a stop on an angle as she went past him. Abrahams stumbled as he tried to avoid slamming into the grey metal beast hunting him.

Tanya was out of the driver's door in a flash and around the front of the van as Abrahams regained his feet and squeezed past the vehicle. He was about to run again when Tanya slammed her right fist into his nose, knocking him backwards as he squealed. He bounced into a brick wall and fell on his knees, dropping his bag as he clutched at his face. Blood trickled between his fingers.

Tanya launched her foot into his crotch and he keeled over, groaning as he assumed the foetal position.

'You pedo piece of shit.' She kicked him again, bent over and took the bag. She opened it and saw the video cassette. 'Sweet. I guess this is mine now, you wankstain.'

Abrahams was still curled up sobbing and leaking blood from his broken nose.

Tanya was about to give him a final kick for good measure when a male voice yelled in her direction.

'Eh, you okay, lady?'

Tanya looked past the front of the van and in the direction she had driven from. She saw two huge, tattooed Islander guys emerging from a gateway to an apartment block. They moved towards her and the fallen paedophile.

Her brain moved as quickly as her body had. 'Yeah, all okay now, guys. This disgusting pervert just tried to grope me and steal my bag.' She held up the plastic bag.

'Want us to call the cops for you, lady?'

'No, guys. Seriously it's fine now. I've sorted him out and got my bag back. Thanks anyway. Must be off, I'm running late for a job interview,' she said as she manoeuvred swiftly back towards the open driver's door. She jumped in, reversed slightly away from the pavement and threw it in first gear, accelerating away.

She looked in the side mirror and saw the two man-mountains laying the boots into Abrahams on the ground. She snickered. 'Now that's karma.'

***

Trev had seen the car in his peripheral vision in the second before impact and his reaction, despite a lack of sleep, had been instantaneous. He was able to jump sufficiently so he landed on the bonnet and bounced off the other side. His self-defence training was ingrained and he knew how to fall so well it was instinctive. He tucked his head in and let his shoulder

225

muscle pack take the impact as he hit the ground, fortuitously landing on the grass verge and not the concrete footpath. As the young woman driving the car sat there looking like a stunned possum, Harry rushed around the front of the vehicle.

'Trev, mate! Talk to me!'

Trev was winded. He gave Harry the thumbs up and wheezed, 'I'm okay.'

'You sure? Looked like a fair wallop.'

'Looked worse than it was, thanks to my amateur acrobatics. Go after Wheeler, brother. I'll call Tan.'

Harry looked at his quarry now making his way towards the intersection with the main drag, Coogee Bay Road. Harry was running hard. If Wheeler got to the main road with a lot more people around, it would make things bloody difficult. That was exactly why they'd selected a café well away from the main business area.

Harry wanted his man desperately and he was now running so hard his chest was hurting. He was closing the gap and was already having visions of getting his hands around Wheeler's scrawny paedophilic throat. Wheeler was tiring quickly now and Harry's visceral determination was giving him Olympic fortitude to fuel his speed.

But it was to no avail.

Harry hollered in anguish loud enough to wake the spirits as Wheeler, under twenty metres from him now, arrived at the main road intersection and at the exact moment a vacant taxi idled past, scrounging for custom. It got the most eager passenger in taxi history.

Harry, still running his heart out, watched as Wheeler frantically waved the cab down and scrambled into the back seat. He turned to look at Harry and gave him the middle finger. The cab pulled away with a screech of tyres as Harry was a mere five metres away from it and his target.

Harry stopped, breathing as if his lungs were on fire, and put his hands around his head. 'Fuck!!!' he screamed at the universe.

Trev was now trotting up behind him.

Harry turned. 'Mate, fricking Murphy's Law. A bastard cab here right at the moment he got to the main road.'

'That'd be fucking right,' said Trev. 'And we can never find a cab when we want one. Which way did it head?'

'West, up the hill. I didn't get a chance to get its number. Not that that would probably help us anyway.'

An engine roared behind them and Trev turned his head. 'Here's Tan. Let's get up there anyway, just in case.'

The VW van pulled over next to them and they jumped in.

'Left onto the main drag, babe, and move it!'

'Where's Wheeler?'

'In a bloody cab heading that way, Tan, a long story.'

Murphy struck again as they got stuck getting onto the main road with a queue of traffic. Tanya moved the van into the road four cars later having forced her way in front of an indignant delivery driver.

Harry, in the front passenger seat, peered desperately through the windscreen, looking along Coogee Bay Road. 'Fuck, not a cab in sight.'

Trev leaned forward from the jump seat. 'I think we should go and punish Abrahams, that double-crossing wankstain.'

The traffic was now at a stop and Tanya was thumping the steering wheel. 'Boys, let's see what's on his video first. Might be useful. We all know what these scumbags are like with their films.'

'What do you mean, babe?'

She tapped the plastic bag sitting in the centre console next to her. 'I got it.'

'How the hell, Tan?'

'Another long story, Trev.'

Harry put his hand on Tanya's thigh. 'As always, young lady, you are truly sensational.'

'Never underestimate girl power.' She turned and smiled.

'I would never, ever do that. Now, team. It's story time at the office me thinks. Plus, we all need a drink.'

'Hell yes,' said Trev.

'Nothing like an early start,' said Tanya.

Harry chuckled. 'What was that about girl power?'

'Okay, smartarse. I'll sort you out later.'

'Ooh, promises, promises.'

Trev groaned. 'Please, no. Not the foreplay again.'

They all laughed as the traffic started moving again.

'Gotta manage a laugh,' said Harry. 'I'd be bloody crying otherwise.'

– 8 –

Tanya parked the van in the access laneway behind the crappy old building housing Harry's office.

Trev turned to Harry. 'Brother, why don't you go and sort some much-needed drinks out upstairs. I need to root around with my gear in here to get something rigged up that'll actually play this old video.' He held up the old camcorder cassette. 'If I can't find the right stuff in the van, I'll need to shoot back to the workshop at my place.'

Harry grinned. 'No worries, always happy to be the bartender.'

'Can I have a look at the gear?' asked Tanya. 'I don't know about all this dinosaur tech stuff.'

'Sure, Tan.'

'See you guys upstairs.' Harry went off into the back door of the building.

Tanya climbed into the back of the van where Trev had some video equipment out on the workbench. She frowned at him as he turned on a small screen device. 'Trev, I thought you needed to root around to find something, but you're up and running already?'

'Tan, I know where every last piece of my equipment is.'

'So, why did you bullshit Harry?'

'Because I have to check this film first, before Harry gets to see it.'

'Oh, of course, Orla.'

'Exactly.'

The film played with an image of a young girl, about ten years old, sitting on a bed. She was scrawny and distinctly undernourished. Her skin was pale white to the point of being anaemic. She barely registered a flicker on her face as two naked men appeared in front of her.

'She looks drugged,' said Trev. 'But it is definitely not Orla. Let's go get that drink with Harry.'

'Think I'm going to need it.'

'And we need to look after Harry. He's going to be hurting inside over losing Wheeler again.'

'Yeah, I know.'

'And, Tan, you don't need to watch this video.'

'Trev, I do appreciate you looking out for me, but yes, I do. I'm part of the team, plus I am doing okay in my head dealing with what was done to me.'

'A couple of nine-millimetre slugs were no doubt part of the therapy,' Trev grinned.

'You bet.'

They hugged and got out of the van.

***

Three drinks each were needed to get them through the twenty-minute video abomination.

Tanya pointed at the now black screen on the video player. 'So, I recognized Wheeler and Abrahams, but who was the third piece of shit that came in halfway through?'

'That, babe, was a very senior cop, Bevan Hayes. Would've been a detective inspector around that time, I think, but now an assistant commissioner.'

'And rising fast,' said Trev. 'I'm so used to seeing the wanker in uniform at press conferences it was a push to recognize him naked.'

'He still had that same haughty sneer to his ugly mug back then. I remember the prick from back in the job before I got the boot.'

'Bet he was a ladder-climbing, back-stabbing wanker,' said Trev. 'Just like his mate, Malcolm Lowe.'

'Yep, Hayes climbed faster than a dose of gonorrhoea up the eye of your dick.'

'Oh, yuk! Gross, Mister PI.'

Harry chuckled. 'Yeah, but I'd prefer the clap to even five minutes in the company of that fuckstain of a man.'

'Well, his stellar career is about to turn into an asteroid burning up as it crashes to earth. I'm going to copy the tape into digital format now. Then it's party time.'

'Yep. And we'll take down Abrahams publicly at the same time. Teach the bastard to double-cross us.'

Trev was fiddling with equipment. 'So, I'll send an anonymous copy to the Feds with the full details of all three rock spiders. And I reckon copies to the media, just to give a safeguard against any cover ups.'

'Good thinking, mate. And let the Feds know Wheeler is on the run and trying to leave the country. That way they'll put a block on him at the airports and probably publicize him. When he hears his name as a wanted man, he'll know he's stuck here in Oz.'

'Then we just have to hunt him down all over again.'

'I like the hunting bit,' said Tanya. 'Actually, I like the torture and death bits, too. Good job I'm not looking for dates.'

Harry laughed. 'That'd be a hell of a profile on Tinder.'

She smiled as she stood and moved to the drinks cabinet. 'I get plenty of action, don't need any of that dating-site shit.' She poured some vodka. 'Guys, I hope we don't have to do any work this arvo, because it's not even twelve yet and this'll be my fourth vodka.'

'No worries there, Tan, we'll throw all the hand grenades from in here and then relax for the day. The rest will look after itself.'

'Yep, plenty of booze in here, and I reckon we grab some pizzas from over the road. Then sit back and watch the show,' said Harry. He lit a smoke. 'The only bit that won't look after itself, of course, is fucking Wheeler. But we'll get back on that chase tomorrow.'

'I think we'll need big Zanza back on the job, 'cos we're going to need that banking hussy to track Wheeler. We need every scrap of intel we can get.'

'Boys, I reckon luscious Lorraine will be very happy to see Zanza again, as soon as her hubby is next away.'

Harry laughed. 'Bet she will. But we might need to speed it up a bit, coffee or drink meet up perhaps with a promise of sex when it suits her. We need to get on this fast, and hubby's next trip could be weeks away.'

'And Zanza will need to sweet talk her big time and persuasively, so she only gives him any info on Wheeler. We don't want her calling the cops as soon as she sees Wheeler's details on the news as a wanted man.'

Harry agreed. 'For sure. Staying ahead of the Feds will be crucial. Last bloody thing we need is Wheeler getting arrested, 'cos they'll keep him in custody and then we're stuffed.'

'I'll be about another fifteen minutes with this, guys.' Trev pointed at his equipment. 'Why don't you go get the pizzas and I should be done by the time you get back.'

'Good thinking, let's go for a walk, babe.'

'No worries, I need ciggies, too.'

'Grab me some, too, please Tan.'

'Cool.'

Harry and Tanya left the office.

They walked back in twenty-five minutes later with four large pizzas and rolls of garlic bread.

'Damn that smells good,' said Trev. 'And I'm done here. I've also done a few still shots from the video, but with the girl and the actual sex pixelated out. However, our three pedo amigos are easily recognizable. We'll stick those out on social media, just to whip up the storm even quicker.'

'Love your work, brother. Start throwing those grenades.'

Trev grinned. 'Roger that. Buckle up, folks, this is going to be a wild ride this afternoon.'

– 9 –

With grenades launched, the sleuths devoured their lunch and, given their all-night job on Abrahams, plus the booze, slumber soon set in. Tanya had booted Trev off the couch, his usual haunt, and she now lay there asleep, stretched out. Her line to Trev had been, 'Beauty over age, Trev, the couch belongs to me for the siesta.' Trev, having pretended to protest, announced his chivalry, to a groan from Harry, and was now reclined in the armchair with his legs up on the coffee table, snoring lightly.

Harry had put his feet up on his desk and leant back in his tatty leather chair, a not-unusual pose for him at his desk, but any proper sleep eluded him as his mind fixated on Reggie Wheeler and his quest for vengeance.

It was a little over two hours later when Harry decided to distract himself and his murderous thoughts by checking the news sites.

'Fuck me!'

His voice roused Trev. 'Mate?'

'Brother, get over here and let's also get the TV on. Miss Universe over there won't be any the less beautiful for waking sooner than she hoped.'

Tanya stirred and opened one eye, rubbing the other. 'If you won't let a girl sleep, then at least get her a bloody drink, boys.'

The men laughed.

'That's our girl,' said Harry.

Trev went over to the drinks cabinet and poured three drinks. He took the glasses back to Harry's desk. 'Come and watch, Tan.'

Harry flicked the television news channel on and up came the faces of Abrahams and Hayes, albeit their professional photos, not the ones from the video. However, certain online sites were focusing in on the naked film stills and putting the professional photos alongside. The entire media was in meltdown.

'Fifteen minutes of fame in style for these two wankers,' said Harry.

Trev was looking back at his laptop. 'Get this for a conspiracy theory wankfest.' He pointed at his screen. 'This idiot is speculating the film is a fake all put together by Islamic State to bring down Assistant Commissioner Hayes, the anti-terror tsar of Australia, and thereby cripple the fight against the Islamic terrorists.'

'What a total fuckwit,' said Harry.

'So, what exactly does this cop Hayes do, guys? I thought he was a New South cop, but he seems to be based in Canberra.'

'Tan, he's the Deputy Director of the federal anti-terror task force. They have cops from across the country on it. So, that's why he's working down there with the Feds. But not for much longer, that's for sure.'

Harry chuckled. 'Apart from savouring every second of watching these wankers fall from grace, there's a delicious irony here with Hayes.'

'Continue,' said Trev.

'Well, you know the great fear factors our wanker politicians latched onto years back when they proposed censoring the Internet, and that they now use every time they want to pass a new so-called security law that further reduces our freedom.'

Trev sneered. 'Yep, terrorists and paedophiles. As soon as those two evils get mentioned, everyone goes into a sheep-like trance, obediently and silently surrendering their liberties.'

'Exactly. And here we have a paedophile in charge of our anti-terror efforts.'

'What a fucking joke,' said Tanya.

***

Assistant Commissioner Bevan Hayes, with his usual cocky strut, strode back into his office at AFP HQ in Canberra following a successful working lunch with the FBI liaison officer from the US embassy.

Canberra was treating him wonderfully and he was supremely confident all his arse licking and slithering sycophancy with the powers above would ensure him the director's position when the incumbent retired in a few months. He was even impressed himself with his ladder-climbing, and smugness oozed from his pores like sweat. There was only one downside to his meteoric rise up the career ladder and the consequent wallowing in the bottomless trough of public money that fed the bloated bureaucracy in the federal capital. And that was the lack of action, at least action to his tastes, as the ready avenues weren't as obviously plentiful as they were as a cop in Sydney, and he had to be far more careful these days about who he was in contact with.

He walked into the outer office where Julie, his young personal assistant, was sitting at her desk. He thought she gave him a funny look, but maybe it was nothing.

'Any messages, Julie?'

'No, Mister Hayes.'

She looked down at her desk. He thought it odd given how friendly and bubbly she invariably was. She was only eighteen and looked fourteen. Which is exactly why he had selected her. He would have preferred a PA who looked about ten, but Julie was the youngest-looking one from the pool offered by the labour-hire company. Precisely because she was eighteen put her well off limits for Hayes, way above his preferred age demographic. But he did enjoy looking at her youthful face and slender body, mentally undressing her and fantasizing that, under the clothing, she was a prepubescent nymph. Then the daydreams ran to having her bent over his desk.

He went through to his office, closing the door behind him. He was feeling so good about himself and his progress he felt the urge to have a look at some porn, his usual form of self-reward. He kept a non-police-issue personal iPad in his office safe for these occasions. Julie knew when he closed his door it meant he was not to be disturbed under any circumstances.

Before he went to get his iPad, he quickly clicked open his computer screen to check for any urgent emails or messages.

There was a message from an unknown source that was perplexing.

> You sick pig fuck. You're going down, cunty.
> Watch the news.

What the hell was that about?

He recognized the next message, from his old mate Simon Abrahams. Hadn't seen him in yonks, let alone been able to party with him.

It's over, Bevan. Run if you still can.

Goodbye, Simon.

How bizarre. He opened his usual news site.

His mouth fell open and he was transfixed by what he saw. Despite the graininess and pixelation, it was his naked self along with Simon and Reggie and that little girl with the druggie mother. Such an amazing weekend. It must have been at least ten years ago. And there was his name in bold upper case on the news page.

He slumped into his leather executive chair and stared out of the window across the Canberra skyline. A few minutes passed, Hayes sitting there as if catatonic.

He heard some noises outside his door. He pulled out his Glock and put in in his lap, one hand on it. The door burst open and two uniformed officers with short-barrelled rifles entered with two other men in suits following them in.

One of the suits looked Hayes in the eye. 'Assistant Commissioner Hayes, I am Assistant Commissioner Ned Kovic from Internal Security. Stand up and step away from your desk, please.'

Hayes looked at him and said nothing. He lifted his Glock pistol from his lap and raised it towards his own face.

'Drop the weapon!' screamed one of the tactical officers, as both rifles were raised and pointed at him.

Hayes shoved the Glock's barrel into his mouth and pulled the trigger.

Behind the desk on the wall was a large glass-framed poster that read 'With Integrity We Serve'. Blood, bone fragments, and mushy brain matter now dribbled down the glass.

***

Back in Sydney in Double Bay, Simon Abrahams had finished tending to his cuts and bruises, having crawled home after the kicking from that girl and those Islander thugs. Aside from the first aid box in his bathroom, he'd also medicated with one bottle of rosé already and he had opened the second. He was sipping the first glass from the new bottle, feeling less in pain, when the news started hitting.

He looked in morose silence at the images of him, first naked with his mates defiling that little girl, and then his official CDPP photograph that was usually used by the media.

They'd be here soon. For him. It was over.

He stood and let his bathrobe slip from his body. He grabbed the wine bottle without bothering with the glass. He stepped out onto his rooftop terrace holding the bottle in one hand and his laptop in the other. He placed the computer on the wide parapet, found the video file for the *Old Macdonald* film, and hit 'Play'. He took a hefty swig of wine and got into spanking the monkey. A degree of urgency took hold of him as he saw four cars stop in front of his building. Two were plain sedans, but two were marked AFP response vehicles.

He cranked faster and harder until he climaxed, as he savoured the farmhands gang-banging the girl. In his second last act of social defiance, he ejaculated over the parapet and onto Knox Street and the police cars below.

There was a banging on his apartment door.

This was it.

He stepped onto a bench against the parapet and up onto the wall itself. He looked at the scene six floors below. Miscellaneous people had stopped to spectate the excitement of the police arrival. He heard one of them shout and a dozen or so faces angled up towards him.

A loud splintering crash heralded the surrender of his front door to the uninvited guests. There was shouting.

Abrahams didn't bother turning around. He took another hefty swig of rosé and bellowed into the void, 'Fuck you all!' Then, still clutching his wine bottle, he swan-dived off the edge.

There were screams from the street level.

Abrahams's last act of social defiance was to spray red graffiti all over one of the police cars as his head burst open on the concrete pavement.

***

Three hours later, the sleuths, now joined by Zanza, called it a day on watching the news.

The death of both high-profile paedophiles was now public, as was Wheeler's mug shot and wanted status.

Harry hit the remote to kill the TV screen. 'Well, team, aside from missing out on Reggie Wheeler, fuck it, it hasn't been a bad day's work in the realm of taking out rock-spider scum.'

'I'll drink to that,' said Trev. 'And I so enjoyed sending that little love message to Hayes.'

He turned to Zanza. 'So, my big friend, you reckon you could get used to working with us?'

Zanza flashed a broad smile. 'What is it you guys are always saying about the Kennedys and being gun shy?'

Everyone laughed.

'Zanza, mate, you are fitting in bloody perfectly and it's great to have you on board.'

'Thank you, Harry.'

'And, babe, a big juicy bonus in your pay packet for that video. You really are one hell of a lady.'

Tanya laughed. 'Except in bed, of course, so not a lady there. But you know that.'

Trev groaned. It turned to blushing when Tanya turned and winked at him.

She turned back to Harry. 'I'll definitely take the bonus, of course. A girl's always got retail needs, and expensive ones.'

'Tomorrow's a new dawn,' said Harry. 'At least for some of us.' He smirked. 'And then it'll be back to the hunt for Reggie fucking Wheeler.'

'Pub?' said Tanya.

Trev, his normal colour again, stood up. 'Do one-legged ducks swim in a circle? Let's go.'

* * *

PART 4

HARRY'S ALTAR

She was like one of those ancient goddesses who tired of their heavenly pleasures and came down to earth for the delights of Man.

- Jim Thompson

Even at this early stage in my career, I had already decided that the only women who interested me were new women. Second time round was no good. It was like reading a detective novel twice over.

- Roald Dahl

– 1 –

Trev put his phone in the centre console and turned the heater up a notch in the grey VW van. July had turned on colder winter weather than usual in Sydney.

'Okay, team, Harry has got some extra info from his ex-Fed mate and will be on his way to join us shortly. He's on his way back to the office to collect the other van.'

Zanza was filling the passenger seat and the Pentax camera looked tiny in his hands as he was taking photos for some practice. He looked at the screen on the back of the camera and showed it to Trev. 'Think I'm getting the hang of this.'

'Yes, mate, nothing wrong with these shots, and no camera shake on the zoomed ones, so good work. You can do the photos any time.'

'Cool. Happy to do any of the work.'

'Mate, you're static in the van only, as far as surveillance like this is concerned. Tan and I can cover any personal following if needed. Foot surveillance requires a high degree of inconspicuousness and blending in.'

Tanya, in the jump seat, put her hand on Zanza's shoulder. 'Big and black is great, in so many ways,' she murmured in his ear, 'but not for tailing a target on these streets.'

Zanza put on an expression of mock outrage. 'Ooh, ouch, such ugly racism from such a beautiful face!' He cracked up laughing, and the others joined him.

'No, I take the point,' said Zanza.

'Yes, mate, on these Aussie suburban streets, especially a snooty up-market area like this, if someone saw a two-hundred-centimetre muscly black guy following someone, they'd be calling the cops, for sure. And that probably would have an element of racism to it. But it's reality, and we have to do our surveillance.' Trev lit a cigarette, cracking the window open a touch.

'No worries. But I can sure help when we need to grab Wheeler.'

'Fuckin' oath, big fella. The expression on his filthy, depraved face at that moment meeting you would be priceless.'

'Bring that moment on,' said Tanya. 'I so want to see our Harry get closure on this finally.'

They went back to watching the house of interest in Cardinal Street in leafy, salubrious Mosman on Sydney Harbour's north shore. The house belonged to an ex-business tycoon and the well-heeled father of a convicted paedophile, Jackson Conroy, who was now out of prison and was in the Feds' records as an associate of Wheeler. They also had bank info that showed Wheeler, or at least Wheeler's bank card, using the CommBank ATM at the Mosman shops twice in the last ten days.

Zanza had had no problems persuading Lorraine to keep feeding him info, on the understanding he would be at her beck and call next time her husband was out of town. He'd also had to agree to entertain two of her friends from the Facebook group. They had seen the photos of Zanza and his tackle and they wanted some of that big time. Zanza had made a half-arsed pretence of that being onerous for him, but in reality he thought he had struck the seam of gold in the mine.

Harry had roared laughing when Zanza debriefed with them. 'Big fella, as the saying goes, if you've got, flaunt it.'

Zanza had grinned. 'It's a tough job, Harry, but someone has to do it.'

Trev put his binos back on the target house. 'Quiet as a grave, damn it.' His observation wandered to the Roman Catholic church a few doors further along the street, and a large building next to it that appeared to be related given the lack of dividing fences.

Over two hours passed with Trev cycling through ELO tracks on the iPod plugged into the van's stereo. He had his head back and was humming along, gently tapping the rhythm on the steering wheel, as Jeff Lynne sang 'Turn to Stone'.

Zanza and Tanya were in the back now, with Tanya showing Zanza the various bits of equipment in the van.

'Lovely!' was his comment when she opened the concealed gun box under the jump seat.

She was demonstrating the video camera with its mounting frame when Trev sat up sharply. 'Movement, gang, the front door's opened.'

Tanya swung the jump seat back and released the back of the passenger seat to allow Zanza to squeeze through. And it was still a tight fit.

Trev chuckled. 'Yeah, I didn't have you in mind when I designed this set up, big fella.'

Zanza grinned. 'Camera, Trev?'

'Yes, mate, happy snaps of anything that moves. It'd be too much to wish for to have Wheeler emerge.'

'If he does, and he's alone, we going to grab him?' asked Tanya.

'Yep, it's broad daylight so bloody risky, but I'm not passing up that chance. Harry would never forgive me.'

'We will have to keep dreaming, guys,' said Zanza, peering through a zoom lens. 'It's not Wheeler.'

A middle-aged man emerged onto the front porch of the house. He was looking back inside appearing to talk to someone.

'That's Conroy,' said Trev. 'Now, into his car or off on foot?'

The question was answered as Conroy walked past his car parked in the driveway and into the street.

Trev's attention switched to the movement of a large black Mercedes sedan pulling out of the church grounds and heading towards them. 'What the fuck?!' he yelled, as the Merc slowly cruised past them.

'What?' said Tanya.

'That was bloody Father Barwick in the back seat, I'll never forget that face, even after all these years.'

'Who?' asked Zanza.

'The priest who raped Trev when he was a kid,' said Tanya.

'We going after him then?' said Zanza.

'Fuck! Of all the times to see Barwick.'

Tanya put her hand on Trev's shoulder. 'It's cool, Trev. I'll go after Conroy since he's on foot. See what he does, if anything. You see if you can tail Barwick. You might never get another chance like this. Go!'

'You sure?'

'I'll be fine, Trev, I've held my own against far worse than Conroy before. And besides, I'm just following.'

'I know. You're a champion, Tan. All right, keep us posted.'

'No worries. Plus, Harry will be here soon as well.'

She slid the side door open and jumped out. Conroy was ambling along the footpath on the other side of the road, heading in the direction of the shops.

Tanya ducked behind the parked car next to the van as Trev pulled out and the grey VW Transporter took off in the wake of the black Mercedes. The van's tyres squealed as Trev hurled it around the corner at the end of the street.

Trev was gripping the steering wheel with white knuckles. 'Gotta catch up with this car. I know it was him, the wanker. Zanza, call Harry, please. Let him know what's going down and tell him to get his arse up here pronto.'

Zanza laughed, picking up his phone. 'Let's hope Harry's not with some lady, naked and horizontal.'

'You've got him worked out, then.'

'A ladies' man and a good man.'

'An understatement on both counts,' said Trev, dropping the van into second to accelerate past a delivery truck that had double-parked.

'Harry? We have a situation, unexpected.' Zanza gave a brief synopsis and hung up.

'Okay, Trev, he was vertical and dressed and is on his way. He's heading for the street with Conroy's house.'

'Cool. Can you let Tanya know, please mate.'

'No problems.' Zanza texted a message to Tanya.

'Trev leaned forward, almost kissing the windscreen. 'Fuck, there it is!' They were on the approach to the Warringah Freeway. 'Looks as if he's going left towards the city. We are not going to lose this wanker, no way.'

They were now only three car lengths behind the black sedan and they followed it onto the downhill ramp onto the freeway southbound. They accelerated as the Merc entered the traffic flow south. 'Looks as if they're heading for the tunnel and maybe the Eastern Distributor,' said Trev.

'Hey, is that your old van?' Zanza pointed out an older VW Transporter model heading north on the opposite side of the barriers.

Trev glanced over. 'Sure is! That's our Harry.'

Harry waved at them from the other side as the two VW vans cruised past each other in opposite directions.

– 2 –

Tanya waited for Conroy to almost get to the street corner before she pulled up her hoodie and walked quickly in the same direction.

Five minutes later she emerged onto Military Road, about thirty metres behind the ped. He was waiting at the lights to cross the road. There was a gaggle of pedestrians also waiting, so Tanya slotted herself into the back of the group.

Once over the road, Conroy headed into the post office. He joined a queue at the counter.

Tanya walked over to the display shelves and pretended to peruse the overseas mailing envelopes, getting herself as close to the counter area as she could without looking strange.

By the time Conroy got to the front of the queue, fifteen minutes had elapsed. Tanya was having expletively unpleasant thoughts about Australia Post and its customer service. It seemed only one of the four staff behind the counter was actively serving the queue. One was absorbed in a passport application, whilst the other two were fiddling with the parcel trolleys whilst discussing their union's latest wage push.

Conroy approached the counter. 'I need to collect a registered letter for a friend who's staying with me. The letter is addressed here as post restante. I've got his ID and a letter of authority.'

'Name?'

'Mine or his?'

The clerk looked at Conroy with an exasperated stare. 'His, of course. The letter will be addressed to him.'

'Yes, sorry. It's Reginald Wheeler. Reggie's sick, that's why he sent me.'

'Okay, ID please, his and yours. And the letter of authority to collect.'

Conroy handed over a passport, a letter, and pulled his driver's licence out of his wallet.

The clerk perused the items. 'Okay, Mister Conroy. Your ID is fine and Mister Wheeler's passport signature matches the letter. I'll go and check out back for you.' She disappeared through a door into the back of the post office.

Tanya had her phone out and was texting Harry and Trev with an update.

Harry replied immediately.

Babe, in Conroy's street. Will wait for you here.

All cool.

The postal clerk returned. 'Sorry, there's nothing here for Mister Wheeler. Maybe try again tomorrow?'

'Okay, thank you.' Conroy turned and walked out of the post office.

Tanya got busy texting.

He's got Wheeler's passport. Want me to try and roll him?

No, babe. Don't want to spook Wheeler. We know where he is now. All good, and great work. You are so good.

Tanya grinned.

Cool. See you in 10.

Tanya left the post office and strolled back to Cardinal Street. She stayed well back as she didn't need to eyeball Conroy any longer.

Conroy was going up his front path as Tanya approached the older VW van and climbed into the passenger seat. She gave Harry a kiss.

'Great work, babe. Now we have a definite location for Wheeler. Just need a plan.'

'Can't wait for this, Harry.'

His phone rang. He answered.

'Zanza?'

He listened.

'Okay, thanks, big fella. I've got Tanya with me and we'll head back to the office. Sounds as if Barwick is going to be on a plane. See you soon.'

Harry hung up and turned to Tanya. 'Barwick's car took the entrance to the international airport.'

'Oh shit, poor Trev. He won't be able to do anything in there.'

'Nope. Too many cameras and too many cops.'

'Well, let's hope the pedo priest goes somewhere exotic.'

Harry frowned. 'Why?'

'So when we track him down, which we will, I get a good holiday somewhere.' She flashed a cheeky grin.

Harry nodded. 'I have always admired your style, young lady.'

The grey VW Transporter followed the Mercedes into the departures vehicle zone of Sydney International Airport.

The Merc stopped at the kerb of the drop-off area. Trev slid the van into a gap a few car lengths in front.

'Zanza, you're going to need to follow him in whilst I park the van.' Trev was looking in the side mirror, watching the Merc and its occupants. 'You fucking piece of shit, Barwick,' he said, as the priest got out of the car.

'What's his description?'

'He's the short, fat guy standing at the back of the Merc, dark grey suit and his dog collar.'

'Dog collar?' Zanza dipped his head to look in the mirror.

'What we call the white priest's collar they wear.'

'Ah, okay. Hadn't heard that name before. Yep, I see him. Brown leather overnight bag in his hand. And the driver's getting a large blue suitcase out of the boot.'

'So, mate, follow him in, and I'll call you as soon as I've ditched this chariot.'

'Cool.'

'And, mate, don't forget, no photos inside the terminal. That'll have cops all over you like a rash.'

'No worries.'

Zanza stepped out of the van and headed towards the nearest entrance doors.

Trev accelerated away in the direction of the short-term car park.

Ten minutes later, Trev was standing next to Zanza in the departures terminal expansive check-in area.

Zanza discreetly motioned with his face. 'He's in that queue, business class, Singapore Airlines.'

Trev turned in that direction. 'Got him. Fricking business class. The Catholic church sure looks after its own.'

'Power and corruption, Trev. Everywhere, my friend.'

'Yep. And bugger it, because all that flight number tells us is he's heading to Singapore. But money on that not being his final destination, so connecting to where, I wonder?'

'How about I try to get close enough to hear him checking in. You know how loud and chirpy those check-in staff usually are. He won't recognize me, plus there's other black guys in here, so not the same issue as those white suburban streets.' He winked at Trev.

'Mate, love your plan, give it a go.'

Zanza sidled towards the end of the check-in counter next to the business-class desk and stepped close to it as Barwick was called forward. Zanza was only five metres away, playing with his phone, ear cocked towards the counter.

'Good afternoon,' said the priest.

'Good afternoon, sir,' beamed the smartly dressed and immaculately made-up young lady behind the desk. 'And where are we off to today?'

'Singapore then Paris,' Barwick replied, placing his travel documents on the counter in front of the lady.

'Oh, wonderful. I do so love Paris. Is it a holiday, sir?'

'More like a retreat with a bit of work for the church.' He tapped his dog collar.

'Ah, I see.' She looked over his documents and passport and tapped on her keyboard.

'Okay, Father Barwick. Here is your boarding pass for Singapore, and here is one for the leg to Paris. And I've checked your baggage all the way through to Paris. Have a lovely trip.'

'Thank you.'

Barwick picked up his overnight bag and walked off towards the gate through to border control.

Zanza walked back to Trev. 'He's going to Paris.'

Trev patted Zanza on the shoulder. 'Mate, you are a bloody champion.'

'And I speak French, so I am coming along when we go, because we will, won't we?'

'Big fella, yes on both counts. But we can't focus on that hunting trip until first we've caught Reggie Wheeler and second we've actually tracked exactly where Barwick has gone. France is a big place.' Trev watched as Barwick disappeared into the restricted zone and out of sight. 'I am coming for you, arsehole.'

He turned back to Zanza. 'Okay, mate, let's head back to the office and get planning with Harry and Tan. There's a paedophile here who needs to be caught.'

– 3 –

Reggie Wheeler sat on the single bed in the spare room at the Mosman house. Thank goodness for friends like Jackson he was thinking. So wonderful of him to invite Reggie to stay for as long as he wanted, and he even ran any errands Reggie needed, so Reggie could stay safely tucked away out of sight. It was now too dangerous for him to venture out anywhere. That damned ex-cop was hunting him like a hungry barracuda. Both Herbie and Bernie had dropped out of any contact with him. Part of him thought that strange, given how close they'd all been. Another part of him suspected that they were dead, if that ex-cop's zeal was anything to go by. And now his prosecutor mate and lifeline Simon, and that senior cop Hayes, were also dead, although by suicide according to the news, and not the vigilante former pig.

God, it felt as if everything was crashing down around him. And it had all been so good, over there in Laos, and occasionally Cambodia and Vietnam. Such easy pickings. Such exotic little virgins for him to initiate into the sweet world of child love.

Life was so bloody unfair. And society simply didn't understand his ilk. He wasn't a monster. He was a child lover, or a 'minor attracted person' in modern language. At least the ever-increasingly powerful woke movement could describe his kind respectfully. Yes, he was a lover of children. Okay, he had killed the cop's daughter and a couple of others along the way, but only because that was necessary to evade capture. At least he could be himself here with Jackson, who had an extraordinarily fine and wide range of child porn films. He even had some still on the old 8mm celluloid. Ah, there was something magically nostalgic watching those oldies on the projector and screen, the clicking of the reels and the flickering image.

So, staying with Jackson was fine, but Reggie desperately wanted to be back in Asia. How was that going to happen now? His face had been all over the news repeatedly, a wanted man. The cops were after him so the border exit points would all be monitored. And, to top it all, that damned Kenmare and his crew were hunting him, too.

And there was a downside to all the evenings he and Jackson had spent masturbating over kiddie films: his urge for live action was becoming irrepressible. He knew the tipping point was rapidly approaching, the point when his urges would trample over any common sense.

What to do? He hoped like hell the registered letter had arrived. Simon had promised him a load of cash to help him out and Reggie was keeping all his fingers and toes crossed Simon had sent the letter before he plunged to his death.

He heard the front door go and instinctively tensed.

'It's me,' sang out Jackson's voice.

Reggie sighed with relief and opened the door into the hallway.

'Sorry, Reggie, still nothing at the post office.'

'Bugger!'

'Mate, it's been nearly ten days since Simon died, so if he had posted you anything, it would have arrived by now.'

'Yeah, I know. I was just desperately hanging on. I need money to get back to Laos.'

'But how? You can't travel. You're a wanted man.'

'Don't know. Can't go through any airport or seaport, obviously, but there must be a way. Stowaway on a ship, or a people smuggler, or something. But they all need payment, that much I do know. Although I've got a tonne of crypto cash if that's useful. I just don't know how the smuggling works.'

'We'll do some research. And I'm sure someone in my network will know something useful.'

Reggie hugged Jackson. 'Thanks, mate, you're a champion. Now, pizza and porn?'

'Ooh, you naughty boy!' Jackson giggled.

***

Harry lit a smoke and put his feet on his desk. 'So, Father Barwick is headed to France?'

'Yes, brother,' said Trev, relaxing on the office couch. 'Now we need to find a way to track him.'

'And then we're going on a trip!' announced Tanya. 'And, boys, I'll be using the company credit card.'

'Aaagh!' groaned Harry, albeit smiling. 'You in Paris with a credit card. That's a truly scary thought.'

Trev guffawed. 'Downright bloody terrifying, I would have thought.' He tapped on his laptop. 'And that building next to the church in Mosman is a Roman Catholic Church premises. From what I can see from the last council paperwork lodged, although it's years ago, it's got boarding rooms and an admin centre.'

Harry snorted. 'Probably their safehouse for all the pedo priests whilst they figure out where to ship them off to to avoid the authorities.'

'Would be good to find out what's in there in the way of records.'

'All in good time, mate,' said Harry. 'Not minimizing your desire for vengeance, Trev, but the priority right now is Wheeler. We need a plan for him.'

'Of course,' said Trev. 'On the bright side, we didn't see any hint of other surveillance for Wheeler at the Mosman address, so I reckon the Feds don't know about it yet.'

'Exactly. But "yet" is the operative word. It'll only be a matter of time, so we need to move.'

'Right,' said Trev. 'So, Harry, pros and cons of a home invasion tonight?'

Harry looked pensive and exhaled smoke through his nostrils. 'A break-in is always problematic: noise and neighbours. Plus, we've got Conroy in there. And he's what we know about.'

'Yeah, but Wheeler is totally unlikely to emerge himself, at least until he has some strategy to escape from Australia.'

'And the only way for him to realistically do that is by boat,' said Zanza.

'What are you thinking, big fella?' asked Harry.

'I've had some dealings with people smugglers along the way. Best method is an overseas vessel out in international waters and then a local fishing boat does the transfer. It's usually done for people coming in, but it's sure the best option for getting out.'

'But he'd need the contacts, wouldn't he?' asked Tanya.

'Yes, or he could find them,' said Trev. 'This is dark web stuff these days. Anything and everything is for sale there. His ped mates will all be on there for kiddie porn, so he'll find contacts, for sure.'

'So, better we go in tonight,' said Harry. 'Yes, there are risks, but this is the first time we've had him pinned to an address here, plus at this stage we're still in front of the Feds.'

'True, this is the best chance we've had since Laos, so let's do it,' said Trev.

'Cool, we need it to be properly dark, minimize visibility by others, so after eight o'clock. Let's talk details,' said Harry.

– 4 –

Reggie and Jackson had wanked themselves half to death over the movie-length delights of *Convent Violations*. It was a veritable masterpiece, had expounded Jackson, a true gem in his collection: so many moments of utter depravity, overlaid with the giggles of young girls getting introduced to cock.

During the course of the movie, Reggie had achieved three orgasms and he was now exhausted. Bed called.

'Night, Jackson, I'm going to turn in.'

'No worries, Reggie. Want a cocoa to take with you?'

'That'd be lovely, mate.'

'I'll go fix it for you.' Jackson walked off to the kitchen.

Reggie sat on the couch, thinking of the little girls in the convent. Jesus, he needed some action.

Five minutes later, Jackson returned with two mugs of steaming cocoa.

'Reggie, I don't want to be alarmist, but I just had a look at the monitor for my cameras out front and there's a silvery van sitting on the opposite side of the road with someone in it, I think. A bit strange in this street at this time of night, don't you reckon?'

A worried-looking Reggie stood up. 'Hell yes. Let's have a look.'

After they had both peered at the monitor screen for the CCTV system, including zooming in on the back of the van and the side window on an angle, Jackson pulled out his phone and made a call.

'This is a code Kentucky Fried,' he said into the phone. He recited the van's rego plate.

A minute later he hung up. 'It's registered to some company name, which is what the cops do with their surveillance vehicles.'

'Shit, how did you get that checked?'

Jackson gave a sly smirk. 'A like-minded fellow in the state vehicle registry. Owes me heaps for a number of juicy films.'

He looked back at the screen. 'Reggie, without wanting to sound paranoid, but you are on the run and the piggies no doubt know we've got some connection. I reckon that's the Feds watching the house.'

Reggie put his head in his hands. 'Shit, I'd better move. Somewhere.'

'Mate, relax, I've got a secret gate in the corner of the back fence. It goes into the neighbour's at the back. I had it installed years ago when that house was empty. Never know when you'll need an escape route. You can scoot up the side of their house and onto the street behind.'

'Bloody perfect, Jackson. Thank you. I'll go grab my stuff.'

Fifteen minutes later, Reggie hugged Jackson goodbye on the back steps.

'Have you got somewhere to go, Reggie?'

'Yeah, I've got an old aunty over in Lane Cove. She'll be happy to see me, and she's on her own, so she won't ask any questions.'

'Okay, you take care, mate. Call me tomorrow, and we can make some enquiries about getting you out of the country. I'll send you a contact in the meantime. Dark web, of course.'

'Thanks, Jackson, you're a champion. Call you tomorrow.' And then Reggie was down the steps and trotting over to the back fence. He found the gate latch under some creeper leaves and let himself into the back neighbour's yard. There was light coming from the back windows and he waited in the shadows, observing. Several minutes went past and he saw no one moving inside. He strode rapidly along the side of the house, up the front driveway and onto the street.

Whilst Jackson was right about the covert vehicle registration set up, what Jackson and Reggie didn't know was the Feds didn't have any silvery VW vans. Nor did the two peds know the human contents of the grey VW van were infinitely more dangerous than any police ever would be.

– 5 –

By eleven that evening, Cardinal Street was cemetery quiet and almost totally dark, thanks to plenty of trees and the typically useless street-lighting in the older Sydney suburbs.

'Okay, gloves and masks on, team,' said Harry, sitting in the passenger seat of the VW van.

'Back door lock is likely to be easier than the front,' said Trev, 'so I'm around there with the lockpicks with both of you.' He motioned to Tanya and Zanza crouched in the back. 'Harry's at the front just in case of a runner. As soon as we're in, Tan you're straight up the hallway to the front to let Harry in. We'll hope it's not deadlocked, although like most people he'd probably leave the key in it.'

'Then, babe, as soon as we've got Wheeler, you're out to the van and back it into the driveway, as far as you can.'

'Anything else for me?' asked Zanza.

'Just try to look bloody scary, mate,' said Harry.

They all laughed.

Tanya put her hand on his shoulder. 'Yeah, two hundred centimetres of muscly black dude appearing in the middle of the night. That should do the trick.'

'Believe me, I can do so much worse than scary.'

'We're counting on that, Zanza. Okay, team, let's roll,' said Harry.

After opening the unlocked screen door, Trev knelt and looked at the old brass door handle on the back sunroom door. He gently tried it, but it was locked.

He pulled a leather pouch out of the zipped pocket on his black hoodie and slid out two lockpicks. He went to work. It took under than ten seconds. He repocketed the tools and pulled his .357 out of its shoulder holster. He turned the handle and eased the door open.

All three faces cringed as the old door hinges creaked.

Trev cocked his ear to the inside that was in almost complete darkness. The internal door between the sunroom and the kitchen was open and Trev could see the green microwave oven clock glowing on a benchtop. There was a clear view along the dark hallway to the front door, with the moonlight glowing through the front glass panels.

A loud snort followed by snoring floated down the corridor.

Trev levelled his revolver and checked the sunroom as he stepped through it. He likewise cleared the kitchen and motioned Tanya towards the hallway.

She tiptoed along it and got to the front door without even one squeaky floorboard. In the dim moonlight she could see a chain below the old night-latch lock. She held her breath as she slowly slid the chain along its runner, pulled it out and lowered it to the door frame. There was a faint click as she turned the latch and then Harry was inside, his .38 in his hand.

There were five doorways off the hall, all of them open.

Trev motioned Zanza, in whose hand the 9mm Beretta looked like a small toy gun, towards the first door. Trev stayed on point at the kitchen end of the hall.

Tanya pointed at herself and then at the door nearest her and nearest the front door. Logically in an old house like this it was the living room.

Harry nodded at her.

She lifted her five-shot .38 and gingerly stepped through the doorway.

Zanza emerged from his room giving the all-clear sign.

The snoring, coming from the front room opposite the lounge, had increased in volume and now sounded like a water buffalo in a mating ritual.

Zanza stepped into the second door along from him and was out in a second, giving the all clear and motioning as if taking a piss.

Tanya came out of the lounge and gave the clear sign.

Trev, followed by Zanza, went to the opposite door towards the back.

Harry held his breath as Trev re-emerged, shaking his head as he walked towards Harry.

He put his mouth to Harry's ear. 'Mate, reckon he's flown the coop. That was the spare bedroom and no sign of a guest in there. This front room will be the main bedroom, and I don't think they'll be sharing a bed.'

'Fuck!' whispered Harry. 'Let's see what Conroy has to say.'

He motioned Zanza to them. As the big man leant down so Harry could whisper, the snoring suddenly stopped.

Trev levelled his Magnum at the doorway and they all paused.

After about ten seconds, there was a gasping noise and the water buffalo resumed its chant.

'Time to be real scary, big fella,' whispered Harry.

Zanza grinned and they followed him into the last room.

Jackson Conroy was sound asleep, enjoying a dream about obscenely young flesh. It was sublime in its depraved way.

Something disturbed his brain. It seemed to be light on the other side of his eyelids. Something tapped his cheek. He opened his eyes as he came out of his deviant reverie. A gloved hand clamped over his mouth. His vision focused and he looked into a large black face.

The black visage hissed at him. 'You make any sound at all, I will hurt you, and hurt you real badly. Understand?'

Jackson nodded, at least as much as he could move his head under the hand that was like a lead weight. He felt as if he were going to shit himself. Then he felt the warmth around his crotch as he wet the bed.

The gloved hand lifted from his mouth. He looked past the black man, who was utterly huge, and saw two white guys and a young woman.

The stockier of the white men stepped over towards the bed. 'Get out of bed, Conroy.'

Jackson slowly complied, sitting on the side of the bed in his greyish stained Y-fronts now soaked with urine.

'Stand up.'

He did so, looking nervously between the four faces all staring at him.

'He's already pissed himself,' said the other white man. 'He won't last long.'

The stocky one stuck his finger, also gloved, into Jackson's chest. 'Now, my paedophile friend, where the fuck is your mate, Reggie Wheeler?'

Jackson looked at the black giant next to him. The ebony face was smirking and the man was flexing his fingers in front of him. He looked as if he were enjoying himself.

Jackson had a visceral fear of physical pain. His only stint in prison—one term of jail was a remarkable run, given his number of victims—had given him that psychological scar for the rest of his life. Not to mention the physical scars. The segregation wing of prison for the peds was usually okay, until two corrupt cops were sent down and also had to go into seg. Jackson hadn't realized who they were until it was too late: after he'd mouthed off over the meal table about the fascist pigs who were obsessed with locking up child-loving men like himself. Later that night he was dragged into the showers and had the living shit kicked out of him and had a mop-handle enema. No, he wasn't having pain again.

He looked away from the black man to the white one. 'He's gone.'

'When?'

'This evening.'

'Why?'

'We saw a van outside in the street. Reggie said it was the Feds. He's wanted, but I guess you know that.'

'Describe the van,' said the thinner white guy.

'A big silver-coloured one. I think it was a Volkswagen.'

The stocky one resumed. 'Where did Reggie go?'

'I don't know, honestly I don't.' He glanced nervously at the black monster.

'Like hell you don't. Give him a tickle, big fella.'

The behemoth lunged and grasped Jackson by the throat.

'Okay, okay,' he wheezed.

The grip relaxed, but the hand stayed.

'So, where?'

'He went to an aunt's place. In Lane Cove. But that's all I know, I swear to god.'

The black guy took his hand away and turned to his white friend next to him. 'Want me to hurt him, make him talk more?'

Jackson dropped to his knees, hands together in pleading supplication. 'No, no, I don't know anything else.' He blubbered. 'I've got Reggie's phone number. Does that help?'

'Where's your phone?' said the thinner white man.

'On charge in the lounge room.'

The thin man walked out and returned with his phone. He came over to Jackson and handed it to him. 'Unlock it.'

The black man bent down. 'And no funny business, or I will enjoy making you suffer.'

Jackson didn't need the reminder. Funny business was the last thing on his mind right now: he simply wanted to survive the middle-of-the-night intrusion. He whimpered involuntarily as he keyed in the code. He passed it back to the man who tapped on the screen.

'And, *voilà*, no more security.'

The stocky bloke pointed at him. 'Conroy, get on the bed and stay there. You move or even make a noise, our big friend here is going to be left alone with you.'

Jackson scampered back onto the mattress and cowered against the wall. The four intruders moved into the hallway and into a huddle. Jackson couldn't hear more than a murmur. The black guy kept looking at him.

'So, Wheeler's gone to Lane Cove, maybe. But I don't think Conroy is lying or knows anything extra,' said Harry.

'Agreed,' said Trev. 'The prospect of Zanza here was more than a weak prick like him was going to risk. So, it's back to bank lady for any updates, that's our best bet.'

Zanza grinned. 'And a sure bet from my end. I think Lorraine is still recovering from out last encounter. But with a smile on her face.'

Tanya chuckled. 'I bet she is. Probably be at least a week before she can walk normally again.'

'At least we know the van in the street was us, and no Feds in sight,' said Harry.

'Yet, brother, yet. But they won't be far off.'

'Now the problem is Conroy,' said Harry.

'Because he's seen us?' asked Tanya.

'No, I'd thought that bit through before. He wouldn't want to call the cops and for them to visit here since I'm sure there's a treasure trove of kiddie porn. Plus, enough threats of revenge from us, and he'd just want to put this visit behind him. No, the problem is that he'll tip Wheeler off as soon as we're out of here, even if we take his phone. He'll find a way.'

'Yeah, there's a landline in the kitchen,' said Trev.

Tanya smiled, with a glint in her eye. 'I'll sort this out.'

'Tan, no gun shots, not even muffled ones.'

'Come on, Trev, do I look stupid?'

Harry grinned. 'Mate, you'd be the stupid one to answer that the wrong way.'

'Of course not, Tan,' said Trev. 'I'm merely acknowledging your enthusiasm at dispatching rock spiders.'

'While I like guns, this girl's got a wider range of skills.' She walked off to the kitchen and turned on a pocket torch. She disappeared from view. She was back a moment later with a heavy-duty, black plastic bin bag.

'You okay to help me, Zanza?'

'You bet.'

Tanya walked back into Conroy's bedroom with Zanza right behind her. She stood a metre away from the bed, the plastic bag behind her back, and glared at Conroy.

'Okay you pedo scumbag, or should I be calling you a "minor attracted person"?' She did the air quotes with one hand, the other remaining behind her back. 'Apparently that's where political correctness has got us to. Fucking ridiculous, these woke wankers.'

Conroy stared at her. 'I can't help it. That's the way I am. Please try to understand.'

She pointed at him. 'Understand? Fuck you. Get over here, you piece of shit, and kneel in front of me. And lose the jocks. I want you naked.'

Conroy looked utterly confused, on top of terrified. He kept staring at Tanya, wide-eyed like a possum caught in the headlights. The competing emotions made him hesitant.

'For fuck's sake,' said Tanya. She motioned to Zanza.

He took one step and said, 'Move, scum.'

'Okay,' whined Conroy, peeling off his underwear and scrabbling off the bed. He knelt in front of Tanya as instructed.

She looked at Zanza. 'Hold his arms and keep him on his knees.'

Zanza stepped behind Conroy and dropped to one knee, grasping the paedophile's wrists together and pulling downwards.

Conroy whimpered and momentarily closed his eyes, expecting some form of serious pain. He reopened his eyes in the second Tanya whipped the plastic bag out from behind her back and over his head. His whimper became a shriek, albeit a short-lived one. It was swiftly stifled by Tanya getting the bag over his head and pulling the edges tight around his throat and neck.

Conroy tried desperately to struggle, but even Hercules would have succumbed to Zanza's strength. Conroy's breathing became more laboured as the oxygen depleted.

Harry turned to Trev. 'She never, ever ceases to both amaze and impress.'

'That's our Tan.'

Conroy slumped.

Tanya held on to the bag for a little longer, then checked for a pulse.

She released her gloved hand from holding the bag. She looked at Zanza. 'Let's move him over to the edge of the bed and turn him so he's propped up facing the mattress, but knees still on the floor. As if he's praying.'

Zanza snorted. 'A bit late for that for him, but okay.'

He lifted Conroy and propped him up as requested. He went to remove the plastic bag.

'No,' said Tanya. Zanza frowned. In the doorway, so too did Harry and Trev.

She knelt next to Conroy and tied the edges of the bag into a knot at the side of his neck. She took his lifeless right hand and wrapped his fingers around his flaccid penis. She checked her handiwork and, satisfied, stood up. 'These gloves are so going in the bin.'

Zanza was nodding. 'Ah, now I see, brilliant idea.'

Trev caught on next. 'Oh, yes, that is clever. Death by auto-eroticism. Such risk-taking behaviour, Mister Conroy.'

Finally, the penny dropped for Harry. 'Like I said, our Miss Roberts never ceases to impress.'

'I'll grab any devices I can find,' said Trev. 'And then we need to piss off.'

'Yeah, I don't think the cops will put too much intellectual rigour into a paedophile's death by misadventure. Since we're here, anyway, let's have a quick search for anything else glaringly of interest. Torches only, and make sure the blinds or curtains are closed.'

'I'll do in here,' said Tanya.

'No worries. Zanza, you take the lounge and the other room on that side. I'll do the spare room. And no sign the place has been searched. We don't want any red flags for whenever the cops finally take a look.'

– 6 –

The smell of coffee and hot croissants filled the Kenmare and Associates office the next morning as the foursome regrouped.

'Nice little bonus,' said Trev. 'Gotta love a guy who doesn't trust banks.' He pointed at the open shoe box on the coffee table, full of wads of banknotes.

'How much?' asked Tanya.

'Two hundred and twenty-five thousand, in bundles of five grand,' said Trev.

Harry, feet on his desk, beamed. He lit a cigarette. 'Sweet. Okay, ten grand each spending money, rest in the safe for a rainy day. All cool with that?'

Everyone agreed.

Trev passed out bundles of cash and went over to the office safe with the rest.

'Big fella,' said Harry, 'your priority is to shmooze with luscious Lorraine. We need Wheeler's whereabouts confirmed.'

'No worries, Harry, she said she'd help anytime I wanted. Only one condition.'

'What's that?' asked Trev.

'Those two friends of hers who want me: I have to deliver ASAP as apparently they are gagging for it.'

Everyone laughed.

'First World problem,' said Trev.

Harry pointed at Zanza. 'Mate, we call that a perk, not a problem. You cool with it?'

The huge African smile lit up the room. 'Of course. They're both hot chicks, too, I saw their photos. Also, I need to do some extra shifts at the club, Mama needs me. The Kenyan guy she's been using has had to go home to visit family.'

'No worries. You keep us posted on anything from Lorraine, and we'll let you know as soon as we're ready to move on Wheeler again.'

'Cool.' Zanza looked at his watch. 'Better run, guys.' He swallowed his coffee and headed out the door.

'Since we have to wait for news on Wheeler, I'd really like to do some work on tracking Father Barwick,' said Trev.

'Absolutely, mate. Let's finish our brekkie and then go snoop on that church building in Mosman.'

'Thanks, Harry. I need this.'

'Yes, I know. And I'm going to call His Eminence. He's got contacts in the Catholic Church, so he might be able to find out more about that building.'

'Cool. I need to sort out some of the surveillance gear after the last couple of days, so I'll shoot back to my place for that and pick you guys up out front in about an hour.'

'No worries, Trev.'

Trev left and Harry got on the phone to Liam. He swung his chair around and gazed out the grimy window. 'Your Eminence, how the hell are you?'

Tanya stood up from the couch and locked the office door.

'Your Eminence, I've got an address for a church premises in Mosman and we need to find out what the building is for. It's next to a church, but looks admin in that sixties or seventies style.' Harry listened and then gave Liam the address. 'Yep, drinks tonight at the Emerald Bar.

It's long overdue.' Harry listened and smiled. 'Yes, Your Eminence, of course it'll be my bloody shout. See you there.' Harry hung up and swung back around to his desk.

Tanya was standing there stark naked.

Harry sat in stunned silence as she paraded magnificently around the two desks, kissed him on the lips and plonked her beautiful behind on his desk blotter, pushing the keyboard to the side. She put a foot on each arm of his chair opening her crotch directly in front of his gaze and slid forwards towards him.

'Now, Mister PI, it's been all work and no play around here recently. Not the company ethos I had grown used to at Kenmare and Associates. And this employee has a ravenously hungry pussy.' She pouted at him.

He began to open his mouth.

She raised her hand to silence him. 'No, no talking. We have plenty of time before Trev gets back here. Eat me!'

'Yes, ma'am.'

Harry dived into his favourite version of paradise, what he had nicknamed 'Xanadu', in tribute to his favourite band, ELO. He set his tongue to work on Tanya's clitoris.

She quietly sang the song, which was her tribute to Harry's devotion to pleasuring her.

Harry was damned well-practiced at this art form and he knew exactly how Tanya liked it, including the teasing of her anus with the tip of his finger. His trousers were straining with his erection.

Five minutes later, she spasmed and yelled her orgasmic delight, although the lyrics to 'Xanadu' had long departed from Olivia Newton John's rendition. She finally pushed Harry's head away. 'Oh, so damned good, my hunky Harry, and I seriously needed that. Now I need a good, hard length. Think you're up to it?'

Harry was already up, in both ways, and he lowered his trousers and boxers in one movement, manoeuvring over his boner.

'Oh, yes!' he sighed as he plunged his cock into Tanya's saturated pussy. He didn't even last three minutes: it had indeed been all work and no play of recent. He groaned as he exploded inside her.

'Fuck, I needed that, too.'

'It'll do nicely for the moment, Harry. But I'm going to need a lot more tonight.'

'At your service, babe. Always.'

'Damned right. Now, back to work.' She gave him a cheeky grin as she reached for the tissue box on the desk.

Trev had swapped to the older, white VW van for the return to Cardinal Street, as he didn't want to risk the bigger grey van being seen back on the street in case someone found Conroy's body.

The three sleuths were now sitting in the van within easy view of the church and its neighbouring building.

It had been over an hour, and nothing had stirred, when Harry's phone rang. 'G'day, Liam.' He listened. 'Thank you, Your Eminence, see you tonight.' Harry hung up.

'Okay, the building next door is, as we thought, a church property. It's an admin centre for the Sydney diocese and also a boarding facility for visiting priests.'

'Great work by Liam,' said Trev. 'Well, judging by the two cars in the front car park, there are some people working in there.'

'And we have movement,' announced Harry.

Tanya hit the start button on the video camera.

A young Thai woman emerged from a side door, pushing a blue wheelie bin. She positioned it in front of an area signposted for deliveries. She went back inside.

Trev peered through his binos. 'It's a secure document bin. I can see the lock.'

'Here she comes again,' said Tanya.

The woman pushed a second blue bin out and set it next to the first one. She returned inside the building.

'Another security bin,' said Trev. 'I'd love to get hold of them, bet there'd be some interesting reading inside. Anything the good old Catholic Church deems worthy of shredding.'

'Yeah, but that won't be happening,' said Harry. 'Here's the document destruction van to collect them.'

'Shit, they've got it timed to perfection,' said Trev.

A red Ford Transit van pulled into the car park and backed into the loading zone. A guy hopped out with a clipboard.

The side door to the building opened and a rotund priest in a cassock stepped out.

The van driver ripped a sheet off the clipboard and handed it to the cleric, who promptly went back inside.

The driver loaded the two bins into the van and drove away.

Another hour of inactivity passed. Both the guys were dozing now with Tanya taking her turn on point.

'Wakey, wakey, boys, hands off snakey. Here comes the Thai chick again, and looks as if she's done for the day.'

Trev sat up. 'Righto, we need to lean on her, bribe her, whatever. We want to know exactly what goes on in that place and what the go is with the document bins.'

'We're not going to grab her in broad daylight, surely?' asked Tanya. 'Poor girl will be petrified.'

'No, of course not. You and Harry are going to follow her. My bet is she'll be heading for the bus stop, 'cos she won't be living in this gold-lined ghetto. Then you approach her, Tan. Use cash if you need to. Always talks.' Trev opened a case next to him and pulled out a thick yellow wad of fifties.

'Shit, a girl could happily go shopping instead,' grinned Tanya, taking the bundle of banknotes.

'And, Harry, you got one of those fake police IDs? On the off chance she doesn't like the cash incentive, I'm sure you can scare the shit out of her over her visa status.'

'Mister Matson, I do so love your devious mind.'

'My pleasure, Mister Kenmare. I smell a priest I need to meet. Father Barwick has a date with destiny.'

Tanya and Harry slipped out of the van and walked in the direction of the Thai girl.

The L90 bendy bus pulled into the stop at Spit Junction. Tanya stood right behind the Thai girl, hoping there'd be two empty seats together on the bus. Harry was a couple of metres away, amidst the group waiting for the bus.

The girl tapped her Opal card on entering the bus and Tanya did likewise, following her target up the aisle. The girl grabbed the first empty double seat and sat in against the window. She looked a bit surprised as Tanya slid in next to her, ignoring the empty seats across the aisle. Harry took one of them. The bus moved off along Military Road heading for the city. In its wake was the white VW van.

'Hi,' said Tanya to her neighbour.

The girl smiled nervously.

'You from Thailand?'

'Yes.'

'A lovely country.'

'Thank you.'

'That building you work in, what is it?'

The girl turned to look at Tanya, a mixture of stunned and anxious written across her face.

'Listen, girlfriend, I want some information about that building, and I can pay you for it.' She opened her small handbag to reveal the wad of pineapples.

The girl's eyes gazed at the yellow banknotes. 'Why you want to know?'

'Honey, I just do. It's part of the church, isn't it?'

The girl nodded.

'And what do you do there?' Tanya folded two fifties and pushed them into the girl's hands resting in her lap.

'Cleaning and helping in the office.'

'And those blue bins you put outside?'

The girl looked alarmed.

Tanya smiled at her. 'We've been watching. Don't worry, we're not interested in you, just the building and what happens in there.'

The girl nodded again.

Tanya tapped her purse. 'You want some more of this?'

There was more vigorous agreement now.

'Where do you get off the bus?'

'Wynyard.'

'Cool, we can talk more when we get off, then.'

– 7 –

Tanya motioned to a bench in Wynyard Park. 'Let's sit. What's your name?'

'Boonsiri.'

Harry stood a couple of metres away smoking, keen to not intimidate the girl too much, at least not unless it became necessary.

'Boonsiri, me and my boss there do investigations.'

'You are police?' The girl's voice quivered.

'No, but like police. So, tell me what goes on in that office and about those blue bins.'

The girl talked.

When she'd finished, Harry stepped away and got on his phone. 'Trev, it seems the place does all the admin for the church staffing across Australia. Those document bins are full of stuff that's been scanned and digitized.'

'Harry, we need to know exactly what sort of copier-scanner machine it is in there.'

'Why?'

'I'll explain later. But she needs to photograph the machine, and then I've got a plan.'

'Roger.'

Harry hung up. He sat next to Tanya on the end of the bench. 'What's your phone number, young lady?'

Boonsiri told him. He tapped it into his iPhone and rang her.

'Cool. Now we can contact you. And if my number appears on your screen, you answer my call, yes?'

'Yes.'

'We can also find where you are at any time. Understand?'

She bobbed her head again, looking even less happy now.

'So, this is what we need, and it's nothing too hard. You at work there tomorrow?'

'Yes.'

'Good. The copier machine that they scan all the documents on, can you take a picture of it for us?'

'I'm not sure I should, they would not like that.'

'They don't need to know. You just wait for the room to be empty and all you need is a few seconds.'

Tanya put her hand on the girl's. 'Best listen to what my boss says.'

'A thousand dollars sound good?' asked Harry.

Boonsiri turned sharply and looked at him. 'Yes.'

'So, you'll take the photos for us?'

She hesitated.

'Do we need to check on your visa?' growled Harry.

Hesitation turned to abject fear. 'No, no, please.'

'Didn't think so. Good. So, the photos?'

'Yes, okay.'

'You send me the photos as soon as you can. Then when you finish work, my colleague here will meet you and give you a thousand dollars. Okay?'

'Yes.'

'Good girl.'

Harry and Tanya walked back into the office.

'Ah, the diplomatic corps return. How are Aussie-Thai relations right now?'

Harry laughed. 'A tad strained, perhaps, but we argued from a position of strength.'

'So, Trev, what's the go with the copier machine?' asked Tanya.

'I have a plan so cunning it almost outfoxed me.'

'All ears, brother.'

Trev pointed at the copier in the corner of the room.

'So, these modern copiers that also print and scan actually have a hard drive in them.'

'So?'

'Harry, you lascivious Luddite, documents that are printed or scanned go onto the hard drive first, and they stay there until it's full and has to overwrite itself or until it's wiped.'

'All right. So, we need the hard drive. But doing an after-hours burg is not on given there are probably priests living there at any given time.'

'Exactly. Enter Mister Cunning here.'

'And why did we ask the girl to photograph it?' interjected Tanya.

'Getting there, Tan. So, as soon as we know the make and model, we source an identical one. Then we get polo shirts made with that company name at the gimmick shirt shop down the street, new magnetic signs for the van, and in we go. The photocopier service crew from hell.'

Harry chuckled. 'Shit, mate, you are seriously good. But how do we arrange a changeover appointment? Surely that would be organized in advance?'

'True. So, we'll just have to bluff our way on that one. Tell them head office arranged it, or something like that. Every big organisation is used to administrative fuck-ups, the church won't be any different. Anyway, we've pulled off much better bluff jobs before.'

'That we have, brother.'

'We copy the hard drive, wipe it clean, and deliver the machine back after it's had its very special service. The replacement machine goes back to our source of short-term rentals, after we've copied its hard drive as well.'

'Cool. So, nothing more to do now until we know the machine details?'

'Yep. And if that photo doesn't come through from the Thai girl tomorrow, then you two will need to lean on her.'

'I think it'll be fine,' said Tanya. 'I saw the look of fear in her eyes when Harry mentioned visas, so I think we hit the right pressure point. He does tend to do that with the ladies.'

They all laughed.

'See, Mister Matson, even Luddites have skills.'

'Point conceded, Mister Kenmare. Now let's head for the Emerald Bar for dinner and a drink with Liam.'

– 8 –

After a fine dinner in the restaurant section of the Emerald Bar, the three sleuths went out to the beer garden, grabbing drinks on the way.

His Eminence, Liam Doolan, was already ensconced at a table enjoying a Guinness and a cheroot. 'Ah, my favourite detective agency, welcome!' He looked at Tanya. 'And you, my angel, are the true oil painting in an otherwise unattractive team.'

'Well, Liam, someone has to brighten up the ensemble.'

'We've got feelings you know,' grinned Trev.

'Righto,' said the big Irishman.

'And lovely to see you, too, Your Eminence,' said Harry.

The all sat down.

'So, Your Eminence, have you had a chance to speak to your church contacts?' asked Trev.

'Indeed, I have.'

At that moment, the bar manager, Shaun, swung past collecting empty glasses. 'Make the most of smoking out here, guys. New rules on the way in a few months. It's going to be no smoking anywhere except the gaming room.'

'What?' said Tanya.

The men sat there looking stunned.

'Yep, the government doesn't want to discourage the gamblers 'cos there's way too much tax revenue at stake there.' Shaun headed back inside.

'Fucking government wankers,' said Harry.

'Never a truer word,' added Liam.

'So, Your Eminence, the church staff? Rather close to my heart, this enquiry.'

'Yes, Trev, I understand. What I have found out is your Father Barwick has likely been sent to France permanently, to hide in plain sight effectively.'

'Why France? Why not the Vatican?' asked Trev.

'Well, it's one of the few truly secular countries that is nominally Catholic. So, the church is there but no one really takes too much interest. It's low profile, if you like. Far less likely to cause waves than if he were in Rome and anything happened or came to light. My source tells me it's likely he'll be sent to some small provincial town in the south or east of the country to help out at the local church.'

'Can your source find out any specifics?'

'Alas, no. But I assume you reprobates will be heading over there?'

'Hell yes!' said Trev.

Harry was smiling.

'Good,' said Liam. 'The bastard church, they have made an art form out of hiding their paedophile priests away from justice.'

'Oh, this piece of shit has a juggernaut of justice coming for him,' said Trev.

'Well, when you do go over there, my contact did mention an investigative journalist at *Le Monde* who has done a heap of work on child abuse in the church there. I reckon she'd be a great starting point.'

A couple of well-oiled hours later, Harry lay naked in his bed. He'd completed his instructed task of inserting the string of anal beads into Tanya and she was on all fours about to straddle his chest.

'Now, Mister PI, all that good stuff we didn't have time for at the office today.'

Harry chuckled. 'I hope you're not expecting to get paid overtime, young lady.'

Tanya smiled as she parked her crotch on Harry's face. 'Payment with your tongue, boss, and nice and slowly with the beads, I want the pleasure to last.'

Harry tried to utter, 'Yes, babe,' but Tanya's swollen, wet labia had enveloped his mouth and a muffled grunt was all he could emit as he plunged into the joy of cunnilingus.

– 9 –

Two days later, at the church centre in Mosman, Father Bernard Firth had finished an excellent lunch of lasagna and salad made by the Italian cook, Rosa, who came in every day to feed the resident priests, of which there were invariably a couple at least, as well as himself. Father Firth's minor part-time job was to assist Father Angelo Puglia in the running of the church next door. His full-time role was as the manager of the rectory and clergy house along with its administration office and records archive.

Visiting priests comprised those attending courses at the Sydney seminary and those whose presence needed to be strictly covert. And Father Firth did enjoy chatting to those ones, given his shared proclivities. Whilst this was one hell of a cushy church job, the one serious downside was a lack of ready access to kids, as it wasn't his parish. Mind you, his last parish was the main reason he was posted here. And he had been told by the Archbishop to 'damned well' keep his head down. And he had.

He belched discreetly, thanked Rosa for the lovely lunch, and went back to his office. The cleaner, Boonsiri, was dusting in there.

'Ah, Boon, nearly all done for the day?'

'Yes, Father. Be done in five minutes, just have to empty the bins.'

'Good girl. And if you'd like some lunch, run along to the dining room. Rosa's lasagna is superb, and as always she has cooked tonnes of it.'

Boonsiri smiled. 'Thank you, Father.' She wheeled her cleaning cart out and disappeared.

Father Firth sat at his desk. As he was reading the latest bulletin from the Vatican, the buzzer for the service door sounded. He sighed and walked out into the hallway. He opened the door. Two men in matching white polo shirts with 'FUJITSU' printed on them, and wearing similarly badged baseball caps, stood there. The thinner of the two had a clipboard.

'Good afternoon, padre. Hoping we've got the right building. Looking for the church admin centre.'

'Yes, that's here. How can I help you?'

'We're from the Fujitsu Maintenance Hub, padre. We're here to change your copier over for its regular service. We've got a temporary replacement so you won't be inconvenienced.'

'Yes, we'd hate to inconvenience the good work of the Lord,' said the stockier one, stony faced.

'I manage the office here and I didn't request this.' He looked past the men and saw a grey van with Fujitsu written on its side.

The slim one looked at his clipboard. 'Says here the Archbishop's office authorized it, and we've got one to do at the seminary after this one.'

'Ah, okay. What do you need to do?'

'We'll bring in the replacement machine. It's the exact same model, so no changeover issues. We'll take the one here for its service and bring it back in a few days.'

'No problem. Follow me, I'll show you where the machine is.' He turned and headed back to the office.

Trev turned to Harry. 'Okay, George, I'll go get the old one and you back the van up to the door here.'

'No worries, Bill,' said Harry.

Trev walked off after the priest. He shuddered. Even being in a Catholic church building made his skin crawl.

Ten minutes and lots of grunting later, and the two machines were swapped over. The guys climbed into the VW van with its magnetic Fujitsu signs on its sides.

Trev grinned at Harry as he turned the ignition. 'Mate, "the good work of the Lord?" I was so close to pissing myself.'

'Yeah, couldn't resist. As usual, the Kenmare sarcasm was lost on its target, but we enjoyed it.'

'Righto, let's do some really good work of the Lord and see what gems this machine has in its brains.'

The van moved out onto the street.

– 10 –

Elsewhere in the city, in a dimly lit hotel room, Zanza was naked, erect, and busy becoming an uncredited porn star, at least for an exclusive social media group. He'd insisted no face shots, of him anyway, under any circumstances, and Lorraine's two girlfriends, Kathryn and Janet, were strictly obedient. Strictly wet and wanton, too, much to the big man's delight.

Janet was currently on her knees, face buried in a pillow, howling with pleasure as Zanza buried his cock in her pussy from behind with an occasional slap on her large butt cheeks, a special request of hers.

Kathryn, also kneeling on the bed, was using one hand to hold the iPhone filming the enormous black rod doing its business, and the other to massage her clitoris, hoping like hell the big African didn't need too long a break before he was hard again and chock-a-block up her love valley.

Luscious Lorraine had promised Zanza to do another check on Wheeler for him as soon as she saw the video of her two friends getting banged. What she wouldn't get to see was Zanza's gargantuan grin as he relished his strenuous work, using his large, rock-hard tool. And he was getting paid for this by Harry. Coolest job he'd ever had.

Zanza was a natural performer in the virility stakes and within ten minutes of unloading in Janet he was holding Kathryn's thighs apart as he eased himself into her sodden pussy. He enjoyed her moaning as he slid further up her, although he couldn't see the look of delight on her face. She'd made a special request as Zanza laid her on her back: Janet was now sitting on Kathryn's face as she ate the jism from Zanza's first eruption. And Janet was squealing on the way to her third orgasm courtesy of Kathryn's tongue.

'Don't forget the camera, baby,' Zanza reminded Janet. 'Lorraine insisted, remember.'

'No worries.' She grabbed her phone from the bedside table and aimed it at the huge black member thrusting in and out of Kathryn.

'God, the girls are going to cream themselves over these videos,' gushed Janet, still moaning as she rode Kathryn's face.

Kathryn, for her part, made some effort at a vocal contribution, but whatever words were intended were drowned in wet labia and jism.

***

Reggie Wheeler was in a flap. He couldn't find his bank card and he was pretty well out of cash after yesterday's late night urgent escape via a taxi from Mosman to Lane Cove. The card sure wasn't in his wallet and he couldn't find it in any pockets or his travel bag.

Aunty Dora's old house in Gamma Road, Lane Cove, with its back yard bordering the golf course, was quiet except for Reggie rummaging in his stuff. Aunty had been asleep when he turned up ringing the doorbell last night and it had taken a long while for her to answer the door. But when she had finally opened it, she'd smiled, taken the safety chain off, and welcomed him in. She'd hugged him and said, 'Oh, my little Reggie. It's been years, at least since we saw each other. But I do love your regular postcards. Asia looks lovely. Have you got yourself a good Asian girl to settle down with, Reggie?'

'You could say that, Aunty. And how are you?' Reggie kissed her cheek.

'Okay, my Reggie, at least for an old bird like me.'

Reggie had always loved his aunt, especially since she was the only close family member, aside from the cousin he'd recently stayed with, who had not disowned him after his prison sentence all those years ago. And so, he had kept in touch, also realizing the value of a safe port of call back in Oz on his yearly visits.

Aunty was now out for the afternoon playing lawn bowls at the local club.

Reggie stared at his total current possessions spread out on the trundle bed in Aunty's back sunroom: one travel bag with clothes, one wallet, one jacket, his laptop, and his phone.

'Oh, shit!' he suddenly exclaimed to the empty room. He now remembered the last use of his bank card: to pay for viewing access on a dark web child porn forum at Jackson's house yesterday evening. They'd been in the dining room using Jackson's laptop and Reggie could even picture his card lying on the table near the computer. He couldn't remember seeing it since then. And he needed it to get cash from the ATM at the shops.

He rang Jackson's mobile. It went straight to voicemail. 'Hey Jackson, buddy. Think I left my CommBank debit card on your dining table. Give me a call, will you?'

He tried the landline number, but it rang out. He tried four more times over the next hour, all with the same result.

The problem was he couldn't go for a visit. Firstly, he had too little cash for a taxi fare and his card was missing. Secondly, and more importantly, the bastard Feds were watching Jackson's house, the very reason he had slipped away under the cover of darkness last night.

Damn it, he'd have to contact the bank and get an urgent replacement. That carried risks, too, since he'd need to give his aunt's address to get the card mailed or, better still, couriered to him. Or maybe, they'd let him collect it from the bank? Yes, yes that would the best way. And hopefully he could make all the arrangements over the phone. That way he'd only have to go out to the bank when the card was ready. He got online and found the number for the local CommBank branch, which was in Longueville Road only about a ten-minute walk away.

Twenty minutes later, he hung up the phone in frustration. It turned out a call to the local branch landed in some foreign call centre, sounded like Bangalore or some such on the Indian subcontinent. Despite the polite call centre person, and her perfect command of English, she had insisted on his address in order to send the card to him. He'd argued unsuccessfully and terminated the call.

Bugger it! He'd have to walk to the branch to make the application and explain his accommodation was uncertain, hence the need to collect the card when it was ready. Surely that would work, he thought, as he considered all the homeless people who had bank cards. Well, at least a bonus was he'd be able to withdraw some cash over the counter. He got all his ID documents together and headed out the front door.

– 11 –

'That's okay, Rashida, you can go. I'll lock up tonight, as I need to stay back for another bloody online meeting.'

'Thanks, boss,' said the branch deputy manager, picking up her handbag and her sports bag. 'I'll be nice and early for yoga.'

Lorraine closed and locked the glass front door of the branch and walked back to her office, shutting the internal door behind her. She'd done her regular check on the Wheeler account shortly before closing and she needed to give Zanza the latest news.

She picked up her phone. 'Well, hello there my beautiful African hunk.'

Zanza chuckled on the other end. 'Good afternoon, lovely Lorraine. How are you?'

'As horny as hell. But unfortunately my husband's next trip has been cancelled and he won't be away again for another six weeks.'

'Oh, baby, you'll just have to watch the videos over and over.'

'I do already. Why do you think I stay back at work after everyone's gone home? It's sure as shit not because I'm one of those managers who thinks they need to be the last to leave.'

Zanza laughed. 'Your staff might think you are.'

'If only they knew.'

'You like the film of me with your two friends?'

'Oh, you have no idea. And those girls can't stop talking about it. They want more, you know.'

'Cool with me.'

'Janet said she'd even give anal a try.'

'Brave girl, she won't walk right for a month after that.'

'Exactly, which is why my arse is off limits. But Janet couldn't care less. She's always been a bit of a cock junkie, and now she's experienced your beautiful beast, she is hooked harder than a crack whore.'

'How many girls are in this group of yours?'

It was Lorraine's turn to laugh. 'Three more. And I reckon after they've watched Kathryn and Janet getting serviced, they'll be lining up, too.'

'Always ready to please. Now, since you can't make another appointment with me, I'm guessing you must have some new information. Otherwise, you are just tormenting yourself.'

'Very smart, my detective friend. Yes, new info today.'

'Shoot.'

'I will, but first you promise to do phone sex with me afterwards.'

'You're on.'

'So, Mister Wheeler went into our Lane Cove branch this afternoon. He's lost his ATM card and had to apply for a new one.'

'So, we've got an address for him?'

'No, he's obviously a bit too cunning for that. He's arranged to come in and collect it as soon as it arrives. The branch has to call him when it does.'

'And will you know what day that is?'

'Yes, but only the day, not the time they'll call him. All cards are delivered by secure courier first thing, before opening hours. The branches usually call people straightaway as those customers wanting to collect the cards personally are usually in a hurry. When your man turns up will be anyone's guess.'

'Probably very quickly, I think. So, will you check each day?'

'No problems. The system will show when the card is to be couriered, so I can call you the day before. It'll be at least three days yet.'

'Thank you, baby. Now, you want to talk dirty?'

'Give it to me, big boy.'

'Close your eyes and picture this beautiful black rod.'

'Ooh, yes. I like that hard, meaty rod.' Lorraine undid her trouser waistband and slid her hand inside her panties.

'Now I'm pushing apart your thighs, nice and wide, so my huge cock can plunge into your pussy.'

'Oh, I'm so wet!'

'The head of my hard cock is pushing your lips apart and you feel the length slide into you, stretching your tight little pussy wide.'

'Oh, fuck yes!' Lorraine's masturbation grew more frantic.

Zanza continued to describe his penetration of her.

Lorraine moaned and groaned as she wanked furiously.

'Baby, I'm going faster and faster, I'm ready to fill you with my load.'

'Yes, yes, yes!'

She cried out as she climaxed, dropping her phone.

– 12 –

Harry put his phone down.

'Brother, that was Zanza. He's got Lorraine on the job. Wheeler will have to go to the CommBank branch in Lane Cove to collect a replacement bank card.'

'We know which day?'

'Three or four days away, at least. Lorraine will be able to call Zanza on the day before the card is delivered. But we won't know what time they'll call Wheeler.'

'Righto, we'll need to be ready to rock and roll and sit off the bank on the day starting before opening time. He'll be in quick smart if he needs the card.'

'Yep. Never know your luck in a big city, we might get a chance to grab him on his way back from the bank to where he's staying.'

'Maybe, but broad daylight in that sort of area? A decent chance will be a very rare creature indeed. More likely we'll have to tail him so we get the address and then wait until after dark.'

'But we'll be staying on him until we do get to grab him, 'cos I'm not losing this fucker again, Trev.'

'Shit no, mate. We'll get Tan and Zanza in a second vehicle so we've got better capability.'

'Good idea.'

'We'll get him, Harry, we will.'

Harry walked over to the drinks cabinet.

'Mate, the waiting game begins yet again. This is shitting me to tears.'

'Brother, I know. But we *will* get him. And you'll get the final justice Orla deserves.'

Harry poured two Jamesons and took one over to Trev, handing it to him.

'Thanks, mate. Here's to imminent victory.'

'Absolutely,' said Harry. 'We may as well get stuck into the church document haul over the next couple of days then.'

'Yeah. I, too, want to hunt down some justice. So, tomorrow we can take the copier back. I've downloaded its hard drive and it's chock-a-block, mate.'

'Shit, how many documents do we have to go through?'

Trev laughed. 'Harry, my lovely Luddite friend, we have software for all these things. So, to start with, I'll run my search software over all the documents. That will probably do the trick for us.'

'Take long?'

'With the quantity of documents, and the range of searches I've listed, it's probably a twenty-four-hour job. But it all just runs in the background. I started it a couple of hours ago, so maybe around this time tomorrow.'

'Very cool, Trev. Now, we could just not bother taking the copier back. I mean they've got a replacement.'

'Mate, that risks raising suspicions, plus I need to get the other machine back to my contact.'

'Okay, fair enough.'

'Pub, mate?'

'Hell yes.'

'By the way, where's Tan?'

Harry chuckled. 'Visiting Longman's niece, Debbie. Bit of girl action.'

'Ah, that's right, they shagged, didn't they?'

'You bet. And good on her. Savour life to its fullest.'

'Yep, we sure do. Drink to that.' Trev swallowed his whiskey.

'Brother, as our company motto says, "Wouldn't be dead for quids".'

Trev held up a finger. 'Yes, love our motto. Just a minute, Harry, let me dig something out, on that note.'

Harry frowned as Trev hit his keyboard.

A minute later, the printer hummed and spat out a page. Trev walked over and picked it up, taking it over to Harry.

'Looks bloody Latin to me, Trev. I remember my Asterix books as a kid.'

'Yeah, I loved them, too.'

Harry read from the sheet. '*Ne mortuus pro quibus sim.*' He looked at Trev and raised an eyebrow.

'Mate, it's the closest translation to "wouldn't be dead for quids", seriously.'

Harry grinned at him. 'Bloody love it, but how the hell did you come up with this?'

'Had it on my computer. A mate back in the job years ago did the original. We ran with the same motto on our team, and he contacted a classics professor at the uni to get it.'

'And it will suit us admirably. Stick it on the wall, brother.'

Trev pinned it on the cork notice board next to the drinks cabinet and above the bar fridge. He turned back to Harry. 'And for the copier, mate, probably best if I do it on my own.'

'I'm happy to come, team and all that.'

'Yeah, and thanks. But I reckon it'd be better not to risk that Thai girl seeing you in the copier van after seeing you on the bus. In case she opens her mouth, never know what hold those bloody Catholics have over her. We do not need her blabbing all.'

Harry nodded. 'Fair enough, I agree. Now, the pub!'

– 13 –

Their fillet steaks devoured in the restaurant of the Emerald Bar, Harry and Trev now sat in the beer garden.

Harry took a sip of his obscenely large Jameson, a huge measure that everyday punters could never obtain from the bar, and he lit a slim panatella. 'Want one, brother?'

'No thanks, mate, I'll stick with my ciggies. Mind you, once we've got Wheeler, I'll join you with one of those big fat Cubans you've got stashed in the office.'

'Don't worry, Trev, we'll be celebrating long and hard then.'

Trev raised his glass of whiskey. 'Here's to victory for you, Harry.'

'Cheers.'

They chinked glasses.

'So, Trev, tell me more about your hunt, as long as you're happy to, of course.'

'All cool, Harry, share anything with you.'

'And that's why I love you like a brother.'

'But not that sort of brother, Harry!'

They both burst out laughing.

'So, mate, you know what Barwick did to me. And I want vengeance but not like yours.'

'Pray tell.'

They both cackled again.

'Lame, Harry, but still funny.' Trev took a long swig of his drink. 'Your brand of vengeance I'm all in favour of, as you know.'

'Oh yes, Trev, seeing you wield that soldering iron is like poetry in motion.'

'Can't deny I enjoy that. And there is a part of me that wants to kill Barwick.'

'And part doesn't?' Harry looked incredulous.

'That's right. Now, look, the scum you're hunting, execution is not only the best option, it's the only option.'

'Here's to that.' Harry raised his glass and took a mouthful. He drew on his cigar and smoke billowed over the table as he exhaled.

'But Barwick is in a position of power and the church has to be exposed, again, and held to account. Killing him, as much as it would satisfy one part of me, wouldn't help that exposure effort. Hell, for some they'd even be sympathetic to him. No, the vengeance must be on a different level.'

'So, exposure, public shaming, and then death?'

'No. You see, with your scum, there's nothing to expose because they're not part of anything systemic. They're abhorrent sex offenders, yes, but not representative of an organisation of power and respectability.'

'I see your point on that. So, what have you in mind?'

'Still making a plan, Harry. But it has to involve maximum public humiliation for the Church. And I'm talking to the nuclear level.'

'I don't want to be cynical, brother, but ...'

'You cynical? Bugger me, who would've thought?' Trev grinned.

'Only on the days of the week ending in Y, mate. But do you think that will make a difference?'

'I do share your cynicism, but I also believe every public disgrace adds slowly to the momentum in the right direction. Harry, thirty years ago, no one, not even the cops, would have contemplated charging a priest as a paedophile.'

'True, and maybe especially the cops. So, we have made some progress.'

'But not enough, mate. The fucking Catholic hierarchy fights tooth and nail, even in the face of blinding-light reality. And their most effective technique is pretty well as heinous and cruel as the original cover ups.'

'Go on.'

'So, when they can no longer conceal the crimes, they dangle, with a coating of reluctance as thick as the Old Testament, large print version, a sniff of financial compensation. A lot, if not the vast majority, of the victims have had seriously screwed lives that has left them financially vulnerable. So, the Church preys on this with all manner of caveats and non-disclosure agreements. Plus, and this is the real kicker, they then litigate, for bloody ever.'

'Yeah, a couple of weeks back there was a story in the paper about a victim from the fifties who had died before his case was finalized.'

'Exactly! And there have been numerous similar cases. There is no limit to the evil of the wankers who run the Catholic Church.'

'I'd venture the same could be said of any religion and of the Establishment generally. Mind you, all the churches are inherently intertwined with the Establishment anyway.'

'Power, mate, as we frequently discuss.'

'Yep, power and corruption.'

'Mate, I know at least two guys from the survivors support group I'm part of who have taken their own lives whilst battling the Church in court. And they were both in my age group.'

'Fricking tragic. I think we need some more booze.'

'Do bears shit? Your buy, Mister Kenmare.'

'Roger that, Mister Matson.' Harry put his half-smoked cigar in the ashtray and went inside to the bar.

Trev lit a smoke and gazed at the stars in the clear night sky.

Harry was back a couple of minutes later with two 'double' Jamesons, extra-special service.

'Cheers, brother.'

They chinked glasses.

'So, what cunning bits of the plan have you come up with so far, Trev?'

'Well, obviously we have to locate the bastard first. But hopefully in the morning when we get into the office, the search tool will have found something in its scan of all those documents.'

'And then I guess we'll be off to France, assuming that's where he has ended up.'

'*Oui, oui, monsieur* Harry!'

'Tanya will love me for that work trip.'

'She loves you already in her own wonderful way.'

'As I do her, mate. In my own Harry way.'

Trev laughed. 'Gotta say, you two have a beautiful relationship that fits in none of the textbooks.'

'Yeah, tried some of them, and they can piss off. All the mind games and power plays and insecurities and self-interest.'

'Don't worry, us gay guys don't miss out on all that shit either.'

'I'm sure. That's because it's human nature. But with Tanya, there's this, well I can only speak for myself, I can't and would never speak for her, there's this mutual respect and an animal magnetism I've never experienced before. About as close to perfection as a relationship can get, I reckon.'

'Well, Tan certainly feels the same way, she's told me. I'm just jealous, brother.'

'Trev, my friend, you'll find happiness again. And probably when you least expect it.'

'Cheers to that.'

They drank.

– 14 –

Friday morning at the office was Kenmare minus associates. Harry sat at his desk with a coffee and surfed the newspapers online. Trev had headed off to Mosman with the copier machine. Tanya was presumably having a sleep in, or morning sex, with Debbie. And Zanza had been on shift at Club Mammary, so would be sleeping until lunchtime.

His phone rang. Tanya. 'Hi, babe. Still in bed?'

'Of course, the sixty-niner action here is to die for. If you don't need me this morning, for work that is, I'll come in after lunch. Okay?'

'Okay? More than okay. I've got myself a visual image of you and Debbie right now.'

'Now, now, boss, no masturbating at your desk.'

Harry laughed. 'Consider it a lawful and reasonable direction of your boss that you spend the entire morning drowning in pussy juice.'

'I'll do that, Harry. Kisses and see you this arvo.'

'Have fun, babe.'

'I will. Oh, by the way, did you ever call that hot Finnish wench?'

'Anna? No, she'd slipped my mind with that's been going down. She did actually leave me her number a little while back.'

'Well, as long as you're not getting too old to chase the ladies,' she teased him.

'Ouch!'

'Ciao, Mister PI.'

Harry put the phone down and smiled as he recalled Anna from the café, the visual of her gorgeous Viking visage replacing the glistening, tangled bodies of Tanya and Debbie.

He lit a smoke and picked up the phone again. It rang half a dozen times and Harry was expecting the voicemail to kick in.

A slightly flustered Scandinavian accent came on the line instead. 'Hello?'

'Anna from Helsinki, with a face so beautiful she could launch a hundred Viking ships. It's private detective Harry looking for you. How does that sound?'

'Harry? I thought you'd forgotten about me. And only a hundred Viking ships?'

Harry could see her mock pout down the phone. He chuckled. 'Definitely not forgotten, Anna, just been incredibly busy.'

'Looking for things?'

'Always looking, you gorgeous girl.'

'Flattery will get you everywhere.'

'Just what I was hoping. At my age, that along with charm are about my only weapons. Oh, and did I mention the tongue?'

'No, but I'm listening.'

'Cool, how about meeting up?'

'Yes, absolutely. I'm actually in the café we met in. I'm waiting for my coffee.'

'Okay, I'm in my office that is three doors up the street, and I'm alone all morning.'

'Oh, cool, I've never seen a detective's office.'

Harry wondered if she'd ever seen a detective's naked body, but he kept that to himself. 'Any chance of another coffee?'

'Yes, of course.'

Harry gave her his coffee order, promising to pay when she arrived, and the directions to his office.

He texted Trev.

> Brother, don't come back to the office until after lunch. Not before 1300.

> What are you up to, you rascal?

> I'm hoping to be up to a whole lot. A Finnish visitor.

> Harry, you are fucking unbelievable. Enjoy. And don't Finnish too quickly! LOL!

> Thanks, mate, and don't you give up your day job! ROFL!

Harry put the phone down. Well, he thought to himself, you've got the place to yourself for at least two hours, probably three. Live a little, Harry.

He saw a shadow through the frosted glass pane of the front door.

He lit a smoke, put a fedora on, pulled his .38 out of the drawer and laid it on the blotter, and swung his feet onto his desk.

The shadow knocked, with rhythm.

'Come in, it's open.'

Anna entered carrying a cardboard coffee tray. She smiled one of those saucy ones that stirs the loins. 'Hello, Harry. The hat suits you as does the cigarette.' She prowled slowly towards his desk, looking him in the eye as he grinned at her, smoke seeping out of his nostrils. She put the coffee down. 'Ooh, is that a real gun?'

'Absolutely. Thank you for the coffee. And you look fabulous. Are you the reigning Miss Finland, or am I confusing you with your twin sister?'

She giggled. 'Fancy two of us, do you?' She sat opposite him.

'I am only human, Anna.'

'She leant over and ran her long fingers along the gunmetal of the Smith and Wesson. 'Any other weapons around here?'

Harry gazed into her sparkling blue eyes, taking in her sleek face and long blonde hair, with some curls added since their first encounter. 'Your hair looks great, too, the curls suit you.'

'Thank you for noticing. But, yes, a detective's eye, I guess.'

'It's on my CV: a keen eye for the ladies.'

She giggled again. It made her cheeks dimple.

'Smoke?' He offered his pack.

'No, I don't.'

'Very sensible. But it's a vice I enjoy. Plus, smoking in the office nowadays is so rebellious.'

The dimples returned. 'I don't mind. It is your office. All you need is a glass of whiskey and the picture is complete.'

Harry thought Anna naked on his desk was more the complete picture. 'Even for me, this is generally too early for a hard drink. But you know your PI scene very well.'

'I love Raymond Chandler.'

'I'm putting you at mid-twenties maximum, so Chandler is not well-read in your generation. And a great shame.'

'Yes, but my dad was a cop in Finland. He read all those authors. He passed on a love of reading. In those long, cold, dark Scandinavian winters, you get to read a lot of books. Plus, I love the films with Bogart.'

'Chandler is one of my favourites, too. And others. I've got a big collection at home.'

'Maybe I can visit your library sometime?' She sipped her coffee and the dimples returned as she grinned.

'I will give you a personal tour, Miss Finland.'

'Cool. Now this morning I have an hour to enjoy your company before I need to leave for a lecture. And while I said I don't touch cigarettes, I am keen on other dangerous things between my lips.'

Harry barred up harder than the Luxor Obelisk. 'Shall I lock the door?'

'Harry, there's not a moment to lose.'

He pressed the switch beneath his desk and the was a solid metallic clunk from the office door as the deadbolt hit home. 'Now, Miss Anna, I do believe you were hoping I could help you find something, if my memory serves?'

That giggle again. 'Yes, multiple orgasms in one session was my wish. And still is.'

Harry looked at his watch. 'Shit, about fifty-five minutes left.'

'I bet you can do it.' Anna was unbuttoning her blouse.

'First, a quick question for my curiosity. You're studying feminism stroke gender studies? At risk of stereotyping, you do not seem to fit that scene.'

She laughed loudly. 'No, I don't, and the stereotype is not far off the mark. The reason is a rich, narcissistic mother. If I pander to her wishes, she pays for everything.' Anna was now in her underwear and standing. 'To be honest, I'd study garbage collection if she wanted.'

As Harry unbuttoned his shirt, he looked at her. 'Second, and last, quick question. I'm at least twenty years older, yet you seem incredibly attracted.'

'Oh, that's simple. Young guys, waste of time, generally. No appreciation of a woman's body or needs. Now, I'm not saying all older guys are any better, but I'm betting you are. I have a radar for it and I can see it in your eyes. Even if I'm wrong, and I'm not, I'll still have some fun testing my theory.'

And with that, Anna's breasts emerged from her bra.

'Oh, Miss Finland, for the next fifty-three minutes I am dedicated to one goal, and one goal only: your ecstasy.'

She smirked and peeled off her knickers. 'Less talking and more undressing, big man.' She turned and walked to the couch.

Harry stared at her perfectly sculpted buttocks as he ripped the rest of his gear off.

Anna sat on the couch and opened her thighs. She said nothing and pointed at her pussy.

Harry almost climbed over his desk in his haste to get there. His awkward final disrobing as he crossed the floor wasn't even fractionally as sexy as Anna's stripping, but being Harry, what he lacked in pizzazz he more than made up for in sensual skill and sheer perseverance.

As he almost fell on her, Anna was still pointing south, now with both hands, so Harry didn't even bother with a kiss or with Anna's pert breasts with large, swollen nipples.

'I want that patriarchal tongue to be a slave to my pussy!'

Harry grinned and went down faster than a Stuka dive-bomber. Her pussy, with its neatly trimmed tuft of pure blonde hair, was glistening and smelt divine. Harry kissed it several times and then he unleashed his tongue.

Anna, both hands now clasped behind Harry's head, groaned. 'Eat me, detective!'

– 15 –

An hour later, Harry sat in his boxer shorts, smoking and now enjoying a large Jameson. After those fifty-three minutes of unfettered, carnal depravity, he reckoned he deserved a stiff drink. Mind you, nothing else was stiff now.

Anna had departed, delighted with her multiple orgasms and promising to visit him whenever he wanted another private tutorial on postmodern feminism and to satisfy her again. She'd headed off to get to her lecture on 'Females prevailing over the patriarchy in the twenty-first century'. She'd said at least having four recent orgasms to reminisce over would make the lecture slightly less insufferable. And, yes, she wanted that appointment to peruse his hard-boiled literature shelves.

Harry looked at his watch and thought he'd better get his clothes on and try to air out the office a bit.

Trev walked through the door at one minute past one. 'Fuck me, Harry, this place smells like a Helsinki whorehouse.'

'Brother, a Helsinki brothel would seem tame by comparison to this morning's activities in here.'

'You really are a complete scoundrel.'

'As I always say, life is here to be savoured, not endured.'

'Never a truer word. Now, Mister Kenmare, if we can possibly get back to work, my search results will be ready.'

'Mister Matson, I am all yours.'

'Actually, I think that Finnish siren took most of you, but I'll settle for the professional bit that's left.'

'Ha ha. By the way, Trev, you look glowingly smug this morning. If I was a gambling man, I'd put money on you getting laid last night.'

Trev snorted. 'That doesn't make you an ace detective, mate. Yeah, I went out with that French guy, Lucien, from the pub.'

'Well, *oh là là*! A good night?'

'Hell yes. Could have done with a bit more sleep, though.'

Harry sniggered. 'Sleep's overrated, especially when there's sex on offer.'

'Damned true,' said Trev, sitting at the side desk where Tanya usually worked. He pulled over the laptop that had been sitting there overnight doing its thing.

He looked at the screen and tapped on the trackpad a few times. 'You little ripper, multiple hits on Barwick.'

'Sweet,' said Harry, getting up and moving behind Trev to see the screen. 'What have we got?'

Trev was flicking through documents. 'All the travel details, so it is Paris as we suspected. And a few letters in French. Some on the letterhead of the Archbishop here and some look like they're from his counterpart in France.'

'And how's your French these days?'

'Not enough to understand all of these. I get a few words here and there, but that's all. I learnt some conversational French from Jean-Louis, but we always talked in English.'

'Zanza might be able to help. They speak French in the Congo, don't they?'

'Yes. Give him a call.'

Harry got his phone. 'Hey, big fella, you speak fluent French, don't you?'

'Well, Harry, the Congolese variety, yes. Why?'

'We've got a batch of church documents in French that we need translated.'

'Sorry, Harry, my French is spoken only. We never learnt much reading at school before we got taken away for the army.'

'No worries, mate, I think I could have a plan B.'

'But Harry?'

'Yes, mate?'

'I am certainly good for a hunting trip to France.'

'Mate, we wouldn't go without you. Count on it. Catch you tomorrow.' Harry hung up.

The door opened and in walked Tanya. She sniffed the air and smiled. 'Oh, Harry! I leave you alone for five minutes and it's as if there's been a bonobo orgy in here.'

'Well, you weren't the only one devouring pussy then, were you?' He grinned at her.

'Fricking spare me, please,' said Trev.

'And how was Helga from Helsinki?' teased Tanya.

'Well, it's Anna for a start, and she was great, and she left entirely satisfied.'

'I don't doubt that for a second. Looking at her Instagram pictures, I wouldn't mind her joining us sometime.'

Harry felt his loins stirring. 'I'll be sure to run that idea past her.'

'Do that. Now, I heard a plan B mentioned when I was outside the door. What goes?'

Trev pointed at his screen. 'Tan, we've got documents aplenty about Barwick headed for Paris.'

'Cool! France here we come.'

'Yeah, but we need them translated before we can plan anything, and by someone we trust.'

'Zanza?' she asked. 'I know he speaks French.'

'That's who I was on the phone to,' said Harry. 'But he doesn't read it. Hence plan B, Sandrine.'

Harry's phone beeped with a message.

He looked at it and cackled. 'What a girl.'

'Let's see, Harry?'

She stepped closer to him and looked at his screen. It was a full-frontal nude shot of Anna.

From Helsinki with love XXX

'From Helsinki with lust, more like,' said Tanya. 'Mind you, I definitely want to her to join us in bed. I would love some of her action.'

'I will suggest a threesome. Just need to figure out the approach.'

'If you can pull that off, Mister PI, I'm there. And you are the best man to pleasure both us girls.'

'Specifics?' said Trev, smiling.

'Trev, I know it's not your thing, but from a girl's perspective you want a guy to delight in going down on you and to eat you as if it's his last meal. And he has to look as if he's enjoying it, too.' She walked over to the bar cabinet and grabbed the vodka bottle. 'And not one of these blokes who does a half-hearted lick job and has a face on him as if he's sucking the lemon after a tequila shot.'

Trev and Harry both burst out laughing.

'Which is why I don't bother with guys my age. They are almost always fricking useless in bed.'

Harry nodded. 'Anna said the same thing.'

'Wise girl,' said Tanya. 'And as for this plan B, Harry's hoping to finally get his dick wet with Sandrine. Or "Miss Carthage" you call her, don't you?'

Harry grinned and lit a cigarette.

Trev was still chuckling. 'If our Harry has his way, as he is wont to do, then it'll be more like "Miss Carnage".'

Harry looked at them both. 'Hope springs eternal, team.'

*　*　*

PART 5

HARRY'S VICTORY

She sauntered out of the room and the close-up view of her undulating bikinied bottom was an erotic symphony all by itself.

- Carter Brown

The magic of sex is its acquisition without the burden of possessions.

- Chuck Palahniuk

— 1 —

Her olive skin took on an amber hue in the soft orange lighting of the boudoir as Harry ran his fingers over the curves of her substantial, firm breasts to the hard chocolate-coloured nipples. With the backdrop of the crimson satin sheets, Harry was transported to a realm of rolling sand dunes in the Sahara at sunset.

When he vocalized that imagery, Sandrine gave a hearty chuckle.

'*Monsieur* Harry, from a lesser man that would be lame. But I know how much you admire me, and from you it sounds poetic.'

'Take that admiration and double it, Miss Carthage.'

'I love it when you call me that.' She kissed him on the lips. 'Now, be a good foreign legionnaire for me. The route through this part of the Sahara is due south. An oasis awaits you.'

'*Oui, ma chérie*! Harry Kenmare PI, at your service.'

Sandrine lay back against a pile of purple and lilac pillows and with her hands propelled Harry southwards. Not that any propulsion was needed, Harry was well and truly on the scent, cunnilingus being one of his predominant skills.

His tongue circled her nipples and meandered down her abdomen to her pubis.

She moaned. 'Ah, Beau Geste finds the oasis!'

'My Tunisian beauty, the wait is over.'

Harry gently parted her thighs and teased her clitoris with the tip of his tongue. He delved inside her. He worked her and she moaned more and more loudly, until she screamed as she came.

Harry made the first move to head back north, but she held him in place.

'It's not only redheads who are double-comers, Harry. Get back to it.'

'Your wish is my desire.'

Harry, his face aching already, returned enthusiastically to his duty station. Slower this time, but with an equally explosive result.

Then he was allowed to surface.

'I'd better let you come up for air now, handsome, because I am nowhere near finished with you.'

'And that feeling is entirely mutual.'

She wrapped her strong hand around his cock, as hard as a rod of granite, and pulled it towards her pussy.

'You, Miss Carthage, certainly will not be needing any lube.'

She giggled. 'Not when a man knows what he is doing. And you, *Monsieur* Harry, are truly an expert.'

'I always aim to please, and to service very well indeed.' He tipped his forehead, grinning.

'Get inside me!'

Harry groaned as he slid his member into her.

'You've been a patient man, Harry. I know you've wanted this for a long time.'

'Miss Carthage, since that very first day in my office. The chemistry was smouldering back then.'

'Yes, yes it was. Now you can let it blaze in glory.'

As she moved expertly beneath him, Harry closed his eyes to savour the ecstasy, then reopened them to admire the beauty of Sandrine and remind himself this was truly happening, finally.

'Enjoy, handsome, but try to make it last,' she purred into his ear.

Harry ran his fingers into her long black hair, with a sheen like obsidian. 'That's a tall order, Sandrine, my excitement levels are at warp factor ten.'

She gave a husky giggle. 'Well, we can always do a couple more rounds this afternoon, unless you have somewhere better to rush off to.'

'A jumbo jet at full throttle couldn't drag me away from here, *ma chérie.*'

Their lips locked and Harry slowly eased in and out of her until he couldn't contain himself any longer. 'Oh, fuck yes!' He released his load.

'That feels so *fantastique,*' she whispered. 'But you are absolutely staying for more. *Obligatoire, monsieur* Harry.'

'I do love a bit of *obligatoire* in the afternoon, *Mademoiselle* Carthage.'

'And I love a lot of it all day. Now, handsome, there's Sancerre in the fridge. Why don't you go and get us some refreshments and I'll take a look at those documents.'

'At your service, *ma belle.*' Harry slid off the bed and strutted naked to the kitchen. He heard the toilet flush in the en suite. He returned with the uncorked Sancerre in an ice bucket with two glasses.

'I see you found everything.'

'I haven't lost all the old detective skills.'

'So true, and you've learned a whole lot more if that tongue action is any indication. Your ability to find and pleasure the sweet spot is awesome.'

Harry winked at her and bowed slightly. 'Again, at your service.' He poured two wines.

'It soon will be again, I am so far from finished with you, Harry. Now, grab those documents and your notebook and we'll get the business out of the way while you recharge your batteries.' She pouted, took a sip of wine, and lit a smoke.

Harry did likewise and grabbed his document wallet from the chair next to the door.

They drank their wine as Sandrine perused the copies of the papers from the church copier and Harry took notes as she translated.

When she'd finished, she lay back and lit another cigarette, holding her empty glass in Harry's direction.

Harry put his notebook down and refilled both their glasses. He looked at her reclining on the satin sheets. 'You are utterly magnificent, Sandrine. No words I could muster would ever do you justice.'

'Then let your tongue sing my praises without words.'

'I'm ready!'

'Lie back.'

He obeyed.

'Now big man, I seem to recall mention of you liking pussy riding your face.'

'Sandrine, that is a scurrilous rumour that is entirely true.' He grinned.

She straddled his abdomen and groaned as she inched her way up his chest. Not a word was spoken by either of them. Then she arrived at her destination and his face was plunged into the aromatic darkness of her wet crotch. She rode him hard, how he liked it.

As Harry slaved with his tongue in the miasma of wetness and perfume, he considered how the only true, unforgettable cunnilingus meant a face that ached more than a couple of rounds with Mike Tyson. He was an expert and it didn't take long at all before Sandrine howled as her body spasmed and her thighs clenched around Harry's face.

When her moaning had subsided, she slid off him. '*Monsieur* Harry, you are the perfect cunnilinguist, without peer anywhere I've ever been.'

Harry beamed, his face shiny with vaginal juices. 'Miss Carthage, helping a lady find a sensational orgasm is right up there in my detective skills, believe me.'

'*Magnifique, mon* stud. Now, after another smoke and some wine, I'm going to roll over, and you will definitely need that lube for the next round.

'Ooh, I like the sound of that.' He poured more wine.

After another cigarette each, Sandrine rolled onto her stomach, looking over at Harry and winking, tapping her own backside.

'Handsome, part those sand dunes and visit a different oasis.'

'Oh, if I must!' Harry reached for the lube.

– 2 –

'That is so Harry's shagged face!' Tanya was pointing at Harry as he stepped back into the office.

Trev and Zanza laughed.

'A Tunisian tryst,' said Trev. 'And how was it, Mister Kenmare?'

Tanya grinned at Harry. 'It's been a long time coming, my Mr PI, and I hope you were, too.'

Harry blushed. 'Bugger off.'

There was more laughter.

'Tell you what,' said Zanza, 'working here is as much sex as it is sleuthing. I like being an employee here.'

'We do also like eating and drinking, big fella,' said Trev.

'Mind you,' said Tanya, 'if we hear Harry saying he's off for a tagine, we'll know exactly where he's going.'

'Yep, cuddles with couscous,' Trev piled on.

Harry plonked himself in his chair and lit a smoke. 'All right, team, I do have the work stuff we need. If anyone's interested in work, that is.'

Everyone cackled.

Harry pulled the folded sheaf of documents and his notebook from his document wallet and handed them to Trev, who eagerly started poring over them.

'Well, hello padre, there's corro between the Archbishop here in Sydney and his counterparts in both

Paris and Bordeaux. All deals with the relocation of Barwick. His need for "a delicate and therapeutic pastoral change of scene" is obviously a euphemism for a pedo priest needing sanctuary. Cunts!'

'Want a drink, mate?' asked Harry.

'Large one, please.'

'Anyone else?' said Harry as he headed over to the bar cabinet.

'My usual,' said Tanya.

'Big fella?'

'A whiskey thanks, Harry.'

Harry made the drinks, played waiter, and sat back at his desk.

Trev put the papers on the desk and sat back with his Jameson. 'So, the upshot is Barwick is headed for the south-west of France, under the auspices of the Archbishop of Bordeaux and agreed to by the head honcho in Paris. Then they talk about openings for "adult pastoral support" in either the Dordogne or the Lot-et-Garonne.'

Harry snorted. 'Yeah, slipping in "adult" is their internal code for keeping the prick away from Sunday School supervision.'

Tanya took the papers from Trev and slid them in front of her. She tapped on her keyboard.

'What you looking for, Tan?'

'Trawling for any news items out of France with any mention.' She kept tapping and scrolling, but not for long. 'Aha! It's in French, but Barwick's name is there.'

'Hit Google Translate, babe.'

A couple more keystrokes. 'Cool. It's a newspaper from France, not one of the main ones I've ever heard of. It's called *Sud Ouest* and is based in Bordeaux. Have to say, this translate function is a bit ordinary.'

Trev was now leaning over looking at her screen. 'Not wrong. If that's what AI has in store, then we haven't got too much to worry about with the robots taking over.'

Harry snorted. 'Illiterate robots, who'd have thought. Mind you, I could nominate plenty of human role models for them.'

'Here we go,' said Tanya. 'It's obviously a local rag, announcing the arrival of an assistant priest to help Father Laurent Massou at a church in Bergerac. The local priest was holding an afternoon tea to welcome his Australian colleague.'

Trev was back on his laptop. 'Here it is on the map.'

Harry stood and moved over to look at the screen. 'You know that area, don't you, brother? Isn't that where the young French barman from the Emerald Bar comes from?'

'That's right,' said Tanya. 'Have you banged him yet, Trev?'

'I may have had some French lessons, yes.'

They all laughed.

'So, Bergerac is in the Dordogne,' continued Trev, pointing at the map. 'The department below is the Lot-et-Garonne where Lucien is from, a town called Villeneuve-sur-Lot. And the whole area is renowned for its cuisine.'

'And wine, of course,' added Harry. 'Sounds like our sort of destination. You reckon Barwick will stay there?'

Trev took a sip of whiskey. 'Yes, mate. They've obviously decided at the top to relocate him to be proactive in avoiding issues here. So, they'll keep supporting him there on the condition he stays put and behaves. That's how the Catholic Church operates.'

'So, he'll see out his days living the pleasurable life in the south-west of France, then.'

'Won't be too many days of pleasure if I have anything to do with it.'

'Which you will,' said Harry.

'Which *we* will,' added Tanya. 'And my passport is ready to fly, boys.'

Harry looked over to Zanza. 'Mate, you got a valid passport?'

'Yes, Harry. My Aussie passport is one of my prized possessions. I'm grateful for the home this country has given me. And it's how I travelled to the US to get my tongue operation.'

'Yep, of course. Well, let's get Wheeler sorted out, or should I say dispatched, and then head for a French holiday. Our sort of holiday, anyway. And Sandrine said she had some useful contacts over there. Old friends of her father from his gendarme days.'

'And Liam mentioned that journalist in Paris, too,' added Tanya.

'Both could be very useful indeed,' said Trev. 'I was starting to plan for …'

He was interrupted by Zanza's phone ringing and the big man saying, 'It's Lorraine.' He took the call and listened. 'Thank you, sexy. Will see you soon, I hope.' He put the phone down. 'We're on. The bank card will be delivered to the branch at Lane Cove first thing tomorrow morning.'

Harry slapped his desk blotter. 'Righto. Ease off on the drinks now, we need to get prepped.'

'Job on!' yelled Trev, smiling like a madman.

– 3 –

It had rained hard overnight and there were puddles aplenty on the roads. It was still drizzling and the windscreen wipers on the big grey VW van swished on intermittent as Harry and Trev sat watching the main street in Lane Cove. They were propped on the same side of the road as the bank, about thirty metres away and facing north towards it. Tanya and Zanza were in a hire-car, a blue Audi A3, on the other side of the street facing south and about the same distance from the bank. They had no idea which way Wheeler would come, so having both directions covered for rapid tailing of him was the logical approach.

Harry was tapping the window ledge of the passenger door with an impatient rhythm along with his foot tapping on the floor.

'Relax, brother,' said Trev.

'Mate, can't help it. I'm more hopped up than a horny lesbian in a female nudist colony.'

***

Reggie Wheeler swallowed his instant coffee and grabbed his house key and wallet. It was nine fifteen and the bank opened at half past.

'Back shortly, Aunty. Got to go to the bank.' He called as he walked to the front door.

'Reggie, my love, can you please get some milk while you're out?'

'Sure thing, Aunty.'

Wheeler closed the front door and walked out onto the street, turning north and heading towards the main shopping street.

He pulled his hoodie up against the light rain and sidestepped a large puddle on the pavement as he came to the first corner. He was itching badly, as if he had a bad dose of crabs, to get back to Laos. Aside from a building, desperate hankering in his loins for some young flesh, he was feeling increasingly out of sorts back in Oz. Things were coming unravelled, it seemed. Simon was dead. Jackson had disappeared, uncontactable. And the Federal cops were on his tail.

As soon as he had access to cash again, he would follow up the people smuggler leads he had from the dark web. It was his only escape route. But it was an unknown world to him, and it all added to his anxiety. He scratched at the niggling stress rash on his chest and quickened his pace as the rain became heavier. He turned onto the main street, Longueville Road, crossed over and walked briskly towards the shops. He pulled his hoodie close around his face to keep warmer.

***

Tanya spotted him first.

'Eyes on!' she almost yelled into the walkie-talkie. 'West side of the street in a dark-blue hoodie and blue jeans. He's just passed you boys. I can see enough of his face, it's him.'

Zanza looked at the photo stuck to the dashboard with Blu Tack. 'Shit, you've got good eyesight.'

Harry's voice came back. 'Good work, team. Now, engines on and ready to roll. My money is he'll go to the bank and straight back the way he came, in which case you guys will be facing in the right direction to follow. We'll have to turn around. And we can't try anything here with all the people around.'

'Roger that,' said Tanya. She giggled. 'I've always wanted to say that over one of these radios.'

Harry came back, 'I love it when you talk dirty, babe!'

There was laughter in both vehicles, breaking the tension.

Trev had binos raised and was watching the bank as Wheeler walked to the door.

Wheeler pushed on the handle, but it was still locked. He peered inside.

'It's nine twenty-eight, two minutes to go,' said Harry. 'Banking hours.'

Wheeler looked at the opening hours on the glass front door and pulled out his phone. He put it back and leant against the wall next to the door, looking out onto the wet street.

Harry's voice came over the radio. 'Okay, look busy and disinterested everybody, he's gawking around until the bank opens in a couple of minutes.'

Trev put his binos down.

The sleuths needn't have worried about Wheeler spotting them.

As Reggie Wheeler stood out on the street, all he was thinking of, in lurid detail, was underage depravity in South-East Asia.

The bank door clicked unlocked and Wheeler was inside in a flash.

Trev was back behind his field glasses. 'Okay, lost him inside now. Think we've got time for a smoke.'

They both lowered their windows and lit up.

'Harry, you spoke to Longman?'

'Yes, the abattoir is at our disposal. As are he and his crew.'

'Cool. A bit neater than going back to Sofala like we did with Schwarz.'

Harry smiled. 'Yeah, the wrong Schwarz. He was bang out of luck that day.'

'No fucking loss, mate, only good ped is a dead ped.'

'Yep. And with this one here, Longman said he and The Ratfucker wanted ringside seats to watch.'

'You cool with that?'

'Yes. Why not? We do have rather a track record with them now.'

'Not wrong there, Harry, who'd have thought?'

'Mysterious ways. Of the atheist variety, of course.'

'Amen to that.'

Both men laughed.

Over in the other car, Tanya was behind the wheel of the hired Audi hatchback, hanging out for a smoke, but strictly forbidden in the rental vehicle. It was her first time driving on a surveillance job, although Trev had schooled her in detail about distance and speed and leap-frogging vehicles.

Big Zanza was in the passenger seat and was assigned with grabbing Wheeler at the first opportunity, if one arose.

He turned to Tanya. 'Hey, you know how you keep a photo of Sasha on your desk at the office?'

'Yeah, I like to look at Sash whenever I can.'

'Is that a bit like looking in a mirror?'

Tanya paused to think before answering. 'See what you mean. Yes and no. We were incredibly close, of course, most twins are. But we never really thought about our physical similarity. Oh …' She smiled at the memory. 'Except the time we originally met Harry.'

'Please, tell me.'

Tanya recounted the trick the twins had played on Harry at the brothel when he was on the assignment for their mother.

Zanza guffawed so loudly he startled a woman walking her coiffed poodle on the footpath. 'Great story. I've got a photo of Sasha on my phone. We didn't go out for that long, but there was a spark.'

Tanya slapped his thigh. 'Oh, yes, I know! She told me about all sorts of fireworks.'

Zanza grinned at her. 'Tell you what, how about we put a framed photo on the office wall as a remembrance of her.'

'That's a lovely idea, Zanz. Harry and Trev will love it, too.'

Before they could continue, there was movement in the bank.

'He's coming out, I think!' called Tanya into the radio. She passed the handset to Zanza and turned on the engine.

Reggie Wheeler had his new card and he needed cash, plus he wanted to double-check the card was all okay before he left the bank. He didn't want to have to make a return trip. He knew he was exposed every minute he was out of the house.

He stopped at the ATM inside the front door. He took the maximum amount he could. All good, he thought. Now, milk for Aunty.

'Where is he?' Harry called into the two-way.

'Just stopped at the cash machine inside. Any minute now, Harry.' There was a pause, and Zanza added, 'Okay, moving now.'

Wheeler stepped out of the bank and waited for a break in the traffic. He crossed the road.

'Where the hell is he going?' said Harry.

'Relax, brother, my money is on the convenience store right there.'

Wheeler disappeared into the store, emerging a couple of minutes later holding a two-litre milk container and a folded newspaper. He turned left and walked south, heading for home.

Tanya waited for a gap in the traffic and pulled out.

'We're rolling,' called Zanza.

'Roger,' replied Harry.

Trev moved out and headed in the opposite direction to find a side street to double-back in.

'He's walking south on Longueville,' called Zanza.

'I'm going to pull over so we don't close the gap too much,' said Tanya, sliding the car into the kerb.

Trev turned left into a side street and did a U-turn as soon as he could. The VW van moved back out onto the main road and headed south as well.

The traffic was steady.

'We need him in a quiet side street for fuck's sake,' said Harry.

'Patience, brother, and let's keep our fingers crossed.'

They slowed and Trev pulled in behind the other team's car.

That was Tanya's cue to get moving again. She let a truck pass and pulled out.

'Still got eyes on,' called Zanza. 'Okay, he's turning left into Dorritt Street.'

'Finally!' said Harry as Trev moved back into the traffic flow.

They watched Tanya and Zanza turn left into Dorritt.

They turned a minute later.

'Oh, fuck!' yelled Harry as he saw the roadwork crew standing around a big hole in the road.

The traffic was reduced to one lane contraflow. Tanya had stopped at the sign held by the hi-vis-clad traffic controller.

'He's crossing the road,' called Zanza.

The controller flipped her sign to 'SLOW' and Tanya moved slowly forward past the roadworks, as their target was ambling right into Gamma Road.

Trev gunned the van to catch up, but caught both the angry glare from the controller and the sign flipping back to 'STOP'.

'For fuck's sake!' yelled Harry.

The traffic girl evidently heard the shout through the windscreen as she was now glaring at Harry instead of Trev.

Harry scowled in return, trying to channel his dark mood at her.

Trev turned. 'Don't piss her off, she'll keep us here even longer just for the hell of it.'

'Yeah, she's got more power with that bloody stop sign than she has with her pussy.'

As the sign flipped again and Trev eased the van forward, the radio crackled into life. 'We've got a house,' came Zanza's voice. 'And we're going to exit out the other end of the street.'

'No,' said Harry, 'don't exit, you'll lose visual on the house. Pull up further along but keep visual. We'll meet you there.'

'Roger.'

Trev swung the van to the kerb and executed a swift U-turn. 'No value in going down the street as well. We can keep the van unseen.'

'Good thinking. Mind you, now we have to face the traffic Nazi again.'

'Yeah, try to look friendly this time, Harry. Pretend you're trying to crack onto her.'

'Mate, you saw her. Those tatts and that haircut, she sure as hell ain't into cock. My charm would be wasted.'

'You may have a point.'

Having gone around the block to enter Gamma Road from the opposite end, Trev stopped the van in front of the car. The side door slid open as Tanya and Zanza transferred vehicles.

'Good work, team,' said Harry. 'Now starts the boring bit: twenty-four-seven surveillance. We cannot lose him this time.'

'And he will have to exit sometime,' said Trev. 'And my bet is on real soon, given he's now holed up again. He'll know his time is limited before the cops find him. But my money's on him waiting until tonight at the earliest.'

'I agree,' said Harry. 'He'll definitely want the cover of darkness. And since he's now got cash and his card again, I reckon he'll call a cab to pick him up and take him wherever he's going.'

Trev accessed Google maps again on his iPad.

'Shit, there's a golf course at the back of these houses. That gives him multiple rear exit options if he needed them.'

'Nothing's ever easy, is it?' said Harry. 'Okay, we need extra troops and fast. I'm calling Longman.'

'Good idea, we'll need the golf course covered at multiple exit points once it closes this evening.' He turned to Tanya and Zanza. 'Meantime, we'll need you two to get eyes on the back fence until the reinforcements arrive, just in case he's desperate enough to do a daylight escape across the golf course.'

– 4 –

Reggie Wheeler wasn't keen on sherry, but it was the only booze in his aunt's place, and she had three full cases of Harvey's Bristol Cream in her pantry. He was on his fourth glass now, calming his nerves before contacting the people smuggler again. He knew nothing of that part of the criminal world and he was scared: scared of the unknown, and scared of failing to get back to his paedophilic paradise in Asia.

And he resented society labelling him a criminal: he just loved children. He was a warm and loving 'minor attracted person'. To hell with Australian society and its judgemental bigotry. So much easier back in Asia. He simply had to get back there. He needed those sweet, young delights again. His testicles were ready to explode from a lack of release. Bugger it, a quick wank before he got back onto the dark web was in order. He got up to close the bedroom curtains. He looked across the back garden to the golf course, now in total darkness.

Back to his laptop and on with one of his collection. The naked little girl on screen had him erect within seconds and he beat his meat enthusiastically until he came into the tissues in his other hand. He cleaned up and poured himself another sherry, right to the brim of his wine glass. Righto, dark web time.

Reggie had a healthy porn business over in the darkness, reaping a solid income in bitcoin from his homemade films from Laos. The market for his depravations with little girls was immense, plus Reggie specialized in some rougher sex with the girls, and his fans paid a premium rate for that material. It was really his dream employment: a massive paycheck for defiling young girls, his passion in life. Couldn't get any better.

Whilst he used bitcoin to buy some porn himself, he'd often wondered if he'd ever be able to fully realize his cyber wealth. Now, it was going to save his bacon. The people smuggler in here wanted payment in crypto. But the bank visit for his new card was still vital, as the cops back in Laos dealt strictly in cash of the folding variety. Along with his introduction from Jackson, emailed to him just after he'd arrived at his aunt's place, yesterday he'd also had to make a good-faith payment before the smuggler, a dark web character under the handle The Travel Agent, would start the full negotiation with him.

Twenty minutes later, Reggie had conversed again with The Travel Agent. He paid the equivalent of about twenty grand in bitcoin, and provided his mobile number to get specific instructions once the necessary marine arrangements were in place. He would get transported by speedboat out to a northbound freighter in international waters and then on to Indonesia, where the freighter was headed. After that, he could make his own way back to Laos.

He poured his seventh sherry and fished his dormant phone out of his bag and turned it on. He'd been avoiding using it in case the Feds were monitoring, even getting the bank to call his aunt's land line when his card was ready for collection. But he guessed as long as he didn't make or take any calls with his phone, he'd probably be fine. At least until The Travel Agent called him, and then he'd be on his way anyhow. And The Travel Agent had been emphatic in saying he would call Reggie: that was the only way the communication was allowed to occur. So, now Reggie had to wait with his phone.

***

Reggie Wheeler guessed incorrectly, of course. In the Feds' electronic monitoring office in Sydney, a young trainee monitor noted an alert on her computer screen.

'Sarge?'

'Yeah?' The Sergeant didn't look up from his newspaper, pen in hand poring over the Sudoku page.

'Got something, Sarge. A phone that has been silent for days just activated.'

'Anyone interesting?' he said as he cracked the first grid block.

'One Reggie Wheeler, wanted for child exploitation offences.'

Now the Sergeant stood and walked over.

'Well, that is interesting. He's the one wanted in connection with that Assistant Commissioner and that Crown Prosecutor.'

'Oh, shit. That one.'

'Yes, indeed. Good pick up, Julie. No calls at all?'

'Not since it became active again and pinged off a tower. That's all.'

She clicked open a different screen. 'No calls since last week when it went silent. It's been switched off.'

'He's obviously lying low, but he must need it on again for some pressing reason. He will know he's being hunted by us, it's all over the news. Let's see where it pinged.'

More mouse clicks.

'Okay, it's pinging to a tower in Lane Cove. Looks like the Gamma Road vicinity by the side of the golf course there.' She pointed at the electronic map.

The Sergeant turned to other staff sitting in the next work pod.

'Okay, analysts, I need any connections between Reggie Wheeler and the Lane Cove area, specifically Gamma Road, but look wider as well.' He clapped his hands. 'Let's move it, please.'

'Yes, Sarge,' came the chorus.

A black Ford F150, V8 engine throbbing, parked in the darkness on the eastern side of the Lane Cove golf course. Archie Longman, in the passenger seat and having received direction on the phone from Tanya, raised night-vision glasses and peered over the golfing greens to the backs of the houses on the opposite side, those fronting onto Gamma Road. He coasted along the row from the end, checking against a map open on his phone screen.

'Got it, Rocco. Give Kenmare a bell.'

'On it, Arch,' said The Ratfucker.

He pressed his phone screen. 'Hey, Kenmare. We're in pozzie and Arch has his eyes on the back of the house and the fence.'

'Fantastic, great to have your assistance, guys. As you can see, the geography's a bit challenging on this one. Tanya and Zanza were watching during the day, just in case, but we need them back on this side so we can cover both ends of the street.'

'Not wrong, plenty of avenues for him to move in. And, Kenmare, I can't wait for you to catch this wanker and then it's party time out at our abattoir.'

'Long overdue, Corsi my friend, very long overdue.'

'And, mate, we've got another truck and crew on the lower edge of the golf course.'

'Good stuff. Now we just wait it out.'

'Cool. Call you if anything moves.' Corsi hung up.

Over in Gamma Road, the VW van was propped fifty metres south of Wheeler's place. A keen eye might have noticed the smoke seeping from the slightly lowered windows.

'Let's hope he moves soon,' said Trev. 'It'll be a lot easier to grab him in the darkness. I don't fancy a snatch in daylight around here.'

'True, although a bit harder to dog him if he ducks and weaves. And why the hell did we have to have a golf course at the back of the house? Talk about Murphy's Law.'

Trev chuckled. 'You wouldn't want it easy, Harry.'

'Actually, to get this business finished and get final vengeance for Orla, I'd absolutely settle for easy. If we lose him again, I'm going to go fucking ballistic.'

'Well, I reckon he'll get going ASAP. He'd be desperate by now, and he knows the Feds are after him. He'll know he needs to get out of Australia pronto.'

Harry picked up his walkie-talkie.

A similar distance to the north of the target house was the Audi hatchback with Tanya and Zanza.

The two-way radio crackled. 'Babe?'

Tanya turned down the Taylor Swift album playing on the mini boombox in the centre console.

'Hi, boss.'

'Hey, how about you do a quick walk past to us and check for lights.'

'Cool, I'll be able to take a piss in the van.'

Harry chortled. 'Yeah, the salubrious joys of surveillance. Trev's already filled one bottle.'

'It's all the bloody coffee,' quipped Trev.

'And, babe, get the big fella behind the wheel, just in case we have to move urgently.'

'Roger that.' She put the radio down.

She turned to Zanza. 'And now big Zed, you need to see if you can slide over here without getting out of the car. Harry said no unnecessary movement out of the vehicle, remember?'

'Bugger me, can we have a bigger car next time, please. This is going to be a move and a half. It's not as if I'm some fucking Congolese dwarf.'

Tanya giggled. 'No, you certainly are not.'

'Ha ha,' he replied. 'Okay, slide your seat back as far as it'll go before you get out. And can you bring me back another bottle, please? As Harry would say, my back teeth are floating.'

'No worries.' Tanya got out of the car and gently closed the driver's door. She walked over the road and headed south on the opposite side to Wheeler's place.

***

'Sarge?' called one of the AFP analysts.

The Sergeant ambled over to the analyst's workstation. 'Got something, Tracy?'

'There's a Dora Wheeler living in Gamma Road.' She pointed to a house on the satellite view. 'House is owned by her, has been for decades. And I've done a search on Ancestry. One of the family trees on there has a Reginald as her nephew.'

'Good work.'

He turned to one of his field agents. 'Paul, you and Kurt get out to Lane Cove, this address.' He pointed at the analyst's screen as the agent stepped over. 'Keep an eye out for any movement. I'll get a couple more crews switched over to assist ASAP.'

'Yes, Sarge, on our way.'

The two agents headed for the car park under the building.

The Sergeant turned to the intercept monitors. 'And watch that bloody phone like hawks, please. I want to know the slightest squeak from it.'

***

Harry and Trev watched the silver Subaru station wagon approach along Gamma Road. They both slunk lower in their seats as it drew close and went on past them.

'Feds!' they said in unison.

'It was only a matter of time,' said Trev. 'They must be tracking his phone and Wheeler must have it on.'

Harry groaned. 'This is a complication we did not need.' He thumped the dash and grabbed the radio. 'Babe?'

'Yep.'

'See that Subaru wagon approaching?'

'Yeah, looks like two heads in it.'

'It's the Feds. Keep an eye open for anymore cruising around and keep as out of sight as possible.'

'Roger.'

Harry picked up his phone.

'Longman?'

'Yeah, mate.'

'Eyes open for cops, buddy. We've had a silver Subaru wagon go past us and they are Feds for sure. There'll probably be others.'

'Cool. Nothing like that on this side so far, but we'll be careful.'

'Longman, if we end up on the move after our man, we cannot let the cops get to Wheeler first. That is simply not an option.'

'Hear you loud and clear, Kenmare. We are in this for all and any action as required, mate, you can rely on us.'

'Thanks, guys, really appreciate this.' Harry hung up.

– 6 –

Reggie Wheeler's phone rang.

'Hello?'

'Listen good, pal, I won't repeat myself. We have an opening tonight. You need to get yourself to the Newport Yacht Club. No later than two AM. You'll be met at the gate. Clear?'

'Yes.'

'I'll call you if there are any last-minute changes. I suggest you get moving.'

The line went dead.

Reggie looked at the time: nine-thirty. He'd need to get a taxi or an Uber to Newport. It was the only way. And he wanted to turn his phone off again, just to be extra safe, but the man had said he'd call with any changes, so that wasn't an option. Still, he wasn't going to be making any calls, so that should hopefully be all right.

Aunty Dora was already asleep, so he'd just leave her a letter to say 'goodbye'. He walked through to the front room, leaving the lights off, and looked out onto the street. He kept himself to the side of the window and watched.

The street was dark and quiet, a couple of inadequate street lamps doing little good. He waited for several minutes. As he was about to turn and walk away back to his room to pack his bag, a set of headlights came into view.

He watched as a silver or grey station wagon went past with two male heads in it. He swore as one of them turned to look at his house.

Fuck! It must be the bloody pigs. And so close to escaping.

He trotted to his room and quickly stuffed his few items into his travel bag.

Fuck!

He sat on the bed with his bag. He couldn't very well call a taxi to the house now. Maybe the back? Yes, he could get over the old back fence and make his way across the golf course, now it was dark. He could get a taxi or an Uber from a few streets away.

His plan made, he went into the kitchen. He grabbed a shopping list pad and wrote a thank you and farewell note to Aunty Dora. He said he'd send her a postcard soon.

He turned off the kitchen light and headed out the back door into the dark garden.

To his delight he found an old gate in the fence and, despite its rusty hinges, he succeeded in opening it enough to squeeze through. The old metalwork squealed a bit, but there was nobody around to hear it. He pushed it closed behind him.

He turned and looked over the dark golf course. He could make out some street-lights over the far side, so that was where he needed to head for.

With a purposeful and desperate stride, he started the traverse. Before he'd gone twenty metres, he promptly stumbled into a sand bunker and fell flat on his face.

He hauled himself up, retrieved his bag, and kept going.

– 7 –

'Get on the blower, Rocco, we've got movement. And he's carrying a bag.' Longman was intently focusing his night vision glasses. He chuckled. 'Stupid cunt just went arse up in a bunker.'

The Ratfucker was on the phone. 'Kenmare, your boy is coming out across the golf course. He's got a travel bag, so this is it.'

'Cool. Any sign of the cops around you?'

'Nope, not so far.'

'Okay. You know what our grey VW van looks like, don't you?'

'Yep.'

'And we've got the second team, as you know. A blue Audi hatchback with Tanya and Zanza in it.'

'No worries.'

'So, anything else enters the fray, it'll be the bloody Feds.'

'Got it.'

Harry put the phone down and picked up the radio. 'Team, we're on. Target has exited out onto the golf course. Longman's got eyes on. Let's move!'

'Roger,' came Tanya's voice.

Trev grabbed the radio. 'And, Tan, you're back driving, please. We need Zanza ready to jump out and grab the prick as soon as the opportunity presents.'

'No worries,' replied Tanya.

The pair swapped places in the car. This time they hopped out and didn't bother with being discreet about it.

As Tanya started the engine, the VW van went past them.

***

At the AFP office, the Sergeant had arranged to get one more car headed to Lane Cove. He'd wanted three more crews, but most of the teams on duty were unavailable for reallocation as there was a large narcotics shipment expected to exit Port Botany into Sydney that night.

'Sarge!' yelled a monitor.

'Got something?'

'Yes. His phone is on the move, judging by a ping off another cell tower nearby. My best guess from the tower locations is he's moving east over the golf course.'

'Shit, he's being extra careful.'

The Sergeant picked up his police radio handset and raised the crew already in Lane Cove. 'Paul, target is moving, out on the golf course we think. And you have Ted and Mohammed joining you pronto. They're northbound on Pacific Highway now. About ten minutes away.'

'Roger, Sarge.'

***

Reggie Wheeler was still wiping sand off his face and clothes when he encountered the creek running through the middle of the golf greens. His introduction was his left foot sinking into mud, followed by tripping as he extracted his foot and going face first into the shallow water.

'For fuck's sake!' he yelled in the darkness.

Longman, watching on, laughed as he saw Wheeler face-dive into the stream. He and Rocco also heard the paedophile's expletive, carrying over the silent greens.

'He's like a fucking clown, this molester.'

'Yeah,' said The Ratfucker. 'But still a molester. Can't wait for Kenmare to get started on him.'

'It'll be poetry in bloody motion, Rocco, and we will have ringside seats.'

'As they say, Archie, the only good ped is a fucking dead ped.'

'Too true, and the same goes for Muslim rapists, as we know from experience.'

Corsi chuckled. 'That we do.'

'Okay, he's back on his feet and heading this way.' Longman called Harry and gave him the update.

'Cool, Longman, we're coming down Dorritt Street now.'

'Shit!' added Trev. 'That's another Feds' car, for sure. White Kia Stinger. It's just turned into First.'

'Longman, hear that? Feds coming your way.'

'Okay,' replied Longman, 'white Stinger, let us deal with them. Can you get eyes on from where you are?'

Trev pulled the van over next to the side of the course bordering Dorritt. He grabbed his night glasses and scanned the greens.

'Not yet, Harry.'

The Audi pulled in behind them.

Zanza's voice came over the radio. 'Harry, where do you want us?'

Harry assessed the situation in an instant, years of detective operations paying off. 'Big fella, as soon as we've got eyes on this prick again, I want you out on foot for the chase. And, babe, you keep mobile and run interference with any cop cars. There's at least two of them now.'

Through the dark stillness, they heard a prolonged squeal of tyres, accompanied by a roaring V8 motor, followed by a huge metallic crunch. There were some shouts, drowned out by more burning rubber.

Longman's voice chuckled over the phone. 'Kenmare, that's one less cop car to worry about. The Stinger is officially rooted.'

Harry and Trev looked at each other.

'I dread to think,' said Trev.

The second Feds' car had pulled over in First Avenue, the two agents peering into the darkness of the golf course.

A black Ford F150 pulled in behind them, The Ratfucker grinning at the wheel, and the headlights went on high beam, blinding the cops.

'Now, Slugger!' Longman called into his phone.

Another F150, primer grey in colour, swerved to a halt in front of the Feds.

'What the fuck?!' yelled the agent behind the wheel of the Kia, drawing his Glock.

His offsider was scrabbling for the radio and his Glock, and making a meal of it.

Before either cop's firearm could clear its holster, there was an infernal screaming of tyres as the grey F150 burnt rubber in reverse gear, at full throttle. It ploughed into the front of the Kia, its large tow ball smashing through the radiator of the cop car. The impact gave the two cops whiplash.

Slugger yelled, 'Fuck you, pigs!', threw the F150 into first and planted his foot. As he accelerated away, the cop car spewed its coolant all over the road.

Rocco reversed their F150 away, did a U-turn across the street, and took off.

The agent in the passenger seat, holding his neck, finally picked up the radio handset.

'Control, we've been taken out. Car's been hit and is totalled. Two Ford F150s, one grey, the other one not sure. Both have decamped.'

'What the fuck?!' yelled the Sergeant at the AFP office. 'Who the hell is trying to protect Reginald Wheeler? And who the hell knows we're out there?'

They were both perfectly good questions, but his staff looked at him in stunned silence.

– 8 –

Reggie Wheeler was only about 100 metres away from the edge of the golf course when he heard the screeching tyres and the metallic smashing noise out on Phoenix Street, his target escape route to his north. He heard some shouting and caught what he was certain was the noise of a police radio. He'd been in a few police cars in his earlier days.

The bloody Feds were closing in on him and they were roughly where he'd wanted to go.

He did a swift turnaround and jogged south instead. He knew from his planning there was an exit out onto Third Avenue, and also onto River Road, at the bottom end of the greens. So, he had options, although he was sure there'd be other Feds crawling around. They must have made the connection with Lane Cove. Must have been his phone call.

Longman and The Ratfucker were now sitting in Third Avenue, with a clear line of sight onto the narrow access opening between the trees onto the golf course.

'Got him,' said Longman from behind his night glasses. 'He's stopped, having a good look in this direction.'

Corsi was on the phone immediately. 'Kenmare, we've got visual again. We're at the Third Avenue spot. He's changed direction, must have heard the car crash.'

'Bugger!' said Longman. 'He's run off heading south now.'

'Get that, Kenmare?'

'Roger that. We'll head for River Road at the bottom. That's the biggest opening out by far and now probably his best option.'

Corsi laughed. 'Cool. But if meeting you lot is his best option, I'd hate to see his worst.'

That got chuckles in both vehicles.

'And our other crew have now got the end of Richardson Street covered, just in case,' Corsi continued.

Harry looked at his map. 'Okay. How about you blokes now take the end of Osborne Road and block off that option.'

'Cool, on our way.'

Harry grabbed the radio.

Zanza answered.

'Team, get yourselves down to River Road. And I want you out on foot, big fella, I reckon we might be in for a foot chase, and we've closed off most of his other options.'

'No worries, Harry. We're on Northwood now, almost there.'

Harry turned to Trev. 'Make haste, Mister Matson. I can almost smell it now.'

'Roger that, Mister Kenmare.'

The VW van turned south onto Longueville Road with a protest from its tyres and Trev hit the accelerator.

The radio fired up, with Tanya's voice this time.

'Okay, Zanza is out onto the golf course. I'm propped at the corner of River Road and Stevenson Street.'

'Okay, babe, sit tight and watch for the bloody Feds. There's still at least one car cruising.'

'Cool. And if they come this way?'

'Babe, improvise. As we've taught you.'

Tanya laughed. 'Harry, do I really have to hang my titties out again?'

'Never a bad move, young lady.'

Trev chipped in. 'Yeah, agreed, and I'm gay.'

'You can piss off, the pair of you. Love you both.' She blew a kiss into the handset.

For a big man, Zanza moved as stealthily as a panther through the trees at the edge of the course. He stopped at the edge of the grass expanse, putting his night goggles to his eyes.

He scanned the fairways before him. In an instant he spotted Wheeler, half walking half running through the middle of the greens with a travel bag in his hand.

He was headed straight towards Zanza's location near the darkened tennis courts abutting the golf course.

Zanza smiled to himself and whispered, 'Come to big daddy, you piece of shit.'

***

In the AFP control room, the atmosphere was frantic. The Sergeant had almost yelled over the phone at his superior, trying to get extra teams to dispatch to Lane Cove. He was curtly reminded by the Superintendent that a narcotics importation was far more important than some suspected paedophile. He was even more firmly reminded of his inferior rank. The Sergeant's face was now so grim all the staff were avoiding looking at him.

A monitor cleared her throat and broke the tense silence. 'Change in direction. Looks as if he's heading south now.'

'What are his exit options?' bellowed the Sergeant.

'Nearest possibility is the cul-de-sac on Richardson street to the east, or a park on the western side. Then it's further down to the bottom. There's another cul-de-sac on

Osborne Road. And there's a big opening on the southern edge, about three hundred metres long, onto both River Road and Stevenson Street running off it. Finally, a big bushland reserve at the very end.'

'He won't want bushland, he'll want a street,' said the Sergeant, now standing next to the monitor looking at the map on one of her three large screens.

He lifted up the radio in his hand. 'Team, get down to River Road, that's my bet. Move!'

'Roger, Sarge,' came back from the remaining car, which did a U-turn and took off west on Dorritt Street, with no idea how far behind the play they were.

***

Trev swung the van into Stevenson Street, waving at Tanya parked at the intersection.

Her voice came over the radio. 'Guys, Zanza is in the tree line at the end of the tennis courts. He's not on radio or phone, keeping silence.'

'Roger, babe. I've spotted him in my goggles. And I can see our target, too. Closing, fast. I'm getting a hard on.'

Headlights raced into the street, past Tanya's car.

'Guys, that's the cops I reckon,' she said into the radio.

'Shit!' said Harry, 'We don't need any commotion right now, it'll have Wheeler running the other way. Let's see what they do.'

The Feds went past the van as well and pulled over in front of the tennis courts a couple of hundred metres away, out of sight of the sleuths.

Reggie Wheeler was gasping for breath as he neared the fence at the south end of the golf course. Fitness wasn't exactly his primary pastime and he'd jogged about a kilometre with his bag. The street the other side of the fence line was in darkness and seemed like an access road, presumably emerging onto a main road.

He worked his way along the fence, amongst the trees and bushes, desperate to find a break in the wire mesh. In his befuddled and exhausted state, he registered too late, way too late, the movement in the shadows to his right.

As he belatedly turned, an enormous figure descended upon him. Even in the darkness, he could see the form was a man and he was black. But also huge, so huge. He didn't think he'd ever laid eyes on a man so gigantic. And the hands that grabbed him were like dinner plates.

The next thing he knew was a stomach-churning sensation as his testicles were crushed and he suddenly found himself prone on the ground with the black colossus kneeling on his back.

He wished for death to come quickly. He wished in vain.

Zanza was grinning as he grabbed Wheeler by the head, swiftly launching his knee into the ped's gonads and dropping him to the ground. The molester couldn't utter more than a whimper. As Zanza knelt on his back, he pulled a pre-cut strip of gaffer tape from his jacket. He peeled the backing off, grabbed Wheeler's hair, and pulled his head up. He slapped the tape over the ped's mouth, firming it around his cheeks.

He extracted two cable ties, securing first Wheeler's wrists behind his back, and then binding his ankles. He hauled his captive to his feet, seized the travel bag from the ground, and almost carried Wheeler to the nearest opening in the fence.

He could see the VW van about ten metres away from the gap in the wire.

Harry spotted the prisoner and his captor in the instant Zanza had his prey.

'Here they are, Trev, I'll get the side door ready.'

'Roger.' Trev started the engine and picked up the radio as Harry got out of the van.

'Tan, we're all systems go. Those Feds might be further down the road at the tennis club, can't quite see around the bend in the road. If you see headlights from that direction, try to run interference until we're clear with our cargo.'

'No worries, Trev.' Tanya started her car and swung it around to face down the road towards the tennis courts.

As Zanza emerged through the gap in the fence hauling his prize with him, the ped's feet clear off the ground, Harry slid the van's side door open.

An engine sounded further down the road in the darkness that was suddenly broken by a glare of light. The engine noise got louder and the light increased.

Zanza saw it and quickened his pace towards the gaping aperture of the van.

Harry was glancing nervously towards the approaching lights.

Trev grabbed the radio handset, but the youngest member of the team was one step ahead and he didn't need to say anything to her.

Tanya accelerated past the van and towards the oncoming lights.

As the Feds' car came around the bend and into sight, illuminating the van and its nefarious activities, Zanza threw the hapless Wheeler into the van with his bag, jumping in after him. Harry followed him and slammed the door behind them.

'Go, brother!' he yelled at Trev.

A police siren pierced the quiet night air with one blast and the police car gunned its engine on its approach.

Tanya swung the Audi across the road and stopped. She stared at the headlights speeding towards her, which dipped as the agent driving slammed his foot on the brakes for all he was worth. The braking was so urgent the wheels locked and rubber screamed on the bitumen as the car slid to a halt, only half a metre short of the passenger side of the Audi.

The cop driving leant on the horn, whilst his offsider leaned out of the window and screamed at Tanya. 'Get out of the fucking way, you moron!'

Tanya waved at them.

'Move your car, bitch!'

Tanya lowered the passenger window. 'Is that how you speak to women?' She smiled to herself. Retarded idiots, she thought. If you can't figure out this is all part and parcel of the same thing, then you really ought to be assigned to parking duties. She glanced to her right and checked the VW van was disappearing. And Trev was not sparing the horses, he was flying.

The Feds threw the siren on again and reversed to try and move around Tanya's impromptu roadblock.

She anticipated their move and jammed her car in reverse as the Feds tried to get past the rear of her car.

The Feds stopped again, the passenger jumping out of the car this time, his Glock in his hand.

Tanya turned the wheel hard right and planted her foot in first gear. The Audi swung back into the direction of the road, spraying a load of gravel from the edge onto the police car and the agent standing outside it. She sped away in the direction the van had gone.

The Fed hopped back into the cop car. They took off after Tanya.

Tanya's radio crackled. 'Babe, some hairy leather-clad assistance is incoming.'

'Thanks, Harry.'

She stopped abruptly. The Feds were closing.

As soon as she saw the shape of an F150 screaming towards her from the other direction, she slammed the Audi into reverse, turned to look over her shoulder and planted her foot.

The move took the cops by complete surprise, forcing them to slam on their brakes again as the rear end of the Audi raced back towards them.

The cop driving desperately threw their car into reverse and urged it backwards.

Tanya swung to the edge of the road and hit the brakes as the dark F150 hurtled past her, a maniacally grinning Corsi at the wheel.

It was game over as the Feds could not reverse anywhere near as fast as the forward moving F150, with its steel bull bar on its front.

As Tanya accelerated away, she heard the crash of metal as the front of the police car was written off by the bikies.

The Ratfucker threw the F150 in reverse and hit the gas as the two cops tried to scramble out of their wrecked car with their guns. Corsi executed a handbrake turn that was as perfect as a ballet pirouette and the bikies screamed away, the V8 engine roaring like a lion.

Longman got on the phone. 'Kenmare, my friend, the Feds are no longer in the game.'

'Great work, Longman, see you at your Dubbo joint in a few hours.'

'No worries, mate.'

***

The AFP Sergeant was going ballistic. 'What do you bloody mean your car's wrecked, too?!' he bellowed into the radio.

'This truck just appeared,' whined the agent standing in Stevenson Street, steam rising from the car's smashed radiator.

'Sarge?' called a monitor. 'Wheeler's phone is tracking north, probably on Longueville Road.'

'Right, notify the state police now, this is an abduction in progress.'

'Oh, shit. The signal's gone.'

'Fuck!' screamed the Sergeant.

***

As soon as the VW van turned onto River Road and headed away from the scene of the crime, Trev called to Harry in the back. 'Harry, get the fucker's phone, we need to ditch it. The Feds will be tracking it.'

Zanza patted down Wheeler's pockets.

'Careful for prints if you find it, big fella,' said Harry, slipping on a forensic glove.

Zanza's hand stopped on the left-hand trouser pocket of Wheeler, who was slumped against a metal cabinet, tears streaming down his face, flowing over the gaffer tape and dripping off his chin.

Harry leant in. 'I love to see sheer terror in your eyes, Wheeler. It's exactly the fear those little kids would have had in their eyes as you put your filthy fucking hands on them.'

Harry pulled the phone out of the trouser pocket. 'We need anything off this, Trev?'

'Mate, probably nothing of interest and anyway we don't have time to examine it now. If we were to hang on to it and turn it on later to look at it, then the tracking could pick it up. Is it switched on?'

'Yep.'

'Okay, switch it off now, and we'll ditch it. I'm pulling over here, I can see a drain in the gutter. Drop it in there.'

The van pulled to a stop. Harry opened the side door and stepped onto the kerb. He deposited Wheeler's phone into the drain and heard it splash in the water below. He got back into the van.

Trev took off again. 'Guys, check if there are any other devices, will you?'

Zanza frisked Wheeler again, more thoroughly this time, as Harry went through the travel bag.

Harry pulled out Wheeler's computer. 'Got a laptop, Trev.'

'That's no problem, it won't have a SIM card, so it can't be tracked. I'm only interested in phones and tablets.'

Harry finished with the bag and looked at Zanza who shook his head. 'All clear, Harry.'

'We're all good, Trev.'

'Cool, RV with Tanya here we come. Now you can spend some quality time welcoming our guest.'

Harry turned, drew his fist back and punched Wheeler square on his nose. There was a whining moan like an injured animal. Blood mixed with the tears over the gaffer tape.

'Oh, that felt so fucking good. I've been hanging out like a desperate junkie to get my hands on you, Wheeler. You know who I am, don't you?'

The ped's petrified eyes stared twitchingly at Harry.

Zanza grabbed him by the throat. 'Answer the man, fucker.'

Harry sneered. 'So, again, you know who I am, yes?'

Wheeler nodded slowly.

'Excellent,' said Harry. 'We are going to have so much fun together. Well, at least it'll be fun for me and my team.'

Wheeler grunted through the tape.

Zanza said, 'I think the arsehole wants to say something, Harry.'

'Well, big fella, let's listen, shall we?'

Zanza ripped the gaffer tape off. Wheeler squealed with pain.

Harry slapped the ped's face. 'Got something you want to say, cunty?'

'Please, just kill me. Please. Quickly. Please.'

The van filled with the guffaws of the three sleuths.

'Reggie, Reggie, Reggie,' said Harry. 'No, no, no! You have to suffer. Appallingly. I am the horseman from the apocalypse who is going to avenge my little girl, Orla. Your death, which will come, rest assured, will be one of the slowest and most painful in all recorded human history.'

'Noooooooo, pleeeease ...' Wheeler blubbered.

The van filled with chuckles again.

Tanya drove onto the slip road in Pyrmont, beneath the Western Distributor flyover and stopped her car. She checked around, once, twice, and three times, as she'd had drummed into her. The place was deserted, as one would expect at three-thirty in the morning. But you never knew when some homeless soul or some wandering party animal could be lurking. She got out of the Audi, pulling her backpack off the back seat.

She lit herself a smoke as the first priority. Then she pulled a screwdriver out of the pack and removed the number plates from the car, being those from Trev's naughty collection. She pulled the real plates from the backpack and reattached them to the Audi, wiping them clean when she was done. She also wiped down the passenger side door, outside and in. She stubbed out her cigarette, got back into the car, and headed for the hire-car company's night drop-off spot next to Darling Harbour.

At the last traffic lights before the drop-off, she slipped a baseball cap on her head, pushing her blonde tresses underneath it. She pulled her hoodie over the top and kept her face lowered as she drove into the car park in one of the hotel complexes. There was no one around. She parked the Audi, slipping on black leather gloves as soon as she had put it in a designated parking bay. She wiped anything she'd touched inside the vehicle. She got out, standing close to the door and discreetly wiped the outside door handle. Still using the space between her body and the car, she wiped the car key and the remote-control switch unit.

Head kept down, she walked over to the after-hours key-drop box and deposited the Audi's key. She walked out onto Murray Street and down the hill to the bottom where the grey VW van was idling.

She climbed into the front passenger seat. 'Hi team! All done.'

'Great work, babe,' said Harry from the rear.

Wheeler had been gagged again and was now prone on the floor and hog-tied.

Trev, looking at her, smirked. 'We pulled into that underpass road right as you were leaving. It is a hell of a good spot for a discreet plate change.'

'Sure is,' she said. 'Now, more importantly, how long is this trip with that wanker?'

'Dubbo is about five hours, Tan.'

'Fuck me. Well, we'd better get a whole carton of Red Bull to last that journey. And more smokes.'

'Yep, we'll stop at a twenty-four-hour servo on the way out of the city.'

Trev turned the van onto the on-ramp towards the Western Distributor and they headed off in the darkness.

***

At AFP headquarters, the failed field agents had now arrived back, their wrecked cars having been towed away and their return journey provided by the local state police.

As the four of them walked sheepishly into the operations room, the Sergeant, red-faced from blood pressure and his facial expression looking homicidal, bawled at them. 'What sort of fricking amateur hour is this? What the hell happened out there?'

The lead agent, credit to him, bit the bullet. Sometimes seniority had its downside, especially when a clusterfuck was the main play. 'Somebody else wanted him, Sarge, and they were better prepared.'

'Yeah,' added his offsider. 'Whoever they were, they were well-organized and completely coordinated.'

'The other word for what you're describing, boys, is professionals. Like we are supposed to be, as the nation's premier police force. Remember any of that?' growled the Sergeant.

The first agent braved the field again. 'Any hits on the plate of the blue Audi?'

The Sergeant scowled at him. 'Nope. Queensland plates and listed to a Ford Falcon utility that hasn't been validly registered in over five years.'

The agent swallowed. 'And that VW van?'

'Those plates don't compute at all, so probably fake. And no clue from any of you on those F-One-Fifties? The ones that demolished you?'

'No, Sarge. Both of them had muck all over the plates, so we couldn't read them.'

'So, in summary then, my team of clowns, we have no Reginald Wheeler and no fricking leads.'

The four field agents stood there nervously as the other staff looked on discreetly. The air of embarrassment in the office was thicker than a stodgy quiche.

***

The grey VW van, with its occupants now well-stocked with snacks, energy drinks, and cigarettes, headed west through the Blue Mountains with its captive paedophile.

As they approached Bathurst and passed the turn-off for the road to Sofala, Trev mentioned it to Harry.

Harry prodded the captive. 'And up that road, Wheeler, is where we took your mate Schwarz. Well, we thought he was your mate, Bernhard. But it was his brother Dieter. Also a ped, of course. Fucking families, eh, Wheeler? Anyway, Dieter suffered terribly before he died and got dropped down an old mine shaft.'

Wheeler moaned.

Tanya spoke for the first time in about an hour, having dozed off. 'So, why aren't we doing that this time? Not as far to drive.'

'Best to get rid of all body parts,' said Trev turning to glance at her. 'And that time, with the first Schwarz, we didn't have the connection with Longman and the abattoir, so this better option wasn't there.'

'And we didn't have any local piggeries,' she grinned.

Harry and Trev both laughed.

'Piggery?' said Zanza.

'Ah, let me explain,' said Harry.

'And you listen in, Wheeler, this is how your mate Bernhard met his fate.'

As the van rolled through Bathurst and then north-west towards Orange and Dubbo, Harry, Trev, and Tanya all contributed to the lavishly detailed recounting of the capture and execution of Bernhard Schwarz over in Western Australia. And why Western Australian bacon was to be avoided at all costs.

The long drive became a pastiche of recollections of their exploits, past cases, and Trev's music selections, a rich panoply of 1970s rock bands. It filled the time.

– 10 –

The chunky electronic gate, hawkishly watched by three CCTV cameras, slid open and Trev eased the van onto the forecourt of the Dubbo abattoir.

Harry, his phone to his ear, leant over Trev's shoulder and said, 'Okay, cruise around the rear.' He put the phone back in his pocket. He kicked the hog-tied paedophile. 'Almost showtime, Wheeler.'

The ped's eyes opened. He twisted his head and looked at Harry.

As the van got to the back of the expansive building, a heavy metal roller door began its clanging ascent. As it cleared head height, a grinning Rocco Corsi stood inside it.

He motioned the van in.

As soon as the VW was fully in the sallyport, the door clattered loudly on its descent.

Tanya hopped out of the van first and was met by Archie Longman coming into the bay.

'Hello, Blondie. Welcome to dastardly Dubbo.'

Tanya screwed up her nose. 'Archie, this place bloody stinks. Don't you ever clean it?'

Longman laughed as he stepped towards the opening side door on the van. 'G'day, Kenmare, Zanza. Now, what piece of scum have you got here?'

Zanza, grinning, grabbed Wheeler and threw him out of the van onto the concrete floor.

Longman sunk his boot into Wheeler's ribs, grabbed his hair and pulled his head up to face him. 'Hello, cunty! Welcome to the Hogs' House of Horrors. And have we got a very special matinée performance planned.' He dropped him back onto the floor.

'And guess who the lead role goes to?' said Harry, stepping out of the van and standing next to Longman.

'But I reckon you'll win the Oscar, Kenmare.'

Harry chuckled. 'Longman, you bet I will. But I'm sure there'll be a few best supporting roles awarded, too.'

'Let's secure him in the processing chamber.' Longman leant down to Wheeler as he emphasized the last two words. 'Then we'll have a couple of coldies in the meal room.'

'Dunnies that way, too?' asked Tanya. 'It's been a long fricking drive.'

'Yeah, Blondie, straight through there.' Longman pointed at a grey wooden door.

Trev followed Tanya.

Zanza hauled Wheeler up and dragged him along as Corsi led the way deeper into the building.

The group stepped into a white-tiled, cavernous space.

'Welcome to the processing chamber,' said The Ratfucker, grabbing a hanging meat hook, sliding it along a rail on its chain to where Zanza was holding Wheeler.

Longman, producing another chain, wrapped it around the captive's ankles and padlocked it.

He looked at Zanza and pointed at the dangling meat hook. 'Big man, hang him up by the chain.'

Wheeler squirmed on the tiled floor as the hog-tie was cut loose.

Zanza seized his legs and lifted him, hooking the ankle chain over the hook being proffered by Corsi.

As Wheeler hung upside down, Corsi pulled on a control chain so the hook rose, until Wheeler's head was about a metre off the floor.

Longman ripped the tape off the ped's mouth.

Harry nodded. 'Yeah, I guess it's the original case of no one can hear you scream.'

'You bet,' said Longman, looking proud. 'Plus, more importantly, if his sinuses block while he's upside down with his mouth closed, he could suffocate. We made that mistake once.'

'And we would not fucking want that,' said Harry. 'Would we, Wheeler?' He punched the suspended ped in the guts.

Wheeler bucked with the pain and grunted.

Corsi bent down to look at the ped's face. 'Don't go anywhere, arsehole, we'll be back.'

Tanya and Trev were already half through their first beer, having located the fridge, as Harry, Zanza, and the two bikies walked into the meal room.

Rocco had closed the heavy insulated door to the tiled chamber of captivity so Wheeler's half-baked cries for help had fallen silent.

Longman pulled more cold stubbies out of the fridge and passed them around. Caps were twisted off and deep chugs of the cold amber nectar followed. It'd been a long five-hour drive from Sydney.

Harry lit a smoke, swallowed his beer, and took the fresh one Longman passed him.

'Longman, wanted to say a big thanks for this. Your help back in Sydney catching this piece of shit was invaluable, and having the means to dispose of his body, in due course, is bloody perfect.'

Longman chuckled. 'Yeah, the dogs of Australia have no idea what's in their tins of food.'

'Pedo Pal,' quipped Corsi.

Everyone laughed.

'And on that note,' said Trev, 'I would advise against eating bacon coming from WA.'

Longman frowned. 'Go on.'

Trev recounted the piggery escapade. When he finished, the two bikies were smiling in approval and admiration.

'Fucking sweet,' said The Ratfucker.

'And good thinking,' added Longman.

'Well,' said Harry, 'necessity is the mother of invention, as they say.'

He emptied his second beer.

'Now, on the subject of necessity, after I've taken a piss, I feel the need for a murderous adventure.'

'Cool!' Longman slapped the table. 'Fucking showtime!'

Beers were swallowed.

Harry went to the bathroom.

Trev picked up his black canvas holdall.

Corsi looked at it and raised his eyebrows.

'Tools of the torture trade, Corsi. And free lessons, mate.'

'I'm intrigued.'

'Just need a power outlet in that room. Brought my own extension cord.'

'No worries there,' said Longman. 'That we can help with.'

Harry rejoined them.

Tanya sidled up to Trev. 'Hey, Trev, my friend, how about I get a go with the blowtorch this time?'

'For you, Tan, anything. Except, of course, the final act. That's Harry, all Harry.'

'Goes without saying. I just feel a need, too. A need to give a ped some pain.'

'Oh, and Corsi, mate,' said Trev, 'a chair and a side-table would be ideal. Or two chairs will do.'

Corsi picked up two metal fold-up chairs from the meal table setting.

'Perfect,' said Trev.

The group walked back into the tiled room.

Wheeler, suspended like a large pale bat, hung in silence.

Harry strode towards him. 'You'd better still be alive, cunty!'

Wheeler's eyes opened and he whimpered.

'Want him on a chair, Kenmare?' Longman poked Wheeler with his fist.

'Yes please, mate. And tied firmly. They sure as hell buck like broncos when Trev gets going with those soldering irons.' He signalled in the direction of Trev who was laying out his collection of items on the second chair.

'And we'll need to give him some regular stimulant injections, because it's no fun when they pass out from the pain.'

'Yeah, we've learnt that one, too,' said Longman, chuckling.

Tanya came back with one end of the extension cord, the other end now plugged into a socket near the door. She handed her end to Trev, with a double adaptor attached.

He plugged in both soldering irons.

Tanya delved into the holdall and came out with the blowtorch.

Longman and Corsi now had the naked Wheeler upright and seated in the chair, Corsi lashing him tight to it.

The ped's eyes were wide open now, like two saucers of terror.

Harry walked over and plunged a needle into Wheeler's arm. 'Just to keep you beautifully awake, Wheeler. Because we simply cannot have you missing all the fun.'

Longman looked at the chair next to Trev, putting his hand close to the irons to feel the growing heat.

'So, Matson, one big boy and one little fella. Pray tell.'

Trev smiled. 'The smaller one goes up the eye of the dick, mate.'

Both bikies groaned in unison and instinctively cupped their groins.

'And it works a treat getting them to talk, believe me.'

'Let me guess,' said Longman, 'the big one is for the arse?'

'Exactly. A red-hot butt plug. Also, incredibly effective.'

Corsi walked over to the far side of the chamber and rolled back the concertina door that formed that wall.

On the other side was another tiled room, but this one with machinery in it.

'Our pride and joy,' said the bikie. 'The mincer!'

'Hey, Kenmare?' said Longman.

'Yeah, mate?'

'When you've finished making him talk, you can finish him off by feeding him slowly and feet first into the mincer. With a massive shot of stimulant to keep them conscious, you'd be seriously amazed how long some of them last. And it's entrainment plus.'

Corsi chuckled. 'So fucking entertaining.'

'Tempting, Longman, but no can do.'

Longman looked puzzled. 'But you are going to kill him, aren't you?'

'Blood oath, mate. But it has to be with my own two hands. I need to avenge my own flesh and blood. Deeply personal, so I need to feel the life evaporate from him.'

The bikie nodded. 'Understood. I'd probably want the same.'

'Thanks again for your help, mate.'

'Our absolute pleasure. We'll be forever grateful for your help with those Jihadi rapist cunts.'

Harry grinned. 'Yeah, and that was our pleasure. Now I reckon we are good to go. Mister Matson of the soldering iron fame?'

'Ready for play time, Mister Kenmare.'

'Me, too,' said Tanya, lighting the handheld blowtorch.

Wheeler cried, 'No!' And a stream of urine sprayed forth.

Corsi got out of its trajectory in the nick of time.

All three sleuths slipped on latex gloves. Zanza hung back with the two bikies.

Harry, side-stepping the puddle of piss, grabbed the prisoner's jaw.

'Now, Wheeler, you despicable, evil piece of shit, you're going to tell me every last detail of what you and your depraved pedo mates did to my little Orla. Or perhaps I should say your depraved dead pedo mates.'

Wheeler stared at Harry. He sputtered at first, no words forming. Then his face hardened noticeably. 'Just kill me, get it over and done with.'

'No!' roared Harry. 'You are going to talk, and then you'll die. How much pain in the meantime depends on how quickly and fully you talk. So, choice is yours on the pain level.'

'Fat choice,' said the ped, sneering. 'No thanks, I'll maintain my right to silence, ex-pig.'

There was a ripple of mirth around the chamber.

'Man,' said Longman, 'I'm really, really going to enjoy this show.'

'Yeah,' said Corsi, 'this is coming together very well indeed.'

'Rights! Rights!' yelled Harry. 'There are zero fucking rights in here. Start talking, you paedophile piece of garbage.'

'We're not called that anymore. I'm a "minor attracted person", get it right,' sneered Wheeler. 'So, fuck off.'

That drew peals of laughter from the bikies and Zanza.

Trev passed Harry the smaller soldering iron. 'It's a weird thing I've noticed with all our peds, Harry. They all seem to go for some last-ditch act of defiance.'

Harry took hold of the iron. 'Yeah, true, but the end result is always the same.'

Trev smiled at Wheeler. 'Massive amounts of indescribably excruciating pain, followed by death.'

'Babe, give him a bit of a singe, just a taster.'

Tanya walked to Wheeler, turning the control knob on the blowtorch so there was now a roaring blue flame.

'Fuck you!' said Wheeler.

'Actually, I think I'm the one that gets to say "fuck you" right now, scum. Or should I say, "minor attracted" scum.'

'Go, Blondie, go!' called the two bikies in unison.

Tanya made the flame do a little dance in front of Wheeler's face, mesmerizing him. She shot the flame to his left ear and Wheeler screamed. She gave him a few seconds to pipe down and hit his other ear with the flame. He screamed again. She stepped back.

'Mister PI, the appetiser has been completed.'

There was applause from the spectators.

'Feel like talking, Wheeler?' asked Harry.

Despite gasping for breath, 'Fuck off' was clearly audible as Wheeler overcame the pain.

'There's just no helping some idiots, Mister Kenmare.'

'No, Mister Matson, there is not, very true.'

Harry stepped over to Wheeler, grabbed his limp penis in his left hand, and slowly inserted the soldering iron into the ped's urethra. This time the shrieks of pain were ear-splitting.

Every other male in the chamber winced. Tanya, however, was all smiles.

Harry stepped back and Wheeler descended back into gasping sobs.

The defiant eyes, still not defeated, looked at Harry. 'Get fucked, ex-pig!'

Harry bellowed as he swung a haymaker, his right fist almost taking Wheeler's head off. The chair and its captive toppled over.

'More pain required, evidently,' said Trev. 'Corsi and Zanza, would you guys please put him on all fours and hold the chair back?'

'Sweet,' said the bikie.

The two men strode over to Wheeler, grabbed either side of the chair and inverted the captive so he was face down on the tiles. The bikie flicked open a switchblade and cut the tape holding the ped's ankles to the chair legs. He pivoted the chair up so Wheeler's arse was exposed.

Trev, holding the large soldering iron, stepped over. 'Wheeler, here's a version of anal sex you've never imagined.'

Wheeler screamed and tried to buck as the hot metal shaft was driven slowly into his anus. Zanza and Corsi had him pinned so his efforts to move were futile.

Longman laughed. 'Well, at least he won't be having any more problems with haemorrhoids.'

That earned a chuckle all round, even from a stony-faced Harry.

Corsi and Zanza set Wheeler upright again.

'Start talking, Wheeler!' shouted Harry.

'You okay, Harry?' Tanya put her hand on his arm.

'I have to hear it. I have to have his confession.'

'I know. I'm here for you, know that. We're all here for you.'

'Including us, Kenmare,' said Longman from the sidelines.

Despite his cauterized rectum, when he'd finished gasping and wheezing, Wheeler surprised them all. 'Oh, how fucking sweet,' he hissed. 'Nice little gang you've got now, hotshot ex-detective. Well, you can bend over and take my cock, just like your slutty little girl did.'

Trev rushed to grab the charging and roaring Harry.

'No, mate! Not yet! This arsehole needs a lot more suffering first.'

Wheeler stunned them all even more with crowing, 'Suffer? You should have seen Orla suffer with me and the boys taking turns.'

The Ratfucker stepped in to help restrain Harry.

Tanya reached into Trev's bag and turned towards Wheeler.

'Don't kill him, Tan,' said Trev.

'No worries there, Trev, I want to enjoy the show to come. But he needs to be shut up in the meantime.'

She forced a rag into Wheeler's mouth and spat in his face.

Harry relaxed a bit and the guys released their hold on him.

Trev lit two smokes and handed one to Harry.

'Brother, I have a plan to raise this to extreme heat for this piece of shit.'

He pulled out his phone.

'No signal in here, mate,' said Longman. 'The meal room out there is fine, though.'

Trev walked out.

'Let's all go for a beer,' said Longman.

They all trooped out in Trev's wake, with a muffled 'Cunts!' audible from Wheeler.

Trev was standing by the window on his phone.

Corsi handed around cold beers.

Trev got off the phone saying, 'Cool, thanks. Name's Smith. Someone will be there shortly.'

He turned to the bikies. 'You got a bloke free to head into town to the pet shop?'

Longman frowned. 'Yeah, sure. But why?'

Trev chuckled. 'Hey, Harry, you remember the notebook we got from Wheeler's room in Laos?'

'Yeah.'

Tanya snorted. 'Regular pedo's little black book.'

'Sure. But there were also plenty of ramblings written down.'

'Yeah,' she said, screwing up her face. 'All his sicko, fucked-up fantasies, or his depraved memoirs.'

'Yeah, that was all there. But on my close reading of it, I also found his talk about his fears, his nightmares. And his biggest fear of all, even more than the shower block in mainstream prison, is rats. He wrote about it repeatedly.'

Harry nodded. 'I remember you mentioned that weeks ago. Probably some horrible childhood experience would be my guess. So, you thinking like that scene in *Nineteen Eighty-Four*?'

'Exactly, brother!'

Longman opened a side door to the room and yelled into the corridor.

A few seconds later, a bald, beefy bikie in full leathers strutted in.

'Yes, boss?'

Longman pointed at Trev. 'Henk, speak to our mate here.'

Henk, a little confused, looked at Trev who motioned him over.

'Mate, here's some cash.' Trev handed him a folded wad of twenties. 'Shoot down to the Dubbo Pet Paradise on the main drag. Your name is Smith and you are collecting four brown rats and three metal cages. They'll be waiting for you.'

Henk looked utterly confused now.

'All will be revealed, mate. You can even watch, too.'

Henk looked back at Longman.

'Just do it, Henk. Take one of the Fords.'

Henk grunted and walked out.

– 11 –

Half an hour later, the little crowd watched in silent fascination as Trev worked away with a pair of pliers and some wire on two of the cages. The third cage, sitting at the other end of the table, was home to four large brown Norwegian rats, all scampering about their compound, squeaking loudly and looking around, noses and whiskers twitching.

'Hey, Trev?'

'Yes, Tan.'

'Before you do whatever you have in mind with the rats, have we got any of that acid in the van?'

'Yep, both sulphuric and hydrochloric.'

'Cool. I want to have a little bit of sport first. That okay?' She turned to look at Harry.

'As long as you don't kill him, and you do have priors let me remind you, then go ahead.'

She smiled at him. 'And for the record, boys, I'm proud of my priors.'

'So are we, babe, but this finale today is all mine.'

Tanya stood up.

'In the bottom cupboard, back left, Tan. Got a warning sticker on it.'

'Thanks, Trev.' She walked towards the door out.

'And Tan?' said Harry.

'Yeah?'

'Nothing in his eyes or mouth. We need him to be able to see and speak.'

She chuckled. 'Of course. I was going straight for his genitals, anyway.'

It was Harry's turn to laugh. 'He definitely won't be needing them ever again.'

There was a loud chortle from The Ratfucker. 'I am so looking forward to the rest of this show.'

Wheeler looked up as the door opened and in trooped the six men and the girl.

He saw a wire cage contraption one of the ex-detectives was carrying. The girl had a metal case with a yellow sticker on it that he couldn't yet make out. But it looked like one of those workplace warning signs.

The girl put the case on the chair next to the soldering irons and opened it. She pulled out two glass bottles and a syringe. She put on thick rubber gloves also from the case.

She looked over at him. 'And would Sir Pedo like hydrochloric or sulphuric today?' She sneered at him.

Wheeler stared at her, speechless. This nightmare got more surreal by the moment.

The girl spoke again. 'Okay, I'll choose, then.' She filled the syringe from one of the bottles and stepped over to him. She dripped some acid onto one of his nipples.

Wheeler shrieked. It was excruciating.

'How's that feel, Mister Molester?'

She did the other nipple.

Wheeler howled again and there was a round of applause from the bikies.

'Go, Blondie!' called the one in charge.

She turned and gave a little mock bow to her audience.

She looked back at him. 'So, fucktard, are you ready to tell Mister Kenmare everything yet?'

All Wheeler emitted was a hiss and some dribble out of the side of his mouth.

'Have it your way, then,' said Tanya.

She sprayed a jet of acid onto his shrivelled penis and scrotum.

This time Wheeler lurched and bucked in the chair so much he keeled over.

That almost had the bikies on the floor with laughter.

Corsi composed himself, walked over, and set Wheeler and his chair upright again.

'Ready to talk yet, Wheeler?' asked Harry, looking and sounding increasingly frustrated.

'Ff …, fff …,' Wheeler choked with a cough. He spat out some mucus and saliva followed by, 'Fuck you.'

'Righto,' said Harry. 'The *pièce de résistance,* then.' He looked over to the bikies. 'Guys, we need a table in front of him and his chair strapped to it so he can't topple over again.'

'And I'll need rope as well,' added Trev.

'No worries,' said Longman. 'Rocco, we'll grab a table from the meal room. Henk, go grab some rope, mate.'

'Yes, boss.'

Longman and Corsi pushed a long wooden table against Wheeler's chest as he sat confined in his chair.

Henk, at Trev's direction, bound rope around the back of the chair, securing it to both table legs.

Wheeler was looking wildly perplexed, wondering what insane version of hell was coming next. His scared eyes were darting around.

'What are you doing?' he wailed. 'Just kill me now, 'cos I'm not fucking talking to you arseholes!'

'The last great act of defiance, Trev.'

'Yep, Harry. Reminds me of that picture of the mouse raising the middle finger to the incoming eagle swooping down.'

Trev turned towards the ped. 'What we have in store now for you, wankstain, will have you singing louder than a Baptist choir in Harlem.'

'Fuck you!'

'You ever read *Nineteen Eighty-Four*, by the great George Orwell?'

'What?'

'Ignorant cunt,' added Harry. 'The closest this arsehole would have got to classic literature would be *Lolita*.'

Trev laughed. 'So, Wheeler, you don't know about Room One-O-One, do you?'

'What's that?'

'Room One-O-One,' grinned Harry, 'is the room containing the thing you fear most in life, the one that really stands out as abject terror for you.'

Wheeler stared wide-eyed at him as Trev placed his cage contraption on the table. He slid it along until the oval hole cut in one end sat in front of Wheeler's face.

Trev pointed to Henk who was still holding lengths of rope. 'Mate, lash the cage to the table first, so it can't move. Then lash around it to hold the arsehole's head against the opening. Nice and tight.'

Henk got busy with his ropes.

Wheeler tried to buck as a rope was passed around the back of his head, but the table and chair were now a solid, immovable edifice.

Henk finished and Wheeler's face, contorted with fear and his eyes flying around like pinballs, was now inside the confines of the cage.

'Now we just need our little guests,' said Harry.

Longman turned to Corsi. 'Mate, given your moniker, I reckon it's only fitting you do the honours.'

The Ratfucker chuckled. 'Shit, yeah!' He walked out to the meal room, returning with the third cage and its scampering and squeaking cargo.

'Nooooooo!!!' howled Wheeler.

Trev slid on a rubber glove, reached into the rat pack, and grabbed one of the squirming rodents. He opened the door on the first section of the cage contraption and shoved the rat inside.

The brown creature immediately ran to the wire wall nearest Wheeler, halfway along the double cage.

The ped's screeching now was so high-pitched as to be bordering on inaudible, except to the neighbourhood dogs. He pissed and shat himself simultaneously.

Harry leant down next to him as Trev activated a video recorder on a tripod at the other end of the table.

'Now, cunty, you are going to talk.' Harry tapped a metal knob on top of the cage where the two cages joined and where the rat was madly sniffing, its beady eyes looking at the distraught Wheeler. 'See this, Wheeler, I pull it up and Mister *Rattus norvegicus* comes straight for your face.' Harry smiled and pulled the knob a tad, creating a centimetre-high gap. The rat's nose went straight under it, but couldn't get the rest of its head through.

The table shook as Wheeler bucked futilely.

'No, no, no, noooooooooo!' Dribble and mucus were now running down his chin.

'Talk, cunty, or meet Mister Rat.'

'Okay, okay! But please, please take the vermin away.'

'No, idiot, you don't get to call the shots here. I'll keep the rat where it is, as long as you keep talking. If you don't comply, I'll let him in and you two can start French kissing.' With that, Harry shifted the cage gate up two more millimetres and the rat's snout pushed a tad closer.

'Hey, Trev, why not chuck the rest of the pack in there with this big bastard?'

'With absolute pleasure.' Trev deposited the other three rats, one by one, into the cage with their mate. They all rushed to join the first rat and Wheeler found himself with four twitching snouts pointed at him, all straining to get under the gate between the cage compartments.

Wheeler looked in desperation at Harry, his eyes swivelling up as far as they could in his strapped head.

Harry pointed at him. 'Talk!'

'Yes, we grabbed your daughter and I had sex with her. We all did. I can't help what I am.'

Harry bellowed, 'Are you fucking justifying it?' Another two millimetres open on the gate and four rodent noses closer to Wheeler. The smallest rat squeezed its head under the gate.

'No, no, that's not what I'm doing.'

'I reckon that's exactly what he's doing,' chipped in Tanya. 'They all reckon rooting kids is normal. We've already heard him spouting this "minor attracted person" garbage. Give him a rat, Harry.'

'Yeah, give him a rat!' yelled Longman.

'Man, fucking do it,' joined in Corsi.

'A rat, a rat, my kingdom for a rat,' said Zanza.

Harry and Trev looked over at the big African.

He smiled. 'So, I know some Shakespeare. In the refugee centre I learned to read English and the big book of the Bard was not in demand, unlike most of the other books.'

The sleuths nodded in approval.

Harry turned back to his prisoner. 'Are you going to give me the details, Wheeler? I'm losing the little scrap of patience I had.'

'I've told you I raped her.'

Harry pulled up the gate a touch and the smallest rat squeezed through.

Wheeler howled as the rodent scampered to his face and sniffed at him. Its three comrades were pushing hard against the gate.

'Details, Wheeler, or the other three join in.'

'Okay, okay,' blubbered the ped. He proceeded with the ghastly recount, of them grabbing Orla on the street, what they did to her back at his place, and the murder at the Royal National Park. When he voluntarily added in the urinating on her, Harry knew the job was done.

He stood back, his hand still holding the gate control on the cage.

Wheeler was bawling his eyes out. 'Please, now take the rat away.' He screamed as the rodent bit his cheek.

Harry, looking into space and speaking to the universe rather than anyone in particular, said, 'Why my little Orla, why her?'

Wheeler took it as a question to him. 'She was suggested to me,' he sobbed quietly.

The tiled chamber fell utterly silent.

Harry was initially lost for any words. He and Trev exchanged looks.

Harry looked back at Wheeler who screamed anew as the rat took another bite, enjoying the blood it had drawn.

'What the hell are you saying, Wheeler? It wasn't purely random? Your mates both said you were just out cruising for a victim.'

'No,' bleated Wheeler. 'They said that 'cos I told them to take the secret to their graves.'

Trev snorted. 'Well, they sure did that.'

'Take this damned rat away and I'll tell you. Please?'

Harry nodded at Trev who opened the top of the front cage and pulled out the rat. He dropped it back into the second cage as Harry pushed down on the gate, persuading the other three rodents to back off. The gate closed.

'Okay, Wheeler, let's have it.'

'There were high-up people who wanted you gone from the police. The task force you were running back then. They wanted it stopped.'

Trev raised an eyebrow at Harry.

Harry nodded. 'It was a trial period for a permanent team working on organized paedophilia, sex trafficking, and the like.'

'Go on, Wheeler,' said Trev, pointing at the rats again.

'So, I got word that a really senior cop, part of the powers that be, wanted you badly damaged, and best way was to rape your daughter.'

'Who?' hissed Harry. 'That fucking mongrel Malcolm Lowe?'

'No, not him.'

'That bloody bastard Bevan Hayes, then?'

'No. No, I never knew this cop's name. We only knew him as Policeman X. But I know, apart from him being one of us, he was close to the Police Minister. They were both into kids.'

'You have any details about this Policeman X?'

'Not really. He was more senior than Lowe or Hayes. I do know he got promoted high and fast because of the Minister and their joint interests. And everyone was shit-scared of him.'

'You ever meet him?' asked Trev.

'No, never. Hayes called me one day for a meet. After I'd handed over my latest kiddie porn tapes, Hayes gave me a sealed envelope. It had a photo of your girl and your address in it. Plus, a wad of cash. Hayes told me the instructions, and said it came from the top, Policeman X, so I had to get it done and keep it quiet. He told me I'd be protected. He said if I didn't do it, they'd bang me up in mainstream to enjoy shower time.'

Harry stared at him and tapped the metal knob controlling the gate.

'Any other connections or clues, Wheeler?'

Wheeler glanced fearfully at the sniffing rats, noses pushed through the wire of the gate.

'Bernie knew him, met him.'

'Fucking hell,' yelled Harry. 'You know Bernhard's dead, so he won't be telling us anything.'

'No, I know. But Bernie had a video. So, somewhere there's something with Policeman X on it.'

'You seen it?' asked Trev.

Wheeler paused, staring at the rats.

'Come on,' said Harry, putting his hand back on the control knob.

'Yes, I saw it. Bernie, Hayes, Lowe, and Policeman X. Bernie had found a girl for them. He knew the mother who was a junkie. They arranged to have the mother arrested. Then Bernie took the girl to his place. The cops arrived and the video is of the four of them gang-banging her.'

'Describe Policeman X,' said Trev.

Wheeler stammered. 'Big man, bald. Some accent in the background, Scottish maybe, but been in Australia for a long time. And there were old-style tattoos on his forearms, like the military used to have, you know.'

'How do you know he had an accent if you didn't meet him?' asked Harry.

'He spoke in the video I saw. Congratulated Bernie on the sweet meat he'd provided.'

'Did you have any contact point for this Policeman X?' asked Trev.

'No.'

Trev scooped a rat out of the cage and moved towards Wheeler.

'No! No! I swear I didn't have any contact details.'

Harry looked at Trev. 'I think we've got all we're going to. You?'

'Yep, I reckon so. That bloody Bernhard held this crucial bit back.'

'Indeed. I thought he'd sung it all, but obviously not. Damned shame we can't go back and torture him all over again.'

Harry headed for the door turning to Henk as he walked. 'Mate, can you completely untie the piece of shit. I'll be back in a sec.'

A few minutes later, Harry reappeared, now in a full forensic coverall suit.

The naked ped was crouched on the floor in the corner of the tiled chamber.

Longman laughed. 'Kenmare, mate, you look like the sodding Michelin man in that outfit.'

Harry grinned at him. 'Go to buggery, mate.'

He raised his right hand from his side, revealing a thirty-centimetre chef's knife.

'Ah, fucking finale time,' said Corsi.

Harry strode past them all and stood in front of the paedophile.

'On your feet, cunt!' he roared.

The cowering molester stared at him. He didn't move.

Harry's left hand grabbed a fistful of Wheeler's hair and lifted him by his head.

'No, no, no ...' whined Wheeler.

'I've got him, Orla!' shouted Harry, plunging the heavy stainless-steel blade deep into Wheeler's guts. 'Vengeance is mine!' bellowed the PI, stabbing Wheeler again.

And again. And again. And again ...

Blood was spurting everywhere, a scarlet spray pattern over the white tiles and Harry's white coverall.

Trev counted twenty-six stab thrusts before Harry delivered his *coup de grâce*, cutting Wheeler's throat from ear to ear.

The ped was already dead before that final knife stroke.

Harry let Wheeler's body slip onto the tiled floor in the pool of blood. He turned to his crew and the bikies. 'Job's done,' he grunted. 'My little Orla is avenged.'

The Ratfucker beamed. 'Nice job, mate. Always a pleasure to see a professional at work. I'll go start the mincing machine.'

'Cool, I won't get cleaned up just yet then.'

– 12 –

The following day, the team of sleuths were back in Sydney.

Harry had insisted they would celebrate out on the harbour, so Trev had hired a large boat with a crew.

They'd enjoyed a seafood barbecue on the massive back deck, washed down with cold beers and wine. Despite it being late winter, the weather had turned on a warm spell.

Now, the stern pointed westward with the Harbour Bridge in the foreground, the four of them reclined in deckchairs as the sun slowly headed for the horizon.

Tanya sipped on a large vodka lime, Zanza was savouring dark rum, and Harry and Trev were well into a bottle of Jameson.

A steward walked over with a silver tray and passed it around, starting with Tanya.

'I'm still happy with ladies first, and the woke brigade can go to hell.'

The steward smiled politely. The guys chuckled.

There were four large Cuban cigars trimmed and ready to go.

With all four duly alight, the steward checked there was sufficient alcohol in the mobile cabinet beside them. 'Shall I leave you in peace?'

'Lovely, Wallis. I'll buzz if we need you,' said Trev.

'Very good, Sir.' And Wallis departed.

Trev turned to Harry. 'So, brother, it's been a long road. How's it feel now?'

Harry half disappeared behind a fog of smoke. 'Bloody good on one level, mate, at least. Orla has been avenged. Those three mongrel scumbags are dead. Finally.'

'Interesting and unexpected gem from Wheeler in his last moments on Earth,' said Tanya, her drawing on the cigar more delicate and elegant than the three men.

'Not bloody wrong,' said Harry, staring at the sinking sun.

'So, what exactly was that task force he mentioned?' she asked.

'Yeah, I was keen to know about that, too,' said Trev. 'But I wanted to leave you in peace during the drive back.'

The reality was they'd all spent the return trip mired in their own thoughts and conversation had been sparser than a politician's ethics.

'Yeah, appreciated the time to ponder everything,' said Harry. 'So, the task force. Messy, in a word. Nasty, in another. Organized sex crime: pedos, servitude, coerced porn, you name it. But it wasn't too long before we identified some of our own. That was the messy part.'

'And I'm guessing,' said Trev, 'that the nasty bit is what followed close on the heels of messy.

'Not bloody wrong, Trev. Bogus complaints about us to Internal Affairs. Late night phone calls and hang ups. Shadowers loitering around, and making it known. But I stuck at it. Until Orla.'

Zanza shook his head. 'So, they'd even go to that extent to shut you down.'

Harry shrugged. 'Yep, they wouldn't just close the task force, because the optics would be too bad and they'd have to explain it. So much easier to destroy the man running it, then you can discredit the whole thing. That's how power works, big fella.'

'And I thought cops stuck together,' said Zanza.

Trev laughed before Harry could swallow his mouthful of whiskey to avoid choking.

'Yeah, no!' they both said in unison.

'Big fella,' said Harry, 'that's how it appears to the outside, and sometimes it's true. But when corruption is involved, that trumps all. And a dirty cop hates a clean cop more than he hates a crim.'

'Because a dirty cop is a crim,' said Trev. 'And plenty of clean cops have been destroyed. You're looking at two right here.'

'Well, I am in fine company, then.' Zanza saluted with his glass.

'Thank you, mate,' said Harry.

There was a lull in the banter as all four drank, smoked, and gazed westwards. The boat bobbed lightly on the swell.

The horizon was turning deep orange as the sun hit the skyline of the Blue Mountains. A smattering of fluffy clouds, now peach-coloured, spangled the sky.

'And now for Barwick.' Trev broke the silence.

'Naturally, brother, or should I say *naturellement, Monsieur Matson*?' Harry made the end of Trev's name silent, French-style.

They all laughed.

Zanza pointed at Harry. 'We need to practice your French, Harry.'

'Really? Oh, I see, you mean the spoken variety!'

Tanya groaned. 'Lame, Mister PI.'

Harry smiled at her. 'Ouch!'

She giggled. 'Nothing lame about your unspoken French, though.'

It was Trev's turn to groan. 'Shit, here we go.'

Zanza looked at all of them in mild bemusement.

'You'll get used to us, big fella.' Harry slapped him on his shoulder. 'And we're looking forward to getting to know you a whole lot better. We love having you in the team.'

'Cheers to that,' added Trev.

'France here we come,' said Zanza.

'And I bloody hope we're doing it business class, guys. A girl wants to look her best upon arrival in Paris.'

'Divine One, you'd look stunning after stowing away on a coal ship for a month.'

She blew him a kiss.

'No worries there, business class it will be,' said Trev looking smug. 'Meant to say earlier, I used Wheeler's laptop in a posthumous final kicking.'

'And?' said Harry.

'Cleared out his bank account and got all his bitcoin. Totalled about eighty grand.'

'Seriously sweet,' said Tanya. 'Because a girl in Paris also needs spending money. So, Mister PI, I reckon you need to increase the limit on my company Amex.' She pouted at him.

'Babe, for you anything.'

'That is the right answer.' She smiled.

'Team, dust off those passports,' said Harry, raising his glass. 'And here's to us!'

'Cheers,' said all four.

They gazed westward again, as the waning glowing orb gave a final blaze of colouring to the sky and clouds. A magenta and deep peach afterglow backlit the Sydney Harbour Bridge.

* * *

Epigraph Sources

Page 1:   (*Harry's Jungle*)

1.   James Crumley © 1993.
        The Mexican Tree Duck, p.257.
        (Edition – Vintage Crime/Black Lizard 2016).

2.   Henry Miller © 1949
        Sexus, p. 458.
        (Edition – Penguin 2015).

Page 61:   (*Harry's Powder*)

3.   Gordon Demarco © 1979.
        October Heat, p.170.
        (Edition – Pluto Press 1984).

4.   Anaïs Nin
        "The Queen", in *Little Birds*, p.83.
        (Edition – Penguin 1991).

Page 173: (*Harry's Sting*)

5.   Raymond Chandler © 1953.
       The Long Goodbye, p.95.
       (Edition – Vintage Crime/Black Lizard 1992).

6.   Kurt Vonnegut © 1969.
       Slaughterhouse 5, p.124.
       (Edition – Vintage 2000)

Page 243: (*Harry's Altar*)

7.   Jim Thompson © 1954.
       A Swell-Looking Babe, p.9.
       (Edition – Vintage Crime/Black Lizard 1991).

8.   Roald Dahl © 1979.
       My Uncle Oswald, p.49.
       (Edition – Penguin 1980).

Page 321: (*Harry's Victory*)

9.   Carter Brown © 1966.
       Blonde on a Broomstick, p.127.
       (Edition – Horwitz Publications 1966).

10.   Chuck Palahniuk © 2001.
       Choke, p.42.
       (Edition – Vintage 2003).

Glossary

For all my readers who are not familiar with the local vernacular and law enforcement jargon, here is a helpful list of the abbreviations and Australian slang and colloquialisms used throughout the text. Some non-Australian ones are also included.

Acronyms & Abbreviations

AC   Assistant Commissioner (senior police rank)

AFP   Australian Federal Police

AGM   annual general meeting

ATM   automated teller machine (cashpoint machine)

CDPP   Commonwealth Director of Public Prosecutions

D (demon) slang for 'detective'

DPP   Director of Public Prosecutions (like the District Attorney)

DUI   driving under the influence

RV	rendezvous
SUV	sport utility vehicle
TAFE	Technical and Further Education (Australian tertiary college system)
UC	undercover police operative
WA	Western Australia (the State of)

Australianisms & Colloquialisms (in the sense they are used in this text)

Note: Some are not exclusively Australian, but are included nonetheless as there are significant variations between the various versions of English in the world.

amber nectar	beer
arvo	afternoon
banknote (note)	bank-bill (in the USA)
bareback	sexual intercourse without a condom
bikie	motorcycle gang member ('biker' in the USA)
binos	binoculars
bonnet (of a car)	hood (in the USA)

boot (of a car)	trunk (in the USA)
bullbar	large bar on front of a vehicle to protect against animal impacts
burg	burglary
bush (the)	the Australian countryside
cab sav	cabernet sauvignon
Canberra	the national (Federal) capital of Australia
chicken	child victim (paedophile slang)
colours	(for bikies) the gang logo worn on the leather jackets
CommBank	Commonwealth Bank (Australia's biggest bank)
Commodore	a very popular, large car made by the former Holden (GM Australia)
corro	correspondence
demon / D	slang for 'detective'
dogging (to dog)	to follow (in surveillance sense)
dogging	engaging in or watching sex in a public place

drum	information
fair suck of the sav	fair go, fair chance
Feds	Australian Federal Police
flashbang	stun grenade
Garda	the Irish police force
gat	a gun (handgun)
gear	hard drugs (usually heroin)
good sort	attractive girl or woman
grog	alcohol
hammer	heroin
intel	intelligence (police or military)
job (in the)	in the police force
juvie	juvenile detention
kip	the currency of Laos
Kiwi	a New Zealander
klicks	kilometres
Logie Award	Australian television industry award

monitor	a person listening to telephone intercepts
note	see 'banknote'
off	(the phone is off) the phone is being tapped
pavement	sidewalk (in the USA)
ped/pedo	paedophile
pineapples	Australian $50 notes (yellow in colour)
piss	alcohol
pissed	drunk
Pom	English person
Port Botany	the main shipping port for Sydney
propped	parked (in surveillance sense)
recce	reconnaissance
rego (plate)	registration number/plate (of a car)
rock spider	paedophile, child molester
'roger' (in dialogue)	police jargon for 'affirmative', usually used over the police radio

root	sexual intercourse
servo	a service station (petrol station)
shadower	a surveillance operative
shag	sexual intercourse
shout	a round of drinks at a bar / to buy a shout
stubby	a 375ml bottle of beer
ute	utility vehicle (like a pick-up truck)
windscreen	windshield (in the USA)

Foreign words (all French)

belle	beauty
bien sûr	of course
chéri / chérie	beloved or darling
chez moi	at my place
coup de grâce	the final or defining blow or strike
département	department (like a county)
fantastique	fantastic
français	French

ma / mon	my
madame	Missus
mademoiselle	Miss
magnifique	magnificent
merci (beaucoup)	thank you (very much)
monsieur	Mister
naturellement	naturally
obligatoire	obligatory
oui	yes
oh là là	a French exclamation of surprise
pièce de résistance	the most remarkable feature
pruneaux d'Agen	prunes of Agen (a south-west French city)
rez-de-chaussée	ground floor
sous-sol	basement
voilà	there it is

Acknowledgements

So, I finally got the third Harry novel out there. For my growing band of Harry fans, I apologise for the time it took. Life gets in the way when you're only able to be a part-time author.

Delays aside, I've loved writing *Harry's Grail* every bit as much as the earlier novels. Perhaps even more so, as I've got more comfortable with the writing process. And hopefully I'm improving, too. You, the readers, are the judges of that.

For everything it takes to write and publish a novel, I've got plenty of people I wish to thank ...

To my partner Ruth, to my sister Katie, and to my good friend Allan Yates for endless encouragement and reading all the drafts. And especially to Ruth for putting up with my writing stuff spread over most available surfaces. Living with an author looks something like being in a cross between a library and a bombsite!

To my editor in Chicago, Vern Smith. Your insights and support have been invaluable. Thank you, my friend.

And importantly, to my band of fellow indie writers I have had the privilege to get to know over the last ten years. Your encouragement and camaraderie over that time has been inspirational. There are many of them, but special mentions to Scotch Rutherford, Alec Cizak, Vern Smith, Andrew Miller, Jon Zelazny, and J.D. Graves.

And for the professional expertise and services provided during the latter stages of the project …

To J.T. Lindroos over in Finland for the cover design. J.T. is now my go-to cover designer. I just love his work.

To Andy McDermott and his team at Publicious Book Publishing Services up in Queensland for the book production. He has done all of my self-published books from the start.

To Stephen Hill at Dylunio here in Sydney for logo and stationery design.

Merci beaucoup!